PENGUIN BOOKS

THE NUDISTS

Guy Bellamy was born in Bristol but has spent most of his life in Surrey. After National Service in Germany with the Royal Air Force, he went into journalism and has worked on newspapers in Cornwall, Bournemouth, Brighton and Fleet Street. He has written several short stories for *Punch*, and his previous novels include *The Secret Lemonade Drinker*. He is married and has a young daughter.

The
NUDISTS
GUY BELLAMY

PENGUIN BOOKS

Penguin Books Ltd, Harmondsworth, Middlesex, England
Viking Penguin Inc., 40 West 23rd Street, New York, New York 10010, U.S.A.
Penguin Books Australia Ltd, Ringwood, Victoria, Australia
Penguin Books Canada Ltd, 2801 John Street, Markham, Ontario, Canada L3R 1B4
Penguin Books (N.Z.) Ltd, 182–190 Wairau Road, Auckland 10, New Zealand

First published by Martin Secker & Warburg Ltd 1986
Published in Penguin Books 1987

Made and printed in Great Britain by
Richard Clay Ltd, Bungay, Suffolk
Typeset in Monotype Plantin

To the memory of my mother

AUDREY BELLAMY

A book-lover who wanted to read this
one but died before I could complete it

part one

INTRODUCTIONS

Every rational human being starts out every day and hunts for happiness.

Stendhal

I long age came to the conclusion that all life is six to five against.

Damon Runyon

ONE

VENABLES FIRST SAW THE WOMAN he wanted to marry on the day after his wedding. She was sitting alone at a table in the Rueda Bar, eating *tapas* and reading a local English-language newspaper. It was Sunday morning and the church bells of San Luis were sending their immutable message down the long, hot, dusty street.

Venables had been sent from the villa by his bride to buy a bottle of Fanta, but he decided to delay his return now with a beer in the Rueda Bar. At thirty-three he had spent a dozen fretful years sifting the nubile stars of a notoriously permissive generation – or, at any rate, those of them who might be susceptible to his limited charm – before settling yesterday, at the altar of a bleak granite church nearly a thousand miles to the north, for the twenty-eight-year-old owner of a sandwich bar, a brisk business-like girl with brown eyes and short dark hair whose pragmatic approach to life had meant that the decision to marry was barely his. For the great playwright in the sky to dream up this scene and dangle before him the blonde girl in the Rueda Bar just twenty-one hours after he had taken the vows that were meant to last suggested a capricious malice up there which had been diplomatically overlooked by the devout gentlemen who had fought for his soul when he had been sent grumbling to church as a boy.

He went in and ordered a San Miguel. It was a bar in which customers who wanted to spend money seemed to come as a surprise. Old men wandered in out of the sun and sat at one of the dozen or so tables, puffing Ducados and reading the sports pages of *El Dia*. Under one of the whirring fans four men without a drink in sight played dominoes. In a corner six chickens rotated unwanted on a spit, and on the bar itself *tapas* were laid out in their trays: squid, meat balls, prawns, octopus, cheeses.

The blonde had chosen *gambas* and a beer. Venables poured his

3

own into a wet glass and wondered how to introduce himself. The English, who wouldn't dream of addressing others at home, become painfully garrulous with each other abroad, seeking out the language they know and striving to create a slice of Britain in alien territory. But this was far from the tourists' beat and the Englishman who arrived here was more likely to be looking for an escape from his fellow countrymen.

Venables drank his beer thirstily. He had a stocky, athletic figure but with his little moustache and his worry beads he did not see himself as a sexual catch. The moustache was to please Wendy and the worry beads – twenty-eight of them on a brown leather thong – were a wedding present. Venables had the thousand-mile stare of a man engaged in the bitter struggle to give up smoking, and the worry beads were supposed to help. He found that he was playing with them now, counting all twenty-eight for the hundredth time, and he put them back in his pocket before the blonde could notice this public display of his weakness. Across the street the windows of the houses were shuttered against the midday sun, and outside the bar the row of tables on the narrow, red-tile pavement had been deserted in the heat. He strolled through the used napkins, each bearing the Rueda's blue-wheel logo, which lined the floor, to the tiny Spanish fruit-machine in the corner of the room. It devoured pesetas, regurgitating rarely, but he continued to play it because he could watch the blonde in a mirror on the wall behind it.

She was in her late twenties and was wearing yellow jeans and a green silk blouse. Forgetting yesterday's big event, he peered instinctively for a wedding ring but the newspaper she was holding concealed that story-telling part of her hand. He realised suddenly that he had seen her face somewhere before, in a sexual setting. It was round and pretty with a large, sensuous mouth which with her tilted eyebrows gave her appearance a disturbing mixture of the seductive and the sadistic. It was hard to judge a girl across a room – his optimism had been bruised too often – but this one gave him hope. He walked back to the bar to order another beer. He didn't want to drink but he didn't want to leave. He filled his glass, but when he turned round to try to establish eye contact with this vision she had left.

He took his drink, not too quickly, to the door and looked up the street. Two girls on Mobylettes, leaning over their own brown thighs, bounced past at a dangerously high speed, but there was no sign of the blonde. It was a long, straight street of low white buildings that stopped suddenly at one end like a Western film set, and curved round at the other down to the island's southern coast. The buildings were mostly homes but a bank, a greengrocer and a chemist were interspersed among them.

Venables returned to the bar feeling vaguely unhappy and started to play with his worry beads again. A husband for less than a day should not be so easily distracted by a stray blonde.

A man with a huge black beard came in. He was wearing a tartan shirt outside white shorts and expensive Italian sandals. He was seriously overweight. He looked round the bar, scowled, and came up to the counter where Venables was standing.

"*Fresa colada*," he told the barman. "You British?" he asked Venables.

Venables nodded. Afterwards he remembered that even in those clothes the man somehow managed to convey wealth. He picked up his strawberry-coloured drink and asked: "Has my wife been in here?"

Venables shrugged. "Is she a bit tasty?"

"I'll describe her. She's got two hundred and six bones, two hundred and thirty joints, seven hundred and fifty moveable muscles, four billion brain cells, twenty square feet of skin, enough electricity to light a twenty-five-watt bulb, eleven gallons of water and assorted chemicals worth just over twenty pounds at today's prices. That describes your wife as well, of course, if you've got one."

"I acquired one yesterday."

"Well, congratulations. Or not, as the case may be. Ben Brock," he said, offering his hand.

"Simon Venables," said Venables. "Are you a doctor?"

"Good God, no. You can't get rich being a doctor, can you? I operate on the fringe of the medical profession."

An abortionist? thought Venables. A faith healer? An acupuncturist? "Was she wearing a green blouse and yellow jeans?" he asked.

"That's the lady. Where is the bitch? She was supposed to be meeting me here." He tugged on his beard, considering possibilities.

"She waited some time."

"I've done a bit of waiting myself over the years."

Venables put down his empty glass and picked up the bottle of

Fanta. "Well, my wife is waiting for this," he said. "I must hop." He realised that it was the first time he had used the phrase "my wife".

"Are you staying in the *pueblo*? We've rented a villa up there."

"So have we," Venables said.

"I'll walk back with you."

Venables was trying to adjust to the news that the dream girl in the Rueda was linked, inextricably or not, with the big bearded man who now followed him from the bar. Every rose had its thorn. The heat hit them in the street. They crossed the road and went up a sidestreet that took them immediately into the silent countryside to the east of San Luis where a dog's bark or even the bleat of a sheep carried half a mile. The fertile red earth here yielded field after field of potatoes. The low, dry-stone walls that divided the land had been built from the boulders that originally covered the fields. Dotted haphazardly around were small white bungalows with pink tile roofs.

"So you're on your honeymoon?" Ben Brock said.

"If they still call it that."

"I love weddings. It's marriages I can't stand. I've been married five years. I forget how it happened." His voluminous waistline pushed out the tartan shirt so that it overhung his shorts like a soffit. His arms looked immensely powerful and Venables, who in his younger years had studied judo, decided that he would not care to grapple with him.

"Do you like Spain?" he asked him.

Ben Brock waved at some cranes that hovered over the inevitable half-built apartments on the edge of the village. "It will be nice when it's finished," he said. "But this is a most interesting island. It's been invaded by the Carthaginians, the Romans, the Vandals, the Moors, the Spanish, the French and the British. In the Civil War it didn't surrender until 1939."

"You're an expert?"

"We come here a lot." He gave Venables a sidelong glance. "Look, we ought to get together. The four of us. We know some places."

"That would be nice."

"Would your wife like it? What's she called?"

"Wendy. A very serious young lady."

Ben Brock frowned. "How do you mean?"

"She's a great pursuer of obscure causes."

"Gay whales against the bomb? That sort of thing?"

"A little more obscure than that. Clearing the name of Richard the Third is among her new interests."

Ben Brock shrugged this information aside. "It's what they look like when they're cooking breakfast that counts. That's what I tell Pym."

"Pym is your wife."

"Yes, I know. And Wendy is your wife. I think I've got that right."

Out in the country they had come to a cart-track that led down to the bungalow which Venables was renting. He stopped. The Fanta was already lukewarm in his hands.

"I'll tell you what," said Ben Brock. "There's a crazy Englishman called Rupert Puckle who lives in a villa at the end of this lane. Big place with a green roof. He's asked us round for drinks tomorrow evening and he'd love to meet you and your wife. Have you met any of these drunken expatriates? Lonely and homesick most of the time and desperate for company from home. Why don't you come along?"

And meet your wife? thought Venables. "Why not?" he said.

Wendy Venables had at twenty-eight reached that age when women decide that there is something faintly ridiculous about men. Their sexual behaviour had always been absurd, but their mental priorities had by this time begun to pall, too, lurching as they did from a boyish obsession with the sporting achievements of someone they had never even met to a carelessly ambivalent attitude towards their own careers. The important things in this world, like a warm human relationship, were, it seemed to Wendy, seldom acknowledged or even noticed by the adult schoolboys who swapped infantile jokes over mugs of beer. But she was a conventional girl and conventional girls got married – not too soon, but not, on the other hand, too late. She was a short, slim girl with a very clear head. She seldom made a mistake.

"What was the Brock man like?" she asked the following morning when they had caught a bus north to the higgledy-piggledy capital of this brown and rocky island. "Tall, dark and handsome?"

7

"Short, dark and ugly with a big black beard," Venables told her. "But quite amusing."

"And his wife?"

"She wasn't there."

They walked between old, white four-storey buildings leaning precariously into tiny streets that were never meant for cars. A notice on a shop window said: "We spik Inglish".

Venables regarded shops as an elaborate device to separate him from his money and he hardly glanced at the displayed goods, preferring to look at the people. But Wendy couldn't bear to pass a window without gazing at the stuff that was offered. Soon she had bought a pair of sandals, a sweatshirt, a leather belt and a copper bracelet made on the island.

"Now that we're married," Venables said, "I think we should live within our means."

"So do I," said Wendy, "even if we have to borrow to do it."

He knew that she didn't mean this; her financial control would have shamed any government.

"Why don't you buy yourself something?" she asked. "Leather is good value here."

"What I'm going to buy myself is a beer. That's excellent value here, too."

They sat outside the American Bar in the Placa Reial. It was like Paris with sunshine.

Wendy ordered a coffee and said: "Being married doesn't feel any different."

"Did you think it would?" Venables asked, pouring out his beer.

"I imagined that something would change."

"Well, we did live together for two years."

"That's supposed to mean that the marriage will last two months."

"I think we'll do better than that. After all, we're now eligible to go to wife-swapping parties."

"Why don't they call it husband-swapping?" Wendy asked. "I can't see you doing it, anyway. You were never promiscuous, Simon."

He thought about Pym Brock, the blonde in the Rueda Bar, but his wife was right.

"It always rather put me off a girl if she was prepared to sleep with me," he said. "I bet Brigitte Bardot would never have slept

8

with me." He finished his beer and thought sadly about the wasted opportunities of his past. It seemed a curious line of thought for his first week as a married man and he wondered what his wife was thinking. She had always given him the impression that sex was all right as a time-killer, but didn't compare with a concerto by Bach, an historical novel or even an average night at the theatre. She was looking in her purse for pesetas to leave on the table. It meant that they were going.

"No more beer," she said. "There are sights we must see."

"What sights?" asked Venables. The sun-tanned holidaymakers wandering to and fro in front of the American Bar were providing enough sights for him.

"Prehistoric sites," replied Wendy. "This island has got hundreds of them. It also has caves converted into cafés and over there is the largest natural harbour in the Mediterranean."

"Let's go and see it," said Venables.

TWO

RUPERT PUCKLE had achieved the ambition that millions merely dream about: he had made all the money that he was going to need without sullying his hands with work. He was a tall, deeply sunburned man in his middle fifties, with lots of grey wavy hair and a white moustache. He had the sort of good looks that made people think they had seen him some time in a film.

He had got out at the top of the property boom, having bought a cottage in the early sixties for £4000 and sold it six years later for £30,000. He bought a bigger home immediately for £40,000 and sold it in 1976 for £90,000. He then bought a third house for £68,000 when it was already worth £80,000, sold it four years later for £125,000, and bought this villa for £10,000, investing the rest of the money in Sweden which provided him every month with far more pesetas than he knew how to spend.

He had spent some of it, though. His villa was a noticeable improvement on the holiday homes that his guests rented. Their water arrived on the back of a burro, led around the countryside by a wizened old man who spoke only the gruffest Catalan dialect. The water was poured into a cavernous cistern beside the kitchen from where it was pumped by a small motor to a tank on the roof. At this stage the law of gravity took over and the tank's water supplied the taps, the cold shower and the lavatory. But Rupert Puckle had not only installed a modern water system, he also had constant sprinklers feeding his green lawn in the centre of which was a blue swimming pool. The cane furniture on his marble patio was expensive, too. He sat on a wicker sofa, surrounded by jasmine and bougainvillaea, opening bottles of wine.

"This is the life," Ben Brock said, filling his glass for the third time while simultaneously stuffing square pieces of cheese into his mouth. Venables could see the origins of his weight problem.

"You're a millionaire," Rupert Puckle said. "Come out and

join me. Be one of the peeling bodies in Lotus Land reaching for the Cuba Libres while the workers clock on at home."

Venables was so intrigued by the news that his new fat friend was a millionaire that his gaze momentarily left the languid blonde whose body was draped over two chairs with her long brown legs supported by a small glass-topped table. She was a very quiet lady, this millionaire's wife, and as she sipped her wine thoughtfully Venables was wondering where he had seen her before.

"It's tempting, I agree," Ben Brock said. "But I can make a lot of money in England and it's still a free country." He scooped up more squares of cheese.

"It's a free country if you can afford it," Rupert Puckle replied. "I spent most of my time there trying to get from car to bar without getting wet. How is it these days, by the way? Do the bars still shut when the rest of Europe is about to go out for a drink? Do the papers still say 'Phew! What a scorcher!' every time it stops raining? It's funny. Your friends resent it if you go to live abroad. They take it as a personal rebuff."

"Did you ever get married?" Wendy Venables asked him. She was finding this man difficult to classify.

"A woman's question," Rupert Puckle said, smiling at her. "My dear girl, married, cuckolded, deserted, divorced."

"And you don't get lonely here?"

"I only wish I wasn't alone when I wake up in the night, but when I wake up in the morning I'm glad that I am. Funny that. I'm getting old."

"You don't look very old to me," said Venables.

"Old? I can remember when the English cricketers went to Australia by boat. I can remember trams with the drivers standing up. I can remember autocycles and Standard Vanguards and the Triumph Renown. Today they're all the same. I can't tell a Ford from a Fiat."

"That's middle-aged," said Venables.

"The prime of life or the beginning of the end?" Rupert Puckle asked. He not only looked like an actor, he sounded like one. The cultured voice delivered the lines as if someone else had written them for him. "Would anyone care for some *serrano* ham?"

He stood up and went indoors. Venables couldn't decide whether he was a suitable object for envy or sympathy, but another question fascinated him more. How had Ben Brock made a million pounds? It didn't seem right that he should have that beautiful wife and money and it wasn't easy to see, on this short acquaintance, how he had come by either. To Venables the situation reeked of injustice.

Their host returned with five plates, five forks and a dish full of sliced ham. Ben embarked on this new offering like a man who had just abandoned a diet. With a full mouth he asked: "What do you do, Rupert?"

Rupert Puckle had brought back with him several cans of beer, one of which he tore open. "Beer on wine, fine. Wine on beer, queer," he said. "What do I do? I avoid the trying realities of everyday life, old boy. In the mornings I do my Canadian Air Force exercises. I swim in the pool. I learn Spanish. I go out for a meal three or four times a week. I have my bridge club on Mondays. Given the sun and the privacy I have here it is often seven o'clock in the evening before I put any clothes on. My tan is unblemished by ugly white patches."

"It beats going to work," said Venables. He suddenly seemed to be envying everybody. His wife looked at him.

"What's wrong with going to work?" she asked. "A man's job is the only thing that earns him respect."

"If that were true it would be very sad," replied Rupert Puckle. "What about his natural qualities? Charm, personality, generosity. Do they count for nothing if he hasn't got a job?"

"Yes," said Wendy, "because if he hasn't got a job he's a passenger and not a participant."

Rubert Puckle shook his head sadly. "I'm ahead of my time. The five-day week will soon be a thing of the past. People will no longer have to sell their time cheaply and will have to find something more interesting to do."

"I can't think what."

"Read Shakespeare. Get fit. Learn a foreign language. Raise money for charity. Visit Russia. Sit down and think. Create a garden. Stop pretending that they're not going to die."

He's the kind of know-all man who would tell a girl how to insert a tampon, Wendy thought. She said, to be friendly: "If you've just got married the last thing you want is somebody lecturing your husband on the folly of going to work."

"Work kills," Rupert Puckle insisted. "That's child's book, page one."

Ben Brock waved a hand while he swallowed some ham. "It's

not work that kills, but worry. Work is where the money comes from." His estimation of people seldom drifted far from the balance sheet. "If you're so clever, why aren't you rich?" seemed to him to be the most pertinent question an arrogant man could be asked. "I bet Wendy works. I can tell."

"I own a sandwich bar called Morsels," she told him. "Drop in for a salmon and cucumber any time."

"And what do you do, Simon?" Pym asked. The unwelcome question arrived in a rich, soft voice that was deeply sexual. He hated his job, his inability to make money. It was something he never wanted to discuss, let alone with the beautiful wife of a millionaire.

"My career hangs by a gossamer thread at the moment," he admitted.

"And there are plenty of people around with a pair of scissors," said Wendy.

This bleak assessment of his situation brought more questions, none of them welcome.

"I'm a buyer. I buy things," he said. "For a big firm in London. But the recession is hitting us. Jobs are being lost."

"Never work for anyone else," said Ben. "Do you know that the self-employed are healthier? There's less strain involved in working for yourself. The more you are in control of your own life, the less likely you are to succumb to illness."

"There's plenty of strain in your life, darling," Pym said.

"Well, unfortunately I seem to be building an empire. I can't stop the damn thing growing. I now employ more than fifty people."

"I have money-making ideas but they never make any money," Venables said.

"Simon wants the laurel crown without the sweat," Wendy told them.

"Let's hear one," said Ben.

"If everyone in the country lent you ten pounds for one week you could make a million on the interest. Then you return the tenners."

"And what would it cost to do that?"

"Simon's ideas always fall down somewhere and that's where that one did."

The others laughed but Venables felt embarrassed. He had pulled the worry beads from his pocket and was now fidgeting with them. If anyone else had been smoking he would have re-started at once.

"I believe I'm on course to become the poorest man in the world," he continued.

"Oh no you're not," said Pym, and for a moment he felt hopeful again. "The poorest man in the world is called Nick Bannerman. He lives over a garage opposite us and can't afford to eat half the time. He's our token poor friend. We throw him crumbs."

"What does he do?" Wendy asked.

"He's writing something," Ben said. "His only possession is a very old typewriter."

"And what do you do, Pym?" Venables finally managed to ask. "I've seen your face somewhere."

"I usually keep it just here," she said, pointing at her head.

"She used to be a Page Three girl," Ben Brock announced. "Inflaming the passions of *hoi polloi* and sending them home in a state of ferment to surprise their wives. She's been responsible for more erections than Wimpeys the builders."

Simon remembered. Pym in a straw hat and nothing else. Pym on some rocks. Pym on a swing. Pym with a rose in her teeth. Pym waist-deep in a Caribbean pool. Pym, legs apart, hugging a palm tree. Pym and a towel.

"That was how we met," Ben said.

"Ben owns an advertising agency," Pym explained. "A licence to print money. I did some pictures for him."

Ben smiled at the story that Pym would not be telling this evening, but he remembered the afternoon that he arrived, his head full of business, at a photographer's studio in Earls Court to supervise the pictures that would launch a product which promised to improve the health of the nation's babies. The baby, selected from more than a hundred at an agency, was classically pretty. Pym was chosen for her topless talent. The pictures taken that day became famous in their own right, growing larger than their original commercial purposes and winning awards in four countries. Ben didn't know this when he moved in on Pym directly the photographer had finished. He lived in a world of tense creative exercises, brash ad men, cautious medical experts and dark-suited drug-company executives, and this topless beauty had kicked a door open in his mind. Perhaps it was the influence of the baby, perhaps it was Ben's unmissable air of confidence and prosperity that won Pym. That night she stayed at the flat which he then rented in Chelsea, having first made love twice on the primrose floor of the photographer's studio.

Sick with lust, Simon Venables stared across at Mrs Brock and wondered idly what colour her pubic hair was. He remembered the Page Three pictures almost too vividly, especially the one on a swing, both breasts in profile. He looked at her nervously – he could not even glance at another woman without Wendy noticing and although she never commented she managed, mysteriously, to release a little hostility into the atmosphere. Pym stared back at him now and he began to wonder whether she was attracted to him. Her question disabused him of this idea quite quickly.

"What on earth are those beads you're playing with? Is it a rosary?"

"Worry beads," Wendy replied. "He promised to give up smoking when we got married. The beads are supposed to help."

"My wife decided that I should give up smoking three years ago," Ben Brock said. "I put on two stone."

"Your wife makes the decisions in your house, does she?" Rupert Puckle asked.

"He makes the big decisions and I make the small decisions," Pym said.

"But Pym decides which are the big decisions," added her husband.

"Well, I've just made an important decision, people," said Rupert Puckle. "I think you should all come out to live in the sun before it is too late."

"Too late?" said Ben. "I understood it was going to last another six billion years and then vaporise the surface of the earth?"

"Well, why don't you all come out for a holiday this summer and stay with me?"

"Oh, yes," said Pym.

"Simon?"

"Love to."

"That's settled then," said Rupert Puckle. "Just write and give me the dates."

The sun, that only had another six billion years, didn't waste time with dusk in Spain but dipped and vanished quickly, to be replaced by a thousand stars, a crescent moon and a comet with a treble-barrelled surname. At the centre of the bottles of wine on the table Rupert found and lit an oil lamp. It illuminated potted geraniums that lined the patio. The night was still hot.

Pym Brock, simultaneously bored and relieved by the company, was cheered by the thought of another holiday here. It gave her something to look forward to, a date to ring on her wall calendar that was dismally free of the elaborate and brightly coloured circles, squares and asterisks that she used to plot future excitement. Two weeks straddling June and July had been optimistically starred for Wimbledon, and a friend who had once been topless too was marrying a famous but injury-prone footballer in May. Beyond that the future was a barren prospect that frightened her. Not that she regretted the passing of her career and its .ephemeral fame. Despite its sexual aura she had found men intimidated by her image and difficult to attract. It had taken somebody with Ben Brock's confidence to sweep her out of the studio and into the kitchen. She had never liked modelling, anyway, feeling easily capable of a larger challenge, but she never managed to decide what she wanted to do and the modelling offers kept arriving and the money was good. Of course Ben was a disappointment – what man wasn't? – but the fact that he was becoming richer every day was a compensation she could not overlook. His greatest drawback was a temper that occasionally became violent. She had hoped that the birth of a son three years ago might have cured it but the reverse was the case: the additional responsibility seemed to create more frequent explosions. She felt safer when they were not alone and so she found that the company of others could be a bore and a relief at the same time.

In the bedroom of their villa the Venables were chasing a lizard, a nightly visitor who shuffled across the white ceiling with such clockwork regularity that they suspected it of voyeurism. If that were indeed its taste, it was a disappointed lizard. The Venables' honeymoon, cut to seven days by the uncertainties at Simon's office, had not been typical of the post-marriage orgies that reputedly took place under the Mediterranean sun. They had spent the days touring, eating, drinking and sunbathing, and arrived back late each evening almost too tired to talk. Venables had never been keen on night sex, anyway. In the animal world, he told Wendy, sex was a day-time activity, and it was only the repressive requirements of civilisation that had driven it into the dark hours for human beings whose sex drives were highest in the morning and dropped sharply in the evening. He was tired when he went to bed. That was why he went to bed.

The lizard vanished tonight as it did every night behind the ornate Spanish wardrobe in the corner, and Venables went into the bathroom to clean his teeth. By the time he got into bed his wife was already there, engrossed in her new paperback about the Princes in the Tower. He lay back and closed his eyes. They had to be up early tomorrow to pack. The honeymoon was over. Honey plus moon. Meaning a month? He had looked it up on the day before the wedding – he was addicted to words – and discovered that it originally referred to waning affection.

"What do you think of our new millionaire friend then?" his wife asked, putting down her book.

"I like them both."

That evening the four of them had eaten at a restaurant in the port.

"Will we go on holiday with them?"

"I hope so. I like holidays."

There was a long silence and he thought his wife was asleep. But she had another question.

"Do you think many people have honeymoons without any sex?"

He opened his eyes and looked at her but she had her eyes closed herself.

"It's the new fashion," he said. "They have it first these days."

He waited for the peace which would allow him to concentrate on his present preoccupation: his new fat friend with the facial hair, the beautiful wife and the million pounds, and the mystery of why they should have so much when he had so little. Venables had been sent out into the world with a provincial degree and a hunger for success but had somehow managed to achieve nothing. Twisting and turning in bed, he tormented himself with the theory that there was a flaw in his character, his mind, his genes. His father had once been a tryer, a pusher, a man who wanted to get rich, too. But in the end he was as mystified as his son about how some people placed their hands effortlessly on huge financial jackpots while others, who seemed to be equally talented, waited nervously for the monthly bills. He gave up the struggle suddenly and relapsed with whisky's help into a defeated stupor. Venables had half expected to read "acute lethargy" on the death certificate.

He lay in bed now, unable to sleep, asking himself over and over whether the world was unjust or whether the fatal fault was in him.

part two

ASPIRATIONS

Being a husband is a whole-time job. That is why so many husbands fail. They cannot give their entire attention to it.

Arnold Bennett

Caged birds accept each other but flight is what they long for.

Tennessee Williams

THREE

SELLERS COURT BUYERS. Simon Venables was taken to lunch only
in those restaurants that emerged with credit in the food guides.
In dark but classy eateries, invariably in Soho, men in search of
large contracts pitched woo over modest banquets, usually fruit-
lessly because Simon only took up the invitations to escape from
the glass-box offices of Top Toys.

Top Toys had grown from nowhere to multi-million-pound
security in ten years by providing something different for the
children of the affluent society. Their newest project, which would
eventually sweep the western world, was a battery-driven toy car for
boys. Most of the components had already been bought or ordered
by Venables and a factory in south London was being primed for
production. One problem remained unsolved – the batteries themselves, which required special qualities of power, size and weight.

Venables pondered the challenge in the sixth-floor office to
which he had now given four years of his life, and glared through
the windows at the chimneys and gasometers of south London. If
you looked at a map of the world, he thought, nobody in their
right mind would choose to settle here. He flipped through his
diary to gauge the shape of the day and found that he had a lunch
date with a man from the North.

He called through a glass partition to his boss, a short, stocky
man of sixty called Shern.

"I'm meeting Schwarzbaum about the batteries."

Shern, who never spoke more than he had to, acknowledged
this with one upward-pointing thumb.

Outside, Venables felt as if he had shed a weight. He preferred
lanes to streets, hedges to walls, and when he looked up he wanted
to see a wide blue sky rather than the twentieth floor of a speculative development. But even here, in the grimy edges of the
nation's capital, he preferred outdoors.

A new generation of sixteen-year-old girls were flaunting their thighs in the street; it looked like a vintage year. He took a Tube to Leicester Square and walked.

Mel Schwarzbaum, a small bespectacled man with shoulders hunched protectively against a hostile world, stood with his pressed aluminium brief-case in his hand, in the hallway of the restaurant.

"Simon – hallo," he said, switching hands on his brief-case to extend his right.

The pair had met only once before and he was interested to learn that they had leapt this quickly to first-name terms. He was relieved, too; he wasn't anxious to wrestle with his host's surname.

The owner and managing director of Schwarzbaum Batteries had reserved a discreet table which strategically excluded eavesdropping waiters, large-eared fellow eaters or even casual interruptions from old friends. He led Venables to it.

"Well, how are Top Toys?" he asked, when the menu had arrived.

"Top Toys are tops," said Venables.

"You've got to push, push, push," said Mel Schwarzbaum. "Never underestimate the apathy of the public is my advice."

"We push," Venables assured him.

"It's certainly a pleasure to come down to London to see you."

"You've come down specially to see me?" asked Venables.

"I certainly have," said Mel. "Call me Mel."

"London is a good place to get out of, Mel. You live here twenty years, you drink your own recycled urine three times and pay high rates for the privilege."

"That so?" said Mel. "Of course everything is cheaper where we operate. To say that if you pay peanuts you get monkeys leaves too much out of the equation. There are huge profits in cheap labour."

"I'm glad that everything is going well for you, Mel."

"It's not," said Mel.

A waiter took their orders and glided away to be replaced by the wine waiter. Soon a bottle of Mouton Cadet appeared.

"Of course, we've put our costs under the brightest possible spotlight. Our revenue targets are just about being met, but the stories you hear in the trade today turn your bowels to water."

Venables looked at Mel, fearing his salesman's rhetoric. He was wearing a white shirt with a light-blue suit. His nose was so large and discoloured that Venables could imagine it coming off with his glasses, like a clown's mask. It would, he thought, make a good face on a comic poster. Have you seen this man? Do not approach him under any circumstances. He is very boring.

"It's difficult for us all at the moment," Venables said. "But private enterprise put this government in, so it can put up with it. Stay hopeful."

"It's difficult to be optimistic if you're a pessimist," said Mel, shaking his head.

In a spirit of adventure Venables had ordered *anitra allarancio*. It turned out to be duck with orange sauce. His host's life story was replayed slowly at his elbow while he ate. It was a discursive narrative about a post-war refugee, washed up on these shores in the wake of Hitler's hatred, who through nerve and energy had created an enterprise the foundations of which, after thirty years of slow growth, were beginning to creak.

"The prediction is," said Venables, "that the upturn is coming."

"That so?" said Mel. Despite his majority contribution to the dialogue, he had managed to empty his plate some way ahead of his guest. "I'm not that sanguine about it."

"Top Toys are expecting an increase in personal consumption before the end of the year."

Mel looked gloomier than ever. "A consumer boom that is based on borrowing can't last," he said. "In fact, it's counter-productive because when it bursts everyone is back where they were – only with bigger debts."

The waiter removed their plates and took fresh orders. Mel drank his wine and said: "You haven't placed an order yet."

"I ordered *zabaglione*," said Venables.

"I mean the batteries. You haven't decided yet."

Venables was surprised. "How do you know?"

"I've made enquiries."

"You're very well informed."

"You don't like our batteries."

"Don't I?"

"That was interrogative."

"I think they're excellent. We just haven't decided yet, Mel."

"We? Whose decision is it?"

"Well, mine."

The waiter delivered *zabaglione* and trifle. Venables, embarrassed, ate. There was no such thing as a free lunch.

"Simon, it's vitally important to us."

"I imagine."

"What are the odds, would you say?"

"Seven to four? Thirteen to eight? You're right in there. The unusual specifications are flooring some of your rivals."

"That so? We can handle it. Our price was competitive, wasn't it?"

"I've been offered better."

Mel looked so dismayed that Venables felt a surge of pity for him. The orders that he had placed for Top Toys had given him considerable power, but he hated to see its effects at a personal level.

Mel leaned towards him. "We have a slush fund, Simon," he said, as if playing a final card. "In the Channel Islands."

"A what?"

"A slush fund."

"I heard you. Why in the Channel Islands?"

"No tax enquiries."

Venables waved to the waiter. "Can we have the bill?" he asked. To Mel he said: "I'll pay. I have to get back to the office."

Ben Brock lay on a brown sunbed beside his cruciform swimming pool. A glass of gin stood on a small white table at his side, and a plastic bottle, half full of lemonade, floated in the pool itself for mid-swim refreshment. The temperature in the log cabin behind him, which was packed with spare sunbeds, spare chairs, spare costumes and a fridge crammed with drinks, was eighty-eight.

To his right the lawn swept up a slight gradient for fifty yards to his huge house which, in Tudor celebration, had windows of leaded glass and bevelled panes; to his left, on a rise behind a row of pines, was a new tennis court, laid in time for the summer but not much used yet. The whole spread was concealed from its equally opulent neighbours by a high hedge of laurel and rhododendron. Only the privileged lived in this road, a private half-mile drive with "sleeping policemen" ridges laid at regular intervals to dissuade the rest of the world from using it as a public highway. Nobody here worried about the rates or the electricity bills and although for most people one day was much like another, for these people every day was different. In this world, you bought air tickets as often as train tickets, and non-airborne days were normally spent travelling, usually very quickly in a chauffeur-driven Daimler, from one business assignment to another – an interview in the Midlands, a conference in the West Country, a board meeting in London. Ben Brock's neighbours maintained an air of mystery, but they were no doubt equally curious about him. They met warily at the meetings of the residents' association, a quarterly conclave that schemed to keep the world out.

Ben sipped his gin and then closed his eyes against the glare of the sun. The heat created rivulets of sweat which trickled down his chest only to find themselves trapped in his stomach's fat. He liked to spend Saturdays enjoying the things which his success had bought, but that success had not come easily. It was the result of a single-minded devotion to work which had become difficult to lose. So lying by the pool now he was thinking about a presentation he would make in London on Tuesday to win a million-pound advertising account for a new drug that would relieve arthritis. He had no doubt that he would win it – he had become a millionaire by trying harder than the others.

He had learned the lesson early, at his very first interview.

After a false start in insurance he had realised that advertising was where the money was, and he applied for a job in an agency's creative department. Like most of the ageing trendies that year, the man who interviewed him was wearing a blue denim suit and a fringe. Being naturally on a diet, he was drinking orange juice instead of coffee when Ben walked in.

"You want to be creative," he said directly Ben sat down. He emptied the orange into his glass and banged the empty bottle on his desk.

"Be creative about that bottle."

Ben was baffled.

"What do you mean?" he asked.

"You want to be creative. Be creative about that bottle," the man repeated tonelessly.

Ben looked at the bottle. "Do you mean the label or the product or what?" he asked.

The man stared at him.

"Just be creative, Mr Brock."

Ben picked up the bottle, turning it in his fingers. He wondered whether the tedious world of insurance wasn't, after all, his natural home.

"You could do quite a lot with this bottle," he said, "apart from its normal function."

The man didn't move. "Such as?" he asked.

Ben remembered what you did with bottles.

"Send messages in it," he suggested.

The man sipped his orange juice but didn't say anything. Ben stroked his beard and studied the bottle. The silence seemed to be depressing them both, and Ben could see his planned future drifting on to the rocks before it had been launched.

"What I could do with a bottle like this would be quite interesting," he said suddenly. "I could slice it up and make napkin rings from it. I could make egg cups from the base. I could melt it down and make a glass sculpture from it."

I could turn it into a sigmoidoscope and shove it up your arse, he thought.

The man nodded. The interview limped to its uncertain conclusion.

That evening, angry with himself, Ben bought a crate of orange juice, poured the lot down the sink, and set to work.

With blowlamps and tongs he melted, twisted and pulled one of the bottles into a fine piece of sculpture that he called "the orange-juice tree". He found a man who owned a tungsten-carbide-tipped circular saw and turned four bottles into a dozen napkin rings. With both the saw and the blowlamp he made three egg cups. And finally he gave a photograph of his interviewer, which had appeared in a trade journal, to a cartoonist friend who produced an excellent caricature of him with a bottle as a sigmoidoscope protruding from his bottom.

The whole lot, in presentation pack, was on the man's desk by lunchtime the following day and by five o'clock Ben had been offered the job.

Trying just a little harder than the others carried him through the first year but by then he had spotted the gap in the market that he needed: an advertising agency that catered exclusively for the pharmaceutical industry. It took another year of careful planning before he was ready to resign and announce the birth of Ben Brock Advertising.

That was eight years ago and now, at thirty, he was a paper

millionaire. The Bentley in his garage cost £60,000, the sporty Aston Martin alongside more than half that. Even the watch on his wrist, a Patek Philippe bought in Geneva, cost £4000. None of these acquisitions seemed to matter much to Ben Brock who knew that only historians got anywhere thinking about the past. He lay beside the pool rehearsing in his head the patter he would deliver to Pexo, the drug company, on Tuesday.

He was disturbed by a splash in the pool and lifted his head to see his three-year-old son, Gregory, drowning. He jack-knifed off the sunbed and dived horizontally into the water to find the boy. He caught a limb and lost it and then caught it again and propelled both of them to the surface.

Gregory blinked and spluttered.

"Swimming," he said.

Ben carried him to the side of the pool, placed him on the edge and climbed out himself. Then he took him over to the sunbed and dried his head. He was a cheerful, handsome boy with his mother's blonde hair. At that moment she appeared in a white bikini that showed off her Spanish tan.

"Have you been in?" she asked.

"Just to save his life," said Ben. "I thought you were looking after him. You know he's not allowed near the pool."

"But I knew you were near the pool."

Ben tried to control his anger. He didn't want to poison his day off.

"Did you swim, Greg?" Pym asked him. "He seems to find the water fascinating."

"I don't want him near it. Have I got to have it covered up every day?"

"Why not?" said Pym. "Don't start a row. The neighbours might hear."

Pym chose her barbs with care. The neighbours worried her husband who had never expected to find himself in this company. When they first arrived Pym had made discreet efforts to find out who they all were. She eventually discovered that among them were an air vice-marshal, now working in Whitehall, the managing director of an international electronics firm, a knighted civil servant and a stockbroker, but they still didn't know which were which. The only neighbour they could identify was Vaughan, because they knew the penniless bachelor who typed all day in a small flat over his garage.

Ben removed the soaking yellow shirt that his son was wearing and laid it out in the sun.

"Side up down," Gregory said, happy with his father's company. He meant that he had been upside down in the water. Ben was endlessly fascinated by his son's struggle to master the language. Television was "chessavision" and disappeared was "different peared" but his efforts, like the rest of his behaviour, were selective. He was quite capable of saying "I'll throw you in the dustbin" if he was annoyed. He had learned how to do the important things. He couldn't tie his shoelaces or dress himself, but he could turn on the television and operate the video equipment. His talent for finding mice, dead or alive, was prodigious. He presented them, usually alive, to visiting grandparents because that was where he got the best reaction. The grandparents loved him and Ben was surprised at the doting affection shown to babies by the very old. He thought a more natural reaction to the just starting from the soon to die would have been a furious envy.

When he let the boy go he immediately toddled in the direction of the water. But he stopped at the edge and watched as his mother completed two lengths. She arrived back at the shallow end and stood up.

"Are you coming in, Greg?" she asked.

The boy nodded and she lifted him in. He kicked the water over her, shrieking with delight.

Ben lay back on the sunbed, fuming at the disturbance. He dragged his mind back to the arguments which he would be advancing, with that clarity and charm which disarms critics, in his Pexo presentation. His wife made no allowances for the demands of his job. She seemed to have no idea why, when most men were watching their pennies, he was a millionaire at thirty. She treated him just like anyone else. He got back to the graphics and visual aids that he would use on Pexo: they centred on the potentially arthritic joints of one hand.

But the shadow of a hand was now being passed backwards and forwards over his face. He opened his eyes to the new interruption, a man in jeans and an old white shirt. It was Nick Bannerman, the man who lived over a garage.

"I heard some loose talk about a barbecue tonight," he said.

Ben sat up. He had forgotten that he was holding a barbecue. "Hallo, Nick. Yes, the Brocks are lashing out. You'll come?"

"Now you've invited me I'll try to fit it in."

"You'd come even if we didn't invite you. Get yourself a drink from the cabin."

Ben Brock liked Nick Bannerman. For a start, in this privileged enclave he was the only male friend he had. He was also intrigued by his lonely and impoverished lifestyle, his frenzied typing over the road, his dedication to some no doubt receding goal. Best of all he liked the complete contrast of their bank accounts. Being generous to Nick Bannerman gave him a warm glow.

He was a tall man – another contrast – with a round, pale face and startling cobalt-blue eyes. His short hair was seldom combed, and he talked slowly and thoughtfully. He was a man in the grip of an obsession.

He returned from the cabin now with a can of Fosters.

"I thought I might let you admire my crosscourt backhand," he said. "This sedentary existence isn't doing me any good."

"How is your sedentary existence? Scribble, scribble, scribble. I envy you."

"There's no need for that," Nick Bannerman said, opening his lager. "Give me the beautiful home, the beautiful wife, the swimming pool and the tennis court, and you can go and live over the road and get a headache staring at my typewriter. No need for any envy, Ben."

"Property shackles, Nick," Ben said, standing up. He went off to the cabin to find his tennis shoes and racket, as Pym came out of the pool with Greg.

"Hallo, Greg," said Nick.

"Take your face away," Greg told him.

"It's his new saying, I'm afraid," said Pym. "Are you coming to our barbecue?"

But before he could answer she had to turn away to catch her son who was heading back to the pool. Nick Bannerman lay down on the sunbed and tentatively tasted the life of the very rich.

"Nick!" Ben called. "What racket do you want?"

"Ben's calling you," Pym told him.

Sometimes he forgot to answer to the name.

Few things are more vulnerable to pressure than a man's mind, but Nick Bannerman felt that he had withstood it very well since he disappeared five years ago and emerged in another part of the country with a new name and the clothes he stood up in. He survived now in a small flat over a double garage that didn't quite join the Georgian mansion of Vaughan, the pet-food millionaire. Vaughan had let the flat cheaply to Nick because in an age of burglaries, muggings and sexual offences of increasing horror, he felt happier with a man within shouting distance when his wife was alone all day. Nick occasionally cast a dutiful glance from his window in search of muggers but seldom even saw the Vaughans.

He sat at his desk in his flat, the victim of a compulsion to cover blank sheets of paper with words. He was a writer, or he was trying to be a writer, and the income from the words that he poured out occasionally put his new bank account into the black. He wrote articles for any publication that asked him and received acceptances from quite a few that hadn't. But his real creative energy went into a potentially big book that he was desperately trying to complete, a massive assault on the feminists' delusion of male domination. It contained a thousand reasons for suggesting that men were sorely treated in the fourth quarter of the twentieth century, condemned to lives that were filled with work, social restrictions, family duties and endless obligations at the expense not only of their happiness but also their health.

It was called *Battered Husbands*.

Planting a boot up the plump bums of the dungareed feminists was now, for Nick, a compelling mission. His files spilled over with ammunition for his cause: newspaper cuttings, court cases, government statistics, quotations from marriages past. The divorce courts were a rich source of material on the subject of women's inhumanity to man, much of it bizarre.

WIFE TOOK FIRST HUSBAND'S ASHES ON HONEYMOON

said a headline on his desk. It partly concealed a more sinister one:

GOD LOSES MALE IMAGE.

He looked out of the window at the Vaughans' immaculate lawn which, just like Ben Brock's, dropped down to a swimming pool. In his cheerier moments he imagined that the royalties from *Battered Husbands* could provide him with similar facilities.

He typed.

Margaret Mead, perhaps now discredited by her Samoan adventure, once wrote that throughout history females have picked providers for mates, and males have picked anything. What conclusions are we to draw from this?

What conclusions was he to draw from this? He lit a cigarette. Once, in an attempt to give up smoking, he had saved every empty packet so that he could frighten himself with the hugeness of his consumption. But at that revealing moment a free offer arrived from the manufacturers – two cartons of cigarettes for anybody who sent off the fronts of 100 packets. He smoked on.

The nicotine delivered his next sentence.

It is obvious.

But little was obvious to him this afternoon and, as always in his unproductive moments, he began to pace the room. Both the garage and Nick's flat perched above it were built, surprisingly, of cedar. The flat consisted of one large room, with a small kitchen and bathroom at one end. Since it had been permanently abandoned by a chauffeur who had been dispatched reluctantly (and fatally) to the war in 1939, its contents had changed considerably. There was now a fridge and a washing machine in the kitchen, a pink shower stall in the bathroom and even, in one corner of the big room, a cocktail bar. The Vaughans had not, however, provided a television, and Nick couldn't afford one. His only luxury, necessary for work, was an ex-directory telephone. His bed, neither single nor double but something in between, fitted unobtrusively in a corner. This was a work place.

In this wood cabin the words multiplied, breeding uncontrollably, despoiling sheet after sheet of the finest Croxley Script paper before joining many thousands of others on the floor that were waiting, perhaps optimistically, to be legitimised by print.

He returned to his desk and wondered how he could twist Margaret Mead's words towards the defence of his beleaguered gender. He thumbed through some cuttings. In Spain 1000 men committed suicide every year, but only 300 women. But there were no dungareed feminists in Spain. For a moment he wondered whether the Women's Movement might not, after all, be about to save men's lives. He found another cutting: seven out of every ten people aged over 100 were women. This looked more fruitful. The lot of the male: work, stress, worry and an early grave? He wrote:

It is obvious. Women are the realistic sex, the harder – far removed from the soft, romantic image that is projected on their behalf. It is the simple and straightforward male whose head is turned by an attractive face, while the woman quietly sets her tender trap to catch her distracted prey.

For some minutes his mind strained after a metaphor about the female spider who devoured her mate after sexual frolics, but he didn't want to over-egg the pudding.

His next chapter would deal with money. He had a powerful cutting in his files about a man who bought himself a house and then met and married a girl. When the marriage broke up the man was kicked out of the house. Stuff like this was meat and drink to Nick. He had plenty of other material to go with it: an old *Hansard* containing a parliamentary debate about the rights of divorced women; a divorce-court settlement that put a father of three in prison; a piece from the women's pages of one of the serious newspapers asking,"Is Castration The Answer?"

But the next chapter would involve a lot of preparation and it would have to wait.

He pushed his typewriter away on his desk and stared, chin in hand, at the Vaughans' garden. The truth was that he felt sluggish. What he needed was a woman. Perhaps the Vaughans had a pubescent au pair girl, preferably with limited English, lurking around the property.

He felt sluggish quite a lot these days. Although the discovery would not be included in the pellucid pages of *Battered Husbands*, he had found that celibacy made him torpid.

Nick Bannerman needed a night that he would never forget, even if he couldn't remember it the following morning.

The exhaustion brought on by the swelling manuscript was now accompanied by a neurotic fear that a fire in the flat would destroy it. A fire-proof safe was the answer, but he couldn't afford a fire-proof safe.

In a cupboard over the sink, where bleach and disinfectant nestled alarmingly with Branston pickle, corn oil and gravy mix, he found a small bottle of Teacher's whisky, a portion of which, he decided, had now been earned.

The drink nudged his memory – tonight the Brocks were holding a barbecue!

Lovely ladies were about to disport themselves by the side of the pool, while romantic music played, jokes flowed and the food and the drink were free. He would arrive early, ostensibly to help with the preparations, and get first crack at the sherbet. By the time he had taken a shower, the whisky bottle was empty. He dressed in a new blue shirt that he had been saving for a special occasion, and a pair of jeans that were several years older.

He left the flat and walked along the private road to the Brocks' house. The long hedge-lined drive to the house concealed a car park; its emptiness told him that he was ahead of the field.

At the back of the house Ben was carrying tables and chairs down the lawn to the pool.

"Give us a hand, Nick," he said.

Nick picked up two small tables. "I only came early to get at the booze."

"You sound as if you have taken a small refreshment already."

"I'm refreshed out of my mind."

"I suppose you writers have to drink to unwind?"

"Trouble is, I tend to unravel."

Ben put down the table that he was carrying and looked at Nick. "I think tomorrow is going to be one of those mornings when you wake up fully dressed."

"I hope so," said Nick.

Fairy lights had been draped through the trees by the cross-shaped pool which was itself lit from within. When darkness arrived it would present an impressive picture. They set out the tables and chairs and brought glasses from the house. They found the barbecue kit at the back of the poolside cabin and lit it now to provide the right red-hot glow later. Finally they transferred crates of champagne from the house to the cabin, along with paper plates but silver cutlery.

"Who's coming?" asked Nick.

"Friends, neighbours. Employees."

Pym appeared, walking down the lawn to the pool with her son.

"Hallo, Nick. Greg wants to come to the party."

Greg stared shyly at Nick, hands clasped together.

"Hallo, Greg," said Nick. "Want some champagne?"

"Take your face away," replied Greg.

"Well, we do," said Ben, opening a bottle and filling their glasses.

"What do you think of this, Ben?" asked Pym, turning round. She was wearing a new short, yellow dress with halter top.

"Fine," said Ben. "How much was it?"

"I dress to please Ben but he never notices," Pym told Nick.

"If you dressed to please me you'd wear last year's clothes," said Ben.

"If you dressed to please me you wouldn't wear anything," said Nick.

"You can't fob her off with a mink coat. She wants wolf or lynx," said Ben. "Do you want an orange juice, Greg?"

Greg ran over to his father and took the drink, and they all made their way back to the house with full glasses.

"We've got a new digital record player that uses a laser instead of a needle," Pym said.

"I don't have a record player," said Nick.

"Nor a television. Nick is cut off from the world's news."

"Anything been going on?" he asked.

"Good news from Mafeking," Ben told him. "And they've given women the vote."

The news produced in Nick an expression of outraged horror. "That's a slippery slope they've climbed on to there," he said. "There'll be a woman in Downing Street next." But he secretly wondered whether, at the treadmill of his desk, he couldn't manage to trace man's misfortunes back to that abject day when angry, demonstrating women won access to the nation's ballot papers.

The first guest to arrive was Mr Anderson, a loud young man who sat – in the way of all progress, as it were – on the county council.

"You're the mysterious chappie who lives over the Vaughans' garage, aren't you?" he said to Nick who escaped from his waffle in seconds and reappeared, via the bathroom, on to a full patio five minutes later.

He headed for a couple in the corner who seemed as isolated as himself. The man, in his early thirties, was wearing a blazer and tie. He had a small black moustache and was swinging what looked like a rosary round in his hands. The woman with him was a short, dark attractive creature with sexy eyes and a firm intelligent mouth.

"Nick Bannerman is my name," he said, offering his hand.

"Simon Venables," replied the man. "My wife, Wendy."

"Are you the couple Ben met on holiday?"

"Pym met us, too," said Wendy. "Why are couples always referred to by the man's name?"

"*Touché*," said Nick. "Or ouch for short."

Confusion over the etiquette of barbecues had resulted in a strange variety of dress. Dinner jackets stood alongside naked shoulders and long dresses, while others, less touched by the past, wore short-sleeved shirts and jeans. No longer surprisingly, these apparently separate factions merged sociably over the drinks: clothes today revealed few clues about their wearers. Right next to Nick, a short girl with Channel-swimmer's shoulders and a man's torn green shirt was proudly relating the saga of her family's misfortunes.

"We lost the title two hundred years ago and then the money," she said. "We had to sell thirty farms."

"How awful," said a muscular lady beside her.

"Oh, we got the money back," continued the girl, her jaw jutting. "It's in the blood."

Venables looked at Nick Bannerman cautiously. "These friends of yours?"

Nick raised his eyebrows and shook his head. "I haven't got any friends," he said. "And if I had, these wouldn't be."

"Not even the girl with money in her blood?"

"I know of her. On a scale of one to five I'd give her minus fifty-four. The number of men who have had her can be counted on the fingers of one continent."

Wendy Venables, standing between them, gave Nick Bannerman a cool, appraising look. He seemed to be wild to her, but perhaps he was drunk. "I thought a rich over-sexed woman was what you men were looking for?"

"Opulence, yes. Herpes, no," said Nick. "I'm glad I've met you. You've sobered me up."

This observation, clearly intended as either a compliment or an insult, was hanging in the air awaiting classification when Ben emerged through the guests.

"How is everyone? Still sober? The champagne is by the pool and can't possibly run out. Her Royal Lowness is helping me

35

with the barbecue so there will soon be steaks. How are you, Simon? Have you met anybody?"

"I've met him."

"My unconventional neighbour? He sits alone in a little room scribbling all day, you know. Very odd."

"That's me," said Nick.

"Where is Pym?" asked Wendy. "I'll go and help her."

When she had gone, Ben led them through the crowd to a small man with red hair and huge Elton John spectacles who was sitting on the edge of a table. He was wearing a cream linen suit, Italian cut, a silk shirt with a flowery tie and burgundy emu shoes.

"This," said Ben, "is Johnny Fix-It, an appallingly vulgar creature impoverished by fast cars, slow horses, strong drink and weak women."

"Where's your wife?" asked Johnny Fix-It. "She makes my pants stick out." He spoke with a genuine Cockney accent.

"The man in the blazer is Simon Venables," Ben told him.

Johnny Fix-It studied him through his saucer-like glasses. "I've been sold second-hand cars by men dressed like you," he said.

"And this is Nick Bannerman."

"Johnny who?" said Nick.

"Johnny Fix-It," replied Ben. "He is a truly amazing man, a miracle-worker. He can fix anything. Anything. His services are highly valued by my firm and highly paid for. I only wish he was on the staff."

"Thanks for the commercial," Johnny Fix-It said. "If I can ever help either of you gentlemen, just call. I need the money."

"What for?" asked Venables.

"I want a motor yacht in Banus."

"What can you fix for me?" Nick asked him.

"Anything," replied Johnny Fix-It simply.

"Just try him," said Ben, slipping off to weld other guests into sociable groups.

"Ben Brıck!" said Johnny Fix-It.

"Isn't it Brock?"

"I call him Brick. Short, square, solid, a bit red. Doing little jobs for him helped to pay for my Ferrari."

"I've never met a miracle-worker before," said Nick. He was trying to remember what it was that he had always wanted to do, an unrealised ambition that had always niggled him. Perhaps Johnny could fix it.

"I can arrange anything except my own sex life," said Johnny Fix-It. "I am hoping that money will eventually solve that problem."

"Why can't you fix that," asked Venables, "if you're a miracle-worker?"

"I don't look like Robert Redford, do I? But I nearly pulled it off last week. I met a really stunning girl in an afternoon club in London and she was very friendly. I asked when I could see her and she said come round that evening. She gave me her address and I thought I was made. So round I went and a big, burly sod opened the door. 'I've come to see Marie,' I said. 'Okay,' he said, 'have you brought the bread?' 'The what?' I said. 'The bread,' he said. I must be going soft in the head. She was a hooker and he was her pimp. 'I'll go and get it,' I said. I went round to a friend of mine who runs a bakery in New Cross and bought sixty two-day-old loaves cheap. Then I drove back and built a wall of loaves on their doorstep with a hole in the middle so I could ring their bell. When the door opened, I gave the whole lot a hell of a push. 'Here's the bread,' I shouted."

"What happened?"

"I was gone. A Ferrari is a useful vehicle."

"I'll tell you what you can fix for me," said Nick, remembering now the schoolboy ambition that had lain dormant since long day-dream hours in the classroom. "I've always wanted to be on television. Practically everybody else in the world has been on television at one time or another. Why not me?"

Johnny Fix-It shrugged and looked up at him. The lights from the trees bounced off his huge lenses. "I'll get you on television, kid," he said. "Write your name and number in this book." He produced a black leather notebook and a gold Cross pen from his cream suit.

"Really?" asked Nick, writing.

"Johnny Fix-It has spoken," said Johnny Fix-It. "There's no money in it for me but I'll do it just to prove a point."

The smell of sizzling steaks floated into the spring evening, and music from Genesis burst suddenly from hidden speakers in the trees. The smell reminded Nick that he had eaten very little all day and he strolled down to the pool where Ben was now busily introducing steaks to bread rolls. "I've got a hundred fillet steaks in the fridge," he said. "Get stuck in, Nick." Marvelling at the extravagance, Nick got stuck in. Simon Venables, whose eating requirements were catered for more adequately by a wife, sought further champagne. As it bubbled in his glass, Wendy arrived.

"You ought to see their kitchen," she said. "It's amazing."

"Kitchens I keep out of. How is the lovely Pym?"

"You must come and see this one. Some day you may be able to afford one like it." She took his arm and led him away from the crowd at the pool. "Pym is all right," she said. "Except that she thinks she has a broken rib."

"How did she do that?"

"She said she fell over on the tennis court."

"That isn't how you break a rib."

The kitchen when they reached it seemed to be all mahogany: mahogany units with terracotta tile surfaces, beautiful mahogany cupboards at eye-level with concealed lights, a breakfast bar in mahogany that had mahogany stools with backrests, armrests and cushions. There were two sinks, one with a waste-disposal unit; two cookers, one split-level electric, the other gas; two fridges; and a spotless copper hood over the hob that included a deep-fat fryer. On a high shelf near the beamed ceiling stood a row of copper saucepans, and the floor, in lacteal white Italian tiles, must have provided a full-time job for the Brocks' cleaning lady. Behind a plant-strewn arch there was a utility room with an eight-foot freezer, a washing machine and a tumble dryer. The final touch in the kitchen was a marble-inlay surface on one of the units, not only for rolling pastry but also for playing with chocolate.

Even by the luxurious standards which Venables fancifully hoped would eventually govern his life there were one or two bits and pieces here that he secretly regarded as unnecessary. Great wealth was not, in his view, something to be thrown around heedlessly: ethical as well as economic considerations counselled restraint. Disapproval, however, would have seemed inappropriate from somebody in his restricted financial condition. It would be misunderstood.

"It's marvellous," he said.

"It would be marvellous to cook in," agreed Wendy. "Why don't you make some money?"

"I'm trying, wife. I'm trying. Where's the bathroom in this castle? Or did all the money go on the kitchen?"

He half expected to find mohair toilet rolls beside a solid gold lavatory, but he was disappointed. As he walked back along the upstairs corridor on a purple carpet of energy-sapping thickness,

38

he glanced through an open door and saw Pym sitting on a bed.
He stopped.

"There's a barbecue downstairs," he called. "I'm sure you're
invited."

"I've just found the most extraordinary thing," she said.
"Come in, Simon, for a minute."

He approached her warily – a meeting in here with both their
partners downstairs made him nervous. Then he realised that in
the solitude of her five-star bedroom she had been crying.

"I came in here to look for a leather belt, then I remembered
that Ben borrowed it once to wear under a sweater, so I went
through one of his drawers and found some nude pictures."

"Nude pictures?"

"Of Ben."

"Of Ben and who?"

"Just Ben."

"That's odd."

"That's what I thought. Who the hell took them?"

"And why?"

"Quite."

She sat on the bed, her hands in her lap, looking sad and
confused.

"I can't understand it," she said.

"Are they recent?"

"I think they are. The suntan, the haircut. Isn't marriage
wonderful?"

She had never looked prettier to him, and he wanted to put his
arm round her and comfort her. But in this room such gestures
could be misunderstood.

"I think your marriage is wonderful," he began. "Ben is some
provider. Wendy and I have been admiring your kitchen."

His implication that money could somehow forgive the discovery
in the drawer made Pym's eyes narrow.

"Kitchens are an investment," she said. "He's too mean to flush
the loo half the time. Do you know what he calls our wedding
anniversary? The AGM. Do you think that's romantic? Sometimes I feel lonelier when I'm with him than when I'm alone."

The revelation of these secret sorrows thrilled him, providing
hope.

"Well, if you don't get married," he suggested breezily, "how
can you taste the pleasures of adultery?"

Pym seemed to be considering this, but was evidently thinking about something else. "He didn't have this money when I married him, you know. Some people seem to think I married him for money but he wasn't that well off then. It's all happened in the last two or three years." She ran a distracted hand through her blonde hair. "I'm not going to mention it."

"What?"

"The pictures. I've decided to ignore them. Don't tell anyone, will you?"

"Not a soul."

"I shouldn't have told you. I was upset." She stood up now and touched her lower ribs gently. "We had better go downstairs."

He held the door open for her. In spite of everything, she had given him no encouragement at all. Determined to make some headway, he said the first thing that came into his head.

"I'll be getting some good tickets for Wimbledon. Would you like to come? Wendy, unfortunately, will be working."

"I'd love to, Simon." She gave him a cautious smile. "What a mess life is!"

"You'll never get out of it alive." He put his hand on her shoulder. "Let's go and find some champagne. Life looks different through the bubbles."

"Only temporarily. He had a hard-on, you know."

"What?"

"In the pictures."

Tired finally of waiting for her husband, Wendy had made her way back to the barbecue alone. But down at the pool the sound of strife was rising above the music. Nick Bannerman was now face-to-face with Mr Anderson, the county councillor, who had provoked his fury with some unheard remark.

"It's been going on for thirteen years and with idiots like you running things it will go on for another thirteen years," Nick shouted, jabbing Mr Anderson in the chest with a finger. Mr Anderson, not much older than Nick and just as tall, didn't budge.

"No, it won't, old boy, because we are going to smash them," said Mr Anderson suavely. "Do you think the British government can listen to the voice of violence? It would give terrorists the green light all over the world."

"Violence is the only thing the British government has ever listened to," Nick retorted, trying to keep his voice down. "Don't you know anything about people? If you've got violence, you've got frustration. Get rid of the frustration and you get rid of the violence."

"Talk to the gunmen?" asked Mr Anderson.

"The gunmen?" Nick said. "Do you remember Bobby Sands?"

"Very well."

"He starved himself to death last year. Would you call him a gunman? He never killed anybody. His family were driven out of their house with garbage cans being thrown through the front window and shots fired outside their door. They had to move, and Bobby Sands got himself a job as a coach builder. After two years he was persuaded, at gun-point, to give up his job. Menaced out of his home. Menaced out of his job. What was he to do?"

"You tell me."

"I will. He was driven to his death by people like you, Mr Anderson."

"I rather resent that."

"Because with your way the violence will go on for ever. As there isn't a God, I think both sides are a bit short of marbles, but I can see where justice lies, and I can see what the answer is. You've got to buy off the Fascist Prots in the north and send them away with huge financial compensation from an international loan in Dublin. Bombs don't work. They're counter-productive. Diplomacy doesn't work. It's all porridge. But money works. Money always works."

"Shit," said Mr Anderson.

"I don't mind you being a bloody twerp, it's the harm that you do," said Nick, and pushed him in the pool.

The splash caused quite a stir.

"What's going on?" asked Ben, hurrying over.

"We were discussing the Irish problem," Nick explained, "but Mr Anderson only understands violence, so I had to use his language."

"Jesus!" said Ben. "Can you swim, Mr Anderson?"

It wasn't clear from the councillor's gestures in the pool whether he was swimming or drowning. Somebody held out the mattress of a sunbed to him and he grabbed it and was hauled, spluttering, to the edge of the pool. With some help he achieved a wobbly perpendicular and stood there dripping, his urbanity dismantled.

41

"Nice guests you've got here, Mr Brock," he said wanly.

Ben interposed himself between pusher and pushed, an exercise in damage limitation.

"Come with me," he said, taking a wet elbow. "We have ways of making you dry."

"That was hilarious," said Wendy, who had watched it all with a quiet excitement. "Do you behave like this often?"

Nick glared at her, his anger still not gone. "It's bastards like that who have made this country a laughing stock abroad. India, Kenya, Cyprus, Ghana, Nyasaland. In we went and locked up the villain and it always turned out to be the next prime minister or president. We haven't got anything right since 1945."

"Come and have a drink with me."

"Thanks –"

"Wendy."

"Ah yes. Wendy. You're married to –?"

"Simon."

"A nice chap, Simon. No call to go and marry him, though."

With their glasses refilled, they found seats by the pool. Nick gazed round critically at the guests, restored now to a calm and well-fed contentment after the unfortunate incident over poor Mr Anderson.

"It's a different world, isn't it?" he said.

Wendy found herself staring at him, fascinated by his wild blue eyes, his mysterious lifestyle, his taste for confrontation.

"What is?" she asked.

"Well, I don't know how you live but I live in a tiny flat over a garage up the road. Rented."

"I live in a flat as well."

"But life for Ben is different, isn't it?"

"Is it?"

"Of course it is. It's champagne by the swimming pool and your own tennis court. It's jacuzzis and saunas and sunbeds. It's double gins on marble patios, and triple garages with Aston Martins, and reserved tables in the best restaurants. It's living in a golden ghetto with a very exclusive residents' association to keep the barbarian hordes from your private road. It's having a bank manager who calls you Sir."

"You're not a Trot, are you Nick?"

"That bunch of wankers? You can't pigeon-hole me. I hate the bloody lot of them."

"You don't wish to confiscate Ben's property?"

"Of course I don't. I love him. Did you notice just now? Not one critical word from him to me. No, my reaction to great wealth is to work harder. I want some of it. But if I worked myself to death I don't know whether I could come by this lot."

"Ben did."

"Advertising is a funny game. There are not many little capers that can produce great wealth very quickly. Pop music is another."

"And what's your little caper?"

"I write. At the moment I am trying to write a book."

"I've read of people making money doing that."

"And lots of others who don't. Do you know what Shakespeare got for Hamlet? Ten pounds. Of course, that was before decimalisation."

"What's it about? The book?"

"Women."

"You know about them, do you?"

"I know they're the same dangerous animal as I am."

"Oh good, you respect them."

"I respect them like I respect the anaconda, an attractive resident of South America that crushes you to death with its embrace."

"Oh bad, you're frightened of them."

"They rule the world. The trouble is they mislead dumb males with this veneer of helplessness."

"Dear me. Whatever happened to you? Did you get married once?"

"Not me. But I did do a survey of a dozen married men. I asked each of them if they would erase their marriage if they could, so that it had never taken place and nobody was hurt. All twelve said yes."

"Well, they would say that, wouldn't they?"

"Macho, you mean? I don't see why. It made them look complete idiots."

"Which, on the whole, men are."

"Oh, I'm not denying that. But it's time somebody spoke up for the poor bastards. There are enough books out on the rights of women, but the men have been too busy, trying to feed five or six mouths, to reply."

"Not you, though," said Wendy, offering him an empty glass.

"Not me. Satyriasis ain't my problem. I've got the sex drive of a rice pudding. I once read that Warren Beatty was a three- to five-times-a-day man. I need a calendar to work out when my next erection is due." He took her glass and bowed. "May I fetch you a drink? I know my place."

She watched him go over to the bar that was now surrounded by people washing down their steaks with Pol Roger. He had the intense blue eyes of a bay scallop, she decided.

Behind her a group of people were betting a lot of money that one of their number could not name the seven dwarfs. At another little group a man in a lurid check jacket said: "I love Suzanne. He wanted to get to the core of nature." Spotting a lady on her own, he moved immediately towards Wendy. She realised that he was talking about Cezanne.

"I wouldn't mind drinking champagne out of *your* slipper," he said.

The single track of male conversation still surprised Wendy. She looked at the man – at his jacket rather than his pale, unsuccessful face.

"You'll have to speak up," she told him. "Your jacket is so loud I can't hear you."

"Mal," said the man, offering his hand. "Ah, here is your husband."

Nick returned with the drinks.

"This is Mal," said Wendy. "Apparently."

"Not Mal Function?" asked Nick. "How much did you pay for that jacket?"

"Fifty pounds."

"You could have got a new one for that."

"Your husband is very witty."

"So am I," said Nick.

Conversationally, Mal was in a bunker, and he retreated uncertainly into the crowd. It was buoyed up now by the free champagne, and noisy outbreaks of laughter bounced back and forth across the pool. Genesis had been replaced: the music from the trees was now a selection of haunting songs from Jacques Brel.

"Don't all these beautiful ladies mellow your attitude towards my sex?" Wendy asked.

"No, they don't," replied Nick, looking round at them. "Mutton dressed up as dog, most of it."

"Did you notice the Chinese girl by the cabin?"

"They're no good. Half an hour later you want another one."

"You're difficult to please, Mr Bannerman."

"Call me Nick," said Nick. "You're supposed to say 'Call me any time'."

"Here comes my husband," said Wendy, "with Ben and Pym. He even talks to his wife as if he were trying to sell her something."

"Hallo, people," said Ben. "Are we all having a wonderful time?"

"Splendid," replied Nick. "Aren't we?"

"Yes," said Wendy. "I was sitting here thinking how lovely it would be to be rich."

"I'm planning to be rich," said her husband.

"I'm going to be rich," said Nick Bannerman.

"I am rich," said Ben.

FOUR

A BRITISH ARMADA of ninety-eight ships was sailing 8000 miles to throw 10,000 Argentinians off a chilly archipelago in the South Atlantic. Preparations were well advanced for the World Cup in Spain. The Derby had its third ante-post favourite in as many months, none of whom would win. Hurricane Higgins was world snooker champion again.

Simon Venables, on his way to work on a sunny Monday morning in May, assimilated these nuggets from a discarded newspaper as he cruised below ground towards some very bad news. He hated the Underground trains: they seemed to epitomise all too graphically how his life had been taken over by timetables and clocks. He arrived blinking in the sunshine.

Top Toys' tower block – or the tower block in which Top Toys leased a dozen floors – stood out as intrusively modern in this down-at-heel *arrondissement*, beloved by immigrants, street traders and thieves. Simon picked his way through pungent, litter-strewn streets to the deceptive security of his office.

He shared the lift with one of the secretaries, Sheila, who clutched a small toy.

"Look what I bought in Italy," she said. "I wondered if Top Toys would be interested."

She held up for his inspection a rotating musical crucifix with a gaudy Christ wobbling round squeaking "Come Back To Sorrento". It was so far removed from the upmarket products launched by Top Toys that he was amused that the girl could be so wrong. Top Toys had recently given the world a yard-high sophisticated robot, a plastic polymer chess set with two-foot pieces that withstood the weather better than any metal and a board that covered an average garden lawn, and a radio-controlled model plane which, although it did not travel faster than a bullet, was built in the image of a plane that did: Concorde.

"I doubt it, Sheila," he replied.

"I think it's cute," she giggled.

Ensconced in his sixth-floor office, he turned his mind, despite its normal Monday morning opacity, to Top Toys' forthcoming sensation: the battery-driven toy car. The choice of battery manufacturer had still not been made, but Mel Schwarzbaum's reference to a slush fund had not only offended him – he had never accepted more than a lunch – but also frightened him off. The choices which this left him created a new puzzle of price differentials, delivery dates and, in two cases, the uncertain component of industrial relations.

He decided that a visit to the factory where this project was about to hatch would clear his thoughts, and reached across the desk for his phone. As he did so, the smaller internal phone buzzed at his elbow.

"Simon? Have you got a minute?"

It was Shern, his boss, in the next room. As if the phone call was not adequate in itself, he beckoned to Venables through the glass partition that divided them. His manner, which was never overly friendly, had a certain aloofness or brusqueness which today had, ominously, disappeared.

"Sit down," he said. "Put your feet up." He leaned over his desk and studied Venables carefully, even sympathetically. "I'm afraid I have some bad news." Papers on his desk were shuffled, and a yellow sheet extracted from them.

"Have you seen the figures?"

"The figures?"

"The first quarter. It's a disaster. Sagging sales, dropping profits. The interest rates don't help. I don't see how they can blame us. It's a world-wide phenomenon. Car production in the States is at its lowest level for thirty years, steel shipments are at their lowest for forty." He put the paper down. "But they do blame us and they want some economies."

"When do I leave?"

"I'm sorry, Simon. It's last in, first out, really. There's nothing I can do. Never mind tumbling profits. If we go on like this it could be outright losses by the autumn."

"I understand. That's why there are three million out of work. Who else is going?"

"One from each department."

"Cartwright is staying?" People were split into two camps

47

over Cartwright: half of them hated him, the other half loathed him.

"He was here before you were. It's as simple as that," Shern said.

"He isn't any good, though. The economy you are making is a false one."

"I know it. But I have instructions."

Simon stood up and shrugged. He was surprised to discover that his initial reaction was relief: escape loomed. The harsher truths would no doubt filter through later.

"What's the money?" he asked.

"I don't know that. Isn't it a month for every year? Ring Accounts."

Venables went to the door. "If I'm going I might as well go now. There's no point in hanging about, is there?"

"Go when you like, Simon. I'm sorry about it. But before you do go will you order those bloody batteries? I don't want to be left with my bum in the butter."

Back at his desk he rang Accounts but a girl explained that it would take a little time to work out the size of his final cheque, what with years done, holidays owed and bonuses earned. He rang a friend in Marketing to suggest a final drink, but he was out. For half an hour he cleared his desk, appropriating the odd biro, and began to feel a tremendous surge of relief that he was about to abandon this grim, formalised world where you tried to guess where you stood by the size of your boss's smile. He wrote out a comprehensive order form for the batteries, put it in Shern's wire tray at the window between their rooms, and left the office. There was nobody around to say good-bye.

Outside, the sun was still shining. Some alcohol by Youngs of Wandsworth seemed a suitable prelude to the rest of his life, but the sour squalor of the pubs in that part of town changed his mind for him after only one pint.

He bought a paper and caught the train. His attention eventually landed on those pages which, despite soaring unemployment, always carried a feast of jobs. "This is a difficult vacancy to fill," he read. "Who could possess the efficiency, technical knowledge, education, charm, financial *nous*, optimism, wit, commonsense, flexibility and firmness of our present manager? Flippant responses will not be welcome; the problem is a serious one. The department is small, but the throughput is large. Applicants should be able to think conceptually while getting the details right. They should be able to work long hours but display resilience under pressure. Relevant experience is desirable but we doubt if it exists. Salary will depend on the learning curve required to achieve it."

It was a long time since Venables had read rubbish like this and it seemed to him that if this was the language used in today's job advertisements his involuntary sabbatical would not be brief. Before he decided that it was easier to buy than to sell, he had worked briefly as a sales rep, which, in his youth, had provided him with a sexual tour of Britain. ("Bedding them in Bedfordshire," he used to say. "Rutting in Rutland. Wilting in Wiltshire.") But that was not something that he wished to return to. As the Tube train rattled home, the size of his problem began to grow in his mind.

Instead of going to the flat, he decided to head for Morsels to share today's news with his bride of six weeks. He was curious about how she would react.

Morsels was something that Wendy had started eight years ago when she was twenty with money borrowed from her father. Working with her characteristic efficiency, the money had been repaid in three years. Morsels stood out through its brightness. The Morsels sign outside was in white on green, the white being steam from a cup of tea. Inside, the brightness was like walking into sunlight, and the green-and-white theme was pursued down to the last napkin. The floor was green tiles, the walls were green and white. The china cups were green, and the twelve tables were glass-topped with white-cane edging. Baskets of green plants hung along one wall. On the counter down one side of the shop were dozens of trays of sandwich fillings: salad, fish, paté, chicken, cold meats, coleslaw, relishes; at one end of the counter there was another hanging basket, this one containing fruit.

Behind the counter, in green tee-shirts with the Morsels logo across rising breasts, were Wendy and her young assistant, Sally.

"Smoked salmon," Venables said, "and a piece of cheesecake."

Wendy gaped, but seemed pleased to see him. "What are you doing here? Go and earn your living, like a proper husband!"

"I'll tell you later, lady. Hallo, Sally." He put a five-pound note on the counter, collected his food and change and found a table. Only three other customers were in the place but it was not yet twelve o'clock. Looking round now he felt a twinge of guilt at how little attention he had paid Morsels; it had merely been the place where Wendy worked. It was more impressive than he had thought. The theme behind the decor, he realised dimly, was that of a conservatory and it worked well.

"What's happened?" asked Wendy, slipping into the next seat. "You're not on strike, are you?"

"I've just become one of those statistics you see on the television news."

"What are you talking about?"

"Have you heard of monetarism?"

She glared at him. "What's happened, Simon?"

"You know this new exciting economic experiment that's closing down firms from Inverness to Plymouth and throwing millions out of work?"

Wendy was non-committal: he was tilting at the party that she loved.

"Well, it's just thrown me out of work. Top Toys have just made an economy and it's me."

"Why you, for God's sake? You're the only one there who knows what he's doing. I know that's true because you told me."

"One in each department – last in, first out."

Wendy shook her head sadly. "You see it on the news all the time but somehow never expect it to touch you."

"Welcome to the leisure society."

But when she had been recalled by the demands of clamorous sandwich hunters, he began to consider what direction his life should now take. Just married, and with a mortgage on the flat, leisure was fine but money was finer. He had never had any money to speak of; on the other hand he had never been short of it. Work had produced sufficient to cater for all needs and a few luxuries. If work disappeared he would be in a situation that he had never known before. The thought didn't alarm him. He still felt a sense of escape from the Colditz of Top Toys, and even gratitude towards them. They were insisting that he should be free. There were no doubt millions of workers who could be laid off to the benefit of their firms which would immediately become slimmer and more profitable. The government understood that. What the government seemed so far to have overlooked was who was going to feed the unemployed when there were ten million of them.

Wendy brought him a cup of tea. "Cheer up," she said. "I expect Morsels can support two of us."

Left with this thought, he found that it grew. If one Morsels could support two people, why not two Morsels to keep them in luxury? Why not ten Morsels? Why not a chain of Morsels across the land to provide cheap midday snacks for the nation's workers? If the nation had any workers by that time.

The idea excited him and it had arrived at the right moment. He had learned some lessons from studying Ben Brock under the Spanish sun. Some people sold themselves into slavery and security. Others became rich. Some people talked about what they were going to do, while others kept their mouths shut and got on with it.

He took an envelope from his pocket and started to make a few calculations. The capital he would need was difficult to guess, but the pay-off from Top Toys, which would be a lot less than £5000, would be only a small part of it. The solution to this alarming discrepancy was blindingly obvious. He only knew one millionaire.

In his eyrie atop the Vaughans' garage Nick Bannerman hammered out words like a terrorist with an automatic. It was time to blast cowering males out of the kitchen.

The evidence accumulated but was becoming difficult to marshal. Women couldn't play chess or paint pictures or conduct an orchestra; they spent their lives cooking but the best chefs were male. Where did these facts, lovingly collected over the years, belong in his book? If it was all due to a hormonal imbalance, a physiology that left women prone to emotional disturbance, unexpected tears and the turmoil that interrupts serious endeavour, what place did it have in *Battered Husbands*? He picked up a cutting whose bizarre headline was equally irrelevant: LESBIANS CALL FOR ALL-WOMEN CEMETERIES. He screwed it up, threw it on the floor and started to write.

Roman women died at twenty-four. Victorian ladies were lucky to reach forty-three. Today the life expectancy of women has reached seventy-five while a man who survives sixty-eight years has beaten the average. And when he expires in his prime, the insurance man cometh – and just watch his widow. With years of fun and freedom

51

ahead of her, she has collected the boodle, invested in a blue rinse and flown off to a second life so quickly you can't see her sexy new shoes for dust!

He lit a cigarette and stared at this for some time. It seemed to belong to a different part of the book. He put a new sheet in his typewriter and started again.

The feminists' battle for a notional equality flouts a law of nature. Winning the right to stand up on buses and buy their own theatre tickets isn't necessarily the secret of contentment. Urged on by their dubious cheerleaders, they could find themselves filling a role that suits them neither physically nor psychologically.

He was distracted at that moment by the sight of Mrs Vaughan in a red bikini heading for the family pool. She was a short blonde woman of around forty, at least twenty years younger than her successful husband. Perhaps he could write her into the book. Somewhere, in a sunless office, old Vaughan was probably answering three telephone calls at once while his wife swam a few leisurely lengths in the family status symbol.

Nick flicked through his pile of notes. It was twenty-seven times more dangerous to be born a boy and, if childhood was survived, a man was more vulnerable to two-thirds of the 300 main diseases. Stress was a male problem. Drowning in a sea of facts, few of them helpful, he watched Mrs Vaughan gliding down the pool. It seemed unlikely that she would ever man the barricades in a campaign against sexism. Woman the barricades? Person the barricades? He consulted his file on language and found a sheet that read:

Since very few jobs or roles are exclusive to one sex, work titles which incorporate "man" are inaccurate.
Statesman – statesperson;
Milkman – milk deliverer;
Fireman – firefighter.

Personkind is going a little loopy, he thought.
He typed on:

With a hundred gadgets reducing housework to a minimum, a woman's work has decreased as the man's job becomes more time-consuming. The woman can relax with her friends in the afternoon, and then create hell when her husband wants to do the same thing in the evenings. She has the priceless pleasure of her children's company while the father often remains a stranger for years. So loaded is the system in favour of women that in Britain if a man receives a knighthood his wife becomes a Lady. But if it is the woman who is honoured with the title of Dame, the man receives nothing.

Mrs Vaughan was rising from the pool via some underwater steps and reaching for a white towel that lay on the grass. Nick caught the blonde hair and the bare shoulders and wondered whether forty wasn't pitching her age too high. The legs looked young. Like the youthfulness of the madhouse, it was probably the under-use of everything that had protected her from the years. The rich aged slower.

He stubbed out his cigarette and wrote on.

It is, of course, the historical swing of the pendulum. In the nineteenth century the bosses walked all over the workers; in the twentieth it is the other way round. Similarly, in the home the woman was once a chattel, and today's reaction was predictable. But there is reaction and over-reaction, and the screaming hordes of today's militant women, pushing hysterically at a door that is already open . . .

He found a new cigarette and lit it.

. . . are going to destroy the balance of our society and produce consequences that they cannot foresee. Already a survey has revealed that in a modern marriage it is more often the man who does not want sex. This is not what nature intended. But battered at work and bullied at home it is hardly surprising if procreation is beyond his powers.

He went through his files again in search of the relevant cutting, another little hand-grenade awaiting its moment. One of the recent nuggets in his collection was a news-agency report which suggested that the Women's Movement was actually depopulating the earth:

> FEARING the extinction of their culture, Scandinavians seek to avert a dramatic population plunge in the 21st century as the sexual revolution and Women's Liberation take their toll.
>
> Despite subsidies to encourage babies, recent government statistics

53

> predict an alarming drop-off in birth
> rates that could drastically shrink the
> Nordic area's 22 millions within two
> generations.
>
> In Denmark alone – where the
> birth rate is among the lowest in the
> world – statistics indicate the
> country's five million people could
> be halved within a century.
>
> Norway's net population increase
> last year was only 0·2 per cent, the
> lowest figure since the famine of the
> Napoleonic Wars, according to the
> country's Central Bureau of Statis-
> tics.

This cutting was absorbed gleefully into the pages of *Battered Husbands*, and then Nick began to think about the chapter that followed. It was going to be about violence in the home, violence directed at men. He had a lovely story about a friend who had a glass door broken over his head by his wife. The chapter would be called "For batter or for worse?"

But first Nick decided to make himself a coffee. Why can't a woman, he wondered, be more like a woman?

High over Chelsea, Ben Brock sat in his office and listened to a tiny alarm bell in his mind. It had been set off by a brief item in the morning newspaper that arrived with his coffee at eleven o'clock. Today's paper was full of news. The Queen – in a summery turquoise dress and elbow-length white kid gloves – had played hostess to Pope John Paul II. Five ships had now been lost in the South Atlantic and the death toll had long since passed 100. But a short story on an inside page brought his leisurely journey through the headlines to a halt.

The government, in its determination to cut public expenditure, was going to scrutinise the National Health Service, and the leak in Whitehall was that one of their first moves would be to order drug companies to cut their costs. Ben knew that when companies cut their costs the first casualty was advertising.

But the more he thought about it, the less he was worried. Business was good. His turnover last year had topped six million pounds, and he had some very solid accounts.

Ben's biggest client was Shackleford Ciderhouse Inc., a vast American conglomerate that had made its early money out of an alcohol-free party drink and gone on into supermarkets, magazines and drugs. Drugs were the preoccupation of the European subsidiary, based in London and headed by a bright and amiable New Yorker named Glen Nardini.

Glen Nardini had given Ben his entire advertising budget which in the last financial year had totalled one and three-quarter million pounds. The American contribution to the agency's billing was nearly thirty per cent and so when Glen Nardini mentioned one day that, like many Americans, he was addicted to Paris, Ben bought him a small apartment in the Latin Quarter, near the Sorbonne. After a while this seemed hardly enough and now Ben Brock bought his client holidays in the Seychelles as often as he asked for them. These hidden backhanders taxed the ingenuity of his financial director who, with his accountant's credentials at risk, endeavoured to keep straight books. But Shackleford Ciderhouse and Glen Nardini were so important to the agency's budget that methods had to be found for retaining their loyalty.

"This is the advertising jungle, not the Boy Scouts, Cliff," Ben had told his financial director. "If you want to run jumble sales you'd better go and do it elsewhere."

"I'll work something out," Cliff had said. "They never taught me to syphon money."

Ben read the newspaper report again and filed it away in his mind. Before he could do anything else, the phone rang.

"Simon Venables, Ben. What are you doing at this very moment?"

"Talking to you on the phone, Simon."

"I'd appreciate the opportunity of a chat. Are you free?"

Ben looked at his desk diary. There was a conference in the creative department at half-past eleven. A new product, which stopped diarrhoea stone dead, was proving difficult to project in the colourful graphics which the agency favoured.

"I could meet you for lunch. There's a wine bar in the King's Road . . ."

Venables got there first and was kept waiting. The idea began to feel like a mistake. He bought a bottle of Vina Real, and watched a chattering foreign lady who only stopped talking when she laughed. After one whole day of being unemployed he was beginning to sense the insecurity which can gnaw at a man who has no job. He didn't seem to carry the same weight as the fully employed. Earlier it had felt quite wrong to be strolling up the street in a pair of old jeans in the middle of the morning. Paranoia lurked as he imagined the disapproval – or, worse, contempt – of the men in bowler hats. He knocked back the wine, though (a light treat discovered in Spain), and assembled some thoughts on his approach to Ben Brock. The move had been resisted on the previous evening by Wendy, who liked the idea of an expanding Morsels empire, but was against borrowing the money from Ben.

"Never borrow from a friend," she said. "It will alter your relationship."

"Who else can we borrow from? The bank isn't lending any money this year. Not that mine ever did."

"He probably hasn't got it, anyway. People who surround themselves with such conspicuous evidence of wealth usually don't have any left to lay their hands on."

"My God!" exclaimed Venables. "The man's a millionaire."

Waiting in the wine bar he began to wonder whether he was letting hope run away with judgement. But when Ben arrived he was in such good humour that Venables could see a chain of Morsels stretching all the way to Scotland.

"Welcome to SW3," Ben said. "This is the bit of London that is flash rather than smart."

Ben was experiencing one of those brief moments of private satisfaction that come occasionally to men who toil in the creative field. The talented team whose exalted lifestyles were sustained by Ben Brock Advertising had failed to produce a single acceptable idea for the anti-diarrhoea pill advertisement. Drawings had been produced and discarded; ideas, tentatively flown, had crashed on take-off. Finally it had been Ben who produced the image they had all been groping for: the centre of the advertisement would be a huge cork.

Venables looked at Ben and thought of Pym.

"How is married bliss?" he asked.

"Mostly an acrimonious silence at the moment. How's Wendy?"

"Oh, Wendy's all right. Will you try this wine?"

Ben held the bottle up. "Memories of Spain. Are you eating, too?"

They bought salads and found a table. Now that he was here, Venables felt nervously anxious to avoid getting to the main subject for as long as possible.

"Talking about Spain," he began, "do you ever hear from Rupert Puckle?"

"We correspond," said Ben. "At least, he does, and I might."

"What does he say?"

"He wants to make sure that we are all on for the holiday. Are you still on?"

"I'm looking forward to it."

"Great. Great." Ben started on his salad by spearing a sardine. "Why aren't you at work, by the way? Given it up?"

"Matter of fact, I have."

"Good. It never got anybody anywhere."

"It seems to have got you somewhere, Ben."

"I was talking about working for somebody else. You always end up trying to steal back the time you've sold them. The self-employed work harder and make more money. That doesn't happen to most people. They get the same wages whether they work or slack."

"I want to be self-employed," said Venables.

"What happened to the job?"

"I was made redundant. There seems to be some sort of recession."

"I read about that. I forget how many working hours this government has taken out of the economy and the funny thing is it hasn't made any difference. Somebody couldn't have been working very hard, could they?" He drank what was left of the wine and beckoned for another bottle. "What sort of self-employed thing are you going to do?"

"You know that Wendy has a sandwich bar called Morsels?"

"Yes. How's it doing?"

"It makes a small profit. What I thought was, why not several of them? Tooting, Clapham, Fulham, Earls Court . . .'

"Good idea. Get on with it. Don't waste a day, that's my advice."

A waiter appeared with the new bottle of wine and filled their glasses. Venables took a large drink.

"There is a problem," he said.

Ben looked at him. "What's that?"

"I haven't got the capital."

"That's no problem."

"It isn't?"

Ben shook his head. "A friendly bank manager."

Venables could see that this conversation, which he had thought was headed in exactly the right direction, had glided off the edge of the target and was about to vanish, like a bad moonshot, into outer space.

"My bank manager isn't friendly," he said. "I got married. It cost money. I'm out of work and probably overdrawn, not quite the combination a bank manager is happiest with."

Ben stroked his beard and smiled indulgently. "Simon, if you're going to become a much-envied entrepreneur, there are one or two economic facts of life that you'll have to learn. Nobody has got any money. The government hasn't got any money. Why do you think it keeps talking about its borrowing requirement? Why do you think it keeps going to the International Monetary Fund to beg for readies? Why do you think people in business never stop talking about the interest rates? They're all in hock up to their eyebrows, that's why. Even the people you think have got money don't have any. Most prime ministers leave Downing Street with an overdraft. Did you know that? That's why the first thing they do when they get out is write a book. If you've got a dud bank manager, change your bank."

Venables nodded glumly, feeling the purpose of his mission slipping away. If Ben had suspected what that purpose was, he had handled it very cleverly. By the time they had finished their meal the conversation had drifted far away from the territory which he had pegged out for it, and he found himself, once again, playing with his worry beads.

"What did you think of Nick Bannerman?" Ben asked as they got up to leave.

"I liked him."

"I was thinking of asking him to Rupert Puckle's if he can afford it. I thought I should check with you first."

"A good idea. He'd love it."

"Johnny Fix-It has got him on to television, by the way. He can fix anything, that boy."

Simon got out his wallet and paid the bill. As they went out a thought occurred to Ben.

"Why don't you come over and play tennis some time? Mixed doubles."

"Thanks."

"Nice to see you, anyway. Why did you come over? Was it just a social call?"

"No. I came over to borrow some money."

"Blimey," said Ben, laughing. "I don't have any money."

On the day that British troops landed in San Carlos, Venables found the courage to visit the bank. The empty days had given him time to visualise an expanding Morsels empire. He even had ideas about how the places should be run – it annoyed him that Wendy did not serve soup – but mostly he concerned himself with the pace of a slow but steady development. In the first instance, he decided, he needed £10,000.

He put his notes into a brief-case that had sat in on much larger deals and left the flat. He could already see the astounding story of his success recounted in meticulous detail in the Business Section: "Simon Venables rose from bobbin boy in a cotton mill to his present financial impregnability because the fourth Earl of Sandwich invented a snack which enabled him to stay at the gaming table." He would have to invent the bit about the cotton mill: the truth would make dreary company for the success that he planned.

In the street, androgynous youths with delusions of adequacy, solvent abusers, young men with fearful identity crises, coped with boredom by the megaton. It was gruesome to think that in a mere sixty years the whole lot would be dead and buried and replaced by an even bigger crowd of no-hopers. Venables dissociated himself from this rabble. He had a plan, and he was doing, not talking. It was going to be pleasant, he reflected, to introduce a little extravagance into his life: crystal glasses, out-of-season strawberries, weekends in Paris. He moved purposefully through the crowds and realised that with energy to spare he was noticing pretty girls a lot more than usual. Most men worked too hard to enjoy that sort of thing.

The bank manager was called Mr Mackay. His short hair was greying in front of his ears but he had a black moustache. He stood up and shook hands, uncertain of what was coming. There were gradations of greeting in the bank.

Venables sat down and outlined his problem. He described the history of Morsels, produced its accounts, and spoke hopefully about its prospects. Mr Mackay listened, revealing nothing, but making occasional notes. When Simon paused, Mr Mackay nodded rather than fill the silence with words of his own.

"What it all adds up to is that I am looking for a loan," he told the bank manager. "We could put the flat up as collateral."

"What do you owe on the flat?"

"Ten, but it's worth thirty."

"It seems," said Mr Mackay, looking at some papers in front of him, "that you are edging towards an overdraft situation."

"As I said, I've been made redundant. I'm owed severance money."

"How much?"

"I don't know. Perhaps three thousand. There is money in my wife's account."

"It isn't your wife who is asking for a loan. I wonder why, Mr Venables, you think that the profit from the first shop justifies the opening of a second?"

Venables didn't like the sound of the bank manager's voice.

"The profit would increase proportionately if there were two shops. Many costs would be halved."

"I see."

"I'm what you call chronically under-funded."

This would have been the moment to talk about his investment portfolio, he thought, if he had an investment portfolio.

"You are," Mr Mackay agreed. "But if this proposition is all you hope it is, shop two would be launched to some extent on the profits of shop one."

Simon was wondering how somebody who had worked as hard as he had and didn't even possess a car could be "edging towards an overdraft".

He said: "If one shop makes a profit of one hundred pounds a week, ten shops, with certain shared costs, would presumably make a profit of more than a thousand pounds a week."

"Quite possibly, Mr Venables. But if you have borrowed the money to open the other nine shops it won't do you much good. Interest rates are cruel and you can over-extend yourself. How much money did you think you would need?"

"About ten thousand."

Mr Mackay shook his head very quickly. "That would be out of the question. It would be a different situation if you still had your job."

"Well, I wouldn't need it then, would I?"

Something which might have been a smile lurked behind Mr Mackay's moustache.

"My advice, Mr Venables, would be to work hard at the shop you already have and increase the turnover and, more important, the profit figure. One hundred pounds a week really isn't very much at all. Produce some figures we can look at. This is a bad year to ask for a bank loan, but if you were to come back in the spring with a story of increased profits – who knows?"

This brief speech, Simon could see, was intended to bring the discussion to its end and he felt too demoralised to continue it. He cashed a cheque on the way out for a hundred pounds and hoped that it took him into the red. A Wayside Pulpit on the other side of the street said: "The tongue cuts where the teeth cannot bite." It seemed an appropriate message for people leaving Mr Mackay's company.

For a moment he wondered what to do, but the answer came quickly. He bought a newspaper and slipped into the first public house where a pint of unspecified bitter was soon gripped firmly in his right fist. The entire future which he had painstakingly assembled in his head over the past week had evaporated, but the beer tasted good. What particularly inflamed him, from the fiasco of the last hour, was the contempt which Mr Mackay had barely hidden for Morsels' profit figures, as if his wife's intelligent part-time hobby was a multi-national corporation. Morsels made more profit, anyway, than many nationalised industries, which made none. The future now looked so unappealing that he decided to block it out with his newspaper. His horoscope said: "Refuse to become either excited or discouraged by today's feedback. Today's birthday: Actor Freeman Gosden." Who the hell was Freeman Gosden?

He ordered another beer and folded up the newspaper. He needed to think, not read.

At his elbow, a hard-faced young man was attempting to ingratiate himself with a pale young girl. "What you need," he told her, "is a young man, a man with engines in his buttocks."

"Yeah," the girl agreed. "What put me off was when his glass eye fell in my beer."

Momentarily reassured that some people's lives were even more disagreeable than his own, Venables steered his thoughts towards the only bright date in his future: on Sunday they were driving down to the Brocks' for a game of tennis. A picture of Pym in tennis shorts lifted his spirits briefly, but when his thoughts moved on to the projected holiday they were all to spend with Rupert Puckle the nightmare possibility that he would not be able to afford it plunged him again into a mixture of gloom and panic. He was a downwardly socially mobile failure with a fiscal haemorrhage. Sweet misery of life, at last I've found you!

Driving down to the country on Sunday morning in the limited comfort of Wendy's van, he could see that the awesome affluence of the Brock household would be harder to take than usual. He didn't envy wealth, he didn't begrudge it; but he felt that it was time for some of it to flow in his direction. The Brocks' Persian carpets, antique furniture and family photographs framed in hand-worked silver were acceptable enough, but their luxurious bedroom, with His and Her bathrooms, jacuzzi and sauna, provided too stark a contrast for comfort with his third-floor rabbit hutch in Wimbledon. It was emasculating in a way that he had not anticipated. The husband, the provider, the ham who brings home the bacon, was being driven by his wife, in his wife's van and would very soon be living on his wife's money.

The interview at the bank had shifted her attitude to him. While he planned an extension of Morsels she could overlook the fact that he had stopped earning money, but now a note of concern had entered her conversations.

"What's your next plan, husband?" she had asked in bed the following morning. "There's no time to waste, you know."

He had moaned an incoherent reply.

"Don't do that," said Wendy. "You've been moaning all night."

"My soul was wrestling with the devil."

"Your stomach was wrestling with the beer."

But by Sunday no fresh ideas had occurred to him, and to fill the strained silence of their journey he flipped on the van's old radio. A new word had entered the language: yomping. British troops in the Falklands, having taken 1400 embarrassed prisoners at Darwin and Goose Green, were "yomping" the forty-eight miles across East Falkland to Port Stanley. It was showdown time in the South Atlantic. In Buenos Aires young men chanted in the street: "*Las Malvinas son nuestras!*" Like most chants, it missed the point.

Ben Brock greeted them in tennis shorts.

"Welcome, city-dwellers, to the health-giving properties of the countryside. That," he said, pointing, "is called a tree."

"I saw one on television," Wendy said. "Big, aren't they?"

At the back of the house Pym, in a cotton top and wrap-over cotton skirt six inches above the knee, was sunbathing on the patio. "Anyone for tennis?" she said.

Simon and Wendy had played a little tennis in the early days, but it was a year or more now since they had picked up their rackets. When they had changed, Nick Bannerman arrived to do the umpiring.

"I don't want any McEnroe tantrums," he said. "My brain hurts."

"How is the book?"

"Slow, very slow."

"What is it going to be about?" Venables asked.

"It should be about seven quid."

They made their way up to the green composition court that was almost hidden among the pines at the top of the garden. At one end was a machine that fired balls across the net for players in training. Ben banged a ball the length of the court to loosen up.

"I play a sort of serve and volley game," he said. "I believe Borg got the idea from me."

Nick found a chair and placed it beside the net. He spun a racket and announced that Pym would serve. Her serves arrived with a considerate slowness, inviting punishment, but Venables returned them to her at the same pace. Wendy was more competitive, serving on tip-toe as well as any of them. She was very nimble in covering the ground. Soon she was carrying her husband on the court as she would shortly carry him off it. Ben played with more force than accuracy, swatting the ball with a frustrated energy and attempting ambitious two-fisted volleys that whistled between the Venables on a rising curve. He kept coming forward, playing an aggressive game, but Wendy's forehand passed him again and again.

"Is it rude for guests to win?" Venables asked.

"A bit of a social gaffe," Ben told him.

At a set each they called it a draw. The sun drove them down to the pool where Pym produced champagne from the fridge in the cabin. As she handed Venables his glass he noticed a poorly disguised bruise on her left cheek-bone.

"There are costumes in the cabin if anyone wants to swim," Ben told them. He settled down on a sunbed at the pool with a glass of champagne resting on his chest. "We've got a cat," he said. "We got her for the mice and they adore her."

"Have you got mice?" Wendy asked.

"We've also got bats," said Pym. "A colony of them in the roof."

"Either we've got bats or the mice have taken up hang-gliding," said Ben.

Nick Bannerman came out of the cabin in borrowed swimming trunks and carrying a new bottle of champagne. "I do love dropping in on these domestic scenes," he said. "Cats, mice, bats – where's Greg?"

"He's visiting his little friend up the road," replied Pym. "When are you going to try this domestic bliss, Nick?"

"Sod that," said Nick. "I had an erection the year before last and it made me dizzy and I fell over."

Ben helped himself to the new champagne. "Marriage is a bed of nails, Nick."

"A bed of toe nails, in your case," Pym added.

"Women don't like to do the things that I enjoy doing," said Nick.

"I imagine that pouring gallons of beer down your neck and lying on the floor belching isn't everybody's cup of tea," Wendy told him.

"They want to go dancing, see shows, visit restaurants."

"Extraordinary."

"I'm glad you agree."

He eased himself into the pool and soon Pym and Wendy joined him. They grabbed his head and pushed it under.

"You understand that?" Ben asked Simon. "The women are fascinated by the challenge of a male who is still at large."

Venables didn't like the sound of that. He wanted Pym to be fascinated by him. He looked at her lovely body and wondered whether she would ever be available to him. These days anything could happen. After all, men were now spraying themselves with a scent which attracted women without them being aware of it.

"Did you go to the bank?" Ben asked.

"It was a waste of time." The thought made him fill his glass, the medicine for jobless poverty.

"I suggested that if your bank was no good you should try another."

"My own was discouraging enough."

"I'm sorry I couldn't help you."

Venables shook his head. "It was cheeky of me to ask."

"Not at all," said Ben. "But ready cash isn't what people have lying around. You haven't found a job yet then?"

"They all seem to require training I haven't had."

"You used to sell. I see salesmen jobs."

"Only with specialised knowledge. Word processors, business systems, the new technology. It's a closed book to me."

"I hope this isn't going to affect our holiday plans?"

"So do I, Ben. It's the only thing I have to look forward to at the moment."

To his delight Pym climbed out of the pool and came drippingly towards him. She pushed her wet hair off her face with one hand and grabbed his ankle with the other.

"What musical am I?" she asked.

He thought of Esther Williams and remembered a very old one.

"Dangerous When Wet?" he suggested.

"Wet Thighed Story!" She laughed and pulled at his leg. "I hope you lot are all staying for lunch?"

"Well," said Venables. The invitation to tennis had been infuriatingly vague.

"Of course they're bloody staying to lunch," shouted Ben. "Let's get to it."

He stood up and produced from beneath his sunbed a yellow Giorgio Armani sweater which he pulled on as he led them up his freshly mown lawn.

In a large room that overlooked the garden, Pym, or some hidden minion in the kitchen, had laid out a cold lunch: Vichyssoise; slices of smoked salmon rolled and stuffed with prawns; a wooden salad bowl full of lettuce, chopped nuts, raisins, slices of avocado and cucumber; granary loaves and a dish of mayonnaise.

"Christ," said Nick, "I was going to have beans on toast."

"Beans on toast?" Ben repeated. "Is that what passes for gourmet cuisine in your dust-caked atelier?"

"A boiled egg perched on a soggy pile of mashed potatoes is another gastronomic sensation," replied Nick. "Why don't you come round for dinner some time?"

"I've got an important meeting that night," said Ben.

"Food without guilt," said Nick. "Do you realise that nine million children will die of malnutrition this year while the stuff we throw away would have kept them alive?"

"It's a logistical problem, Nick. The council can't take our garbage to Africa. You sound like a Socialist to me."

"I am," said Nick. "It's not illegal yet, is it?"

"I'm SDP," Venables told them. "The wave of the future."

"It looks more like a trickle," Ben said, scooping up soup. "Pym's sister is a bloody Socialist."

"I didn't know Pym had a sister," said Nick. "Can I borrow her?"

"Not yet sixteen," said Ben, "and men are already ramming it in orifices that she is barely familiar with herself."

"She's not like that," protested Pym.

"She is," Ben told her. "She offered me her breasts in the cabin when she came for a swim. 'Are they as good as Petronelle's?' she said."

"The little bitch," said Pym. "What did you say?"

"I said no."

"That was nice of you."

"I was frightened. She was fifteen, for God's sake."

"Who is Petronelle?" asked Wendy.

"It's what Pym is short for," said Pym.

Ben had raced ahead to the smoked salmon. "I learned to eat quickly at boarding school," he said. "Otherwise you never got any second helpings." He leaned over the table to fill their wine glasses. "I've been poor and I've been rich. I can tell you, rich is better."

"How do you join?" asked Nick. "I'd like to get as lucky as you."

"You don't think it's luck, do you? What's lucky about working fifteen hours a day? Do you think I enjoy it? I'm a Rupert Puckle, really. I want to be in the Terraza Bar at the Club Nautico, not bashing my brains out in an office block in London."

"I think he is saying that his money has come from hard work, Nick," said Wendy.

Nick resented the reproach. He had never worked so hard in his life as during the last few months. Occasionally, exhausted by the effort, he had fallen into a deep sleep for only five or ten minutes in the middle of the day. He said: "Wealth might be proof of industry, but poverty isn't necessarily proof of indolence."

Ben swirled his wine round in his glass. "I'm not lecturing you chaps," he said. "I'm sure you work jolly hard at your typewriter, Nick. But if in the end hard work doesn't produce lots of money it's a misguided endeavour, isn't it?"

"Perhaps not everyone is as obsessed with money as you are," Pym said.

Venables hated to contradict her. But he thought he valued money even more than Ben Brock. Sometimes he yearned for it with a lust that was almost overpowering. He admitted: "I'm obsessed with it. I really believe it can buy happiness."

"Happiness for me is being half-way through a good book," said Wendy. "That's not extravagant."

"Happiness for me is being half-way through a hundred-pound bottle of champagne," said Ben. "That is."

Pym brought in a large white china dish shaped like a wine glass. It was piled high with fruit: strawberries, raspberries, peaches, bananas, kiwi fruit, mangoes. A smaller dish contained whipped cream.

"I have a new ice-cream-making machine," she told them. "I can make any colour you like. Pink for the strawberries, green for the kiwi fruit, vanilla for the bananas." But they all chose the whipped cream; it tasted faintly of brandy.

"Does anyone want any cheese?" Ben asked.

"I have to leave room for the beans on toast," Nick told him. He wanted to emphasise the contrast between his penny-watching existence and the riches which filled this mansion. When the phone rang on the wall and Venables answered it, it proved to be cordless so that he could take it over to Pym at the table.

A gold palace lantern hung from the ceiling above them and there were picture lamps over paintings of unknown value on the walls. The leather sofa against one wall would have cost at least £2000. Opposite it was a carved mantelpiece, bearing Victorian candlesticks, over a real fireplace. The room seemed to have been furnished as the money rolled in with little regard for what had been bought before.

Casually conducting this inventory, Nick realised that Venables was doing the same thing.

"I've got to fetch Greg now," said Pym, returning the phone to the wall. "Why don't you go back to the pool? You're wasting the sun."

They all walked back to the pool and found sunbeds. Ben fell asleep almost instantly. Wendy read a Sunday magazine article about instant food shops.

"What a pad," commented Nick.

"I want one like it," said Venables.

"So do I," added Nick. "I'm hoping success is contagious."

Ben woke with a start. "I didn't go on about money, did I?" he asked. "Honestly, I'm living on a knife edge. It could go as quickly as it came."

Slumped on his second-hand bed, and masturbating casually into the women's page of the *Guardian*, Nick Bannerman was beginning to wonder whether he had overlooked something in life. The list of omissions was ominously long. It included not just television, video recorders, freezers and credit cards which people increasingly regarded as prerequisites for normal living, but other much more fundamental gaps in his ascetic existence: a house, a car, a wife. Money. Omissions, emission. He threw the *Guardian* into his bin. If masturbation didn't have such a bad name there would be fewer rapists.

His sex life, sabotaged by a jealous mother in the early years and subsequently bedevilled by poverty and pessimism, was becoming one of the great non-events of the twentieth century.

It had started promisingly enough in East Anglia where his parents owned a small restaurant near Fakenham. Beautiful girls, often weekend waitresses, were taken off in his battered three-wheeler Reliant to Brancaster Bay or Cromer.

He had been disgracefully slow to realise what was happening.

The girls that he took out were sooner or later dismissed from the restaurant's staff. The restaurant was run by his mother, a dominating lady who consigned her husband to the kitchen where he occasionally plucked up the courage to joke with Nick about "the old dragon". Nick tried to joke back, but grew sadly to despise a man who failed so disastrously to be one.

Twice in his last years there Nick had taken girls back to the restaurant for a late drink and his mother had refused to allow them in. He knew what the problem was now: he was an only child and his mother's view of the future did not include another woman claiming him and taking him away. At first he was tortured by the divided loyalties involved. He presumed that the problem was not unique and would solve itself in time. Like many people who discover that their future has been decided by the success of their parents, he had worked in the restaurant in the expectation of owning it, but now, to help resolve the problem, he did what he had always wanted to do and became a reporter on the weekly paper. His mother took this surprisingly well. He still lived at home, he had no girlfriends, and she was proud when his name appeared in the newspaper.

The traumatic turning point in Nick Bannerman's life was precipitated by the arrival on the reporting staff of a girl called Helen. She was a rather beautiful dark-haired girl with saucer eyes, fresh from some provincial university, and destined later to make her name on television where her brutal charm shook unexpected truths from unwary politicians. Nick grabbed her on her very first day and within three months was planning marriage.

One May evening when he arrived at her flat to take her to the theatre in King's Lynn, she opened her door clutching an envelope.

"Are you ready, doll?" he said, kissing her. "We're pushed for time."

She shook her head, but didn't say anything.

"What's up?" he asked, walking past her into the flat. "Aren't you coming?"

"No, I'm not," she said, and sat down. "I'm sorry, Tony. I didn't know."

Nick sat down, too. "What? Didn't know what? What are you talking about?"

She handed him the envelope without looking at him. When he saw what was inside it, he cried with shame.

The letter, to Helen from his mother, said that Tony had a weak heart, a very limited life expectancy, and it would be in his best interest if she brought their relationship to a close.

He stood up, humiliated, unable to speak, and made for the door.

"That letter . . . a lie," was all he could get out.

In a public house in the country, unused by his friends, he had two large whiskies. By the time he left he had changed his name to Nick Bannerman.

He returned to the restaurant after it had closed, packed a suitcase, stole £100 from the safe, and caught a taxi to Norwich station. The following morning he was in London.

And now, in his bolt-hole in the country, he was a freelance writer, eking out a precarious existence with occasional articles, and pinning his faith and his future on an anti-feminist tome which had its psychical roots deeply embedded in his past.

Now that it seemed that you could reasonably expect a coronary occlusion at sixty, he had to regard his life as half gone with nothing to show for it. Today's piece of advice on his desk calendar said: "He has achieved success who has lived well, laughed well and loved much." A triple failure.

For a few work-delaying moments he thought back to the girls he had known – to Helen, of course, and to earlier, younger claimants to his heart. He could even remember a young girl who had excited him in the coffee shop every Saturday morning back in his teens. Those were the days when last year's nymphomaniac was this year's pram-pusher. It wasn't like that now.

The other extravagant paraphernalia, coveted by millions, concerned him less. What use did he have for a video recorder? If you have never seen a red double-decker bus, you won't want to ride on one.

His route to financial security lay on the desk in front of him, in the form of blank sheets of paper that were waiting for words. Unusually for Britain, there were huge blue patches in the sky outside, but his place was here until his daily word target had been met. The target was becoming almost impossibly difficult, and he would do anything to postpone the moment when he must start even though he knew it would mean working late in the day to keep to his schedule.

Stalling for as long as possible, he picked up a days-old copy of the *Daily Mail*. The news was difficult to digest. For the first time in centuries, Iran was busy burying Iranians chest-deep in the ground and pelting them to death with rocks the size of oranges. In America, that cradle of exciting ideas, they had become squeamish about the electric chair and instead had pumped a man full of potassium chloride, sodium thiopental and pavulon which had carried him off to that shining city on the hill almost immediately. At home it was a bunch of women rather than men who were involving themselves in the debate about nuclear missiles. He wondered whether there was a chapter for his book in their activities, but what did he care about cruise missiles, SS20 warheads, zero options and interim concepts? A death was waiting for each of us and for most it would be many times worse than the instant oblivion of a nuclear explosion.

He turned inside the paper and struck gold. A whole page was devoted to the subject dealt with in his book!

"The domineering, dissatisfied, affluent, emasculating house-wife undoubtedly survives in our richer suburbs and her power can be vicious," wrote the columnist.

The first witness was an accountant from Manchester:

> WOMEN don't know the harm they do. I feel I am on a permanent treadmill forever trying to give my wife what she wants but with a continual, nebulous feeling that I have failed. She acts out the role of little woman in public. All our friends would say, if asked, that I was the boss but she has a devious way of making me believe that I have let her down, that she is resigned to life with me not fulfilled. She makes me feel that sex is my reward for having provided some transient material advantage, rather than a mutual sharing. As a result I want to make love to her less and less and possibly the saddest comment I can make after 27 years is that I have absolutely no idea whether this is a relief or a sorrow to her.

A male schoolteacher from Lancashire accused the paper of perpetrating the myth that women were always the underdog, forever anxious to please:

> THERE are thousands of men treated like dirt in their own homes. My children are encouraged to regard me as a rather inconvenient

> lodger with an unfortunate job that
> doesn't pay enough and brings me
> home too early. I get the impression
> that everybody is relieved when I
> have the decency at weekends to get
> out of the way and spend a few hours
> digging in the garden.

The woman columnist concluded that bullies of either sex could "successfully disparage achievement, indulge in psychological warfare, withdraw favours, make sex seem a reward, not a mutual joy. They take pleasure in the diminishing phrase, the sarcastic rebuttal to a loving approach."

Nick gleefully filed this stuff away. Perhaps he should go to talk to the columnist on the *Daily Mail*. She looked rather pretty in the pictures.

He shifted his typewriter to the centre of his desk. He was in the middle of a chapter called "The Century of the Common Woman", but when he tried to remember where his chapter was supposed to take him his thoughts returned to Helen, the girl he had loved and lost.

Forcing himself, as he had to every morning, he opened one of his notebooks in search of inspiration. "Why can't women play darts?" he read, "or snooker or any other game that requires no physical strength?" But in a beautiful little pub on the Broads Helen had regularly thrashed him at darts. He drew a thick line through these irrelevant questions which had nothing to do with the lot of the human male. The hardest thing about writing this book was keeping his eye on the target.

He could see already that this was going to be one of those days when the words were extracted like teeth.

FIVE

THE PROSPECT OF POVERTY was not something that Ben Brock had ever seriously considered. He joked about it occasionally out of kindness to his less successful friends, but the turnover of his firm, despite the fluctuating figures on the balance sheets, told him that he would never be poor.

The day after the tennis, however, the worry began.

An unnerving episode opened the week for him. He was going over the details of the new Pexo account in his Chelsea office when there was a knock on the door. Pexo were about to spend a million pounds launching a new drug which they claimed would relieve arthritis. Ben had been awarded the account after a dazzling presentation. It meant another £150,000 for Ben Brock Advertising at a difficult time. This recession was getting to parts that previous recessions had failed to reach.

He called to the door and his financial director came in.

"Have you got a minute, Ben?" he asked.

His financial director, Cliff, was a lean, pale young man of thirty-five. His contribution to Ben Brock Advertising had been immense since Ben stole him from a firm in the city where lower, more realistic salaries guaranteed business stability. While Ben made money, Cliff made the money make money.

"Sit down, Cliff. What's up?"

"It's a bit embarrassing, actually," Cliff said, putting a folder on the desk. "I want to insure your life."

"Don't I look well?"

"You look fine, Ben. But this firm depends on you. You know that. Without you . . ." He waved a hand. "Frankly, I'd be a bit over-exposed. Well, I'd like to stay here."

"I want you to stay, Cliff."

"Well, here's how you can help. I've been updating the firm's insurance policies and it gave me the idea. I can insure your life

73

for the next ten years for a hundred thousand. It'll cost me forty pounds a month."

"You can't insure another man's life, can you?"

"No, you can't. That's the point. You'd have to make me the beneficiary of the policy. That's what I've come in for."

"Would our insurance people accept it?"

"They would if I tack it on to all the other policies and tell them it's all or nothing."

"That's okay, Cliff. Go ahead."

"Fine. Thanks." Cliff stood up. "Congratulations on the Pexo account, by the way. We needed that."

When he had gone Ben didn't know whether to feel flattered or depressed.

On Monday mornings he made a tour of his tiny empire to keep in touch with his staff. It was all very informal, but he wanted them to know that he was watching them. It always irritated Ben when non-advertising friends visited his agency and laughed at the proliferating departments and the grand titles that even quite mediocre people took for themselves. The Creative Department, with a creative director and two associate creative directors, was a favourite target of criticism. Even Pym was less than impressed by the mystique of the business.

"He doesn't look very creative to me," she said on one visit. "Why is he picking his nose?"

"He's thinking," replied Ben. "He doesn't know he's picking his nose."

In the Creative Department today they were thinking about arthritis. In the Copy Department men were writing words, screwing them up, and drinking coffee. In the Studio, two artists sat in front of drawing-boards, staring selectively at brushes, chalks and crayons. In the Production Department they were looking at job bags – large, over-printed envelopes containing the order, the correspondence, the dockets and the time sheet. In the Research Department the staff were always on the phone, discovering market needs of new products so that Ben was well briefed when he pitched for a new account. With the market well researched and the problems identified, Ben knew more about the client's product's prospects than the client knew himself. In the Account Handling Department, account executives and account directors discussed accounts and planned lavish lunch dates to sweeten the men who awarded them to Ben Brock Advertising.

74

Sometimes Ben himself wondered whether the whole edifice wasn't a little top heavy, but his doubts were assuaged annually by the profit figures. Apart from the generous salaries, the biggest drain on the profits was an unsuccessful bid for new business. Ben had spent £20,000 on an elaborate presentation to a drug firm and failed to get their advertising. It was money lost. Once, in pursuit of what piece of business he had now forgotten, he had had twelve London taxis painted pink (and subsequently black again) at more than £1000 a taxi. The drug firm had praised his initiative, admired his idea, and been frightened off by his extravagance. The account went elsewhere.

Back in his office his secretary had left his coffee and that morning's *Times* on his desk. This intended break in his morning rarely went uninterrupted and the phone rang as soon as he had picked up his cup.

Linda, his receptionist-telephonist, said: "It's Mr Parker of Pexo."

"Okay," said Ben, and heard a click on the line. Mr Parker, the marketing director of Pexo, was the most important person in the world at the moment so far as Ben Brock Advertising were concerned. Ben gave him a warm greeting.

"Hallo, Ben," said Mr Parker. "Have you seen *The Times*?"

"It's in front of me."

"Try page three."

Ben turned the page and the headline hit him: DRUG FIRMS TOLD: CUT COSTS. The leak from Whitehall had turned out to be true. It was war on public expenditure, war on the rising costs of the Health Service, and war, specifically, on the rampant spending of the drug companies.

"I'm sorry, Ben," said Mr Parker. "This isn't the moment to spend a million pounds launching a new drug."

Ben felt cold. "What do you mean?"

"We're cancelling the launch. I'm sorry but there's no choice."

"You can't do that. We have a deal."

"Well, I wouldn't take that attitude. When things improve there will no doubt be other business."

Ben didn't want other business: he needed this business.

"Do you mean you're pushing the drug out without advertising it?"

"No, we're not going to launch the drug this year. The

government wants to save money, so the public can put up with arthritis."

Ben felt dizzy. He was glad that he was sitting down.

"Thank you," he said, and replaced the phone.

He sat with his head in his hands while the coffee went cold. The phone rang several times during the next quarter of an hour but he didn't answer it.

Simon Venables had always been an early riser, leaving his bed soon after waking, eager to start the day. Wendy found it more difficult to throw off the duvet, and quite impossible to do so until her husband had brought her tea. But the deadening effects of depression had reversed their roles. He had lost the impetus which once propelled him from his bed and he would lie there, awake but eyes closed, contemplating an empty day, a melancholy bank statement, a job application ignored, a bleak future. Wendy, finding no tea, eventually fetched it herself.

Sometimes it would be ten o'clock before he reached the bathroom to confront in the mirror a face that was settling too easily these days into an expression of defeat. By that time Wendy had gone and freshly cut sandwiches were piling up on the polished counter at Morsels. Simon felt no guilt at this development – self-pity leaves no room for guilt.

One morning, after rising even later than usual, he found jeans, sandals and an old shirt with few buttons left, and made his way to the kitchen to boil an egg. In the days when he had left the flat at 8.15 in a smart suit, and carrying the obligatory brief-case, he had often resented the hours of his life that were slipping away, as it were, in the custody of somebody else, but now that all the hours he wanted were his he didn't know what to do with them. There was nobody to play tennis or golf with; other people hadn't been awarded this much leisure. Activities which cost money had to be discouraged. He propped up the morning newspaper and decapitated his egg. Perhaps a restrained visit to a licensed hostelry would help to shorten the day.

As he was washing up he noticed that the morning's post had been left unopened on the fridge, and he scooped it up, more to stall boredom than in the hope of hearing anything interesting.

The post arrived these days with a brightly coloured collection of leaflets, designed to separate the recipient from his cash and replace it with things he never knew he needed. Burglary! The odds are against you. Order our electronic automatic burglar-alarm system now. Or how about a new fitted fireplace in the natural beige of Cotswold stone? Just the thing for a third-floor rabbit hutch. Home extensions . . . double glazing . . . cavity wall insulation. There was even a leaflet to tell him that back pain was no longer a problem.

Dispatching this gaudy and presumptuous literature to the kitchen's pedal bin, he took the genuine mail into the living-room, found a knife, and slit open the envelopes that had been sent to him personally. The first was a water rates bill for nearly £50. The second was a reminder that his television licence fee would be due at the end of the month, but he could already see that the third envelope was the only interesting arrival that morning. Re-directed to his house unopened by Top Toys, it bore a Cheshire postmark.

"Dear Mr Venables," he read. "This is to thank you for your great kindness in placing Top Toys' battery order with us. It will save the life of my firm and, indeed, I am now taking on staff for the first time in two years. Now that the contracts are signed I am in a position to show my gratitude to you as I promised at our lunch which I so much enjoyed. I have accordingly placed fifty thousand pounds for you in a nominee account in the San Remo Bank of Credit and Commerce in St Peter Port, Guernsey. Perhaps some time you will let me have a sample of your signature. I look forward to doing more business with you in the future. Yours very sincerely, Mel Schwarzbaum."

During the next half hour, Venables read this letter eight times, pausing between readings and sometimes during them, to consider its ramifications – legal, moral, domestic, professional. At the end of that time he threw the letter into the air and jumped around the room in his favourite imitation of an excited ape, complete with noises.

It was another thirty minutes before he had calmed sufficiently to write a letter of thanks, with sample signature, to Mel Schwarzbaum. "I am writing from home because it is better that you use this address," he wrote. It didn't seem necessary to reveal that he and Top Toys were no longer batting in the same team.

His next move was to phone Mr Mackay at the bank and ask for an appointment.

"I'm afraid I can't alter my decision," said Mr Mackay's humourless cadence.

"There is a new situation," explained Venables.

"Come in at twelve fifteen," said Mr Mackay.

The jeans, the sandals and the old shirt were discarded; the suit, the black shoes and the persona of a successful businessman replaced them. He left the flat with his letter to Mel Schwarzbaum, slipped it into the very first pillar-box, and walked, mostly on air, to the bank.

The arrival of money brings with it the need for decisions. Venables made the first one as he reached the bank – he would not tell Wendy about the money just yet. Its source would be difficult to explain. The bank's staff looked as dour as ever. He thought that he hadn't seen such a hard-faced, uncharitable-looking bunch of people since the last religious hymn-singing programme on television.

Mr Mackay's secretary arrived to beckon him in at twenty past twelve. In his office her boss rose briefly with a peremptory smile.

"What can I do for you this morning, Mr Venables?" he asked, as if he already knew that the answer was going to weary him beyond reason.

"I've got some loot."

"Some –?"

"Loot," said Simon. He liked to get these conversations on to his own ground. "What you chaps call liquid assets."

"Do you mean money?" asked Mr Mackay.

"Dough. Cash. Money is another word." He felt slightly light-headed, and realised that he was still on some sort of high from the morning's news. "I have fifty thousand pounds in Guernsey."

"Guernsey?" asked Mr Mackay. He looked as if he had never heard of Guernsey.

"In a nominee account."

"Ah."

"I suppose what I want to know is how I can bring it here so that I can get on with the business venture I discussed with you."

Mr Mackay looked at him as if he was having some difficulty in taking this in. "Well, the first thing I should tell you," he said eventually, "is to be careful."

Venables shook his head and looked puzzled. Mr Mackay put

one elbow on his desk and his chin on his fist. "We have something in this country called income tax, Mr Venables. If you have fifty thousand pounds in the Channel Islands I should leave it there. If you bring it here you will lose forty per cent. Twenty thousand pounds."

Venables felt confused and then angry. In the last euphoric hour income tax had not occurred to him.

"Is that true?" he asked. "Would they know?"

"The Inland Revenue can always ask to see your current account. And if the money is on deposit we're obliged to notify them of any interest over a hundred and fifty pounds. They can work it out."

"What are the chances of their looking at my current account?"

"It's not a risk I'd take," said Mr Mackay, flashing a rare smile. "And anyway, when you started to invest it in your wife's business they'd ask where the money came from. They are always on the look-out for big spending. So is everybody else, come to that. I always tell my customers that everybody lives next door to a spy from the Inland Revenue. I'm not against income tax but it's my duty, as your bank, to warn you."

Venables sat motionless in his seat. First the good news: you have fifty thousand pounds. Now the bad news: you can't spend it.

"All problems have an answer," he suggested.

"No, they don't," said Mr Mackay. "Some are insuperable."

But Venables ignored the innate pessimism of the bank manager and looked around for a solution. "Supposing we leave the money in Guernsey," he said. "Could I borrow against it here?"

"Ah, now there we might be able to help you," Mr Mackay replied, nodding thoughtfully. "If you give the bank in Guernsey permission to confirm that the money is yours and that x thousand pounds will be held to cover an overdraft in England. Proof of title is the thing."

Venables considered this idea, distracted at the same time by a suspicion that Mr Mackay did not really believe in the existence of the Guernsey money or, at least, not in his ownership of it.

"If we get confirmation from the bank that the money can be held to our order," said Mr Mackay, "I think we might be able to arrange something."

Venables smiled. "That seems to solve the problem."

"What is the name of the bank?"

"The San Remo Bank of Credit and Commerce."

"I've never heard of it." He reached for the *Bankers' Almanac and Year Book* on the shelf behind him without leaving his seat, and flipped through the pages quickly. "They're here," he said, surprised.

"Or rather there," said Venables. "It's the age of the off-shore account."

"Of course, there is another factor you shouldn't overlook," Mr Mackay said, returning the book to the shelf. "If the Guernsey money has to be remitted to us, or any part of it, tax would have to be paid at that point."

"You mean if I borrowed twenty-five thousand from you, and then had to pay you from the Channel Islands, ten thousand would go in tax?"

"Exactly that. You're very quick, Mr Venables. So you would bring in another ten thousand from Guernsey and then have to pay four thousand tax on that."

"So I'd get another four thousand over and have to pay sixteen hundred on that. I get the picture."

"It would depend, of course, on whether you were going to repay us from here or there."

"How can I know? Business ventures are always a risk."

"Exactly, Mr Venables. I tell ten customers that every day."

Venables stood up. "I'll go away and think about it."

As he walked out of the bank he imagined that he was the only man in the world with £50,000 who had no money.

Just after he had decided that things couldn't possibly get any worse, Nick Bannerman discovered that his penis had turned purple.

He was overdrawn at the bank which had taken to sending him begging letters; and he couldn't find the right note on which to end his book. He had written sympathetically to the bank, saying that he was unable to help them, but he hoped that they pulled through; and the bin at his feet was full of crumpled and rejected pages which constituted a day's hard work. And now his penis had turned purple, perhaps from neglect. Suddenly nothing was going right. He was even becoming neurotic about the passing years – too many people in the street were now younger than he was.

Lately, in a popular and quite probably misguided gambit to fend off age, he had taken up jogging. In his Nike shoes, bought second-hand at a jumble sale, and his old St Michael tracksuit, he ran most mornings, stumbling half awake over the "sleeping policemen" in the drive outside but clearing his head wonderfully for the day's positive thinking.

This tentative quest for fitness had taken him last night on to Ben Brock's tennis court where a straight-sets victory for the host had, Nick hoped, softened him up for a conversation about money.

"Why do you keep talking about money?" Ben had asked, over a fruit drink at the pool.

"I don't have any," Nick told him. "I need a loan to finish the book."

"If you were in America you could go begging to the Guggenheim Foundation."

"I'm not in America, Ben."

"So you've come to me. You're not the first, Nick, and I'd like to help, but things aren't going too well for me at the moment."

Nick looked at the pool, glistening in the evening sun, and the tennis court in the pines, and wondered how well Ben wanted things to go.

"Anyway, lending a friend money is a bad idea. Sometimes you lose the friend, sometimes you lose the money, and quite often you lose both."

"Forget I asked," Nick said. "Mind if I swim? That tennis was a bit warm."

"Jump in. I'll join you."

Nick peeled off his tracksuit, shoes and socks and dived into the pool in his new purple underpants.

Remembering the swim now as he sat forlornly at his desk, he realised why his penis had turned purple – it was the dye from his new, cheap pants.

With this growing concern banished, he began to feel more hopeful. He picked up his pen as if words were imminent, but eventually put it down again and swivelled in his chair.

Two posters, acquired from the jumble sale along with the running shoes, were Pritt-sticked to the wall at his side. One, which he liked very much, said:

NATIONAL PARKS:
SOLITUDE FOR
THE MASSES.

The other, a memento of the general election of 1910, said:

TARIFF REFORM
WILL TAX
POOR MEN'S CUPBOARDS
TO SAVE
RICH MEN'S POCKETS.

It was, he knew, the year in which George V replaced Edward VII on the throne. Those fiery old men who held an empire in the palms of their hands! His mind wandered up and down the corridors of Buckingham Palace and he suddenly found the paragraph he had been seeking to end his book. He picked up his pen again. Sometimes he typed but today, thinking slower, he used a pen.

Here in the United Queendom, with a warrior queen in Downing Street and a thousand more females outside lobbying on every cause from missiles to menstruation allowance, it is time for men to reassert their traditional role ... for the sake of both the sexes.

He put his pen down and gazed at the pile of pages that he had written. It seemed to be about right. For a few minutes he considered a coda on some celebrated court cases, tucked away in his files, featuring the horrendous wounds inflicted, usually with scissors, on fine husbands the world over, but memories of the Yorkshire Ripper made the point topple. He pulled a fresh sheet of paper from his box and typed:

BATTERED HUSBANDS
by Nick Bannerman

This encapsulation of months of hard work cheered him enormously. Finally here it was – a book. Well, a manuscript. A smile which mingled pride and hope was aborted by the ringing of his phone.

"Simon Venables here, Nick," the phone said.

"Hallo, Simon."

"Do you remember at Ben's barbecue that we met a chap called Johnny Fix-It?"

"Amazing man."

"Is he? What's the strength there, do you think? I mean, can he fix things? He said he'd get you on television."

"He's got me on television. I'm on next week."

"You rate him then?"

"I certainly do, Simon. He's a miracle-worker. Have you got a problem?"

"What's his background? Sort of legal-financial, isn't it?"

"I think he's an accountant. Do you want his number?"

"That's just what I want."

Nick thumbed through his own private phone book and read out the London number of Johnny Fix-It.

"I bet he'll be able to help you," he said.

"I hope so," said Simon. "Good luck on television. What's the programme called?"

"I think it's called *Tell The Truth*."

"I'll look out for it."

Nick returned to his desk. Perhaps he would soon be able to afford a new green steel one that would encourage him to start writing all over again. He had a good title ready for a novel in his head: *Memoirs of a Streaker*. All he needed was the other 100,000 words to go with it. He picked up a magazine and started to look at the publishers' advertisements and the type of books that they published. Some care would have to go into selecting the recipient of the vitriolic opus in front of him.

From the window he could again see Mrs Vaughan enjoying a morning dip in the pool. Perhaps one hot day it would occur to her to invite her impecunious tenant to enjoy crumbs from the rich man's table. After that, he joked to himself, he could have a swim.

Watching her tanned limbs dangling in the water a thought arrived that made him reach for his pen: *Even in sexual intercourse it is the man who does the work!*

During revision, he would work that into his book.

"Do you know Hampton Court?" asked Johnny Fix-It, when the

fifth phone call finally found him.

"You mean the Cardinal Wolsey job near Richmond, or is it a pub?" asked Venables.

"The area. You're sort of SW in Wimbledon, aren't you? Can you get tickets for the tennis, by the way?"

"As a matter of fact, I can "

"Good. I'll know who to come to if anyone asks me. Listen, there's a wine bar over there where I've been known to destroy the odd bottle of dry Montilla . . ."

His red Ferrari arrived punctually, trailing cassette music. Venables, watching him through the window, had a bottle of dry Montilla open and ready.

"Well, kid, nice to see you," said Johnny Fix-It, sitting down. "How is Ben Brock? Still prospering?"

"I believe so," said Venables, pouring wine.

"What can I do for you?"

"Live up to your nickname. You have quite a reputation."

"Shoot," said Johnny Fix-It, picking up his glass. He was wearing a very conventional pin-stripe suit today, complete with waistcoat and shining black shoes. With his big Elton John glasses and wild red hair the impression was a strange mixture of the respectable and the raffish.

"The problem is rather an unusual one," said Venables slowly. "There is a man who has fifty thousand pounds in an off-shore account. In Guernsey, actually If he brings it to England he will lose nearly half in tax. But he needs to bring it to England. And when it's here, it has got to be legal, legitimate money which the tax people can see but not touch. Otherwise he could just fly over and fetch it."

"The man is you?" asked Johnny Fix-It.

"As it happens."

"Well, I need to know who I'm dealing with. I should tell you, I think, that I live on percentages. They are very small percentages of very large amounts of money."

"Whatever you say," said Venables. "The problem is insuperable, isn't it?"

Johnny Fix-It shot him a searching look. "Who told you that – a bank clerk? No problem is insuperable, Simon. Not if you want to drive a red Ferrari and own a motor yacht in Banus." He picked up the bottle and stared at the label. "What we are talking about is turning black money into white money."

"Can it be done?"

"Of course it can be done. Let me tell you something. There isn't anybody in Britain today who is making a lot of money without having some fiddle or other. It just isn't possible. That's an economic fact. But there are a lot of people in Britain today who are making an awful lot of money."

"Find the fiddle," said Venables.

"Well, I must admit that I don't know off the top of my head how to turn black money into white money, but it wouldn't take me a day to work it out. Of course, you would lose something in the transaction, and probably not just my percentage. Would it be acceptable to you if I turned fifty thousand black into forty-five thousand white?"

"That's a lot better than the Inland Revenue," said Venables.

"I'll proceed on that basis. What account is the money in?"

"It's a nominee account in St Peter Port."

"I know it well. You'll have to go there in person with your passport." He finished his glass of wine and poured himself another. Venables' glass stood untouched. "I've never laundered money before. It's an interesting challenge."

"How did you get Nick Bannerman on television?"

"That was no problem. I know the producer. I don't like doing things like that – I don't make any money. Still it brought you to me, didn't it?" He smiled at Venables. "Look, I've got a meeting in town. A little consultancy work I do on the side. Can you meet me tomorrow?"

"Where?"

"Here? Nice place. Same time? I'll have it all worked out."

Wendy was playing Bach and ironing shirts when he reached the flat.

"Had a nice day?" he asked, but the reply was slow in coming. The suspense was bearable. He fell on to the sofa and picked up the evening newspaper she had brought home. Two months of marriage seemed to have poisoned their relationship nicely. It had all seemed so much bouncier at the start of the year when he had jokily asked her father: "Before I ask for your daughter's hand in marriage, can you tell me what your prospects are?" They had all laughed then, but now the laughter had stopped. While he had fantasies about Pym, Wendy wondered, usually aloud, why he hadn't found a job. The drabness of the flat didn't lend itself to hilarity, either. The money that it cost would, 100 miles from

London, have bought them an impressive detached house with lawns and garden. Ten miles from Piccadilly Circus it got you a third-floor rabbit hutch.

As usual, he sought refuge in the newspaper. A forensic pathologist was examining the Turin shroud, and the present was also catching up with the past in other, distant corners of the world. In the Pacific islands, motor accidents had replaced falling out of trees as the most common cause of injury.

"Any job news?" Wendy asked, slipping a newly ironed shirt on to the hanger, "or are you still going to raise the capital to extend Morsels?"

He ignored her sarcasm, and produced a letter of rejection he had received that morning. "That firm in Kent seem to think that they can survive without me," he said. "The feeling is quite mutual."

"I'm glad you're so confident."

He returned the letter to his pocket. "It's always nice to feel the full support of your wife when hard times arrive."

"I've been working all day for both of us. I've cooked the dinner. I've spent two hours ironing your clothes. Where have you been?"

"Drinking wine at Hampton Court. It was a business meeting." He realised with both shock and relief that she wasn't even interested enough to pursue it.

The following evening, with time to spare, he arrived early at the wine bar and ordered a gin and tonic. Wine, he decided, was for meals. You got a good class of girl in this privileged corner of the capital and he sat at the bar listening to them.

"My next husband's going to be a Swede," said one blonde damsel who looked no more than twenty.

"What's wrong with the British?" her friend asked.

"They haven't got the style, unfortunately."

Venables took this rebuff personally, and decided to tune in to another conversation. A plump, middle-aged lady with a contorted accent and a caftan that concealed the damage that chocolates had wreaked on her figure, had been to see a play that was apparently called *Luke Bech in Ongar*. It sounded vaguely familiar.

He finished his gin and tonic and was ordering another when he saw the red Ferrari arrive outside. Johnny Fix-It, wearing a bright pink shirt with his suit today, came in quickly, a man hurrying from one deal to another.

"I've got it together, kid," he said. "It was obvious directly I thought about it." He peered at Venables' glass through his comic spectacles. "What's that?"

"Gin."

"I'll have one."

Venables ordered a gin. By the time it had arrived, Johnny Fix-It had withdrawn to the quietest corner of the room.

"Now then," he said, when Venables had joined him with their drinks, "have you ever heard of Carltons?"

"Carltons? No."

"They're credit bookmakers in the city. Not as big as Hills or Ladbrokes but they haven't been going so long. They're doing very nicely. Jack Carlton is a client of mine. In fact, it was him I was dashing off to see last night."

Venables nodded, mystified.

"A lucky chance, really. Sitting in his office I suddenly saw the answer to your problem. Here's his card." A black card with gold lettering appeared from Johnny Fix-It's top pocket and was handed across the table. "First thing tomorrow morning you will write to that address and say that you want to open an account. To get it off on the right footing you should enclose a big bet."

"What on?"

"Anything. Connors is going to win Wimbledon, isn't he? Brazil will win the World Cup. On second thoughts, it had better be horses. Do you know anything about horses?"

"I would recognise one."

"There's a horse called Soba coming down from the North to run in the Stewards' Cup at Goodwood next month. I'm told it is going to win but it doesn't matter whether it does or not. The point is you have to establish your credentials as a punter in case anyone ever looks at the books. Put five hundred quid on to win."

"I don't have that much."

"It's credit, isn't it? You don't owe till you lose and by then you'll have your money."

"What's it called?" Venables asked, taking a pen and envelope from his pocket.

"Soba. That's S-O-B-A. Do it tomorrow."

"Fine. And then what happens?"

"You'll fly to Guernsey and present yourself at the bank with your passport. Collect a banker's draft for the whole amount, fifty thousand pounds, payable to J. Carlton. You've got his card. That banker's draft you deposit with me. I am the intermediary, trusted by both sides. Okay?"

Venables nodded.

"Jack Carlton will provide an ante-post certificate backdated on a winning horse. He will owe you forty-five thousand pounds on the bet and he will deposit a cheque with me."

"I see."

"Clever, eh? You will receive a legal, tax-free forty-five thousand, Jack Carlton and I will share five thousand."

"It's brilliant. What can go wrong?"

"When I'm involved, nothing goes wrong. It will take a week or two while your credit account is established. Then Carlton has to find a winner at the right price. A fifty-to-one shot on which you had a grand would do, because the ten per cent betting tax would knock that back to forty-five. The important thing immediately is for you to get your account open with a big bet. It's no good betting in tenners and then putting a thousand pounds on. Somebody could get suspicious. So five hundred as a starting bet is what's needed."

Venables nodded again. He was trying to ignore a slight whiff of doubt that came drifting across the table.

"Of course Mr Carlton will be able to set the forty-five thousand loss against tax," he said.

"That's true. And he will no doubt put your banker's draft into his own off-shore account which will suit you, too, because the money will never be seen in Britain. But that's the way it is with me – everybody wins."

"I'm trying to spot the flaw."

"Flaw?" Johnny Fix-It looked hurt. "There isn't a flaw."

"It can't be that easy, can it?"

"Well, now I've thought of it, it's extremely easy. Of course, not everybody would have thought of it."

Venables ran through the project again in his head. One flaw was sitting up, begging for attention. It emerged at that moment when Johnny Fix-It had £95,000 of other people's money in his custody, with nothing to keep it company but an ambition to own a motor yacht in Puerto Banus. It was hardly something that Venables could discuss. He looked at Johnny Fix-It contentedly sipping his gin. The man had professional qualifications, but then so did a high proportion of the prison population. With an effort he pushed these thoughts from his mind. It was only the people who never saw any real money who comforted themselves by harbouring unworthy thoughts about the rich and successful. With the clients he had, Johnny Fix-It had to be honest, even if that wasn't how the Inland Revenue would characterise him.

He offered Johnny Fix-It his hand.

"You've got a deal," he said. "And thank you very much."

SIX

On a sunny morning in June, Nick Bannerman approached a green skyscraper beside the Thames.

"*Tell The Truth,*" he said to a bored lady who sat smoking at reception.

"Third floor, green room," she replied, without looking up.

This did not seem to Nick to be the right way to greet a television personality, but standards, he knew, were falling everywhere. He took the lift. A dozen people sat uneasily in the green room, like hypochondriacs in a doctor's waiting-room. Nobody spoke. Nick found a cigarette and a seat and stared across the river at St Paul's.

Fifteen minutes later, a small, busy man with a clipboard arrived and filled the green room with his apologies. He introduced himself as the producer and explained that he had been held up downstairs where they were still fixing the set.

Just after that, Nick was introduced to a yeti-hunter, a small, dark-haired man with piercing eyes.

"Bick Ford," said the yeti-hunter.

The producer grabbed a third person from the crowd, a plump, solemn man in a black sweater, called Barry. The three of them were ushered to a table in the corner of the room.

"You will pretend to be Bick Ford," said the producer. "The panel is going to have to guess which of you is the yeti-hunter. Barry and Nick have got all day to learn what you do, Bick. Okay?"

He hurried away to organise similar groups.

Bick Ford was a fast-talking, intense man, who had spent months alone in the Himalayas looking through his binoculars in search of his elusive quarry. Barry, it emerged, was a musician in a well-known dance band, lured out of the television canteen to make up the numbers.

"I don't even know what a yeti is," he said. "And if I did, I wouldn't believe in it."

"You will by this evening," said Bick Ford. "The yeti is known as the abominable snowman, and it's a hulking great ape, about seven foot tall and covered with hair. What we are really talking about is the gigantapithicus, the largest anthropoid ever seen on earth. Fossil remains found in the rocks in south-east Asia tell us that it was strutting around five hundred million years ago."

"Is there anything more recent," Nick asked, "any developments in the last five hundred million years?"

Bick Ford looked at him. "In Russia in 1925 they found a relic hominid."

"A what?" said Barry.

"A relic hominid, an almasti. It was a wild man covered in hair that rushed out of a cave and was shot by Russian soldiers. It had a protruding jaw and a flat nose and a doctor reported that it was not human."

"Anything else?"

"In 1951 Eric Shipton took a photograph of a yeti's footprint."

"How do you know it was a yeti's footprint?" asked Nick.

"There was nothing else it could be. Lord Hunt has heard a sharp, piercing cry."

"So have I," said Barry. "Often. How many yeti hunts have you been on?"

"Three."

"Have you ever seen any trace of a yeti?"

"No," said Bick Ford.

At lunchtime a salad was wheeled in so that the briefing of the imposters would not be interrupted. Over food, Bick Ford became more persuasive.

"You must remember that ten per cent of the earth's surface is still unexplored. The terrain is too difficult to traverse. We didn't discover the gorilla until 1846, and the yeti is its brother. It could have been driven up to above fifteen thousand feet to survive. It could have been forced to adopt a new way of life."

"What does 'yeti' mean?" Barry asked. "That's the sort of question a panel would put."

"It means 'the wild one'," said Bick Ford. "Let me show you some pictures I took in Makalu. You'll get an idea of the environment."

"Any pictures of the yeti?" asked Nick.

"No," said Bick Ford.

All round the big room the would-be television stars were huddled in groups of three, gradually becoming airship pilots, gold-miners, Channel-swimmers. By the end of the afternoon Nick knew all he needed to know about yeti-hunting: what you wore, what you ate, what you carried, how many yaks you needed and how to make a plaster of Paris footprint.

"The danger is altitude sickness, the killer is apathy," said Bick Ford, putting away his colour slides. "The panel will never pick you, Barry. You're much too fat to be an explorer."

"I always put on weight between expeditions because I lose so much weight during them," said Barry.

"Very good," said Nick.

The producer came over and pulled up a chair.

"Nick, what's a big foot?" he asked.

"Never heard of it," replied Nick.

"I haven't told them that yet," said Bick Ford. "The Americans call the yeti Big Foot, and the Canadians call it Sasquatch."

"This is getting complicated," said Barry. "What are you going to do when you find the yeti, Bick? Kill it or bring it back to the zoo?"

Bick Ford raised both hands in horror. "I don't even carry a gun. All I want to do is prove that it exists. I shall photograph it, film it, take its footprints."

"Good luck," said Barry.

At five o'clock, meal vouchers appeared and they were ushered to the canteen. From there they were escorted to make-up, where their faces were moistened and powdered.

"I've always wanted to be a famous television star," said Nick. "It's the only thing that counts today."

They took a lift down to the studio. The audience had already been shown in and were being entertained or "warmed up" by a Scottish comedian. "We were going to have Yul Brynner on the panel but he had an accident in a bowling alley," he said. "He bent down to do up a shoe and somebody stuck two fingers up his nose."

Nick treated this material with the contempt that it deserved, and made himself comfortable in his seat. Any minute now his face would be flung invisibly across the country to land simultaneously in six million homes. A panel of celebrities were introduced to the studio audience and then took their seats at desks opposite.

The floor manager, in a shimmering orange shirt and rimless glasses, made up on his jaw for the hair that he lacked on his head. He pressed a hand to his ear as secret messages arrived.

"Five seconds," he shouted.

A light shone in Nick's face. Fame at last!

"My name is Bick Ford and I am a yeti-hunter," he said.

The lights changed.

"My name is Bick Ford and I am a yeti-hunter," said Barry.

"My name is Bick Ford and I am a yeti-hunter," said Bick Ford, who was a yeti-hunter.

"Three people all claiming to be a yeti-hunter," said the chairman, a well-known comedian who was performing panel-game duties, as it were, between jokes. "But only one of them is going to ... *Tell The Truth!*"

The programme titles came up on a far monitor and a bouncy signature tune filled the studio briefly.

Nick gazed across at the panel like a yeti-hunter who has come face to face with a snow leopard.

"Number one," said a beautiful lady journalist who wrote long unreadable articles in one of the Sunday papers. "What do you pay a sherpa?"

"Forty rupees a day," said Nick.

"Number two, what is that in English money?"

"About two pounds," said Barry.

"Number three – what does a yeti eat?"

"We believe that like the gorilla he's a vegetarian," said Bick Ford.

Five minutes later a unanimous panel picked Barry the musician.

When Nick left the flat the following morning in search of food, he was intercepted by Mrs Vaughan. "I saw you on television last night," she said. "I thought you were very good."

"Well, it was fun."

"Look, any time you want to use our pool don't bother to ask." It had taken the magic of television to extract the invitation that he wanted.

In the musty village store half a mile away Pym threw her arms round him.

"You were marvellous, Nick. They should give you your own show."

Nick bought tinned mince and potatoes, a bachelor's diet. Pym was buying the mysterious ingredients of a casserole.

"How are things?" he asked, when they left the shop.

"Jump in. I'll give you a lift back." She opened the passenger's door of her Golf and said: "They're grim. Why don't you come round and cheer us up some time?"

"I've been very busy revising my book. What's grim?"

"Business is grim, according to Ben. The government is waging war on the drug industry and its wild, wild costs. He's had three big accounts cancelled at the last minute."

"Oh dear."

"Actually, it's beginning to look serious."

"Can't he diversify? Plug cornflakes, or something."

"That's what they're all trying to do. It's a very competitive business."

"Well, when I've finished the big job I'll drop in with a bottle of champagne and cheer you up."

She dropped him at his gate and he hurried in. There would be no peace for him now until the book was finished.

But two more distractions awaited him before he could get back to his bulky manuscript. The first was a phone call from a friend, a magazine editor who commissioned the occasional article from him.

"Do you want to make a quick hundred?" he asked.

"I need the money," Nick said. "But I'm trying to finish a book."

"There's no travelling, no interviewing. You can write it now off the top of your head. I saw you on television last night."

"Who didn't?"

"A thousand words on what it was like, what happened behind the scenes, that sort of thing. Light, amusing, you know?"

"Yeah, thanks. It'll be in the post tonight."

"This magazine exists to subsidise you authors. I wish I had time to write a book."

Nick replaced the phone and balanced the day he would lose on the book against the hundred pounds that he would make in the next six hours. His hand had barely left the phone when it rang again.

It was the producer of *Tell The Truth*.

"Mr Bannerman? We've had a strange call from a woman claiming to be your mother."

"Oh God!"

"She wanted your address."

"You didn't give it to her, I hope?"

"Certainly not. We only have your phone number."

"You didn't give her that either?"

"We never do that sort of thing. But we did say that if she wrote to us we would forward the letter."

"But you haven't got my address."

"No, but you're going to give it to me now or you won't get your hundred pounds appearance fee for appearing on *Tell The Truth*."

The idea that his mother might catch his TV debut had been considered by Nick at the beginning, but discounted because his parents were always too busy running the restaurant in the evenings to watch television. The possibility of their friends spotting him had not seemed very strong either. They had few friends who had known Nick and he was five years older with a different name.

He gave the producer his address and hung up. His mother could write to him but she couldn't find him. He let more cheerful thoughts take over: in the space of twenty-four hours he would make £200.

Simon Venables' sex life had gone from regular to spasmodic, spasmodic to intermittent, and intermittent to non-existent, all in six months. It had finally vanished along with his job. Grappling with the unemployed was not to Wendy's taste.

The withdrawal of this pleasure, accompanied only occasionally by excuses, came as a blow to Venables who found that now he was relieved of the strain of earning a living he had energy to spare. It was only the men in the smart suits who left home at eight in the morning and returned, white-faced, eleven hours later who thought celibacy was fun.

"Is this the end of sexual intercourse as we know it?" he asked one night in bed.

Wendy recalled an agamic honeymoon, a man who had once been too tired by work to enjoy sex at night. "Never mind that," she said. "What about that job in Wembley, advertised in the

95

Telegraph today? You should be getting the early edition of the *Standard* every day and be first in with a job application."

"Are we having a conversation or taking minutes?" Venables asked. He considered inventing an impending interview, but Wendy could spot a lie at 400 yards in a fog.

She turned her back on him. "Your lack of resolve disgusts me, Simon."

He took the rebuke in silence. It probably seemed well deserved from the other side of the bed. He couldn't tell her that he was now craftily engaged in getting their hands on more money than they could earn, after tax, in four years. In his frustration he began to picture the big art mistress who lived in the flat downstairs. She had the gait of a giraffe, the manners of a goat, and the halitosis of a camel, but at least she liked him. The picture changed to Pym, Pym on a swing, breasts in profile. The heavy breathing at his shoulder told him that his wife was already asleep – the well-earned sleep of the gainfully employed – and he found his mind wandering back to the day they met. He had been on his way to negotiate with a man who sold plastic balls, the crucial component of some long-forgotten toy, when he first dropped into Morsels. Wendy was attractive, lively and twenty-six, a disturbing age, even in these emancipated days, for a girl. Venables had recently ended an affair with a school-teacher on the grounds that she was bossy, pedantic and dim, and was looking around. Wendy was looking, too. In the first hour she reached a peak of flirtatiousness that was never to be attained again.

"You can have it on the house," she told him when he tried to pay for his sandwiches. "I like your face."

The least he could do was ask her out. They wound up at the National Theatre where titled actors delivered a restrained performance of a resuscitated Hungarian epic, while the Thames flowed dankly by. They followed it, of course, with dinner in Soho.

"I'm a buyer," he told her when she asked him to explain exactly how he lived.

"I'm a seller," she said, smiling.

"We have the makings of a deal here."

"I come cheap."

She had pushed from the start and he had never assembled his thoughts sufficiently to resist, or even to know whether he wanted to. Within a month he had moved into her dainty flat; within six he had got himself a mortgage and bought this one for both of them. And that spring, to the evident relief of her parents in Worthing, they had married.

Lying in bed now he did not regard her new gift of celibacy as his main problem. His main problem was going to be how to explain to her the sudden arrival of money, if money suddenly arrived. The origin of this windfall was not something that Wendy was going to appreciate. He fell asleep and the dilemma infiltrated his dreams. "You must return the money, Simon," she told him. Luckily they were in the best room of an hotel in Grand Bahama, so at least they had got something out of it.

The following morning he took the paper and the post from the top of the fridge and settled down to his lonely breakfast. The war, he discovered, was over. Argentina, having lost to Belgium in the World Cup on Sunday, had lost to Britain in the Falkland Islands on Tuesday. It wasn't their week, but when millions of people allowed themselves to be ruled by soldiers, whose professional tastes leaned towards invading other countries, what could you expect? Venables had always been attracted to Argentina – the climate, the beef cattle on the rolling pampas, the glaciers of Patagonia!

He turned to the sports pages and was cheered to discover that the tennis began in a week. He seemed to remember that at Ben Brock's barbecue he had promised to take Pym to Wimbledon.

The post consisted of one plain envelope from Top Toys. It contained a cheque for £3104.72. It was his redundancy cheque. How they arrived at that figure he would never know. It occurred to him now that most people in his situation would have applied for some unemployment money, and probably a tax rebate as well, but he had been shooting for bigger fish in the gloomy portals of Mr Mackay's office.

After breakfast he wrote a letter to Jack Carlton asking to open an account and requesting a bet of £500 on a horse called Soba in the Stewards' Cup. Then he took his cheque round to the bank and paid it into his account. It was a pleasure to drop in without having to chat to Mr Mackay.

Two days later Johnny Fix-It rang.

"Is that Venables the big punter?" he asked. "I'm sorry I haven't phoned you."

"I didn't expect you to phone me."

"I like to keep in touch with my clients."

"How's things?"

"Everything's fine, just fine. Jack's got your bet. He's opening an account for you and will send you the stuff."

"The stuff?"

"Your account number, your credit limit, the book of rules, conditions of acceptance, forecast betting, ante-post betting, deposit accounts, computer tricast rules . . ."

"It all sounds very complicated."

"Don't bother your head with it. Listen, Jack would like to meet you. It's a good idea, for the reassurance of all parties."

"Okay. Reassurance would be nice."

"Jack says that. I'm the go-between."

The go-between took them for lunch in a noisy Italian restaurant in the City. Jack Carlton had that pale, overweight look which would induce an alert life-insurance salesman to take to the hills. But in the fat, weary face, adorned with a plump grey moustache, the eyes were constantly working, gauging chances, judging prospects, weighing odds. Venables was studied.

"Nice to meet you, Mr Venables," he said. "I've brought your ante-post voucher." He produced a pink slip from his wallet which gave Venables twenty-to-one on £500 on Soba in the Stewards' Cup.

"Ten thousand pounds coming my way," said Venables.

"Soba isn't going to win," said Carlton. "There are better horses in that race."

"Johnny thinks it will."

"There's chartered accountants and turf accountants," replied Carlton. "Johnny is the wrong sort."

"What are you both starting with?" asked Johnny Fix-It, studying the menu.

The waiters, shouting cheerfully, hurtled past carrying spaghetti and cannelloni. They wore very short green aprons, presumably to accommodate tips. Carlton ate quickly while his eyes covered the room.

"It's a licence to print money isn't it?" Venables said to him. "Bookmaking?"

Carlton wiped his mouth with a red paper serviette. "Not entirely, Mr Venables. We've been known to lose."

"I don't see how the punter can win in the long run."

"Oh, he can. Believe me."

Venables wasn't sure why he should believe Carlton. But the

mechanics of gambling, with which he was now temporarily involved, interested him.

"When do they?" he asked.

"You take politics," Carlton said. "If you've got the time and the money you can't lose. You've got five years to back both horses in a two-horse race. Back them when they're unpopular and not expected to win next time and you get the right price. Whoever wins, you win."

"I'm SDP," said Venables. "We like to think that's not a two-horse race any more."

"You can have hundreds on them forming the next government. I'll give you fifty to one they don't get twenty seats."

Their host interrupted this. "Let's talk business," he said. "Have you fixed up a trip to Guernsey yet, Simon?"

"I don't even know where it is."

"You turn right at Southampton. When do you propose to go?"

"When do you suggest?"

"Now that you've opened your account let's get on with it," said Carlton. "We need a fifty-to-one winner and there aren't that many of them."

"Do it as soon as possible," said Johnny Fix-It. "And get the banker's draft made out to Jack Carlton."

"Jack Carlton personally. Not Jack Carlton Limited," added Carlton.

Venables nodded. "Nothing can go wrong with this scheme, can it?"

"Like what?" asked Carlton suspiciously.

Venables wondered how to answer this without appearing rude. Bookmakers the world over might be the essence of integrity, but that wasn't their public image.

"The only thing that could go wrong," said Johnny Fix-It, "would be for Simon to fly to Guernsey and find the money wasn't there after all."

"Don't say that," said Venables, feeling suddenly uneasy.

"Why don't you phone the bank?" asked Carlton. "They've got telephones in the Channel Islands, haven't they?"

"They wouldn't answer questions like that on the phone," Johnny Fix-It said. "You have to appear in person, with identification."

Venables could see the possibility of disaster. After all, he only had Mel Schwarzbaum's word for the existence of the money.

"I'll fix it tomorrow," he promised.

Ben Brock's instinct now was to sell and run. He had spent eight years building up an agency that was sufficiently admired by competitors in the business for there to have been many hints fed back to him that if he wanted to quit, they wanted to buy.

He wanted to quit. The strong sense of intuition that had brought him this far told him that for him the tide had turned. He had made his money through luck and hard work and the luck was running out. It would take more than hard work to swim against this tide.

Sitting at his desk one morning he ran over the salient facts. The most important was that if the government succeeded in cutting drug companies' costs he was sitting on a diminishing asset, and the sooner he sold it the better the price. The second fact, he reminded himself, was that he had never intended to be the richest man in the graveyard, working until he dropped, while piling up huge amounts of money in the bank that not only would he never spend but that neither, thanks to death taxes, would his son. The third fact was related: he had always suspected that there was more to life than sitting in an office but he had never had the time to find out what it was.

He rang through to Cliff, his financial director, and asked him to call in.

"They've accepted the life insurance," said Cliff, shutting the door. "But I had to twist their arm a little."

"Sit down, Cliff," said Ben. "And you can forget about the life insurance."

"Forget about it? Why?" asked Cliff, dragging a chair towards Ben's desk.

"Confidentially – this is to go no further – I'm going to put out a few feelers and see if I can sell up."

Cliff looked at him sharply. "I don't recommend that, Ben," he said. "This is definitely not the moment to do it."

"It might be a bad moment to do it, but there are worse moments coming, I suspect. We've had the cream. The game's up."

"I don't think the staff are going to like it."

"My staff confuse kindness with weakness. They will be looked after. To tell you the truth, I'm getting a bad feeling about the future. It seems to me it can only get worse. Why not sell now while there is still something to sell?"

"The loss of the Pexo account will bring the price down."

"We've still got Preil, the anti-rheumatism drug. That's a very big account."

"We've still got Shackleford Ciderhouse, too. Glen Nardini is asking for another three weeks in the Seychelles."

"Well, buy it for him quick. If we lose Shackleford Ciderhouse we really are sunk."

"I'll fix it this afternoon. But in the meantime I strongly urge you not to even try to sell until things improve."

"Who says they are going to improve, Cliff? The government is out to cut the drug business down to size, and you know who gets hurt when anybody starts making economies. The one above the bottom line is advertising."

"I know," Cliff said. "I always thought we should diversify, but I'm only a humble accountant, not one of your ad-men whizz-kids."

"Into what?"

"The future is home computers. That's where the growth will be. We could handle it. All we need is two or three scientific writers. We could be the agency that understands their products."

Ben barely listened. "My background's medicine. I feel too old to learn new tricks."

"You don't have to. You hire people."

"And who makes the presentation that actually wins the account?"

"Somebody else."

Ben shrugged. "Fact is, Cliff, nobody else does it quite as well as me."

This time Cliff shrugged. He knew it was true.

Ben leaned forward at his desk. "What I want you to do is prepare the accounts for me to show to a prospective purchaser. Don't look so worried. I'll make sure you come out of it all right."

"Thanks."

"I mean it."

"I know you do. It's you I'm worried about. You won't get the price you would have got at the beginning of the year."

"I know that. But if I wait it will be even less."

After Cliff had gone, Ben felt a weight lifted from his back. He began to wonder what those other things were that life held apart from a job, a desk and an office. Travel, he thought. A forty-foot sloop heading for Antigua; a Range Rover to Istanbul; the orchid flight to Bali. He reached across for his morning newspaper in search of similar ideas, but a double-column headline on the front page leapt at him:

ANTI-RHEUMATISM DRUG BANNED AFTER 8 DIE

He read the story that followed with a fear that gripped his stomach.

A DRUG taken by more than 75,000 people with rheumatism has been banned by the Department of Health after reports on the deaths of eight patients.

The Department said yesterday that it had received reports from doctors about 230 patients suffering side-effects from the drug, Preil. Eight of the patients had died.

It advised anyone who has been prescribed the drug not to take any more tablets and to consult their doctor about an alternative. The drug's product licence is being suspended immediately.

Preil is an Italian-made anti-inflammatory drug used for the treatment of rheumatism and for the relief of mild to moderate pain.

It has been available in Britain since September last year. About 10,000 people are thought to be taking it at present.

Side-effects experienced by some patients have included stomach upsets, irritation of stomach ulcers and internal bleeding. Others have suffered dizziness and headaches.

The side-effects came to light in a

study of patients carried out by the manufacturers and were reinforced by adverse reports by doctors.

A Health Department spokesman said: "Doctors are advised neither to start any new patients on the drug nor to prescribe it without good reason. Pharmacists are advised to contact the prescribing doctor about any prescriptions they receive for the drug."

The phone was ringing as he finished reading. It was one of his account directors.

"Preil has been banned, Ben," he said.

"Yes," said Ben. "I know."

The moment that Nick Bannerman had waited for during long and solitary months was marred before he could make his usual, reassuring cup of tea. It was the day that he would finish typing his book, wrap it up, select a publisher, and fire off the little missile that would, he hoped, scatter not only women but docile fifth columnists in trousers as well. But the erratic postal service reached him first. The letter from his mother, redirected by the television producer, was written in large but firm handwriting on cheap, lined notepaper and filled many sheets.

My dear Tony,

I hope that you can imagine what a great shock it was for us to see you on television the other evening when for five years we have been worrying about you and wondering where you were. To turn up with a new name, unless it was adopted purely for the programme, was particularly hurtful to your father who is a sick man. In my opinion it is a sickness that was brought on by your disappearance, as he has not been the same since you left. We had to sell the restaurant and now live on the interest from the money.

The television people say that it is not their practice to reveal the addresses of people who appear on programmes so we have no idea what part of the country you are living in. My guess is that you are in London. And I hope you are happy.

It is difficult to imagine anything crueller than the way you walked out on us, or anything more ungrateful. You have undermined your father's health and caused me five years of hideous embarrassment. And in five years – not a note from you, not a message. You haven't even thought to return the money you stole from the safe. It seems poor thanks for the sacrifices we made when you were a boy. You seemed so happy then, on daytrips to Blakeney and Cromer. Even later when you tootled off to Brancaster in your Reliant there was no hint that you hated us so much. I wonder what went wrong? Now people say, "I saw your son on television". You can imagine what fools we feel. We have left your room as it was, and looked after your clothes and books, the camera, the typewriter and the rowing machine. The painting of Castle Acre that you liked so much is still on the wall, but we had to sell the Reliant eventually, and for a lot less than the hundred pounds that you took.

It would be nice to think that one day you will come back to see us. There is no telling how much longer your father will last.

We naturally wonder whether you have got married and whether we are now grandparents. We know that you are not married to Helen, the reporter you "took out". She is on television quite a lot herself now, and we read in the newspaper about her marriage to an MP. But if we have grandchildren aren't we entitled to know? It is so cruel of you to keep these things to yourself.

Your father asks me to say that he would appreciate hearing from you.

In spite of everything,
your loving mother

Nick laid the letter out in front of him, page by page. It took an effort of memory to ensure that history was not being rewritten: for a moment, somewhere in mid-letter, he had the shameful impression that his mother was the wronged party in this awful domestic melodrama. But the fact that she had managed two references to the money reassured him that this was the same scheming, selfish, malicious and domineering woman he had finally shaken from his life five years ago. Of course, she would be older and perhaps mellower today, but there was no hint in her pained whine that she thought herself to be remotely responsible for what had happened.

He collected the letter up and was poised for a moment to drop it in his waste bin. Instead he put it in a desk drawer.

He resented the distraction that it had brought to his big day. The elusive trick of concentration was too fragile for emotional turbulence. The mention of Helen stopped him cold for more than half an hour, as he wondered how she could have found a man she could marry in that monstrous menagerie of egos beside the Thames. The news that she appeared regularly on television delayed him further. Was she to return to haunt his middle years through the modern miracle of broadcasting?

Eventually the same ruthless dedication that had got the 100,000 words in front of him on paper in the first place enabled him to exorcise all thoughts of his mother, Helen, and randy politicians, and he fed a page of Croxley Script into his ageing typewriter. Page 425. He typed quickly but carefully for two hours until he came to the magic words – the end. He corrected the day's typing without the aid of a dictionary – Shakespeare, he always reminded himself, had done fairly well without the help of one. Then he scoured old notebooks for an epigraph that he had been saving to stand at the entrance to this literary experience. It was from Samuel Butler and seemed to him to hit the right churlish note:

Brigands demand your money or your life: women require both.

He typed this on a separate sheet and put it at the front of his manuscript, and then typed the title and his name and address on another sheet. He slid the whole lot into a cardboard folder and wrapped it up, nervously now, in an untidy parcel of brown paper and Sellotape.

The feeling of exultation that swept over him was so over-powering that he almost forgot that he had no idea who was going to be the grateful recipient of this vituperative message. He had collected a list of publishers that was so long he barely knew where to start looking. It even included Gallimard in France, Unieboek in Holland and Mondadori and Longanesi in Italy. There were even Iron Curtain publishers – Czytelnik, Europa, Narodna Kultura – but would he ever get the roubles? With a pin, as it were, he picked a famous London publisher, copied the address on to the parcel and stood up, the job done. His flat, he realised, was filthy. His idea of cleaning it had been to pick up the balls of fluff with his hands, but now, perhaps, he would have time for something more thorough.

With the parcel tucked proudly under his arm, he walked the half mile to the village post office. As he pushed it through to the surly lady behind the grille he felt like giving it a good-luck kiss, but this would have required an explanation that he didn't wish to provide.

Next to the post office was the village pub and he decided that he had earned the writer's traditional reward. Sitting at the bar, cradling a pink gin, was Mrs Vaughan.

"It's the television star," she announced. "Good morning."

"Good morning," replied Nick, and ordered a gin.

"Let me pay for that," said Mrs Vaughan. "When are you going to use the pool?"

Nick realised with a shock that she was flirting with him. "I've been very busy," he said.

"Doing what?"

"Writing a book. At least, it's just a manuscript at the moment, but I hope it will emerge as a book."

"Really?" said Mrs Vaughan. "I wondered what that clattering typewriter was up to. What's it about?"

"Women."

"Really?" Mrs Vaughan repeated. Her skirt moved an inch up her knee. "You know about women, do you?"

"I've got their number."

"What are you doing in here then, writer? Get back to your desk."

"Oh, all proper writers drink like mad," said Nick. "If Scott Fitzgerald and Dylan Thomas had been teetotallers they wouldn't have written a word."

"Cheers," said Mrs Vaughan.

"Cheers," said Nick.

When he escaped from the Valiant Sailor, as the village pub was mysteriously called, he remembered a promise to take champagne to the Brocks when the *magnum opus* was completed. He prowled the liquor department of the village store and found a bottle of Lanson Black Label.

Back in his flat he was greeted by the shrill cry of his phone.

"Pym here. I've been ringing you regularly."

"I've been out to post the book."

"It's finished?"

"Absolutely. And I am clutching a bottle of alcohol which I'm planning to share with you."

"I was ringing to ask you round, anyway. The Venables are dropping in tonight to sort out our holiday in the sun."

When Nick arrived at the pool the others were, at Wendy's instigation, drinking a toast to the royal baby, a future king, who had arrived that day. Greg was holding an orange juice.

"He's going to be your king, Greg," Pym told him.

Nick raised his glass of champagne, but it failed to stifle his reservations. "I'm not sure all this breeding is necessary," he said.

Pym frowned. "It's absolutely essential, Nick. Didn't you hear that the German government is pleading with people to have children? The way things are going now there won't be enough workers in twenty-five years to pay the pensions."

"It will happen here, too," said Ben from his sun-lounger. "Look at the five of us. All we've produced is Greg. Poor old Greg! We'll need big pensions by then and Greg will have to work for the five of us."

"I'm quite prepared to do my bit," said Nick. "But you can't breed on your own. I read a book about sex once."

"How's your book?" asked Wendy, who was sitting at a table with Simon. She was wearing an attractive yellow sweater, and Nick decided to sit next to her.

"He's finished it," said Pym. "Let's drink a toast to it."

"May it find a publisher," said Wendy.

"It had better," said Nick. "How are things with you, Simon? You seem a mite quiet."

Venables nodded. "Life gets a bit complicated when you're out of work."

"Did you reach Johnny Fix-It?"

"Yes, thanks."

"Is he the chap who was at Ben's barbecue?" Wendy asked. "What did you want him for?"

"Bit of advice."

Ben asked: "What's complicated?"

"There are a lot of balls in the air at the moment."

"And two of them are yours?"

"That's about it."

"What are you talking about?" Wendy asked.

"My future," said Venables. "Don't you worry about it."

"I didn't know you had any."

"You just concentrate on Morsels, dear."

"Pile it high and sell it cheap," said Ben. "I may need a job myself soon."

"Are things not going well?" Wendy asked.

"They could hardly be worse," Ben told her. "The question is, can any of us still afford this holiday? Nick?"

"I can't afford to eat half the time, but I'm still coming. I've never had a proper holiday."

"Where's the money coming from?"

"I'll go out and do some work," Nick said. "They pay you money then, don't they?"

"Simon?"

"We're coming. What will it cost?"

"The air fare is about a hundred. Then we'll have to pay Rupert Puckle something. I thought we'd go for three weeks."

"That's settled then," said Pym. "How lovely!"

"What about Greg?" Venables asked her.

"My parents are having him. Greg is holidaying in Theydon Bois."

Venables felt relieved at this news. He saw the holiday as his chance to advance his claim on Pym, and a three-year-old boy hovering demandingly on the edge of the stage could spoil the plot. At his most optimistic he could imagine some civilised partner-swapping at the heart of this sun-filled expedition.

"Theydon Bois, Greg," he said. "You'll love that."

Greg scowled at him. "Take your face away," he said.

Pym filled their glasses.

"We've drunk to the future king. We've drunk to Nick's book. Now we'll drink to our holiday in the sun."

They raised their glasses to a sky that was already clouding over.

SEVEN

GLIMPSING HOPE, Simon Venables resumed his troglodytic habits and caught the Tube one morning to Earls Court. He changed trains with a smile on his face and sped west to Heathrow Central where men with mysterious talents plucked him from his subterranean trolley and, with barely a hiccup, hoisted him 12,000 feet over southern England.

On the ground at Heathrow, the two small black-and-white propellers of the Air UK Dart Herald seemed barely sufficient to lift a packed plane off the runway, but now they were chugging along like an old car at 220 miles an hour, skimming a low carpet of cloud. The passengers all looked like men on questionable financial missions, with poker faces and brief-cases that Simon half expected to be padlocked to their wrists. Sipping a coffee, he reflected that he was a man on a questionable financial mission himself.

As the Dart Herald wheeled over murderous rocks, Guernsey was seen to be a green island set in a green sea – and covered with green houses. Gazing down through diminishing clouds, he could only wonder why, if Argentina was prepared to spill blood over the Falkland Islands, a marauding army speaking fluent French had not already stormed the tiny island of Guernsey, tucked as it was between Brest and the Cherbourg peninsula. They landed with a bump in a field in the south of the island, and Venables hurried past a policeman, who scrutinised arrivals in this conservative haven, and headed for the taxi rank outside the airport building.

The driver filled the journey to St Peter Port with answers to his questions. In Guernsey the bars closed on Sundays and, because there was spirit in petrol, the petrol stations closed as well. There was no gambling, no caravans – and very little taxation.

"That," said the driver, waving his hand at some large houses on their right, "is the English millionaires' ghetto. Fort George. When they give the shops that address, their bill goes up. When they find out what is happening they move out of Fort George. Fort George is for newcomers."

They drove down a steep, pretty, winding hill into St Peter Port. Simon paid off the driver, and stepped out into a picture postcard: a straight half-mile row of tall white buildings facing a multitude of little harbours full of small boats with French names. Beyond the harbour this off-shore island had off-shore islands of its own: Herm, Sark, Alderney, and ticket offices along the front offered trips there. Simon ducked into the tourist office on the quay and emerged with a handful of literature. He had six hours on the island before his flight home and didn't imagine that his visit to the bank could last longer than an hour. Sitting on the front he learned that the French had, over the centuries, made many bloody assaults in attempts to win the island for themselves, but the inhabitants, who had been British since 1066, insisted on remaining so. It was an echo of the South Atlantic.

He left the quay and climbed narrow stone steps that led up to the High Street. The pillar-boxes were blue and the telephone kiosks yellow. Every business seemed to be either a bank or a perfumerie, offering colognes and sprays and dusting powders at a lot less than would be charged at home. Wendy's tastes, he knew, ran to Madame Rochas toilet water and he bought her a bottle for £10. In the street a man was selling lottery tickets for £1, to fund a new leisure complex in the town. It seemed to Venables to be an intelligent breach of the local laws on gambling. He found the San Remo Bank of Credit and Commerce next to a jeweller, but decided to delay his visit; the thought of walking around all day with £50,000 in his pocket made him nervous. His nerves, not helped by a renewed craving for nicotine, betrayed him when the single shot of a cannon boomed round the port, a local tradition at noon that he only read about in his tourist leaflets later. For a second he had thought jumpily that the French, with Britain's shrinking forces on the other side of the world, were about to lay siege to the island again. The huge digital clock outside the Midland Bank told him that it was midday, and he found himself, without even thinking about it, in the Ship and Crown on the quay. Men in thick blue sweaters that suggested, accurately or otherwise, associations with the sea, were drinking Guernsey Brewery's best bitter. He ordered a pint. It was so good that he wondered, sitting at a table in the window and watching the hundreds of boats bobbing gently in the harbour, whether he shouldn't join his money here. St Peter Port was nicer than Wimbledon. Why not invest the money and laze? But a notice over the bar had a peremptory tone:

LAST ORDERS
15 minutes to the hour – and the
premises vacated by the closing hour.

Perhaps this wasn't quite the fun-loving place that he needed. The *Guernsey Evening Press* on his table had a story about an islander who had been "blacklisted". It meant that he was forbidden to buy alcohol. His escapist idea faded.

He left the bar and looked for food. He found a place on the front called the Steak and Stilton, and had both. The restaurant seemed to have been carved out of the rocks, with the semi-circular roof of an air-raid shelter. The leaflets collected at the tourist office and absorbed over his meal told him of a different Guernsey and of a real air raid. Thirty-four islanders had died in a raid on the port in June 1940, the month when the five-year German occupation had begun. The Channel Islands had been the only British territory to be occupied by the Germans during the Second World War, an occupation, said the brochure, endured with impotent rage. Food was scarce, radios were confiscated, and all islanders not born in Guernsey were deported and interned in Germany on Hitler's orders. The Channel Islands became the most fortified section of his Atlantic wall. It was chilling to imagine those strutting lunatics in such pleasant surroundings, and Venables turned his mind to other matters. The San Remo Bank of Credit and Commerce.

It was a small building but its sandstone front and tall, ornate front door gave customers the feeling of solidity that was conveyed by much larger establishments. Venables found his passport, cleared his throat, and marched in.

"I want to draw a banker's draft on money that has been deposited here for me," he told a young girl at the service counter.

The girl nodded as if this sort of thing was going on all the time. "May I have your passport?" she asked. She took it and disappeared, leaving him in a cold sweat. Was he really about to get his hands on £50,000? Was it a joke? The situation was rich with possibilities of awful mistakes, clerical oversights, missing documents, absent signatures. The worry beads came out of his pocket.

"Our Mr Duquemin will see you," the girl said when she returned. She pointed to a door at the end of the counter.

Mr Duquemin was a short, young man with a tanned face. He lived in a small room with a desk and two chairs. The document on his desk, Venables saw reading it upside down, was about a "Swiss Mutual Fund with an International Investment Portfolio".

"My name's Duquemin," he said, offering his hand. "I'm the assistant manager."

"Simon Venables."

"Sit down, please. You have some money here?"

"I *hope* I have some money here."

Duquemin sat down and stared over the desk, awaiting further information. Nobody would believe the stories he had heard in this room. Nobody even knew any more exactly how much money there was in Guernsey. It was coming in so fast that even the British government had to be polite.

"Some money has been put into a nominee account for me with your bank."

"How much?"

"Fifty thousand pounds."

"Who by?"

"Mel Schwarzbaum of Schwarzbaum Batteries. An English firm."

"It rings a bell," said Mr Duquemin. He picked up Venables' passport and started to read it. "Do I gather you want to take the money away?"

"I want a bank draft for the entire amount."

Mr Duquemin stood up. "Wait here, please," he said and vanished through a back door. He was gone a long time. In the end Venables was driven to reading the document about the Swiss Mutual Fund. "The Fund's portfolio is subject to market fluctuations and to the risks inherent in all investments," he read. It was much safer, he thought, to back horses.

A quarter of an hour slipped past and then a girl he had not seen before came in holding a blank sheet of the bank's notepaper.

"Would you put your signature on here, please, Mr Venables?" she said.

She handed him a Sheaffer pen that was all gold, and he scribbled his signature nonchalantly as if dropping into banks to pick up fifty grand filled a large part of his week. He looked at what he had written and hoped it bore a passing resemblance to the signature he had sent so eagerly to Mel Schwarzbaum. The girl smiled and pulled the sheet of paper away from him.

Left alone again, Venables scanned the room for reading matter. Beneath the brochure about the Swiss Mutual Fund he saw a typed sheet and edged it in his direction. It was headed "A proposal from W. Duquemin (St Peter Port branch)". The proposal was brief and brilliant. "Guernsey is a fortress," he read, "and it would lend itself to the safe-deposit no-questions-asked type of business more than almost anywhere in the world. Even in London these type of safe deposits have been robbed, but here in Guernsey, where the airport can be closed and the coast watched, thieves would have no chance of getting away. My proposal is that we build one thousand safes beneath the bank where there is plenty of unused space, and advertise their availability world-wide. Confidentiality would be guaranteed, and no customer would reveal what was in his own safe. The rent would be only £250 a year, but this would produce for the bank an annual profit of a quarter of a million pounds."

Good on you, W. Duquemin, he thought, returning the sheet to its original position. Not for the first time, he was surprised at how easy it was for some people to make money.

The author of this proposal appeared at the door.

"I'm sorry to keep you waiting, Mr Venables," he said. "It's a lot of money and we have a bit of internal checking to do."

"Is there a problem?"

Venables had begun to get a bad feeling.

"Not so far. But a bank draft, as you know, is drawn on the bank itself." He disappeared again before Venables could explore this aspect of the transaction with him. Again he sat alone wondering how a sane man could endure the tedium of solitary confinement.

After ten minutes Mr Duquemin returned. This time he was all smiles.

"Yes, that's in order, Mr Venables. I'll get the bank draft typed up. Is it payable to you?"

Restraining himself from dancing round the room, Venables said: "No, to Jack Carlton."

Mr Duquemin slid a piece of paper across the desk and a pen, this time a silver Parker. "Will you write his name on there?" He watched Venables writing and asked: "Does this gentleman live in England?"

"London."

"I hope he's *au fait* with your tax laws."

"He's heard of them."

"Most people prefer to keep their money here."

"Perhaps he'll bring it back to you. He doesn't have to cash it in England, does he?"

"That's true." He made for the door again with the piece of paper. "Your interest and our charges cancel each other out, so the draft will be exactly fifty thousand."

"Fine."

Mr Duquemin returned quickly this time with the bank draft. Venables took it and felt a thrill that was almost sexual. This was probably the most money that he would ever hold in his life. He read it twice.

"There is a receipt here for you to sign," said Mr Duquemin. "Sign here, here and here."

Venables scribbled. Then he folded the bank draft up and tucked it into his wallet.

He left the bank as quickly as possible, as if further checks would reveal that there had been a terrible mistake. Once in the street he was anxious to get home. With £50,000 tucked against his heart he found it difficult to relax, imagining pickpockets, muggers, street accidents. His flight wasn't due for two hours but he decided to make his way to the airport – carefully. He walked up the High Street and into a street called Le Pollet, a concession to the neighbours across the water. It led down to the taxi rank on the front.

Cruising through the country lanes to the airport, he began to warm to Guernsey, even if you couldn't get a drink on Sunday. He wanted a drink at the airport, but had tea instead. The document in his wallet deserved a sober companion. Sitting in the sun, his hand moved unconsciously to it, for ten-minute checks on its presence.

But when the Dart Herald from Heathrow came curving out of the sky to fetch him, he realised that he had lost something that day. Somewhere – in the bar, in the restaurant, in the bank – he had mislaid the bottle of toilet water that he had bought for

Wendy. It was just as well, he realised, as he went through to check in for his flight. How would he explain to her that he had spent the day in the Channel Islands?

Ben Brock's search for a possible purchaser of his agency took him one cloudy morning to an upstairs restaurant in Chancery Lane. Mike Prentice, of Spedding Advertising, was Ben's greatest rival in the drug world which was why he had not until now accepted his repeated invitations to lunch. Arranging the date on the phone, Ben had not revealed that he wanted to sell his firm; he intended to see how the conversation went. But lurking in his mind was the unwelcome possibility, even probability, that Mike Prentice wanted to sell Spedding Advertising to Ben.

As in so many of his recent ventures, Ben was stymied almost immediately. Mike Prentice was not a man to waste a lunch date on only one person, and a second guest appeared as soon as they had sat down: Timothy Talbot, who was responsible for the advertising of a large drug company, Dibley Pharmaceuticals. Talbot threw the odd crumbs to both Ben and Mike Prentice, but the really huge accounts, the products whose names were known to everybody in the land, seemed to drift elsewhere.

Ben decided, studying them both, that by Chelsea rules, Mike Prentice was flash, and Timothy Talbot was smart. Mike Prentice wore an Italian mohair suit with a crocodile-skin belt, and soft-leather foreign shoes. A gold bracelet dangled superfluously from his wrist. Timothy Talbot wore an old check suit that was beautifully cut, and a Viyella shirt. Of course, Mike Prentice was probably as rich as Ben and he evidently believed that there was no point in making it if nobody knew, whereas Timothy Talbot was only a paid employee of someone else, although in this company he was fawned on by men who were much wealthier than he was. It was firms like Dibley Pharmaceuticals that kept them in champagne.

"How goes it, Benjamin?" Prentice asked, when a small, swarthy waiter had brought their steaks. "Do the shekels still roll in?"

"Not in the same quantity as hitherto," Ben replied. "Haven't Spedding Advertising noticed a recession?"

"Oh, we've noticed it. I blame Timothy. The bloody drug firms won't advertise, and when they do their products get withdrawn. They could bring people like us to our knees."

"You two gentlemen are hucksters," said Talbot, dabbing his mouth primly with a napkin. "You never believe in the efficacy of the product, anyway. With you it's only money. With me it's a vocation."

"You bet I don't believe in them," said Prentice eagerly. "Bromides, placebos. My father-in-law has been bed-ridden with arthritis for years. It's made him deaf, blind and dumb and now it's frozen him completely rigid."

Timothy Talbot picked at his food diffidently. "He doesn't sound too well to me," he said eventually.

"I had an aunt who was blinded in one eye when a baboon pissed in it at the zoo," Ben told them. "What did the drug industry have to offer? Nothing."

"You gentlemen are ribbing me," Talbot said. He looked as if he had never laughed.

"It's the poverty that's making us bitter," Prentice replied. "We address you from our beam ends."

"I think not," said Talbot, flicking the gold bracelet on his host's wrist. "I, on the other hand, can't even afford a holiday this year. I was going to dump the children on my mother-in-law and take my wife to the Mandarin Hotel in Hong Kong in September. You can do a four-day tour of China from there – Seven Star Crag, ancestral temples, Canton."

"I always thought you were rather well paid?" Ben suggested, encouraged to hear of someone else's hardship.

"I am. But we've just bought a big house in Kent and I'm having a ten-thousand-pound extension put on the back. So no holiday this year."

Mike Prentice said: "You shouldn't have all these children, Timothy. I have no children. Neither has my wife. If we want to go to Paris, we go to Paris."

"As a matter of interest," said Talbot, "and given the business I'm in, what form of birth control do you use?"

"Sodomy," replied Prentice.

Talbot nodded solemnly. "I believe you," he said.

As the waiter took their plates, Ben realised with a silent anger that he could not discuss the sale of his agency in front of Talbot. If the drug industry knew that Ben Brock Advertising was up for sale he would never get another account.

"Let's have some more wine," he said, contemplating a wasted lunch. "We'll drink our way through the recession."

But over the cheesecake that followed he determined that the visit to Chancery Lane would not be wasted. In the taxi back to Chelsea he made a brief stop at a travel agent in Knightsbridge, emerging with an armful of brochures. Back in his office he worked his way through them, a pleasurable scenic tour of palm-fringed beaches, luxury hotels and twinkling foreign capitals that took him much longer than he had intended.

"Every city has one great hotel," he read, "and in Hong Kong it is the Mandarin. On Hong Kong Island, overlooking the harbour, this de luxe hotel is just thirty minutes' drive from Hong Kong International Airport, and only a few seconds from the famous Star Ferry, linking the hotel with the Kowloon peninsula."

This time he rang his own travel agency who granted him a minimal discount, but the prices were still as de luxe as the hotel. A holiday for two in September would cost his agency a little over £2000.

"I want the written confirmation this afternoon," he told a harassed clerk.

An hour later he had the yellow reservation slip in his hand. It guaranteed a fourteen-day holiday at the Mandarin Hotel, Hong Kong, for Mr and Mrs Timothy Talbot. On a sheet of the agency's headed notepaper, he wrote: "Have this one on us. Ben Brock." He sealed both in an envelope addressed to Timothy Talbot at Dibley Pharmaceuticals and sent a secretary off in a taxi to deliver it.

He had forgotten about it the following morning when a large white envelope, with Dibley Pharmaceuticals' baroque logo in the top left-hand corner, lay on the top of his post. He opened it quickly, sniffing a new product, an invitation to pitch for a new and lucrative piece of business. But when the contents fell on his desk he was reinforced in a comparatively recent belief that he could no longer do anything right. Pinned to the holiday reservation slip was a note that said: "You know better than to expect me to accept this. Tim."

*

Nick Bannerman had disliked so much of his life that by the time he was thirty he wondered whether misery had become a habit. It had been a life whose shape had been decided by influences beyond his control: teachers, parents, employers; and when he had escaped all of them he found that new factors placed fresh restrictions. They were mostly financial, and as he began to consider his holiday in the sun he realised with disgust that not only had he never been abroad, but neither could he afford to go there now. The up-and-down state of his bank account had made the manager at first edgy and then irritable. A loan to pay for a holiday seemed an unlikely gesture from the man whose terse notes of exasperation arrived so frequently.

He felt curiously drained after the efforts on his book and, waiting in a vacuum for some reaction to it, he had no appetite for work. He thought about *Memoirs of a Streaker*, the novel that he wanted to write, but couldn't bring himself to confront all those empty pages again. Doing nothing more energetic than thinking, he came up with the idea of the world's first sponsored novel. Sponsors were sponsoring everything else – why shouldn't they sponsor a novel? He imagined Mitsubishi, Benson & Hedges, Volkswagen and Trusthouse Forte signing large cheques every time their product was mentioned in a book. But this idea went the way of many others, and as the prospect of his first foreign holiday began to shake, he phoned an editor he knew and asked for work.

The editor, an enthusiastically shirt-sleeved young man who lived permanently among page proofs and deadlines, said: "You've picked the right day, Nick. There's a new television series coming up on great boxing matches and they're starting off with Cooper's fights with Ali. We want someone to interview Cooper about those fights. We'll pay three hundred and exes."

The thought of meeting one of his heroes made the prospect of money seem unimportant. But plodding the grimy streets of north London's cement jungle that afternoon, after the magazine had phoned the great boxer and arranged the interview, he decided that men should be paid just to visit that part of the world.

In a quiet grove where the houses were big but built just a little too closely to their neighbours, Henry Cooper lived with his wife, two sons and a dog. Nick was big but Henry was bigger. He was wearing a white short-sleeved shirt and fawn slacks. He shook Nick's hand. The fist that decked Ali remained passively in a pocket. Nick remembered that fight, and he remembered, too, what the left fist had done to an Italian who kept hitting low. The Italian, unconscious standing up, had pitched forward into his opponent, finally ending up with his face on Cooper's boots. Joe Erskine had been counted out draped alarmingly over the bottom rope so that the back of his head rested on the canvas outside the ring. Cassius Clay, before he became Muhammad Ali, had been so disorganised after Henry hit him that his manager had torn his glove to stretch a one-minute break between rounds into two minutes while a steward ran off to find new gloves. The architect of this mayhem was gentleness itself. The pictures on his walls were of boats and trees, not savage moments in the ring. On a long bookshelf there was a volume called *Great Punchers*, but it was next to *Little Women*.

"Clay used to cuff and hit with the heel of the gloves," said Henry Cooper as Nick scribbled. "He was a clean fighter but his punches were the sort that cut you, not like short, sharp punches."

They were sitting in an elegantly furnished room that overlooked a patio and, beyond, a small swimming pool. In seventeen years in the ring Henry had made £300,000. His father had never earned more than £11 a week.

"What do you think of Ali now?" Nick asked. "Did he take one punch too many?"

"No," said Henry. "He says he's got an illness similar to diabetes and I believe him. The sweet and starchy food that he loves poisons his system and makes him sleepy. He's also got a fluid retention problem which used to blow him up to eighteen stones between fights. He may have taken too much medication during his career, but he's not punch-drunk. You've only got to look at his face. No lumps or bumps, no scar tissue, no flat nose. He rode the punches."

Nick steered the talk round towards the phial of ammonia that had been used illegally to revive Clay after Henry had flattened him in 1963.

"The referee couldn't see what was going on," Cooper said. "With four big guys round Clay in the corner you couldn't see it, but you can see it on the film afterwards. Still, that's what managers are paid for, to think quickly. They only have fifty seconds between rounds."

"Or, in Clay's case, two minutes."

Henry smiled. He smiled a lot. "If the boot had been on the other foot my manager would have done the same for me."

In less than an hour Nick had much more than the 1000 words he had to write about this encounter. It was the easiest interview he had ever done. Henry was off to play golf, so Nick left quickly and walked down a long straight road that took him away from the expensive areas where retired champions lived to the grubby environs of Hendon where dogs and traffic wardens prowled with equal malevolence.

At Hendon Central he bought himself a southbound ticket for the Northern Line and began to cheer up. He had made £300 in a day. If he did that every day he would earn £75,000 in a year. In four years he would make as much as Henry Cooper had earned in his entire career. It was little dreams like that which kept him going, and if things went wrong he always had the words of John Maynard Keynes, scribbled in one of his notebooks, to fall back on: "If you owe your bank manager a thousand pounds, you are at his mercy; if you owe him a million pounds, he is at your mercy."

Johnny Fix-It's scabrous language and outrageous behaviour, temporarily shelved when the discussion involved the fate of £50,000, was back in full employment. "I can't make it, I'll be in Cambridge," he shouted into the phone. "Cambridge, you deaf berk! Clap, Aids, Masturbation, Bunions, Rectum, Impotence, Diarrhoea, Gonorrhoea, Enema. Got it?"

Venables stood in his small sparsely furnished office in Fenchurch Street, having been sent on in by a pretty, blonde girl who was painting her nails in an even smaller outer office. Johnny Fix-It evidently ran his wheeling-and-dealing operation with a minimum of equipment: a steel desk, two filing cabinets and three telephones. The Elton John glasses had slipped down his nose in the heat of this exchange, and he raised them to their rightful place with his left thumb as he replaced the phone.

"Good morning, Simon," he said. "Pull up that chair." He collected many sheets of paper together on the desk in front of him and slid them into a green folder. Behind his head was an aerial picture of London that was intended to convey the impression of a window, and below it was a wall safe.

"That's a very tasty greeter you have out there," Venables said, sitting down.

"Debbie?" said Johnny Fix-It. "Eyelashes that could clean your teeth at twenty yards, and the cranial capacity of an amoeba. Still, you can't have everything. I'm going to take her to Banus and change her entire personality with the force of my sexual energy."

"Good for you."

"Of course, it's more speculation than ejaculation at the moment. She probably wouldn't come within a yard of my underemployed pieces. What I need is a Sexfam shop. How's life with you? All booze, screws and snooze, I suppose?"

Venables shook his head. "None of those things. In fact it's so inactive at the moment that my automatic watch keeps stopping."

Johnny Fix-It, palpably offended by the spectre of sloth which Venables had innocently evoked, outlined how his own life, in contrast, was moving at a velocity that was difficult to control as unnamed, greedy men with multifarious problems picked at his brain to find the resolution of financial situations that teetered at the edges of the law. His conversation was sprinkled with words that Venables had never heard before: ricks, scams, megabucks. He had to work out the meanings for himself as Johnny Fix-It's high-speed description of the opportunists, entrepreneurs, gamblers, nervous investors and incompetent traders, whose dubious interests he protected with intrepid zeal, filled the room. "Ricks" were mistakes that people made to their own financial detriment, he decided, and "scams" were barely legal financial coups. "Megabucks" meant big money, the motivating force behind the Johnny Fix-It operation.

"Have you found your way to the bailiwick of Guernsey yet?" he asked, remembering that Venables, too, was a client.

"What a nice place it is," said Venables. "If only they could tow it south a bit into the sun. Have you been?"

"Been?" said Johnny Fix-It. "I have a company registered there. It's going to fund my yacht in Banus."

Venables pulled a white envelope from his pocket. "I've brought you this."

Johnny Fix-It opened the envelope and laid the banker's draft on his desk. He studied it with infinite attention, like an art lover gazing at a Miró.

"Congratulations," he said. "It's in order. We're in business." He picked up the nearest phone and dialled a number. "Jack Carlton, please," he said. "Tell him it's Johnny." He waved the draft at Venables while he waited. "I bet this is the most money you've ever held?"

"So far."

A voice on the phone distracted Johnny Fix-It from this piece of optimism. "Jack? Mr Venables has delivered the draft." He paused, listened and nodded. "Your name, yes. I'm putting it in my safe. Yes. Of course. Good-bye." He put down the phone and picked up the draft. "I'll give you a receipt for this."

"What does Jack Carlton say?"

"He says quite rightly that we can't do anything now until a horse wins at the right price. As soon as it does, he'll be in touch."

"And you'll ring me?"

Johnny Fix-It scribbled a receipt on his own headed notepaper. It said: "J. M. Henderson."

"I'll ring," he said. "Don't worry."

"I always thought your surname was Fix-It?"

"Ben Brick started that."

"Ben Brock. You're both bad at surnames. What's the time?"

"Noon. Where are you headed?"

"The tennis."

But outside in the street he was so worried about his casual separation from £50,000 that he could not get himself into the right mood of anticipatory pleasure for his first date with Pym. On the train he pulled Johnny Fix-It's receipt from his jacket pocket. It said: "Received from Simon Venables: the sum of £50,000" followed by an illegible signature. This seemed to rather leave open the question of current ownership of the money. Its ambiguity frightened him. He folded it up and tucked it into the innermost recesses of his wallet, not knowing whether it was worth the paper it was written on. The original plan, he recalled, had been for Jack Carlton to deposit his money with Johnny Fix-It when Venables delivered the draft. That had not happened. Was it impracticable without a race date, or was something funny going on? He considered phoning Johnny Fix-It, but as the train rattled south he realised that things had gone too far now for him to lose his nerve. The bank draft, if he reclaimed it, wasn't even in his name.

Time, which is always helped by a selective memory, erases all worries, and when he reached the All England Club he was once again a man with £50,000 at his disposal. With his tickets in his pocket, he swept past the crowds to the main entrance in Church Road where he had arranged to meet her. She wasn't there but his watch couldn't tell him whether he was early or late. He stood on the pavement wondering why Wimbledon, more than any other event, attracted such a good-looking crowd. It wasn't just the sun, the bronzed skins, the summer dresses; even the men looked like models from those glossy adverts designed to persuade you that ownership of a BMW will enhance your appeal to women and render them captive.

Pym arrived in a flowery dress that stopped at the knees. She extended her hand theatrically to be kissed.

"Ben doesn't know I'm here," she whispered. "Aren't I naughty?"

"You realise that this is the most televised spectacle in the country," he said. "There are cameras everywhere. See?" He pointed at one on the outside balcony of the ivy-clad Centre Court building that was picking up some action long-distance on one of the outer courts. "Your beautiful face could be beamed at any moment into twenty-six countries."

"Let's hope not. My husband has a jealous streak."

The news that Ben did not know he was meeting Pym raised Venables' spirits. It put an exciting tinge on their meeting, lifting it from the commonplace to the clandestine. He led her down one of the crowded narrow pathways between the outside courts where beautiful young girls with brown legs and straight white teeth bounced around on the virgin grass. There was a powerful aura of sex in the air which was why the local magistrates' court was kept busy during the tournament dealing with a predictable variety of sexual misdemeanours perpetrated by the paying customers. Venables was tempted himself, but Pym was more excited by the famous faces as world stars made their way self-consciously through the gaping crowds for first-round matches on outer courts. "I always thought Betty Stove was bigger than that," she said. "Look, there's Jimmy Connors!"

Insisting that they could become separated in the crowd, he held her hand and got a bigger kick out of the contact than he had done since he first left school. He remembered the first moment he had seen her, sitting in the Rueda Bar. It seemed at the time to be the biggest find since Clyde Tombaugh discovered Pluto, and now, three months later, he was holding her hand!

They stood for a while watching a hopeful pair, one from Rumania, one from Korea, on Court Eight, and then made their way to the Centre Court where McEnroe was scheduled to infuriate the umpire and delight the crowd. They had a good seat in the third row, and McEnroe subdued the opposition without the use of tantrums. Venables wondered whether he had spotted a flaw in the game: all else being equal, the left-hander had an advantage.

When they left the Centre Court there was only one place to take Pym – to the Pimms Bar near the Wimbledon Museum. Thousands of people, exhausted by the efforts of others, were sitting on the grass. The massive results board by Court Two showed the expected names moving towards epic collisions in later rounds.

"It's all so much faster than it appears on television," said Pym, when he had bought her a drink. They sat at a little table near the bar. "I shall go home and thrash Ben in straight sets."

Venables was glad that she had brought the conversation away from the highly paid antics on the grass to where he wanted it to be – to Ben, to her, to him. The problem was that she never gave the slightest hint that she fancied him. Her days as a Page Three girl had seemed to inure her to the blatant enthusiasms of panting men. Plato ruled.

A fleeting picture of Wendy working in Morsels lingered before him, produced, he saw suddenly, by the surprising number of people who were carrying Morsels picnic boxes in preference to the All England Club's expensive fare. This was the sandwich bar's busiest fortnight, and Wendy produced a special package for tennis *aficionados*: a cardboard box, bearing the green Morsels logo, and containing smoked-salmon sandwiches, strawberries and cream, and a quarter bottle of Moët & Chandon.

But looking at Pym he found it was quite easy to forget about Morsels. He decided to get to the heart of the matter. He had never had Pym to himself before. He asked: "What happened about the nude pictures? Did you ever mention them?"

"Good Lord, no. What could I have said?"

"You might have asked who the hell took them?"

"I think," Pym said, staring into her drink, "that questions like

124

that create a crisis. Don't you?"

"Possibly. But if you have a husband who is posing for nude photographs with person or persons unknown, I'd have thought you have a crisis already." Venables felt that he had a lever, and was reluctant to let go.

But Pym laughed. "You haven't been married very long, have you, Simon?"

"Three months."

"How is it?"

"Pretty bad."

"Why?"

"I don't know. We just sort of drifted into it. And losing my job didn't help."

"When you've been married as long as I have, you'll know that there are a lot of things you have to overlook. Marriage is a delicate commodity."

Venables listened to this unexpected defence of marriage with mounting panic. He had always had a secret feeling that one push would separate the Brocks for ever. It was just a question of getting himself ready, especially financially. In every other way he was over-ready. The sexless weeks had lifted him to peaks of frustration that made him dizzy. He was quite certain that he could make love to a dozen women and still be robustly eager for more. Lust on this scale was rare: it seemed a crime to waste it.

"The trouble is," he said, "I'm in love with *you*."

The words seemed to escape without consulting him.

"You're what?" asked Pym.

"I'm in love with you. I fell in love with you the first time I saw you."

Pym put her glass down and looked at him. "Don't be ridiculous," she said.

But Venables was committed now. "It's true. You were sitting in the Rueda Bar on that Sunday morning. I thought, 'That's the girl I've been looking for all my life.'"

"Wasn't that the day after your wedding?"

"As it happens, yes."

"That seems extraordinary to me."

"Well," said Venables, "I was fairly surprised myself."

"I think I'll have another drink."

The Pimms was expensive, but Venables fetched two more

glasses. He was alone with her now and would happily buy it by the jug. On the tea lawn hundreds of people sprawled with flasks and sandwiches. They had paid a lot of money not to watch any tennis.

"This has come as a bit of a shock," Pym said, sipping her new drink.

"I thought it might. I've been very discreet."

"Does Wendy know?"

"Not an inkling. I don't think she'd notice if I was sleeping with the Luton Girls' Choir."

But Pym was not in the mood for a joke. "Simon, I have a husband and a son. Whatever you may imagine about ex-models, I'm a very conventional girl."

"I know. I know you are. How is Ben?"

"He's a bastard."

"But you married him."

"Evidently."

Venables picked up his own drink and wondered where this conversation was going. "I'm just putting my cards on the table, Pym. I'm here if you need me. Of course," he said, trying to joke, "I can see that there is a considerable difference between a penniless man with no job, and a man on his way to his second million."

"Don't get bitter."

"I was joking."

"Are you sure? Anyway, Ben isn't on his way to his second million. In fact I don't think he still has his first million. He looks worried to me."

"What's happened?"

"The drug industry has a headache."

"Physician, heal thyself."

"I think it's quite serious. Ben tells me nothing, but I hear phone calls and endure his temper."

"I read about government cuts in the paper. I wondered whether they would hurt Ben."

"I gather they are. Look, shouldn't we wend our way? I have to collect Greg, and Ben rather likes hot food to be waiting when he gets home. It's what wives are for. And I have had my afternoon at Wimbledon, while he's been slaving in an office."

Venables stood up. "You sound like an ideal wife to me," he said.

126

"Do I? When I got married, Simon, I decided that if I was going to be a wife I would be a good wife. It's as simple as that. Any idiot can do things badly."

It seemed to Venables that she had more virtues than even he had imagined. Her only vice was failing to see any virtue in him.

"I made that decision on our honeymoon in Greece," she said, standing up. "We spent it in an hotel called the Panoramic. Everybody called it the Ram and Panic." She laughed at the memory.

"Your honeymoon is at the top of a long list of things I don't want to hear about," said Venables, guiding her to the exit. Crowds were waiting for the tickets of early leavers, so that they could see the last hour cheaply.

Across the road an entire golf course was being used as a car park. They walked across the grass as Pym tried to remember where she had left her car. In huge marquees on this side of the road caterers hired by giant corporations served expensive food to business guests who often finished up watching the tennis on television in the marquee rather than stumble across the road to see it in the flesh.

Pym's yellow Golf was several hundred yards from where she thought she had left it. She unlocked the driver's door and threw her handbag on to the passenger seat.

"Do you want a lift?" she asked.

"No. It's a short walk. Why did you marry him, Pym?"

"He asked me. I loved him. We were fun together."

The reply relieved him. It was all in the past tense.

"Thanks, Simon, for . . . a memorable day."

She smiled up from the car.

"Kiss?" he suggested.

She shook her head. "I don't think we should, do you?" She slammed the door, but wound the window down a few inches. He leaned towards the opening that she had created.

"Won't you throw a crust to a starving man, lady?"

"Not if his wife owns a sandwich bar."

EIGHT

THE DAY that Nick Bannerman always remembered arrived with a broiling sun in the first week of July. At this time of the year, encouraged by the bright light, he would leave his bed a full hour earlier than in the long, dark days of winter, and now that the desk-bound marathon was behind him he increased his jogging to a two-mile run before breakfast. In a day devoid of work, this breathless exertion seemed to appease those gods who demand that all of us each day must suffer a little, and Nick was able to face his first meal with the satisfaction that other men experienced after eight hours of hard but successful toil.

On this morning, however, he had only just broken into a trot when he was confronted by the postman who handed him a letter. It was a large, white envelope that was unmistakably more important than his usual mail, and turning it over he saw printed in raised blue letters the name and address of the publisher to whom, only three weeks previously, he had dispatched his bilious epic. His heart began to pound as if he had indeed completed his run – what was supposed to arrive in the post at this stage was a large brown parcel containing his own rejected manuscript. He sprinted back to the flat and sliced the envelope open with his kitchen scissors. Then he sat himself comfortably at his desk and, not familiar with the succinct missives of busy publishers, prepared himself for a long, literary discussion about the merits of his work.

"Dear Mr Bannerman," he read. "We are interested in publishing *Battered Husbands*. Can you ring me? Yours sincerely, Theo Benson."

Feeling an elation that actually made him lightheaded, he reached for his phone and was half-way through dialling the number before he realised that it was not yet half-past seven. He abandoned the phone and re-read the letter several times, searching for hidden meanings in its choice of words. He settled on the phrase "interested in publishing", and worried at it while he waited for the world to start work. Did it mean they might not publish it? What did it depend on? His appearance? His suitability for a chat show? His price?

He put the letter down and made tea. He had a strong urge to ring the Brocks but a native superstition decided him to delay the celebrations until a contract had been signed. He rang Theo Benson at half-past eight, nine o'clock and half-past nine, but there was no reply. At five past ten he established contact and an hour later he was on a train to London. He bought *The Times* to calm himself down, but the only item to hold his restless mind was the discovery by excited palaeontologists in Ethiopia of the fossilised remains not of a yeti, as he had hoped, but of man's oldest direct ancestor, a four-foot-tall creature who walked upright four million years ago. It did not seem to Nick, given the timespan, that man's progress since had been as sensational as man liked to imagine, an impression reinforced when the train broke down, holding them up for half an hour.

A taxi took him to Bloomsbury, an area he had become familiar with when he first left home. In this quiet hinterland, between the museum and the zoo, publishers squabbled over manuscripts like chickens over corn. He found his in a splendid Regency house that looked more like a rich man's home than an office. Across the road, in an identical building, was another even more famous publisher.

Theo Benson looked as if he had been kept alive in the Kremlin hospital's reanimation unit. His dark eyes stared from a cadaverous head, and his body twitched. He worked in a surprisingly cramped room, the walls of which were totally covered in books. Glancing fascinated at the names of the famous authors on the spines, Nick realised that all of these literary lions had been dead for some time.

"I very much enjoyed your philippic, Mr Bannerman," he said. He was an old man in a black suit. "Do sit down."

Nick sank into a leather chair and looked across a cluttered antique desk at Mr Benson. "Do you think it's going to change any attitudes?" he remarked conversationally.

Mr Benson twitched and shook his head. "In my experience neither books nor newspapers have any effect on anybody."

"Isn't that rather pessimistic, coming from a publisher?" Nick asked with what was meant to be a smile.

Mr Benson stared back. "In a conservative country like Britain it takes twenty years to get an idea into our heads and a hundred years to get it out. I've no illusions. Tell me about yourself, Mr Bannerman. How old are you? What do you do?"

"I'm thirty. I write. Freelance journalism, that sort of thing."

"Have you plans for other books? If we launch a new writer we like to know that he's not just a one-book man. Names catch on slowly in this business."

"I'm planning a novel. Called *Memoirs of a Streaker*."

Mr Benson managed to conceal his enthusiasm for this project. "A novel?" he said, staring at the ceiling and twitching.

Nick's elation had now gone. He did not like this room or this conversation. He was not sure that he liked Mr Benson.

"You see," said the old man, "what you have written is non-fiction. Didactic, readable, a certain mordant wit. But non-fiction."

"I don't see your point, Mr Benson," said Nick, feeling a growing impatience. "All the other writers seem to do fiction and non-fiction. Orwell, Greene, Hemingway."

"Not any more they don't," said Mr Benson. "Have you got an agent?"

Nick shook his head. "Do I need one?"

"It's a matter for you. Well, look. I'd like to publish *Battered Husbands*. I believe it will cause a stir. What I propose is an advance of five hundred pounds, half payable now and half on publication, and then the usual royalties on sales."

"Five hundred pounds?" said Nick, feeling sick. "I can earn that in two days."

"I'm sure we'd sell the paperback rights and that would provide your major source of money later. You would get sixty per cent of the paperback money."

"Where does the other forty per cent go?"

"We get that. It's standard practice in publishing, Mr Bannerman."

"How many copies would you print in hardback?"

"Fifteen hundred."

"Fifteen hundred?" said Nick, standing up. "I think I'm in the wrong office, Mr Benson." He reached over and picked up his manuscript. "I'm going to try the firm over the road."

Amazed and frightened by his own temerity, he walked out of the room. Was he turning down publishers already?

As the door shut, Theo Benson picked up his phone and dialled a number.

"Give me Arthur Scott," he said. There was a pause. "Arthur? Theo. You were reminding me the other day that I owe you a favour. I'm about to repay it. There's a temperamental young man called Bannerman heading in your direction. He's got a certain bestseller under his arm. Be nice to him."

Nick was so surprised by the cordial reception he received from the second publisher that he would probably have signed away his book for an advance of £5.

"Mr Bannerman?" said the girl at reception, as if she was expecting him. "Our editorial director, Arthur Scott, will see you now." She left her desk to guide him up the stairs. A door at the top opened and Arthur Scott came out with a pretty dark-skinned girl. He shook her hand and said: "You'll have the dust jacket next week." He turned and gripped Nick's hand. "Mr Bannerman. Do come in." He shut the door behind them and pointed to an armchair. "Do sit down. Marvellous girl, that. Hitch-hiked to India and got gang-banged in the mountains by some trachoma-ridden Kurds. It's going to make a wonderful book. Would you like a coffee, or something stronger?"

Arthur Scott was in his thirties. He had a small, pleasant face and receding hair, and he had a quiet, cultured voice. Nick was thrown by the contrast between this office and the last. Although their exteriors were identical, Arthur Scott's firm had torn the inside of this one apart and built a 1980s office in a Regency shell. The walls were lined not with books but with bulletin boards, posters and press cuttings. "A coffee would be nice," Nick said.

Arthur Scott sent this message into an intercom and, ignoring his high-back swivel chair, perched himself on the corner of the desk. He was wearing jeans and a dusty-pink cotton-voile shirt with rolled-up sleeves.

"You've written a book," he said. "I can tell by the manuscript on your lap."

Nick gathered it up and handed it across. "I would like you to publish it," he said.

"*Battered Husbands*," read Arthur Scott. "I like the title already. What's it about? No, don't tell me. I'll read it."

"It's a male answer to the feminist movement," Nick said.

"Is it?" said Arthur Scott. "Is it really? I was only saying yesterday that there is a gap in the market there. I'm excited."

"If you're excited, I'm excited," said Nick. "The man over the road offered me a five hundred pounds advance."

"Theo? I'm afraid they haven't quit the nineteenth century yet. All their authors are dead."

"I noticed."

"They haven't. I'll give you a five thousand advance and make sure it's sold in the States. But I'd better read it first."

"How long will that take you?"

"When I ring you tomorrow I'll have read it. Let me have your number."

A girl came in with the coffee. As he drank it, Nick studied the posters on the wall, each of them featuring an author and a book. All the authors, according to the newspapers that Nick had read, were millionaires, all the books bestsellers in several countries. It seemed to him that he was sitting in the right office.

He was dreaming about a poster that featured his own face and his own book when the telephone rang the following morning. It was seven o'clock.

"I hope I didn't wake you?" Arthur Scott's voice said. "I've been up all night reading your book, Mr Bannerman, or may I call you Nick?"

"Please do," said Nick, waking quickly. "Did you really stay up all night?"

"Work comes first with us, Nick. That's why we get the bestsellers the others miss. Your book is tremendous and the potential is frightening. I see it as being big on both sides of the Atlantic. It'll be the vade-mecum of demoralised family men, the bible of defeated males everywhere."

"I like what you're saying, Mr Scott."

"Arthur, Nick. Listen, I'll print twenty thousand copies, and fix a deal in the States. Have you got a carbon?"

"Yes."

"Let's have it. I'll put a contract in the post this morning. Read it and ring me with any questions. I'll pay you the five thousand I promised, half on signature, half on publication."

"When would that be? Publication, I mean."

"I was thinking about that as dawn crept over West Hampstead. It normally takes a year to bring out a book, but yours has a topicality which makes it urgent. We could do it in the autumn and catch the Christmas market."

"The sooner the better," said Nick.

"I shall aim for October. We could just do it in three months. When you've signed the contract, bring it in with your carbon copy and I'll take you out to lunch."

"Thanks."

"Not at all – and congratulations."

Nick put the phone down. It took all his concentration to keep the tears from his eyes.

The blacker his future looked, the more determinedly Ben Brock pursued the life of a millionaire. To start trimming at the edges of his extravagant lifestyle now would somehow be an admission of defeat, a tacit encouragement to the fates who plotted against him, a conscious acknowledgement that he was on the skids. Breakfast on the patio today was only scrambled eggs and grilled bacon, but it was accompanied by what Ben regarded as the ultimate early-morning luxury: freshly squeezed Spanish oranges and a bottle of Dom Perignon. He sat in the sun watching a blue tit land precariously on a swinging cage of peanuts that hung from a beam above his head.

"This is the way to live," he said.

"But can we afford it?" Pym asked, guiding scrambled eggs to her son's reluctant mouth. "What's happening, Ben? Is it going to be all right?"

"The prognosis ain't that delightful."

"What does that mean?"

Ben drank Buck's Fizz. No husband was less communicative on the subject of his work. He had once had fancy ideas about keeping his family and his firm in separate compartments.

"No one will buy it," he said.

"Buy what?"

"The agency."

"You're selling up?" Pym was surprised.

"I'm trying to sell, aren't I, Greg? But no bugger wants to buy it. Not that I blame them. It's a long time since we had good news."

"Isn't this just one of those bad patches that you will pull through?"

"Not with this government in power for the next ten years, and I think the Falklands is going to set them up for a long innings. They've got a thing about public expenditure. That means the Health Service. That means drugs. That means me."

"Get out of pharmaceuticals."

"We've tried. We haven't won a single account. All our eggs-pertise is in one basket." He poured some more Buck's Fizz. "The Health Service has made me a millionaire. It's not exactly what Aneurin Bevan intended."

"Ben, there must be somebody who would buy the agency."

"What would they be buying, Pym? The last seven years of a lease in Chelsea."

"What's going to happen then?"

"I don't know." He looked at the immaculate lawn that rolled down to the cross-shaped pool and at the new tennis court beyond and wondered whether he could hang on to them. But he was saved from further contemplation of the possible horrors in store by the arrival of a wild, singing, dancing figure on the patio.

"I've made it! I've done it! I'm rich!" he shouted.

Pym stood up. "Good morning, Nick."

"What's he on about?" asked Ben. "Has he been sniffing glue?"

"The book," sang Nick. "It's going to be published!"

"It's not!" said Ben, leaping up. He had got used to the idea of Nick writing a book. Nearly everyone he knew was writing a book. The thought that Nick's would actually be published had never occurred to him. "Who's doing it?"

Nick whispered the publisher's name in reverential tones.

"They're great," said Ben, deeply impressed. "In fact, the best."

"That's wonderful, Nick," Pym said. "You may kiss me."

"You can't kiss me," said Ben. "But you can help me to drink this champagne."

"Quite right," said Nick. "In the old days when I was poor I used to have a cup of tea for breakfast."

"When did you hear?" Ben asked him.

"About five minutes ago on the phone. This man stayed up all last night reading it. He says he will get it published in America. You heard of America?"

"The land of the topless shoeshine?"

"They also invented the brash, ball-kicking wife. The book should go down like a bucket of cold vomit over there."

"Perhaps it will help to liberate the ulcer-ridden American male," said Ben. "Actually, I'm not too sure about America. Any country that was carrying out public executions as recently as 1936 and could bring itself to elect Eisenhower rather than Stevenson, and Nixon in preference to Humphrey can't be all good."

"I won't hear a word against them," said Nick. "That vast, literate country, thirsty for ideas, with its educated millions who actually read books without their lips moving! I shall probably have to tour the country and plug my work in obscure television stations . . ."

"Before having your balls cut off and rammed down your throat by the Sisters of Feminist Advance, Alabama chapter."

"On second thoughts, I may make a video here and send it over instead."

"Harangue them in your absence," said Ben. "Much safer." He stood up. "Well, congratulations, Nick. I'm really delighted for you. But I have to go to work. I'm sure Pym will find some scrambled eggs for a famous author."

Nick played with Greg on the patio while Pym cooked him breakfast. She returned with a plate of eggs and bacon and, as she bent over, he saw her eye.

"What happened?" he asked, pointing at a bruise.

"A little keepsake from Ben. I went to Wimbledon with Simon and he didn't like it."

"How did he know?"

"The television cameras picked us up in the crowd. We were in the third row."

"And he *hit* you?"

"You've never noticed before? For a writer you're not very observant."

Nick was shaking his head disbelievingly.

"Don't let's talk about it," Pym said. "This is your big day. What wonderful news! What is the book called?"

"*Battered Husbands*."

*

Speeding up the A3 at a little over 100 miles an hour, Ben flicked the Bentley's radio on, trying at the same time to gauge the shape of the day ahead. The setbacks and disasters of the past few weeks had forced him to take one day at a time; he could remember when he planned in weeks and months. From the car radio a man with a heavy Ulster accent was saying: "My reaction is one of complete horror" and Ben nodded in agreement as he swept past a line of cars, marooned nose to tail, in the middle lane. The programme's topic changed, and soon another interviewee was eliciting further signals of agreement – a man from the Institute of Fiscal Studies pronounced portentously: "Eight billion pounds sounds a lot." The world's news poured into the car – in San Diego a girl of five was dying of senility; there was a seven-year waiting list to climb Everest, at the top of which, somebody suggested, there was probably a Coca-Cola stall – and when he reached London he was glad to turn it off. He parked in his own reserved space in a small car park behind the offices, and took a lift to the floor where Ben Brock Advertising were now struggling for survival.

At his desk he buzzed through for two coffees and then rang Cliff.

"How do things look this morning?" he asked when Cliff had sat down.

"No better than yesterday. I've been reading about Preil, though. They never should have withdrawn that drug. Three of the eight deaths were counted twice, one man died of cancer, and a woman of eighty-four was on several drugs when she died."

Ben drank his coffee. "Thalidomide made everybody nervous," he said.

"Naturally. But most European countries are still using Preil, and the US have only suspended it."

"Sometimes I really think that it is us they are out to get. What's going to happen is that drug companies will withdraw their products from Britain. You'll have women screaming for valium in the street."

"I've been looking at some figures," said the financial director. "Research costs and so on. The end of it is a forty per cent benefit to the country and the patients, and a sixty per cent benefit to the drug companies. It seems fair enough to me. What about all the expensive research that doesn't come up with anything?"

"Don't tell me. I know," Ben said. "We're all going down the

136

plug-hole. My attempts to sell the agency haven't exactly brought a queue to the door."

"My figures were right."

"Nobody liked them."

"I told you it was the wrong time to sell, Ben. Hang on in there. Diversify. Home computers. You have to keep going to get anywhere."

"I've got a rendezvous with a brick wall. As for computers, I don't even know what they are. I'm going to leave that to the next generation. Any fifteen-year-old already knows more about them than I could ever learn."

"You're only thirty, Ben."

"I know, but I've got a lot on my shoulders. Dandruff, mostly." He smiled at Cliff. "You see? I can still joke."

Cliff arranged his papers in a neat pile. "That isn't necessarily a bonus point."

"What's going on here today?"

"Phil's department are sending out a mail shot."

"What's that? Some new form of ejaculation?"

Jokes were anathema to Cliff. His financial instincts resented them. There were no laughs in a balance sheet. He said: "As you're in such a buoyant mood, perhaps you are strong enough to face another little piece of bad news that appeared in the papers this morning?"

"Show me."

Cliff opened Ben's copy of *The Times* that lay on the desk between them, drew a ring round one story and pushed it across.

"Britain's drug bill," Ben read, "could be cut by almost £150 million a year if doctors changed their prescription habits, says a study of 50 London GPs by the Royal College of Practitioners. It says savings could be made if doctors issued original, unbranded versions of drugs, prescribed only the amounts needed for a course of treatment, and stopped handing out drugs which can be bought over the counter at the chemist's."

"That is tantamount to telling doctors to ignore our ads," Cliff said.

Ben nodded grimly. "Don't think I'm paranoid, Cliff, but they really are after us. Short of making it a capital offence to run a pharmaceutical advertising agency, I don't really see what else they can hit us with."

"It's only a study by a few doctors," Cliff suggested.

"It'll be manna to this government. They'll grab it. How did I ever help to elect this bunch of cheapskates?"

"They want to cut public expenditure, and the public agrees. They think they'll pay less tax."

Ben hurled the newspaper across the room. "Nobody can be that bloody stupid. The defence budget will take it all. Deterrents not drugs, missiles not medicine. I don't know how I got into this bloody business."

"I don't know how you are going to get out."

Wendy Venables picked up and embraced causes news of which reached her compassionate soul through the medium of television documentaries. Each week she spent a few hours being upset by some fresh blemish on the social order, brought to her by courtesy of the cathode-ray tube: road accidents, school closures, house shortages, hospital inadequacies all produced a predictable sequence of sorrow, anger and action. The action took the form of letter-writing and, occasionally, money collecting, but in a sad world there always seemed to be a new and bigger outrage in the pipeline to shoulder aside the scandals of yesterday. This week she had a new obsession: kidney transplants and dialysis machines, and was now writing a furious letter to her Member of Parliament demanding to know why the government appeared to favour expenditure on the former at the expense of the latter.

Venables sat in an armchair reading *Penthouse*. He had long abandoned any attempt to keep up with the shifting loyalties of his wife's campaigning nature. Recently, feeling neglected, he had launched a sarcastic campaign of his own.

"How is the single-parent battered black homeless lesbians' department?" he asked. "When do we march?" If silence is the most perfect expression of scorn, Wendy's reaction was suitably demoralising. "What about jobless, sex-starved husbands in third-floor rabbit hutches? When do we get air time?"

Tonight, choosing silence, he read his magazine. He was curious about what *longueurs* of sexual deprivation had propelled him into the newsagent to buy *Penthouse*. It was nearly ten years since he had done such a thing. He turned the page and read, glassy-eyed:

I am a 24-year-old unmarried man. I have been trying super-hard to fellate myself. Although I'm getting closer every time, it seems to be impossible. Do you have to be double-jointed to perform this feat of sex? Please give me your advice. It means a lot to me.

Zeke

Venables didn't feel well enough to see what reply this cry for help had received, but for a few minutes he seriously considered the possibility of copying it out on Wendy's notepaper and switching letters before she sealed the envelope to the politician. They were desperately in need of new ideas at Westminster, and the spectacle of them all rolling round the green benches trying out this nutcase's bizarre fantasy would have important historical consequences, clearing the befuddled public's mind in seconds.

"You ought to read this," he said. "It's most unusual."

When she eventually answered him, she said, "You're carnal, I'm cerebral" in a manner that was so strongly reminiscent of one of his old schoolmistress girl-friends, that he wondered how she could possibly have missed her vocation and wound up in a sandwich bar.

"I'm cerebral sometimes," he said. "I was reading about Thomas Carlyle this morning when you were at work. His marriage was totally celibate, you know."

"Now you're being carnal."

He remembered why he had bought the magazine. It had occurred to him that he might find some old pictures of a retired topless model he knew. But Pym's days were long gone and today's models were bottomless, too. He put the magazine on one side, and switched on the television. Now that he couldn't get it, sex seemed to be everywhere – a very deep voice was talking about screws, kisses, balls and bits of bottom. When the picture caught up with the sound, it turned out to be a snooker match.

"Do we have to have that on?" asked Wendy. "I'm trying to write a letter."

"I know you are, sweetness, and more power to your elbow. What I say is free foreign holidays for underprivileged, doped-up granny-muggers."

He turned the sound down: it was better without it. But as soon as he had settled again into his armchair the telephone began ringing in the hall. It was clear that Wendy was not going to answer it.

"Simon? Nick Bannerman."

"Hallo, Nick."

"A most extraordinary thing has happened, Simon."

"Oh good. It's so boring up here in town."

"My book has been accepted. It's going to be published. So tonight I am buying drinks for my friends."

"I'm your friend, Nick."

"There's a pub at the end of the road I live in called the Valiant Sailor. Ben and Pym are coming."

"So am I."

"Bring your lovely wife."

"I'll try. And congratulations."

Wendy was consulting *Who's Who* to see what honours had been heaped on their comatose MP. She showed no curiosity about the telephone call. Her plan for the evening, once she had straightened out the politician, was to persuade her husband that any job was better than no job. His idleness affronted her now; it conflicted with all she had been taught. Sally, her assistant at Morsels, had a brother who ran a mini-cab firm and was looking for a driver. Wendy thought that even if it took an hour she could persuade Simon to take the job. His apparent disinterest in work was beginning to worry her, and, at the same time, the flat was just starting to depress her. With its inherited wallpaper, its old-fashioned kitchen and its pre-war bathroom, it was never intended to be anything but temporary. Wendy imagined a little house with a garden, perhaps with a greenhouse, where she could grow summer salads, strawberries and ornamental plants. Her husband's joblessness delayed this dream.

He came back into the room and sat down to watch the silent snooker. He didn't want to show too much excitement at the news that he would soon be seeing Pym, and his wife's mood suggested that he would be facing stubborn opposition to the idea of jumping into the van and driving thirty miles down the road to get drunk. She had begun to comment on his expenditure lately – the money going out, when none was coming in. He couldn't tell her that he had £50,000 up his sleeve, and he still couldn't imagine how he ever could. His most recent idea had been that he would have to invent a mysterious aunt who had, sadly, passed away, preferably on the other side of the world, leaving everything to a nephew she had never met, but Wendy's enquiring mind was unlikely to accept that without copious documentation.

He stood up and turned the snooker off. There seemed to be only about twelve snooker players in the world who kept playing each other over and over again in tournaments invented by sponsors and given grandiloquent titles like "Grand Prix" and "Classic".

"That's better," said Wendy. "I want you to be a kidney donor."

"I've only got two."

"One's plenty. Anyway, I mean when you die."

He walked over to the table. The envelope to the House of Commons was sealed: it was too late to introduce self-fellation to all those upright Members.

"Isn't this conversation somewhat premature?" he asked.

"Well, we can hardly have it when you're dead."

"Okay. I'm a kidney donor. Listen, you don't seem very curious about the phone call."

She turned to him, interested. "Was it a job?"

"No, it wasn't. It was Nick Bannerman. His book is going to be published."

She jumped up. "Oh, wonderful!" He was surprised at how pleased she was.

"He wants us to go and have a drink with him tonight."

"What are we waiting for?"

Driving west in the Austin van with the sun in their eyes, he recalled that he hadn't seen Pym since his embarrassing declaration at Wimbledon. He wondered how she would react to him now. Wendy, a passenger tonight, turned on her radio. The royal baby, it said, was to be called William Arthur Philip Louis.

The Valiant Sailor, a hostelry that drew its business largely from a very affluent neighbourhood, was crowded to the doors and beyond so that several groups sat at tables outside. Inside, it was old-fashioned, low-ceilinged and belligerently resistant to the plastic modernisation that had been quietly accepted by more submissive drinkers elsewhere. Through the crowd they could see Nick, brandishing a bottle of champagne.

"How indescribable to see you," he shouted, kissing Wendy on the cheek. "Champagne for two? I don't suppose you get invited to a lot of literary shindigs, do you?"

While Wendy congratulated Nick, Venables' gaze wandered beyond them to where Pym was waving and smiling at him. He waved back uneasily. Next to her, in a short-sleeved check shirt, her bearded husband signalled a kind of military salute for which his forefinger touched the centre of his forehead.

"Are you going to be rich and famous, Nick?" Wendy asked, taking her champagne.

"Both," replied Nick. "But if not both, rich."

"I don't know how anybody can write a book," said Venables. "All those words."

"Desperation," said Nick, handing him a full glass.

Wendy was enthralled. "When does it come out?"

"In the autumn," Nick told her. "We're going to fill the Christmas stockings. Cheers!"

Venables made his way over to the Brocks. Ben had disappeared.

"I'm afraid you were right about the television," Pym said. She was wearing a low-cut white blouse and green jeans.

"The television?"

"Ben saw us at Wimbledon and wasn't all that thrilled."

"I thought he was at work?"

"They show highlights in the evening, remember? I was watching it with him at the time and he suddenly said, 'Look, there's Simon.' Then he said, 'Christ! That's you.' I was in the wrong. I should have told him. It looked so deceitful. I was scared he'd say I couldn't go. I've always wanted to see it."

"Shall I mention it to him?"

"Oh, he doesn't blame you. He thought it was nice of you to take me. It wouldn't occur to him that it might be a pleasure."

"It was certainly that."

"How's Wendy?"

"Who?"

In a corner behind them, a girl of about twenty was shouting sociably at two presumably deaf old ladies: "This weekend we're going down to Robert's school for the sports." The information produced no reaction, and the girl changed tack. "How are your geraniums?" she bellowed.

"What do you think of the names of the royal baby?" Pym asked.

"The royal baby?"

"William Arthur Philip Louis."

"I think I heard that on the car radio."

"I love the royal family, don't you?"

"To pieces," said Venables.

"Why don't you have a baby?"

"I'm a man."

"You have a role to play."

"When do we begin?"

"Doesn't Wendy want children?"

"I think all Wendy wants is for me to find a job. If you're talking about my sex life, it's a bit like talking about God."

"Do you mean it's sacred?"

"No, I mean it doesn't exist."

Ben emerged from the lavatory. "Hallo, Simon. We've got some odious creeps living round here. Do you know that turgid prat called Cavendish-Cooper?" he asked his wife.

Pym nodded. "He's standing not a million miles behind you."

"He just said to me, 'At our school we were taught that when we'd been to the lavatory we should wash our hands.'"

"What did you say?"

"I said, 'Really? At ours, we were taught not to piss on them.' Isn't it good news about Nick?"

"Marvellous," said Venables.

"He can turn his royalties into pesetas and buy us Cuba Libres."

The proximity of Pym, her abundant cleavage, her full, sexy mouth untouched by any cosmetics, was making it difficult for Venables to concentrate. He turned to the author and saw that he was kissing his wife. Sex still seemed to be everywhere today – through the window he could now see a large, pale labrador in the car park, aroused by the rejection of a coquettish spaniel, attempting to bugger a girl of about four. The dog stood behind her, a paw on each shoulder, as the girl, her innocence still intact, shouted delightedly: "Get off!"

Mr Cavendish-Cooper, noticing it too, called to somebody at the door: "Get that hound off Tara."

"That's the sort of name we have round here," Pym told Venables. "Tara, Crispian, Tamzin, Saskia. We ain't got no Waynes or Jasons down our street."

They were joined by Nick and Wendy, who were each carrying a bottle of champagne.

"I've been congratulating the writer," Wendy said.

"I saw you congratulating him," said Simon.

"I've got to kiss them now," Nick explained. "They'll never kiss me after they've read the book. Who wants some more champagne? Just remember that teetotallers die younger than moderate drinkers."

"You call this moderate drinking?" asked Wendy. "Your blue eyes are going red."

"It's a special night. Normally I sip cocoa in my room and imagine the sexual antics of my married friends." He filled his glass. "I can tell you this little secret before the book comes out – sometimes I envy them. I am beginning to wonder which is going to arrive first, leg-over or senile dementia."

Ben put a hand on his shoulder. "You know what they say – no man is complete until he's married, and then he's finished."

"Ben is very good at knocking marriage," said Pym.

"It is the duty of all married men to stop bachelors jumping in," said Ben. "It's called humanitarianism."

Pym smiled sadly at Nick. "Subtle as napalm, my husband."

"Pym was thwarted in her teenage ambition to be a young widow," Ben told them.

"It isn't too late," said Pym.

"I think you're safer drinking cocoa, Nick," said Venables, cheered by the Brocks' bickering.

"It's all in my book," Nick said. "The trouble is I can't remember what I wrote."

"You'd better refresh your memory," Wendy advised, "if you're going to become the spokesman for hen-pecked husbands."

"Yes, if you're going to be grilled on the telly you'd better get your act together," added Ben. "We men are relying on you. A cogent, forceful exposition of our continuing raw deal, that's what we want."

"To tell you the truth," Nick said, "I'm beginning to wonder whether I've got it quite right."

NINE

ON JULY 16, in a six-furlong cavalry charge at Thirsk, a horse called Auburn Hill won the 4.45 race in a photo-finish. Its starting price was fifty to one.

The achievement of Auburn Hill went unnoticed by Simon Venables who had found that life retained a better quality if he avoided the sports pages – the semi-literate burblings of overpaid stars, the Lego language of football managers and the clunk of the clichés of the sports writers themselves – and kept his attention on the real world.

In her frustration at his continuing inactivity, Wendy had hit on a new stratagem, to turn the long hours of his leisure into work by filling them with what she called "little jobs". Today's "little job", when his wife had departed for the sandwich factory, involved fitting a new and complicated curtain rail over the living-room windows; the rail had taut cords running down the wall at one side, so that the curtains could be opened or closed without being touched. It was a device which Venables was having difficulty in fixing. And he had a much more urgent job of his own to do: he planned to write to the popular papers to discover whether any Page Three pictures of Pym were still extant.

In the event, both ventures were postponed by the ringing of the phone.

"It's Johnny," said Johnny Fix-It.

"Good," said Venables. "Any news?"

The fate of his bank draft had begun to weigh so heavily on his mind that he had intended to ring Johnny Fix-It himself.

"A horse won at fifty to one at Thirsk yesterday," Johnny Fix-It told him.

"Is that good?"

"It is for you. You had a thousand pounds on the nose."

"I did?"

"A brilliant piece of gambling, if I may say so."

"Have you evidence of this coup?"

"It's in my hand as I speak. Can you drop in this morning?"

"I've already left."

"I'll call Jack now."

Venables arrived in Fenchurch Street in a state of high excitement, wondering whether anybody had ever travelled from the suburbs to the City quite so quickly. Debbie indicated that he should go straight in with one slow sweep of her enormous eyelashes. Johnny Fix-It, as usual, was on the phone, his glasses on the very tip of his nose.

"You've got to learn to look at the doughnut, not the hole," he shouted in a mood of some exasperation. "Yeah," he said. "Take care."

He slammed the phone down. "I hear Ben Brock's on the skids," he said, waving Venables towards a chair.

"What makes you think that?"

"Information. His business is in big trouble."

"I hope he survives."

"Why? Perhaps she'll leave him."

"You fancy her, too?"

"I fancy everybody. Now then." He slapped his desk. This room was for working. He collected his thoughts, grabbed a phone and dialled. "Jack? Simon Venables is here. Okay." He replaced the receiver. "I think we can bring this transaction to a satisfactory conclusion this morning," he said, opening a drawer and searching through it. "Here is your ante-post voucher, dated yesterday, saying that you had a thousand pounds to win on Auburn Hill."

Venables looked at it. "I was rather hoping to collect the money today," he said.

"You will," replied Johnny Fix-It. "But that little piece of paper in your hand is vital and you have to look after it very carefully. That's what proves to the Inland Revenue that the fortune in your bank account was a legitimate gambling win."

After ten minutes Jack Carlton arrived. "Good morning, gentlemen," he said, shutting the door firmly behind him. "Let's talk business."

Instead of talking, Johnny Fix-It plunged into a small safe in the wall behind him and produced Venables' bank draft. He put it on the desk in front of Jack Carlton who studied it for some time, as if the secret of life was there for whoever could recognise it. Then he opened his wallet and produced two cheques.

"Towards your yacht in Banus, I suppose," he said, handing one for £2000 to Johnny Fix-It. "Here's yours, Mr Venables. Forty-five thousand. Luckily that's what you would have got on that bet when betting tax had taken ten per cent."

Venables took the cheque and slipped it into his wallet. His instinct now was to run, head down, all the way to the bank.

"What will you do about betting tax?" Johnny Fix-It asked.

"I can lose it," Jack Carlton replied briefly.

"Well, that's it then," Johnny Fix-It said. "I've made two thousand pounds, you've made three thousand plus the saving on income tax, corporation tax and every other bloody tax, and Simon has saved fifteen thousand from the clutches of the tax man. Am I a clever boy, or am I a clever boy?"

"You have few rivals and no masters," agreed Jack Carlton.

"In a deal like this it's difficult to know who pays for lunch," Venables said.

"Oh, I pay for lunch," Johnny Fix-It said. "I may have made the least, but you are my clients. We'll be doing more business together, no doubt. For instance, what are you going to do with the money, Simon?"

"Spend it?"

"I should hope not. A man can grow rich with that much capital."

"Put it on a horse," suggested Jack Carlton.

"Buy platinum bars," said Johnny Fix-It. "But don't bring them into Britain or you'll pay VAT. My professional investment advice is available."

Venables' original intention of financing an ever-increasing chain of Morsels sandwich bars had begun to lose most of its appeal. He said: "I'm going to join the *nouveau riche*. I wonder why everyone despises them?"

"Because they're bloody envious," said Johnny Fix-It. "No, it's worse than that. In this country they sneer at people who have made their own money, and admire the chinless creeps who inherit it from daddy. Success is a dirty word and you are supposed to feel guilty if you have made it. They haven't got the same social history in America. They worship success now, and don't give a bugger who your grandfather was. That's why they are going forwards, and Britain is going backwards. When I get my yacht in Banus they can call me *nouveau riche* until they turn green. I shall have made every penny myself."

"Good for you," Jack Carlton said. "I was brought up in a slum in Hackney. Last week I made over sixty thousand pounds on the World Cup. All the money was on Brazil. I've always been fond of Italy!"

"And are you a millionaire?" Venables asked. He liked this new atmosphere of mutual affluence that filled the office.

"Just a bit," conceded Jack Carlton. The admission arrived with a wink but no smile.

"It's not that hard, actually," said Johnny Fix-It, "as long as you work for yourself. If you're someone else's employee, you're buggered."

"So Ben Brock keeps telling me," said Venables. He did not intend to be employed by somebody else ever again. He began to see that losing his job was going to be the best thing that had happened to him. Success started here. He now had the two assets that most people lacked: time and capital. But how he would deploy them was not yet clear.

Johnny Fix-It took them to the Gay Hussar in Soho. By the time that Venables reached Wimbledon two bottles of wine had persuaded him to forget about the money until after his holiday.

He went into his bank half expecting a red carpet. He looked round hoping to see Mr Mackay. He would have enjoyed waving the cheque under his disdainful nose. But there was no sign of the manager, and he went up to the counter and filled in a paying-in slip. He watched the girl with a thrill of anticipation as he pushed her the cheque, but she glanced at it and stamped and initialled the slip as if the cheque had been for a couple of pounds. He turned away disappointed, his dislike of banks reinforced, and went out into the street.

Wimbledon Broadway made him wonder, as usual, why he had settled in these bleak concrete areas, and he remembered that when he had bought the flat in Thornton Hill, the estate agent had talked of "southerly views across the North Downs", creating a totally bogus picture of rural tranquillity.

Outside the station, the flower stall was selling red roses. The elation at his bank account, or the wine, or both, decided him to buy one for Wendy and deliver it, in person, to Morsels.

*

The contract which Arthur Scott sent to Nick Bannerman consisted of four pages of tiny type, divided into twenty numbered paragraphs, many of them sub-divided into other paragraphs marked a, b, c, or, sometimes, i, ii, iii.

He sat down, feet on desk, and started to read it. "The Proprietor hereby grants to the Publishers during the legal term of copyright the sole and exclusive licence to produce and publish the said work in volume form in the English language throughout the British Commonwealth as politically constituted at the date of this Agreement (including Canada) and including the Republics of South Africa and Eire. This licence shall be non-exclusive in the rest of the world except the United States of America, her dependencies and the Philippine Islands."

Greatly discouraged, he tried Paragraph Two. "The Proprietor guarantees to the Publishers that the said work is in no way a violation of any copyright belonging to any other party and that it contains nothing of an obscene or libellous character and furthermore undertakes that he shall and will hold the Publishers harmless from all suits and all manner of claims and proceedings or expenses which may be taken against or incurred by them on the ground that the said work is such violation or contains anything obscene or libellous, provided always that the Publishers shall consult the Proprietor before compromising or settling any claim arising under this clause."

Nick's curiosity about the other eighteen paragraphs was less than wild by this time. He put the contract down and searched the drawers of his desk for the carbon copy of *Battered Husbands* which would soon be landing on a glass desk on the island of Manhattan. He put the contract and the manuscript into his old plastic brief-case, found his best grey suit, and set off for London.

"It's a standard contract," said Arthur Scott, pouring him a gin. "Authors aren't supposed to understand it."

"This one doesn't," admitted Nick, "but it sounds so impressive I should like to sign it."

"Just here and here," said Arthur Scott, leaning over his desk and pointing to various dotted lines. "I've re-read your book and it's even better than I thought. Freighted with venom – lovely!"

"I've brought the second copy for you," Nick said, pulling it from his case. "For America."

Arthur Scott took both the contract and the manuscript. "You're going to be a dollar-earner, Nick. But first, the sterling.

As it's your first book I won't let you wait." He left the room and returned a few minutes later with a cheque for £2500. "Half now, half on publication," he said. "As soon as we get proofs, we'll start offering the paperback rights. If they sell the paperback rights in America you'll be driving a Rolls-Royce."

Nick looked at the cheque. It was the largest he had ever received. "I'm beginning to warm to this scribbling business," he said.

"You are going to be taken to a lot of lunches, but let me be the first," said Arthur Scott, putting on a suede jacket.

They went to the Venezia. Pewter clouds marred a midsummer's day and Nick began to dream of his holiday in the sun, a certainty now with his cheque in his pocket. Over chicken and rice, Arthur Scott lifted a curtain on the world of publishing and produced story after story of famous writers, brilliant publishers and bestsellers that had been rejected as no good. Salinger walking out of a publishers with tears in his eyes and *The Catcher in the Rye* under his arm because they wanted him to remove a couple of dirty words; Thomas Wolfe and his 330,000-word novel that stood five inches high in typescript on the publisher's floor; Hemingway crying when his first wife lost for ever the entire manuscript of his novel on a train in France; a friend reading the first typed copy of Tom Stoppard's *Rosencrantz and Guildenstern Are Dead*, and telling him: "Don't give up your job, Tom."

It was clear to Nick that Arthur Scott had told these stories before – and would tell them again – but he could have listened all afternoon. Arthur Scott was accustomed to entertaining authors, but it was still a business lunch and by the time the gâteau arrived he brought the conversation back to his newest writer.

"I've thrown your title to the Art Department and they've come up with some ideas already," he said, swamping his cake with cream. "One I like is a royal-blue dust-jacket with the title in big red letters and the word BATTERED battered. In fact it will be so battered that it will appear to be bleeding. The red of the lettering will be blood. What do you think?"

"It sounds good."

"I shall be taking copies to the Frankfurt Book Fair and I'll sell a few foreign rights. Do you fancy yourself in Turkish?"

"The Moor the merrier," quipped Nick.

"The important thing now is that you keep writing. This book will make your name known and we will be able to sell another.

You've got to get a move on. You know the old saying – the first twenty years are the longest half of your life."

"I want to write a novel."

"I'm afraid that everyone wants to write a novel. You've found something new. Beaten paths are for beaten men." He scooped up some gâteau. "That's another old saying."

"You seem to have a supply of them."

"A vice of the book trade, I'm afraid. What would the novel be about?"

"It would be called *Memoirs of a Streaker*."

"Sounds intriguing," said Arthur Scott doubtfully.

"Superficially it would be about a retired streaker who was now a sort of technical adviser to streakers. But there would be another subliminal message."

Arthur Scott looked as if his ears had decided to deceive him, but he said: "Maybe you can do it. As far as I'm concerned manuscripts like yours are as rare as palm trees at the North Pole. Would you like coffee?" He beckoned a waiter. "I have no idea what your message might be, of course, but there are different dangers for each writer, waiting, like a gaucho's bolas, to bring him down." At this stage Arthur Scott produced two cigars from his top pocket and handed one to Nick. "In your case, I imagine, it is that you could topple into cynicism. You must watch that. Cynicism is the opposite of enthusiasm, and what we need today is enthusiasm."

Nick listened to this with growing admiration. "I've never felt more enthusiastic in my life," he said solemnly. "Do you think I'll get on television?"

Arthur Scott nodded very slowly. "I'm certain you will. Our publicity people will be arranging that. Of course, there will probably be a horde of angry females wheeled on to snap at your heels, wild feminists with men's haircuts, introduced to liven things up. Television is trying very hard these days, and they'll never settle for two points of view if a couple of dozen are available. Do you think you could handle it?"

Nick's performance as a yeti-hunter had not abated his desire to appear on television; he wanted to be on television almost more than anything else.

"It should be fun," he said.

"Talking to some of these chat-show hosts isn't my idea of fun, but it certainly sells books."

"That's what we want."

"I'm going to enjoy working with you, Nick." Arthur Scott drew on his cigar and let the smoke drift slowly from his mouth. "*Memoirs of a Streaker*, eh? You've certainly got a way with titles."

Back in the office he insisted on presenting Nick with three of their recent books: a 600-page epic about a priapic monk who contracts *herpes genitalis* from a ropework designer in Kent (soon to be a major film); a compassionate story about a young, black Londoner who mugs old ladies to augment his social security money; and a Booker Prize-winning political satire about pogroms and genocide in Uganda, written by a Nigerian professor who worked in Madras.

"Lovely dust-jackets," said Nick, expressionlessly.

"Lovely sellers," said Arthur Scott.

Soon afterwards, wandering south, Nick began to feel cheated that the most triumphant moment of his life had no audience. He wanted to grab strangers by the elbow and make sure that they appreciated the size of his achievement. He wanted a ripple of applause, if not a Land-Rover lap of honour. At the very least, he wanted to show the biggest cheque he had ever received to somebody other than a bank clerk.

He reached Oxford Street thinking distantly of his parents. This was one triumph they wouldn't share, although now that they knew his name, they would no doubt try to track him down through the publishers. He would have to warn Arthur Scott about that.

All the shops in Oxford Street seemed to be selling jeans, a strange concentration of products in one of the country's busiest shopping centres. He pushed on through the crowds and suddenly spotted, amidst the sea of denim, a small sandwich bar. He immediately realised where he should be. He had decided weeks ago to drop in on Wendy at Morsels one day. Today was the day. He found a Tube and headed west and south.

When he emerged among the gaunt, white buildings of Wimbledon half an hour later, the sun had emerged, too. The street looked like a 1930s sepia photograph and he was glad that he lived in the freshness of the country. He looked up and down the street, in search of Morsels, and discovered a flower stall outside Wimbledon station. This was the sort of day when he should arrive brandishing a red rose, he decided. He bought one, and asked a driver on the taxi rank where Morsels was.

"It's up the hill in the village," the man said, not looking up from his evening paper.

"Right," said Nick, getting in.

"It's not very far," said the driver.

"Drive on," said Nick. A taxi had been a luxury for years.

Travelling up Wimbledon Hill Road he was taken into a quite different world. Instead of card shops, estate agents, TV rentals and supermarkets, Wimbledon Village, as the locals called their posh end, had art galleries, beauty salons, classy boutiques, antique shops and wine bars. In the middle of them, in green and white, was Morsels.

The lunch rush over, Wendy was sitting on a stool drinking a cup of tea. She was wearing a green tee-shirt with "Morsels" written across her chest.

"Hallo, darling," he said, handing her the rose. "I've come to take you away from all this."

"Nick! What on earth are you doing here?" she said, standing up.

"I've come to take you away from the squalor you live in to the squalor I live in."

She took the rose and laughed. "Tea or coffee?"

"Coffee. I've been meaning to drop in on your business empire so I've come along today to show you my cheque. Do you get many famous authors in here?"

"Hardly any. That's a nice cheque. Shouldn't you put it in the bank before you lose it?"

"I thought I'd flash it around a bit first. I like the decor. Bright and cheerful. Do you make money?"

"You're not the tax man, are you?" She gave him his coffee and he took it to one of the glass-topped tables.

"What are the books?"

"Just a little present from my grateful publisher. This one is about a rogue monk who catches herpes. What we literary chaps call picaresque. Would you like to borrow it?"

"I don't think monks and herpes are my – what's the expression?"

"Bag of nails? Can of worms?"

"Kettle of fish. Are you drunk?"

"Mildly exuberated."

"There's no such word," said Wendy, joining him at the table. "A literary chap like you should know that."

Nick looked round the room. "Get many mapsers in here?" he asked.

"There's no such word as 'mapser', either."

"Where do you think words come from? We literary chaps make them up. Now a mapser is a noisy eater, and I've always thought restaurants should have special areas set aside for mapsing. 'Are you a mapser, sir?' the waiter would ask. 'No, but my wife is.' In the mapsing area you'd have louder music."

She looked at his pale, round face, and the smart grey suit that she had never seen before, and asked: "Why haven't you got married, Nick?"

"You married Simon," he replied with a shrug. "Where is he, by the way?"

"Fixing a new curtain rail, I hope. I'm the devil who finds work for idle hands."

"Somebody like you, small, pretty, shapely, efficient. They're not easy to find, but most people don't find the partner they really want, do they? They settle for something less."

"Are you being serious, or is this part of your cabaret act?"

"*In vino veritas.* I brought you a red rose."

"I expect when your book comes out you won't be short of offers."

"I can imagine," he said, nodding. "Myopic nymphomaniacs lunging at my trousers. Greedy for the flower of my wisdom, the vigour of my body, the use of my chain of credit cards."

"Is life going to be fun for you, Nick?"

He looked serious for a moment. "It's my turn," he said. "I've tried poverty. It doesn't work."

She picked up the red rose that lay between them at the moment that the door of Morsels opened and Venables came in carrying a red rose. He stared at Nick and at the red rose that Wendy held and then moved to the table in a fish-tail dancing step.

"He's been drinking," explained Wendy.

"It's lugubrious Nick Bannerman," Venables said. "Is that the red rose of love?"

"It's the red rose of French Socialism," said Nick defensively. "I'm canvassing for Mitterand."

"Everything's coming up roses," said Wendy. "Do you want a coffee, Simon? You look as if you do."

"Please, Mrs Venables. What brings you to SW19, Nick? Are you chatting up my wife?"

"Somebody's got to," said Wendy. "Have you fixed the curtain rail?"

"She's a slave-driver," Venables said, waving his finger at Nick. "I must warn you."

"She's a lovely lady and you're a lucky man," Nick replied. "I came down here to show her this." He put his hand in his trouser pocket.

"Are you sure she wants to see it in here?"

"My first royalty cheque." He handed it to Venables who read it with interest. "That's the biggest cheque I've ever been paid."

Venables could see that although it was only an eighteenth the size of the cheque that he had just received, it was at least equal in the satisfaction it gave to its owner. This annoyed him, and added to a mild irritation he felt at Nick Bannerman coming round to show off to his wife. That, and the wine he had drunk in the Gay Hussar, made him pull out his own wallet and throw the paying-in slip from the bank on the table.

"I got a cheque today myself," he said. "But I paid it into the bank."

As Nick picked it up, Wendy, arriving with Simon's coffee, read it over his shoulder.

"My God, what's that for?" she asked. "Have you sold the flat?"

Venables sat back smiling, with his eyes closed. Wendy put his coffee down, and picked up the slip herself.

"Simon! Where did this come from?" she demanded.

"A husband provides, darling," he said. "Nick's cheque is only two and a half thousand, but he doesn't have a wife to support."

"There *is* more coming, Simon," Nick said.

Venables smiled at him and stretched across for his coffee. "I'm sure there is, Nick. I don't want you to feel inferior in any way."

"I never feel inferior," Nick said. "Just misjudged."

"Simon!" Wendy repeated. "Where did it come from?"

"Are you following this, Nick? The peremptory tone, the demand for private information that is purely my business? I hope you've dealt with this stuff in your book?"

"She may have a right to know," Nick said mildly.

"A husband earns it, a wife spends it. That's the way our society works. He doesn't have to go through a bloody inquisition as well, does he?"

"Her curiosity seems perfectly natural to me."

"I thought you were the genius who had written a book that was going to drag men off their knees? You're beginning to sound like one of those Greenham Common dykes who rub used sanitary towels in policemen's faces."

"If Wendy came home one day with forty-five thousand notes, I imagine you would ask how she came by them," said Nick. "You would have a right to know."

"I certainly would."

"She has that right."

"Is this what your book's preaching?"

"My book is not an attempt to reduce women's rights," Nick explained. He felt a surge of enthusiasm on this subject – he was rehearsing a future chat show. "It's a plea for equal rights, for an equal deal. At the moment, without question, men get the short straw."

"Okay," said Venables, holding up both hands in surrender. "I've never been against equal rights, equal pay, or anything else. God knows, a few days ago my wife was keeping me, although how she did it on the customers I've seen in here today I'll never know."

"I've usually closed by now," Wendy said. "The rush is over."

"Okay. The cheque was from Jack Carlton."

"Who's Jack Carlton?"

"A bookmaker," said Nick.

"Precisely," said Venables.

"You've been gambling?" asked Wendy, mystified. "You don't gamble."

"A small investment with my redundancy money."

"What on?"

"A horse called Auburn Hill. It won yesterday at fifty to one. You can check it in today's papers."

"Does Morsels have a licence to sell alcohol?" Nick asked. "This doesn't seem to be a coffee occasion."

"Fortunately, no," Wendy said. "We break the law once a year to sell champagne to the tennis crowd. We hide it in a picnic box. But I don't think my husband taking up gambling is a cause for celebration."

"Oh, come on," said Venables. "It was just one little bet."

"Little? Forty-five thousand pounds from a fifty-to-one winner? I did maths at school, Simon."

"You see what happens," Venables said, "when you tell your

wife things? Now you know why wise husbands keep their mouths shut."

"I recognise this slippery slope," Wendy said. "My grandfather gambled."

"I bet he never won forty-five thousand pounds," said Venables. He already believed that he had won the money on a horse.

"No, he didn't. And he ended up selling my father's toys to pay off the bookmaker."

"I've never seen your father playing with toys," Venables said.

"His dad flogged them all," Nick explained.

"He was seven at the time," said Wendy. "You men always stick together, don't you?"

Nick, chastened, said: "I could never resist a joke, Wendy."

But she rounded on him now. "You think this is a joke?"

"Suppose I donated a grand to impotent, bald, one-eyed chimpanzees," Venables suggested. "Would that salve our uneasy consciences?"

"Suppose you took the whole lot back and told them that gambling was the pastime of an idiot?"

"I don't believe this," Venables said. "It's not natural. Any other wife in Britain would be trying on mink coats by now."

"Do you really think I need that sort of show-off prop? You're insulting me by mentioning it."

Nick, embarrassed socially, eclipsed financially, and deflated now instead of elated, sucked noisily at an empty coffee cup. Wendy removed it, refilled it, and slid it in front of him.

"I was going to say that you don't know the first thing about your own wife," she said. "But perhaps it's mutual."

Venables threw his arms in the air. "What have I done? I walk in here with forty-five thousand pounds for the family funds and she treats me as if I had murdered the cat. Well, bollocks to it."

He stood up quickly and walked out of the shop.

In the street he felt better. The sun was shining, the money was in his bank account and soon he would be on a Mediterranean island with Pym. She appreciated money.

He started to whistle.

*

Among the unsolicited verbiage which reached him in the mail almost every morning – the by-product, he imagined, of a long-lapsed postal subscription to a magazine that bolstered its sagging revenue by selling lists of addresses of proven suckers – Venables now retained that high percentage of it which seemed anxious to tell him what to do with his money.

The advice arrived from all over the world. From Arlington, Virginia, he learned that "the Dow will rise to 3000". He discovered that copper prices would soar. He was told that the Cold War would get colder and profits would be made in "the metals of war". Cellular radio was going to be the biggest profit-maker since the computer. There was going to be money in silver – and in sugar. He saved the post until one afternoon, and then read his way through it: antiques, foreign currencies, precious metals, stocks, property. He wrestled with investment cycles, commodity futures, taxflation.

He pored over the gratuitous advice, with its vaunted inside knowledge and its arcane references, in a mood of utter stupefaction. After two weeks, Mr Mackay got in on the act.

"Dear Mr Venables," said his electric typewriter. "I notice that you have recently been keeping a substantial credit balance of around forty-eight thousand pounds on your current account which, of course, is earning you no interest. You may have plans for the use of this money, but should this not be the case, I thought I should write to let you know that there are various types of investment available on which you can get a much better return on your capital. Perhaps you would like to call and see me, and we can discuss the possibilities which would suit your situation. If you are not able to call do not hesitate to telephone me and I will be pleased to help you."

The practice of refusing help when it was needed, and offering it when it was not, was what produced the bank's huge profits, he concluded bitterly. He stamped across the room and flicked on the television to get his mind away from the mysterious world of high finance.

In the uneasy silences which now governed his domestic life he had come to regard his nest egg at the bank – spurned by his wife, concealed from the world – as his own private cache, not to be exposed to the arid arithmetic of economists or the meretricious charms of professional bankers. It had arrived there without their help, and he had yet to be convinced that their interference would do it any good.

The green hills of Sussex came up on the television screen, a panoramic sweep of the South Downs' sunny expanse of gently rolling fields and distant trees with not a building or person in sight. But cutting suddenly to another camera nearly a mile away, the viewer was now alongside the starting stalls of a horse race, and burly men in helmets were pushing and shoving to get the animals into the stalls. The gates flew open as soon as the last horse was in and as they raced into a steep incline viewers were transported to another camera up the course which showed the field gradually approaching over the brow of the hill.

Venables jumped not merely out of his seat but into the air, as if cruelly assaulted from below.

"It's Soba, well away, Soba by two lengths," intoned an ice-cool commentator.

Venables had forgotten all about Soba in the Stewards' Cup at Goodwood which, he now saw through a sub-title on the screen, this was.

Soba had taken a lead at the beginning of the race that it would never relinquish, but Venables watched in heart-pounding excitement until it had reached the winning post and the cheering crowds, and disappeared round an abrupt right-hand bend, turf flying.

There was just time for Venables to dance a complete circuit of the room before the phone rang.

"Congratulations," said Johnny Fix-It.

"Congratulations yourself. It was your tip."

"I had a small investment. The motor yacht moves ever nearer. What are you going to do with all this money?"

"Don't you start. I'm snowed under with advice here."

"Who from?"

"Bank managers, insurance companies, postal investment specialists."

"Don't listen to their crap, kid. If they knew how to make real money they wouldn't be in those jobs, right?"

"I suppose not."

"First you make your money, then your money works for you. That's the system. If you ever want any advice, call me."

The phone rang directly Venables put it down.

"Ben Brock," said Ben Brock. "I have some air tickets here for Friday, August sixth."

"Great!"

"I hope that in your current poverty-stricken joblessness this isn't going to prove an embarrassment?"

"How much is the bill?"

"Two-twenty for the two."

"I think I can manage that. Who's the cheque to?"

"Ben Brock Advertising. We need the money. How's Wendy?"

"Taciturn."

"Which creep invented marriage, anyway?"

After getting rid of Ben, it took Venables several minutes to recapture the mood of joy which had been brutally interrupted by his busy phone. The idea that he had this afternoon made another £10,000 to push up his bank account to the unimagined figure of almost £60,000 seemed so unreal that he had to sit down to persuade himself it was true.

He had always regarded himself as one of that sad majority who had never found the right job for himself, never felt a pull in any significant direction. The jobs that he had drifted into had been accomplished with ease so that he was constantly reassuring himself that he could do much better if only he could discover at what. But his life had continued lazily, and he had paid for it with a loss of self-respect.

But now, at the age of thirty-three, he had been given the chance of a fresh start. His life would never be the same again – that much was certain.

He got out his chequebook and made one out to Ben Brock Advertising for the air tickets and then, seeing the stationery in the drawer, he decided that a swift dart in the direction of his bank manager would be appropriate to his present mood.

"Dear Mr Mackay," he wrote. "Thank you for your letter. When I think that your bank can give me useful advice on how to make money I shall certainly ask for it."

As he sealed the envelope he thought sadly that he would never be able to tell Wendy about these new thousands that had tumbled into his bank account. After all, this time he *had* won it on a horse.

Feeling no more than usually embattled, Ben Brock drew a red ring round 6 August on his desk calendar, and phoned Nick Bannerman.

"I suppose that the cheque for one hundred and ten pounds that you will write out today to Ben Brock Advertising will present no problems to a famous author?" he said.

"You sound desperate for the money, Ben," Nick suggested.

"I am. Don't miss the post."

"What are holidays like? I've never had one."

"Well, you sit around in the sun, sipping exotic drinks, and when you get too hot you stroll into the sea. Evenings you dine out."

"I could put up with a lot of that."

"Do you think Simon and Wendy can afford this jaunt? He's been out of work a while now."

"Are you kidding? He won forty-five thousand pounds on a horse the other day."

"He didn't tell me that."

"I was there when he came back from the bank."

"You were where?"

"In Morsels, Wendy's sandwich bar."

"And what were you doing in there, Mr Bannerman?"

"I was chatting up Wendy."

"I see. It should be an interesting holiday."

"That's what I thought."

The news that Simon Venables had quietly stashed away a small fortune proved so interesting to Ben, obsessed as he now was with money, that it was some time before he could get back to his wobbling empire. When he did, he found that Cliff had left him a morning newspaper which carried the headline: KILLER DRUG STILL ON SALE.

"A drug which has been withdrawn by its maker because of links with deaths in Britain and abroad is being freely dispensed in chemists' shops," said the report. "An investigation has revealed that there were more than 800 prescriptions for Preil, the anti-rheumatism drug, last month – after it had been withdrawn at the insistence of the Government's Committee on the Safety of Medicines. Our investigation shows that doctors are prescribing the drug against the advice of Government advisers and the British Medical Association. A BMA spokesman said: 'While ignorance may account for some prescribing of withdrawn drugs, in other cases doctors choose to ignore the expert advice. They say that for their individual patients the drugs work well and that the risks of adverse effects have to be put into perspective.'"

Ben had no trouble putting everything into perspective: he was the wrong man in the wrong industry in the wrong year. He buzzed Cliff.

"Does it mean that this inept government can't even ban dangerous drugs and we are all back in business?" he asked.

"I think not," Cliff told him. "Preil say the drugs were imported from Europe at enormous cost. It's all part of the joys of belonging to the EEC."

Ben pulled his desk diary towards him, but his heart wasn't in it. "What's happening today?" he asked.

"Marvin Maher are giving us a definite answer on whether they want to buy the agency."

"At our price?"

"They haven't said, but they're the people who have shown most interest."

"They're a big agency. It would make sense for them."

"Keep your fingers crossed."

Ben had spent so much time lately courting potential purchasers of his agency that he had quite overlooked Marvin Maher's professed interest. He perked up at the news that a decision would arrive today: by this evening his troubles could be over. He ordered a coffee and shuffled through the trade journals on his desk. Perhaps he was about to learn how to relax again.

In one of the magazines he found the answers to a quiz that he remembered entering, in a slack moment, many weeks before:

1. A peregrine falcon.
2. They were all rivers in Hades.
3. TBIC means "The boss is coming."
4. Merope is the faintest of those stars in the Pleiades that are visible to the naked eye.
5. John Updike. (The others are Jewish.)
6. About 4000 miles.
7. Valdez, Alaska.
8. No ordinary pocket calculator will give the factorial of a number higher than 69.
9. (a) Pierre de Fermat (b) Homer (c) Wladyslaw Sikorski.
10. Attlee and Wilson. (No other post-war Labour Party leader has ever won a general election.)

None of these answers, so far as he could recall, corresponded to the replies which he had optimistically sent in the hope of winning some vintage champagne, and he took this to be a bad augury. Indeed, gazing at the answers in wonderment, he struggled to think what the questions could possibly have been.

When his coffee arrived he transferred his attention to the six air tickets that had been delivered by his travel agent that morning with a bill for £660. Aside from bank-notes, there were no pieces of paper that gave him so much pleasure as air tickets bearing his name, particularly when the destination was 1000 miles south of his office in Chelsea. They enshrined hope and the promise of fun. They took you to a brightly lit world where ringing phones, incessant rain and the long, wearing grind of professional affability were replaced, in a matter of hours, by sunshine, duty-free shops and guilt-free days of delicious torpor. That was what he needed now. In recent weeks he had developed special techniques for deflecting his tired mind from the nightmare he was living in and now, watching the clouds through his window, he fell to wondering, as he had wondered before, why it should be so much warmer in, say, Kinshasa, than it was in Kensington. Kinshasa, being nearer the Equator, was probably 1000 miles nearer the sun, but as the sun was 93 million miles from either of them why should a mere 1000 miles make so much difference? It was one of those things he had always meant to find out. To keep reality at bay for a few more minutes, he listed others: Why do Eskimos never get cancer? How did the Indians get to America in the first place? Why do jockeys never wear beards? How are you supposed to wash your feet in a shower? Where do flies go in the winter-time?

Cliff came in looking pale. Increasingly, these days, he looked like a man who had forgotten for some weeks to go to bed.

"They don't want it," he said.

Ben felt himself being dragged back from a long way away.

"Who doesn't want what?"

"Marvin Maher doesn't want to buy Ben Brock. They just phoned."

"*Sic transit* Gloria Swanson," said Ben numbly.

Cliff sat down without waiting to be asked.

"You know what this means?"

"Tell me."

"Infrastructure shakedown."

"And what does that mean?"

"It's American for sacking people."

163

"I've never sacked anybody, Cliff."

"You're going to have to start."

"Where?"

"I could give you a list. There are too many people here contributing too little. Tearing around and confusing movement with action. We're going to have to cut back to survive."

Ben was alarmed at this new forceful side to his financial director – normally he listened, advised and submitted.

"And who," he asked, "would be at the top of your list?"

"What about that Welsh bitch, pristine Christine? She does nought point nine recurring of bugger all."

Ben had always rather fancied Christine and so, he suspected, had Cliff. At the back of office politics there often lay a sad little story of callous rejections and unvented appetites.

"Have you got something against the Welsh, Cliff?" he asked.

"Yes, my first wife was Welsh. They're a race of extremes where the women are concerned. They're either on their knees in the chapel or on their backs in the alley."

"And which is Christine?"

"Chapel."

"Well, I'm going to have my holiday, Cliff, and I'll be giving the whole subject a lot of thought. Until then we do nothing."

"Right," said Cliff, standing up. "But you'd better leave me your address."

"I will."

"Anything particular you want me to do while you're away?"

"Just keep buying Seychelles holidays for Glen Nardini."

Cliff left him staring dreamily through his office window. The sky was now a murky grey blanket that covered London. But he could see the sun.

part three

REVELATIONS

*Nakedness is a luxury in which a man may
only indulge without peril to himself when he
is warmly surrounded by the multitude of his
fellows.*

Michel Tournier

No naked man ever lost anything.
Japanese proverb

TEN

When the well-worn Trident, leased cheaply to Broomstick Airlines, climbed jerkily through London's resident clouds and set its nose optimistically towards the south, Simon Venables began to realise why his air tickets had cost so little. As the plane shook like a shed in a gale he reached discreetly for the safety instructions in the back of the seat in front and listened attentively for a change of tone in the aircraft's engines. He looked in vain for the worry beads in his pocket but remembered that he had left them at home, convinced that he had now made the break from smoking. Nick Bannerman, who had never flown before, had seen the airport buildings hurtle past as the Trident strove to lift off, and had then watched in horror when the ground slowed down and stopped as the plane rose. He now imagined that it was the plane that had slowed down and stopped, and he was convinced that it was about to fall backwards on to the runway it had only recently cleared. This was no more than he had expected and he sat silently clutching his thighs, unable to speak. Wendy Venables, whose life had, through her business-like nature, been cruelly short of holidays, decided before she left Wimbledon to close her mind to domestic problems and escape for three weeks, with drink if necessary. She scanned the aisle for a stewardess bearing gin, but the No Smoking lights were still on as Broomstick Airlines grappled grimly with gravity. She looked across at Nick Bannerman, who she hoped would make this holiday memorable, but he was staring ahead like a man who had smelt death. Pym Brock was thinking about her son, Greg, and enduring her customary guilt at having left him behind, but Ben had been adamant that he didn't know the difference between Theydon Bois and Addis Ababa and until he was old enough to appreciate foreign travel it was a waste of money providing it. Ben himself was engrossed in the financial pages of his newspaper, immersing himself in the commercial disasters that were afflicting other people.

They descended into a ferocious heat that hit them like a blast furnace as they left the plane.

"Is this abroad?" Nick asked. "It seems different."

"It's hotter," said Wendy.

Waiting in the small airport building for their luggage, they gazed out at a sky of unblemished blueness, laid over a scorched, flat landscape. Nick's luggage consisted of one old holdall, but the others had larger and more expensive suitcases which eventually required two taxis.

Rupert Puckle, wearing a cashmere dressing-gown and velvet monogrammed slippers, greeted them on his patio with Spanish champagne. The patio, beneath a roof of palm fronds and cane, smelled of jasmine.

"There was no point in trying to meet you at the airport," he said. "No plane has arrived on time since I've been here."

"Just pour out the champagne, Rupert," said Ben. "Let's start as we mean to go on. Can I introduce you to Nick?"

Rupert's villa was sparsely furnished. There was a low white marble table in the main downstairs room, with a dumb cane plant in a terracotta pot in one corner and an orange tree in a white pot in another. The mirror on the wall was framed with pink and white shells.

Rupert took them upstairs to three cool bedrooms. Each had its own balcony overlooking the pool. Nick unpacked quickly, a task involving little more than hanging up a few shirts in an empty wardrobe. When he went down to the patio and the champagne, Venables was already there.

Rupert Puckle had used the intervening time on his land, having joined an agricultural co-operative to alleviate his boredom. He had planted pear trees and avocado trees with an eye to the future and, in the meantime, was nurturing red cabbages, carrots, lettuce, onions, beans and beets. His best paying crop was sweetcorn which he had planted every two weeks so that it ripened regularly. He had studied soil content, pesticides and water control, and was trying to decide whether to buy some pigs.

"The best bet is lemon trees," he said, during a stroll round his grounds, "but you don't get any fruit for three years and it's five years before you have a really good crop. Will I be here in five years?"

"I hope so," said Venables, "or where can I go for a holiday?"

"I'm increasingly haunted by the feeling that time is running out. Perhaps it comes from being alone."

"I thought you preferred living alone?"

"I do really. You have time to think. But I'm not sure all this isolation is good for anyone. That's why I've been looking forward to your visit. I've even been writing some poems this summer. There's nothing like sexual deprivation for driving a man to poetry."

Ben appeared from the villa. He had changed into a gaudy pink-and-orange shirt, white shorts and sandals.

"Rupert," he asked, "why are you wearing a dressing-gown?"

"A very expensive dressing-gown," said Rupert. "The money is piling up faster than I can spend it."

"There have been a few changes in our financial situations since we last met. In the spring I was rich and Simon was poor. Now it's the other way round."

"What happened?"

"Simon won a fortune on a horse and my firm is going bust."

"You'll pull through, Ben. Your type always does."

"Quite," said Ben. "Unfortunately, the present situation doesn't depend on me. I'm a pawn. What's the answer to my question, anyway?"

"The dressing-gown? Actually I never wear anything around here. I'm not overlooked. But with all these lovely ladies arriving I thought I'd better cover up. Don't want to frighten them."

"I wouldn't mind a bit of nude sunbathing myself," said Ben.

The following morning, Wendy decided that before they all slumped around the pool they had a tourist's duty to see the island. Rupert's aged Mehari, a tiny green jeep from the factories of Citroën, was offered, but as it could only comfortably seat two, and as an appropriate air of sloth had already descended on the visitors, Nick found himself alone with Wendy soon afterwards, bouncing along ancient roads through groves of peach trees and palms and pomegranates. The island was criss-crossed by thousands of dry stone walls, and covered with semi-tropical oleander, hibiscus and bougainvillaea. They passed farmhouses with whitewashed arches over the front doors, ancient watermills, dry canals and sixteen-foot letter Ts in stone that had stood mysteriously for 4000 years. Incongruously, on the top of a hill, American servicemen laboured on a secret mission. Wendy decided to head north where, even on an island as small as this one, it was greener than in the south.

Nick took in a lot of this but what he was enjoying most was being driven by Wendy, who seemed to have adjusted quickly to driving on the right-hand side of the road although they were so narrow that it was often difficult to tell which side they were on.

"I find the sun makes me sexy," he said, conversationally. "Do you? Perhaps it boosts the testosterone level."

"That's why there are more Indians than Scandinavians."

"It affects you too?"

"Get your hand off my knee. I'm driving."

"It's a nice knee, though."

"Do you fancy me, Nick?"

"You've got the edge on megalithic remains, Wendy."

Quite soon they reached the north coast. They drove into the gleaming white fishing village of Fornells where the white buildings had white roofs, too. Fifteen stumpy palm trees lined the front of the harbour where the water was so clean that you could read the small print on the labels of discarded beer bottles at the bottom. The shops sold the same things as all the other shops – a sun oil, Fanta, ice-cream, souvenir bags – but Wendy found a top-hat-shaped boutique behind the harbour. At the top of its perilous stairs were pictures hand-made in cork from the forests of south-west Spain, and bookmarks made from the flowers of the island. Nick, his hopes growing, bought her one of each, and offered lunch.

In a genuinely Spanish restaurant which nevertheless managed to have tartan wallpaper behind its cocktail bar, they studied a menu which ranged from rabbit to suckling pig. They sat in a long, narrow room with the sea view at one end appearing like a cinema screen. The premises were so cramped that on a visit to the *caballeros*, Nick discovered staff producing *crêpes Suzettes* with a bunsen burner in the corridor. They opted for Dover sole.

"What is it like," Nick asked, "being married to a rich man?"

"Do you know, that money has never been mentioned since? Perhaps he did take it back."

"I doubt that he would do anything as barmy as that, even if pushed by a lovely lady like you." He was distracted by a life-like painting of a lobster on the wall behind her head.

"At one time he talked of opening a second Morsels, even a third and fourth. But now he has the money to do it he never mentions it."

"How was he going to do it when he didn't have the money?" Nick asked, pouring her wine.

"He went to the bank when he lost his job. The usual thing. The bank said he could have the money if he had a job, and he said if he had a job he wouldn't need the money. He's changed a lot since we married. I think it's Pym."

"Pym?" He had just realised that the lobster in the painting had moved and was not in a painting at all, but a tank. It struggled to scale the blue walls of its cell.

"He met her on our honeymoon and hasn't been the same since."

"Does she fancy him?"

"I've no idea. It's funny. Simon and I were fine until we got married."

"It's a common situation. The unmarried try harder. The married feel caught."

"Do you know that on our honeymoon we had no sex at all."

"That is odd," he conceded, liking the intimacy of this conversation. He fuelled it with more wine.

"And then of course when we got back he lost his job and his whole personality seemed to change. We'd met Ben and Pym and they were so rich."

"Envy?"

"Oh, nothing like that, but discontent with himself."

She looked so sad now as her fingers played thoughtfully with the wineglass that he wanted to comfort her with a very gentle embrace. She was wearing a short white dress and the wind in her hair from the journey and the beginnings of a suntan gave her a very outdoor look.

"I thought you were a bit hard on him about the money on the day that I was in Morsels," he told her.

"I probably was. I have a dread of gambling. Money that comes that easily goes that easily and you never know where you are. Also, with him being out of work I could see whole afternoons in the betting shop, boring, sterile. But he hasn't gambled since. At least, I don't think he has."

"I wonder why you came on this holiday with these people if you think Simon is after Pym. Aren't you rather throwing them together?"

"It was the only holiday I was offered. Anyway, I like Pym. And if Simon was going to chase her he could do it at home. Here I can watch him."

Nick was distracted again by the discovery that the tank behind her head was now empty. The lobster had been removed. Looking round, he was fairly certain that a German couple two tables away were now eating it. He was squeamish enough to be thoroughly disturbed by this development, and changed his mind about the ice-cream he was about to order.

"Actually that's not quite true," Wendy admitted. "I came here because you were coming."

"What a coincidence," Nick said. "Your presence was the main attraction for me."

"We're partners in a conspiracy now. Are you going to be an amazing success, Nick?"

He shook his head. "I shouldn't think so. I'm too nice to succeed, aren't I? Only the unpleasant triumph in this hard and ruthless world. Haven't you noticed?"

"What happens to the nice?"

He looked up at the empty tank behind her.

"They get devoured," he said.

When they got back to the villa everybody was naked.

They didn't realise it at first. Pym was lying face down on a sunbed by the pool, Simon was sitting on the grass with a towel over his lap, and Ben was swimming.

"We've turned this place into a nudist colony," he said, pulling himself out of the water.

"So you have," said Wendy, looking at him. "What for?"

"It looked nice out this morning so I left it out. Why not? There's nobody within half a mile."

"I see," said Wendy. She noticed that her husband was holding a bottle of champagne, and guessed that alcohol had helped to precipitate this nudist paradise, a theory which was confirmed when Ben fell backwards into the pool.

The splash woke Pym, who sat up. Her breasts were as brown as the rest of her body after topless sunbathing by her own pool. However, a triangle of white round her blonde pubic hair revealed that nudism had not yet arrived in the Brocks' back garden.

"Get 'em off, Wendy," she commanded. "Keep me company!"

"Certainly not," said Wendy. "There's too much flesh here already."

"Until you've walked naked in the sunshine, you can have no idea how good it feels. Come on, Nick."

"Not me," said Nick. "I'll get excited."

"I don't believe it," said Pym. "It was only when humans started wearing clothes that the birth-rate soared. If we all walked round naked it would drop."

"Don't bet on it," said Nick. "It's your legs, Pym. They give a man ideas."

"I've seen better legs on a horse," said Ben.

"In your present state, comparisons with horses are what you should avoid," Pym told him. "Your penis makes an acorn look menacing."

"I should check Simon's first," said Wendy.

Venables sat self-consciously by the pool, filling himself up with champagne. He had been coerced into this by the Brocks and once they were naked felt that he could no longer sit there dressed. But his wife was right. Ben's, though small, looked bigger. His discomfiture increased when his wife reappeared in a bikini.

"Have you been showing them your parts, darling?" she asked. "Or did you leave the magnifying glass at home?"

"Screamingly funny, my wife," Venables told the others. "The thing is that most people only ever see the opposite sex naked." He was drunk enough now to stand up and drop his towel. "Do most men have bigger ones?"

"Well," said Pym, studying him, "I've never seen a smaller one. What happened to the rest of it?"

"It gets bigger," replied Venables.

"I should hope so," said Pym, "or you'd never find it."

"Never mind, darling," said Wendy. "It's the workman, not the tool."

"Absolutely," agreed Pym. "I knew a man once –"

"I don't want to hear it," said Ben.

Nick lay back on a sunbed in jeans and shirt. He wanted to sunbathe but was uncertain about what to wear or not wear. He liked the idea of a nude swim, but he didn't want to leave Wendy isolated as the only dressed guest. She was toying now with an armoury of cosmetics that would protect her from the harsh assault of the afternoon sun: a tropical blend by Coppertone that smelt of coconuts, a bottle of Ambre Solaire, and a small sun-protection stick from Germany which promised to prevent peeling.

"Where is Rupert?" he asked.

"He went shopping in San Luis," Ben told him.

"I think we should take him out to dinner tonight."

"Good idea," said Pym. "There are some nice restaurants in the port."

There was a splash as Venables disappeared into the pool.

"Don't lose it!" shouted Pym. "We'll never find it in there."

He came to the surface, scowling. "Your wife is a bit unkind, Ben."

"When she's being really nasty, she waits until I'm asleep and then pulls hairs out of my nose."

Venables climbed out of the water and went over to the sunbed where Pym was lying. He picked her up in his arms and carried her shrieking to the pool. But now, with one hand on her lovely thighs and the other not a centimetre from her superb breasts, he could hardly bring himself to let her go. He held her for a moment too long before throwing her in the pool. When she came to the surface she laughed and pointed at him.

"You're right," she said. "It does get bigger."

They ate that evening in the port, beneath the battlements that had once protected the island. They sat at tables on the pavement and looked across the water to the hills beyond, where Nelson was supposed to have stayed nearly two hundred years earlier. In front of them, on the balcony of the Estación Marítima Bar, crowds watched the big silver ferry from Barcelona ease its way in. Behind them on the rock walls, just a few yards from where 600 local men had been shot at the end of the Civil War, somebody had stuck a VOTE PSOE poster. Democracy at last.

"As a deep-water anchorage this place is second only to Pearl Harbor," Rupert Puckle told them. With his white moustache and his brightly coloured shirt hanging outside white slacks he looked even more like a famous film star.

"This holiday is developing its educational side," said Ben. "Where's the fun?"

"Did you know that a Japanese sub-lieutenant who bombed

Pearl Harbor in 1941 subsequently piloted Japanese Air Lines jumbo jets to Hawaii?" Venables said.

"Do I need to know that?" asked Ben.

"If you want fun, Ben, we'll go on to a flamenco club," Rupert suggested. "The girls can throw their bodies about a bit."

A waiter came out of the restaurant and gave them a menu in six languages. At the next table a woman with huge thighs whined piteously about the heat.

"Be careful what you eat," Rupert said. "They have strange tastes round here. Also, I find olive oil is an aperient."

"Strange like what?" Wendy asked.

"Well, they catch sparrows in traps with worms and hooks and then boil them in cabbage. I doubt that you'll want to try that."

"Bullfights, boiled sparrows. It's a cruel country."

"Well, Torquemada was Spanish. He practically invented cruelty. He was the Inquisition chappie who burned people by the thousand. He was some way ahead of Hitler – he was expelling Jews from Spain five hundred years ago."

"I don't want any more history lessons, Rupert," Ben said. "I'm on my holiday."

"You tourists are all the same. You want to pretend that this is Britain with sunshine. What are you all eating?"

He ordered for all of them in Spanish, and chose the wine.

Ben drank half his glass before the others had sipped. He realised that he was nervous, nervous about what might be happening at home. He had hoped that he could get away from it and forget in the sun. He wanted a holiday that was entirely frivolous, with much drink and no solemn conversations about anything, even Spanish history. But he was finding that the reality of his firm's condition could not be pushed aside that easily. His nervousness was making him irritable. Sitting in the port and eating steak he could imagine that this could be his last holiday for a long time. Pym was chatting happily about flamenco dancing. He resented her peace of mind. If he had told her the whole story, he thought, she would never have agreed to come.

Nick Bannerman was wondering whether he could, would or should have a sexual relationship with Wendy. Accustomed to agonising over ethics, he could see the additional disadvantage of having her husband under the same roof at the same time, and the necessity for keeping at least the appearance of harmony among the party until the flight back. But he could also see that the sun and champagne were going to militate against celibacy. He toyed with an opening gambit: *Would you like to borrow my body for a couple of hours?*

Wendy smiled at him now as if he had actually said it.

"We are eating well today," he said. "My stomach must be wondering where the beans on toast have got to."

"I was supposed to be counting calories," she said.

"So was I," added Pym. "But never on holiday."

When they had finished eating, they climbed up hundreds of steps which took them from the port to the town. Rupert led them to a flamenco bar in one of the narrow backstreets. Admission was free but drinks were expensive. In a long, low-ceilinged room, lit by low-watt bulbs in wickerwork cages on the wall, a cast of four men and two women sat on a row of chairs and took it in turns to dance. They shouted and stamped and clapped to the strumming of guitars, beating out extraordinary salvoes with their feet.

"Clapping as an art form," said Ben cynically. Pym was plucked from her chair by the diminutive star of this ensemble, a man with a lot of black curly hair and a bottom not much bigger than a tennis ball, and she was soon clapping and stamping herself, as if her early years had been spent in the nightclubs of Madrid.

Ben found himself affronted by this exhibitionism. Tonight nothing would please him. He sipped his gin as the flamenco dancer returned his wife to wild applause and then took Wendy who, it appeared, had Spanish blood in her veins, too. Afterwards one of the *señoritas* in a long, red dress danced with that mixture of arrogance and concentration which was the essence of the flamenco. Watching her dismiss him with her flashing eyes, Nick Bannerman wondered whether there was time to get her into his book.

They left the club long after midnight and wound up at a table on another pavement, drinking coffee. It was a country that kept different hours to their own. Children who had slept in the afternoon were playing in the streets now which were as crowded as they had been twelve hours earlier.

"I'm not used to holidays," said Pym. "I think they're something you have to train for."

They were all tired. Unaccustomed quantities of oxygen and alcohol had reduced them to a weary silence.

"It's your second this year," Ben reminded her. "You should be getting used to them."

"Ben sometimes has holidays on his own," Pym said. "He pretends it's work, and leaves us at home. I hate it."

He glared at his wife and it seemed to Venables, watching this scene, that his eyes bruised her.

"You're a chattel," he said. He had drunk rather more than the rest and, for the first time, they could imagine how violence could erupt in the Brocks' home.

"You think that's funny," Pym said.

"It's obvious that you don't," commented Ben.

"Now you're showing your real self, dear."

"That," sighed Ben, looking depressed, "was buried years ago."

"It's sad, really," said Pym. "He really believes that wives are chattels. He lives in the past."

"You're feeling restricted, are you?" her husband asked. "You want to spread your wings?"

"Not spread them. A little flutter, perhaps."

"You can go tomorrow."

An air of embarrassment settled over the table and Rupert Puckle stood up.

"It's time for bed," he said.

Nick Bannerman lay in bed that night and wondered whether to take his clothes off the following day. In this heat the idea of nude sunbathing appealed to him, but he was certain that, with Wendy looking at him and Pym's brown body padding round the lawn, he would get an erection of Olympian proportions. He had read that men never had them in nudist colonies, but he didn't believe it. He didn't see how they could avoid getting one. He had half a dozen a day with a suit on; how many more would he get stark naked, in the company of beautiful, unclad women? He had one now, just thinking about it. There was another, connected problem which he had been aware of since his last years at school: his penis was enormous. After the ribbing that Simon Venables had endured about his anandrous condition, he did not welcome public scrutiny.

At seven o'clock the following morning, when a hot sun was already beating against the window of his room, he decided to conduct an experiment in nudity while the others slept. He crept downstairs naked and went out into the garden. It seemed an extraordinary luxury to slip from his bed and walk straight out into the world without bothering to dress. He realised that never before in his entire life had he been outdoors without a shred of clothing.

He walked up the garden in the sun, passed the pool, and took a leisurely stroll round Rupert's vegetable garden. The feeling of freedom was a delicious surprise. He followed the boundary of the garden as far as the vegetable garden when he saw that Wendy, the early riser on this holiday, was already outside and coming towards him. There was nothing he could do but face her. She was wearing jeans and a man's shirt. He felt at a disadvantage.

"Are you getting the early-morning air?" she asked, looking at him approvingly.

"I thought you were all asleep."

"So you decided to join the nudists? Be careful you don't vasectomise yourself on the century plant." But she couldn't take her eyes off his body and he knew, with the usual mixture of pleasure and embarrassment, that a monumental erection was on the way. He turned to one side but the outward and visible sign of his excitement was more than she could overlook.

"Blimey, Nick. You're huge," she said.

"I'm sorry. I'm experiencing a mild tumescence not dissimilar to a hard-on," he said, and jumped in the pool before this development could reach its full potential.

He had a towel round his hips before they ate a boiled egg breakfast on the patio.

"This is one of those formal places where people dress for breakfast," Wendy told Pym.

"Did I miss you, Nick?" said Pym. "Curse my hangover. Ben, you missed Nick's nude debut."

"Terrific."

"It's Wendy's debut today," said Venables. "Or are you going to be the odd one out?"

"Talking about odd ones out," said Wendy, "what time are you unveiling yours?"

"I knew a man once who made love to a girl through a letter-box," said Rupert. It wasn't possible to tell what train of thought his mind had followed. "She jammed it open with a matchbox."

"Why?" asked Pym. "Was he a postman?"

"A postman? No. Her father had locked her in."

Rupert, eating an orange for his breakfast and wearing his cashmere dressing-gown, smiled proudly at this story and the others were left with the impression that the central role had been his.

Venables and Ben were wearing white shorts but an hour later, as the sun rose in another cloudless sky, they were discarded and the Puckle garden was again transformed into a nudist colony.

As Pym pulled her tee-shirt over her head, Venables gazed hungrily at the feast revealed to him. Her big breasts were already as brown as the rest of her, but today he fancied running his tongue up the inside of her thigh. He rather hoped that the idea would give him an erection or, at least, the beginnings of one. If he had an erection he would be as big as Nick (as long as Nick didn't have one, too). Oddly enough, he didn't resent the remarks about his size, although there had been a time when he would have found them painful. The new condition of his bank account had given him a feeling of security that nothing could dent. Only the inferior felt inferior. He looked over at Pym's naked body stretched invitingly on the grass – the breasts scarcely flattened as she lay on her back, her pubic hair a golden bush that, with the sun behind it, seemed to be on fire – and thought: You are going to need my money soon. He was certain now, from Ben's behaviour, that the Brock family was facing ruin. All I have to do is wait, he thought.

Nick still had the protection of his towel as he sat on the grass and devised a method of keeping his frustrated body under control. He would fill his mind with asexual thoughts and unless his body had a mind of its own that should take care of it. He decided on a word game of shared initials. As Ben, who was studying the exchange rate in an English newspaper, had just announced: "Jesus Christ, it's hot!" he began to look for other people with those initials. Jimmy Carter and James Callaghan came to him at once, followed by two other politicians from the past, Julius Caesar and Joseph Chamberlain. He tried to think of some writers from the hoard of paperbacks in his flat, and came up with a most unlikely pairing: Joseph Conrad and Jackie Collins. Slowly he pulled the towel from his body and spread it on the grass beneath him. Julie Christie, he thought, but he fancied her and hurried on to less attractive names. John Calvin, James Cook, Jean Cocteau. The first syllable of the last name stopped him dead, and he glanced down at his wayward body. It seemed to be behaving itself. He remembered another writer, Joyce Cary, and tried to recall an amusing line he had written. Wendy came out of the villa in a yellow bikini that was so brief she might just as well have left it off. Her bottom, he decided, would have disturbed a eunuch. It disturbed him, and he struggled after the line that he had enjoyed from Joyce Cary. The effort at recollection worked – his body relaxed and the line arrived: "It was as dark as the inside of a Cabinet Minister."

Wendy lay down at the edge of the pool. She had brought a pink pillow from the bedroom for her head. She was facing the wrong way for him and Nick lay on his back and concentrated on banishing from his head all thoughts of sex. He took the initials into the world of sport and came up with one of his soccer heroes, Jackie Charlton. But Wendy had turned over on to her stomach: in this position she was looking straight at him. John Conteh, he thought quickly. Jimmy Connors. But it was no good. He could feel it going up now like one of those films run backwards of a chimney being demolished. He turned over on to his stomach. If John Calvin couldn't stop him getting a hard-on, who could?

"You've got a lovely bum, Nick," said Wendy.

Rupert Puckle came out with a tray of champagne. He looked like a fox who had been thrown into a chicken run.

"Get your dressing-gown off, Rupert," Ben commanded.

"Certainly not. I'm the factotum round here." He placed the champagne in an ice-bucket on a table and began to fill the glasses from the last bottle. "But I must say your wife looks very attractive, Ben."

Ben got up to fetch a drink. His big beard and his fat belly were such prominent features that his genitals were overlooked. "Seen one, you've seen them both," he said.

"Bring us a drink, Ben," said Nick.

"Why? Too embarrassed to get up?"

"I've got up. That's the trouble."

Everybody laughed, but Nick continued to lie face down on the towel. Jack Carter, Jakarta, he thought. It didn't seem to be working any more. His predicament delighted the girls who sat up to bait him.

"I'll show you my naughty bits if you show me yours," Pym shouted.

Face down on the grass he knew that this was an erection that would not admit defeat, and the sun was burning his back. He had to move now, or spend the rest of the holiday in bed. He stood up and ran to the pool.

"Privates on parade!" Pym shouted.

"Members' enclosure," said Wendy.

The water treatment worked, but Nick stayed on in the pool to cool his burning back. Cold at first, the water was actually warm and swimming naked was such a sensual experience that he feared he might soon be back where he started. Venables joined him in the water, and throwing a ball to each other finally relaxed him enough to get out.

Ben seemed to be asleep, but the girls were drinking. The champagne in Rupert's bucket disappeared in a couple of hours and more was collected from the fridge. Rupert himself was washing the Mehari. Presently the sun was so hot that Pym found a sunshade in his garage and erected it on the grass.

"You've come all this way to find the sun and now you hide from it," said Venables.

"Remember you said that tomorrow when your skin falls off," Wendy told him, joining Pym in the shade. They sat together, one naked, the other in brief yellow, working their way through the champagne and watching the men doze. In the dry fields beyond Rupert's property there was a silence they had never known. As the sun reached its peak, the men turned over, roasting on a spit.

Ben gave up first, retreating with a drink to the shade of the patio where the cane chairs had comfortable tie-on cushions. Venables joined him, dazed by the heat. Nick, for whom the permanent use of a pool was a novelty, decided to cool off in the water. By the time he climbed out, Pym and Wendy had joined the others on the patio, and he had a long naked walk to join them. But there was no problem now: the sun had cauterised his libido. He poured himself some champagne and sat down.

"I think Nick has got the biggest willy I've ever seen," said Pym, studying it with approbation.

"How many have you seen?" asked Ben. "I don't think you should talk like that in front of your husband."

"Tongue in cheek," said Nick, embarrassed.

"Foot in mouth," said Ben irritably. "It doesn't look that huge to me."

"It did this morning," said Wendy. "He was quite enthusiastic when he got up."

"He was scratching his nose with it," added Pym.

"He was hiding behind it," said Wendy. "I wondered who it was. Then he peeped round the side and I saw that it was Nick. 'Get on the end of this and walk towards me,' he shouted."

"I'm afraid my wife is drunk," said Venables, covering himself with his towel. He did not like the drift of this conversation.

Pym was drunk, too, laughing uncontrollably at Wendy's remarks.

"If I was a man," she said, when she stopped, "I would want one of those African jobs that bang against your knee-caps."

Ben fixed her with an expression in which disgust and disbelief vied for control.

"Why is it," Nick asked one evening as they sat watching the boats bobbing at Cala Fons, "that the bars in Britain close just when everybody wants a drink?"

Ben stirred his Bloody Mary and sucked the swizzle-stick. "The British are deeply suspicious of pleasure. They regard it as a distraction."

"From what?"

"I've never found out. But they only shut the bars in the afternoons during the First World War because drinking was hitting production in the munitions factories, and a supine public have never managed to restore the original opening hours."

"Who wants to drink in the afternoon?" said Nick. "I'm talking about shutting them half-way through the evening. It's not civilised. It's positively totalitarian."

"That's why the British are such disgraceful drunks abroad," Wendy suggested. "They're repressed at home."

"Another thing," said Nick, still fascinated by the ways of abroad, "they don't keep asking for money here after every drink. Such trust! In Britain they often want the cash before they've served the drink."

"We can't be trusted to pay. We can't be trusted to drink. We are treated like children," said Venables.

"One more thing," added Nick. "The sun here is a source of heat instead of just light."

"Nick likes abroad," said Pym. "You can tell."

"I'm going to spend a lot of time here," Nick said. "Living in Britain suddenly seems rather silly to me."

They had left Rupert Puckle to attend his weekly bridge club and made their way down to the tiny harbour which had dozens of white rowing boats, with names like *Tauro*, *Neptuno* and *Fiesta*, at its edges. Among them were several fishing boats and one only slightly larger pleasure boat with eight blue wooden seats. On one side of the harbour new dainty white houses perched on the top of a low granite cliff, but on their side they could sit at the water's edge in front of a row of bars and restaurants that were buried in the harbour wall, caves with electricity. Sitting there, smelling the oil from the boats and listening to the gruff voices of the local fishermen, they could watch the big passenger ships pass the harbour on their way up the estuary to the port, sending waves into Cala Fons that made the rowing boats dance long afterwards.

"Think of what you would miss, Nick," said Wendy, "if you lived abroad."

"Rupert says kippers and cocoa," replied Nick. "I could survive."

"Television," suggested Pym. "West End theatre."

"Judas Iscariot, Megastar," said Ben. "I wouldn't miss the theatre."

"You'd miss the tradeweighted Index," Pym said.

Nick asked Wendy: "What would you miss? I can't think of anything."

"Umbrellas?" she suggested. "The smell after rain?"

"Poetic, my wife," said Venables. "I'd miss sport on television."

"They have sport on television here," Nick said. "Wendy's right. Umbrellas is what you would miss. Umbrellas and wellies."

"The trouble is," said Ben, "I don't much care for the people who emigrate. Do you want an emigré as a neighbour?"

Pym put her feet up into Venables' lap, brown feet in white, plastic shoes. "What's the matter with them?" she asked.

"They're either people who couldn't make it at home or boring, right-wing old farts who are still wondering what's happened to the Empire."

"We would constitute a third category," said Nick. "People who have made it at home but prefer to spend the winnings where it doesn't piss with rain twice a day, where the bars don't throw you out just as you are beginning to enjoy yourself, and where the government hasn't invented so many taxes that one way or another they end up with about ninety per cent of what a lobotomised public has earned."

"That sounds like a man who is off," said Ben. "That sounds very much to me like a man on his way to Heathrow with a large suitcase."

"Watch me go," said Nick. "I've never been to abroad before. I think it's a nice place."

"Beats Battersea on a wet Monday," Venables conceded. Newly rich, he was wondering about abroad himself.

"Of course there is a fourth category of exile down here," added Ben. "The career criminal. No extradition treaty. The place is jumping with British villains."

"Looking for friends, generous with the vino," said Nick. "Up to here with charisma."

"They're worse than the other lot who are wondering why half the map isn't red any more," said Ben. "Do you know the five most reactionary groups? Bookmakers, publicans, criminals, gipsies and dogs."

"Who says so?" asked Nick.

"I do," said Ben.

"That's good enough for me."

"*¿Quisiera un vaso de cerveza?*" asked Pym.

"Wave at the man," said Ben. "I can wave in five languages."

The waiter came over and took their order. It was getting dark quickly.

"After this, I'm going to buy us all dinner," said Venables, removing Pym's shoes.

"Ben, Simon is undressing me," she protested. "I was just thinking, the best thing about being naked all day is that you don't have to keep washing clothes."

They had adjusted to nudity quickly. That morning Nick had gone into Pym's bedroom to borrow some Nivea cream for a tender, sun-damaged area on his shoulders. She was sitting on the bed in jeans and bra, getting fluff off a skirt by rubbing it with a jumbo hair-roller wrapped in Sellotape, sticky side out. From the room's white walls hung what looked like a very amateurish painting, showing two lopsided piles of hay, outlined for some reason in blue and watched by someone who appeared to be a milkmaid. It turned out to be a print of Vincent Van Gogh's "Haystacks in Provence", a discovery that so outraged Nick that he made Pym study the painting's imagined flaws and listen to his furious views on the delusions of the art world, a speech lasting fully five minutes and delivered, he realised with amusement afterwards, completely naked.

It was almost strange for them to be sitting around now fully dressed.

Ben had moved on from the Bloody Mary to sample a bottle of Xoriguer, one of the locally distilled gins, brewed from juniper berries to a British recipe, left behind along with the Georgian buildings in the eighteenth century.

With appetites that had shrivelled in the heat, they sat in the restaurant in the cave and picked at small steaks and bits of fish. Only Ben, whose shape demanded it, could handle a large meal. He ordered a seafood mixed grill, and was working his way through a forest of *gambas*, lobsters and mussels, relating between mouthfuls the amusing story of an alcoholic friend. "Each evening he would arrive home drunk in the early hours and creep into bed without waking his wife. Half the time, she didn't even know he had been drinking," he said, peeling a prawn.

"I know that story," said Pym. "I never realised my husband drank until he came home sober one night."

"Shut up," said Ben, glaring at her. "This isn't a joke. It's a true story. It happened in Woking. One night he arrived home and the key wouldn't open the front door. He didn't know whether he had picked up the wrong keys in the pub, or whether his wife had changed the locks, but he knew how to get in without waking her because he had done it before. He crept round to the back where they had built a ground-floor extension they called the breakfast room. He got on to the dustbin, and then on to the roof of the extension. From there he could get through a window that brought him on to a hallway outside his bedroom. Once inside, he decided to undress outside the bedroom, in case the rattle of coins and keys woke up the dreaded wife. It was only when he was naked that he remembered that they had sold this house two years ago."

The laughter that this story produced was cut short by the unexpected arrival of Rupert Puckle.

"Rupert!" said Venables. "You're supposed to be playing bridge. Has your memory gone?"

"A cable arrived just as I was leaving," he said, waving an envelope. "I thought I'd better find you."

"Who's it for?"

"Me," said Ben. "I just know it."

He took the envelope and looked at it with hatred. He knew already that the seafood mixed grill would remain half eaten.

"Open it," said Pym. "It might be serious."

"Oh, it'll be serious," Ben said, slitting the envelope open. The message read: GLEN VAPORISED ESSENTIAL YOU RETURN CLIFF.

He passed it to Pym.

"What does it mean?" she asked.

"It means that Glen Nardini, our biggest client, has been sacked, and one of the remaining legs of Ben Brock Advertising has been kicked away. I'll have to fly home. Is there a phone in this cave?"

"I'll show you one," said Rupert.

"Finish your meal first," Pym suggested.

Ben stood up and shook his head. "I just lost my appetite. Sorry, Simon."

It seemed cooler now as he walked along the harbour front with Rupert, past alfresco diners on one side and rowing boats on the other, to a bar that did have a phone. Rupert was familiar with its provocative mechanism and in less than fifteen minutes Ben heard Cliff's voice.

"It's Ben," he told him.

"Thank God. Look, Ben, this is serious. Get a plane –"

"What happened?"

"A big purge at Shackleford Ciderhouse, that's what happened. Glen was out in a day. Car keys on the desk. The whole works."

"Any repercussions?"

"Immediately. The message we got said: Stop all work in progress and bill us up to date."

"Jesus!"

"It's grim, Ben."

"I know it."

"You'd better get here."

"I'll see you tomorrow."

He put the phone down and turned to Rupert.

"I'll have to fly home tomorrow. Pym can stay. I don't want to waste two return tickets."

"What a bloody shame, Ben," said Rupert. "Is there anything I can do?"

"Buy me a drink. I think I've just gone bankrupt."

ELEVEN

IN A BAR in a silent, sun-bleached backstreet, where small dark men in black berets sipped mysterious potions from tiny glasses and coughed occasionally into *tapas* of braised squid and seasoned meatballs, Nick Bannerman sat drinking San Miguel, waiting to become famous.

He was finding that no matter what happened on the island, his mind was never far from his book – or the manuscript that would soon be his book, with a shiny, colourful dust-jacket that bore his unsmiling picture. His last job, before he flew out, had been to drop into a local photographic studio where a tubby man, with many limp-wristed gestures, took forty-eight pictures of him in fifteen minutes, all of which were dispatched to Arthur Scott's publicity department who produced their own copies and enlargements and were now thoroughly prepared for the demands of a voracious media. Nick decided to prepare himself as well. He felt like a politician who needed a firm grasp of the party manifesto before he took to the hustings. The fact that his proximity to the Brocks' marriage had cast painful doubts on his central proposition no longer disturbed him. After all, he told himself, there could no longer be a sane Socialist who believed that nationalisation produced either profit or efficiency, but their reformist zeal induced them to chunter on about it long after everyone had stopped caring, like the eagerly ticking watch on the wrist of a dead man.

He glanced round the small, white-walled bar with its bright neon lights, and wondered what stories the customers could tell him about their country's turbulent past. He knew that this island had resisted Franco to the end, but who knew what horrors occurred on the long, sad journey to surrender? In one small village on the mainland the local priest had been put into the bull-ring with a bull which had eventually gored him to death. The crowd had then cut off the priest's ears and presented them to the bull. Elsewhere, priests were shot without trial, and buried without coffins, defenceless cities were bombed, prisoners massacred in jail, brother killed brother. The old men at the bar, he knew, would never discuss the war even if he could talk their language. From the papers they were holding, it seemed likely that they were more concerned today with the victories of Atlético Madrid or Real Mallorca, but Nick yearned for the stories he would never hear. He had read the history books, but here were the people who knew. The manifestations of democracy, which had reached these parts suddenly, were, on the face of it, depressing. The streets were no longer crime-free, brandy was no longer ten pesetas a glass, and the pornography in the shops was stacked to the ceiling. But strikes were now legal, exiled politicians had returned home and Chaplin's *The Great Dictator* could be shown in the cinemas. Armed police no longer roamed in pairs. None of this was reflected in the impassive faces of the locals: they had seen so much that there was nothing left to move them. In a way Nick envied them their rich and tragic history. Great events had been played out in their lifetimes – drama, turmoil, upheaval. The long, damp days of boredom that constituted life in northern Europe were unknown to them. Their sunny homeland, Europe's dark ages only a dozen years ago, was now, with its crime, its legalised pot and its pervasive sexuality, the continent's liberal spearhead. The interesting thing was, Nick thought over his beer, that if the Commies had won the Civil War, the country would not now be a parliamentary democracy and on the verge of electing a Socialist government. He formulated the Bannerman Theory of Armed Conflict on the strength of this thought: Although it might not appear so at the time, in any war the right side will always win.

He finished his beer and ordered another. In these backstreet bars that were used only by the locals the beer was so cheap that he felt guilty. The barman, a surprisingly pale young man, smiled and said nothing. Lacking any means of communication, they had resorted to the exchange of funny little smiles which embarrassed them both. Nick lit a cigarette and noticed that his packet of English Silk Cut carried a health warning in Spanish: *La Direccion General de la Salud Publica advierte que el uso del tabaco puede ser perjudicial para su salud.* Perjudicial – the message was clear. Some young soldiers came into the bar and ordered beer. They were from the barracks in the town and, according to Rupert Puckle, earned £5 a month. Unlike British soldiers, they pulled their berets down on the left side of their heads, a reaction perhaps to the long, dark years of the right.

Through the window he suddenly saw Pym, laden with shopping, and went to the door to call her in. She was wearing a yellow tee-shirt and white shorts, and the soldiers turned to enjoy her.

"Have I spent some money!" she said, dumping her purchases on a chair.

"It rather looks as if you have," Nick said. "What will you drink?"

"A beer."

She opened her bag to reveal a pair of Charles Jourdan shoes, with matching handbag, belt and sunglasses.

"The shoes are expensive but they cost twice as much in London," she said. "I must try to get Ben to see the economy of it."

"How is your holiday," Nick asked, "without Ben?"

"I'm enjoying myself." She sipped her drink. "Did you know that Simon has a thing about me?"

"I sort of noticed."

"And you have a rather bigger thing about his wife?"

"Well," said Nick.

"You really have got the most enormous organ, Nick. If you put it in Wendy it'll knock her hat off."

"Two points there, I think," said Nick, filling Pym's glass up. "Mrs Venables is married. Also, she doesn't wear a hat."

"Bare-headed housewives are getting laid from Sunday to Saturday, Nick. It's what keeps them sane."

"Does that mean you are contemplating mischief with Simon?"

Pym held up her new shoes, imagining her feet in them. "I think not. He doesn't make me fizz."

"Fizz?"

"Bubble."

"Would you say that you liked him well enough to take him away for an afternoon on the beach?"

"To leave you with Wendy."

"I suppose that would follow," said Nick. "I hear the beaches are very clean."

"And Simon could hardly be too pressing in front of several hundred people."

"That's settled then," said Nick. "Any news of Ben?"

"He can't ring me, can he? He never tells me anything, anyway. I'm his chattel – you heard him the other night."

"Why do you stay with him if he hits you? I've often wondered."

"He's a great guy when he's not hitting me."

"You mean he's good in bed?"

"Since you ask, yes."

Nick drank his beer and wondered how he could reconcile the tolerance of women with the venom in his book. "Do you think he will go bust?" he asked.

Pym nodded slowly. "Something terrible is happening. Oddly enough, I've never cared about money. I'm not extravagant except, perhaps, on holiday."

"You'll care about money when you haven't got any," Nick told her. "It can become quite an obsession."

"If Ben loses his money, he'll make some more. He's very single-minded."

"It's easy to make it if you already have some. It's not such a pushover if you're starting from nothing."

"Why's that?"

"It's easier to turn fifty thousand into a hundred thousand than it is to turn fifty into a hundred, because fifty is too little to do anything with."

"You're beginning to sound like a financier, Nick. Any chance of financing another beer for a girl?"

"*Con muchisimo gusto*. Let's drink to your afternoon on the beach."

Venables was having his hair cut by a veteran barber who kept a small cigar in his mouth and one eye on the television throughout the operation. Recently he had grown sensitive about his appearance and had studied the hairstyles of the rich and the famous as he wondered what appearance to present to the world. Pop stars had gone from long hair to short hair. Footballers were shaving off their sideburns and letting the hair grow down the back of their necks – but who wanted to look like a footballer? Venables' new hairstyle was eventually decided by the heat. But when he looked in the barber's mirror he decided that, without the moustache, he would look rather like an American tennis star, so he had that taken off, too.

"Where's your moustache?" asked Wendy. She was waiting for him at a table outside the American Bar where they had last sat months earlier on their honeymoon.

"On the floor over there," Venables said, pointing at the barber's shop. "What do you think?"

"It makes you look younger."

Gratified by this verdict, he sat down and ordered himself a *café con leche*. From the Calle de la Infanta, Mobylettes and Seats zoomed into the town with little attention to pedestrians, mostly old ladies in black who showed an intrepid disregard themselves for the age of the motor vehicle. The newest thing in this old square, with its ancient four-storey buildings toppling towards each other, was its own nameplate: Plaça Reial. In even quite recent maps it was Mola Square, after Franco's murderous sidekick.

They were in town to buy some presents, which was what Wendy said you were supposed to take home from holidays. She was equipped not only with credit cards and travellers' cheques, but also, being suspicious of all foreign specifications, her own pink tape-measure which she produced and used in every clothes shop.

Venables was more interested in buying some bottles of Rioja wine at a quarter of its price at home – the more money people had, the greater their interest in bargains. He now saw his wife's disinterest in his financial coup as a considerable advantage. Most women, glimpsing gold, would have compiled a yard-long shopping list by now, he thought, but Wendy behaved as if he had been involved in an unsavoury court case, probably involving small boys, that she had determined they would put behind them.

"I've seen some shoes that I am going to buy for Dad," she said. "And I thought I would get Mum some jewellery."

"What are you going to buy me?" Simon asked.

"What do you want? Apart from Pym?"

"Do I want Pym?"

"You look at her as if you want her."

"She's an attractive lady," he said.

"Particularly with no clothes on."

"With or without clothes."

"Is she the reason," asked Wendy, "that you took your moustache off?"

"Come on," he said, pushing his chair back. "Let's do the shopping."

The sea, choppy today, was turquoise towards the horizon but gloomily khaki nearer the shore. Venables didn't like that khaki.

"You know what they call the Mediterranean?" he said. "The sewage farm of southern Europe. You go swimming out there and turds the size of marrows will float past your ear."

"I'm not going to swim," said Pym. "I'm looking for sea shells."

They had driven to this sandy cove, surrounded on three sides by pine-clad hills, in Rupert's Mehari. Others had found it, too, and an ice-cream salesman was making his way among the prostrate sun-seekers.

"That's the sound of a Spanish beach," Pym said. "A man shouting 'ice-cream' in four languages."

"It's better than the sound of an English beach," remarked Venables. "The deafening rat-a-tat of windbreaks being hammered into the ground." He laid a rug on the sand and removed his shirt and jeans. "This is ridiculous," he said. "We've come all this way so that you can put a bathing costume on. If we'd stayed at home, I could have admired your body without it."

Pym wore a smart white bikini. "This was very expensive. It would be a waste not to wear it," she said, flopping on the rug. "Anyway, you never meet anybody at the villa. I want to meet a dark, handsome Spaniard with a name like Orlando Romero."

This wasn't what Venables wanted to hear. "Would you be unfaithful to Ben, if you did?" he asked. Perhaps unfaithfulness could become a habit.

"I'd never be unfaithful to Ben. He's nasty when he's cross."

Venables, lying down now in a three-year-old pair of French swimming trunks, raised himself on an elbow to ask: "Are we talking about love or fear?"

"Both," said Pym. "Aren't you in love with Wendy?"

"I'm in love with you," Venables said bleakly.

Pym baulked at the directness of this reply. She sat up and

scanned the beach. "Don't be silly, Simon. Come and help me find some sea shells."

"I sort of drifted into marriage," he said, standing up. "It happened when I wasn't looking."

Pym stood up, too. "You seem a bit young for a mid-life crisis to me." He looked so miserable that she added: "I like you without a moustache."

"Good."

"All you need now is a willy transplant."

She ran away laughing and he chased after her. Noticing the topless sunbathers, he pinned her arms and removed the top of her bikini.

"You look for shells and I'll look at you," he said. He enjoyed the unblemished smoothness of her brown back. His wife's back was marred by two spots which seemed to have taken up permanent residence on her right shoulder-blade. Pym's chest was so spectacular that even men with topless girls found it necessary to look.

Walking the length of the beach they found many shells, only a few of which Pym kept. She held them out in her hand before dropping her final selection – pale pink, mother of pearl, orange and cream – into her bag.

"What are they for?" Venables asked.

"Do they have to be for anything?"

"Yes. What are they – a hedge against inflation?"

"I might make a necklace out of them, or earrings. I might stick them on to a jewellery box or a photograph album. I've got hundreds of them. I don't know yet what I am going to do with them."

"I don't understand women."

"Well, we knew that already. Why don't you buy me an ice-cream?"

He left her in search of the multi-lingual ice-cream man, burdened with a heavy sense of failure. He had hoped that getting her away from the others, particularly with Ben marooned in Britain, would produce a quantum leap forward in their burgeoning relationship. But the truth which faced him now as he plodded barefoot across the hot sand was that their relationship wasn't burgeoning at all. He couldn't understand this. Most women, twinned with a husband who hurt, would be drawn instinctively, if not emotionally, to a man who offered comfort, admiration and love. But Pym didn't seem to take him seriously. He did not impress her. When he returned with two chocolate ices, his aggravation was increased by the discovery that Pym was now surrounded by men. There were about twelve Germans in knee-length swimming trunks gathered round her. Why was it that on holiday the Germans were never found in groups of less than twelve? One of them was even sitting down on Venables' half of the beach rug. He eased his way through the crowd and handed Pym her ice.

"Are you starting a fan club?" he asked.

"What's German for gang-bang?" she asked. "I'm trying to figure out their plans."

"None of them looks like a Spaniard called Orlando Romero," Venables said.

"They just arrived, like ants," Pym told him. "I think they've taken a fancy to my chest."

"Up," said Venables to the man on his rug.

"Up? Up?" the man said.

Venables indicated with his hands that the man should vacate the rug so that he, Venables, could sit on it.

"*Nein*," said the man, smiling and pointing at Pym.

Some German conversation followed this and Venables got the impression that the man on the rug was being urged to move by the others, some of whom began to drift off.

"What have they been saying?" he asked.

"Don't ask me," said Pym. "I think they have been discussing my body in a foreign language."

Venables tapped the head of the man on the rug and said "Up" again. He could feel his anger growing now. He could also see the opportunity he wanted to impress Pym.

The man said something in German and waved Venables away. He continued staring at Pym, transfixed, apparently, by her breasts. Venables leaned over him and pushed his half-eaten ice-cream in the man's face. The man got up quickly now and rushed in a fury at Venables who took his right wrist, bent forward, and using the man's arm as a lever across his own back threw him seven feet across the beach. The man sat on the ground and looked at him. Then he jumped up and rushed at Venables again. The same thing happened except that this time, landing awkwardly, the man broke his ankle. He complained in German to the two friends who had remained and watched this performance in near hysterics. When they could stop laughing they made a seat for the man with their hands and carried him away up the beach.

Venables lay down.

"That was very clever, Simon," Pym said. "You don't look the sort who could do that."

"Too small a penis, you mean?"

"You don't look a brawler."

"That's not brawling. That's science. I used to go to judo classes. Do you know you can kill a man like this?" He raised his flat hand to her face until his little finger was touching the bottom of her nose. "It pushes the bone into the brain."

"Would you like me to rub some sun-cream on your back?"

"I think I would."

They lay in the sun for an hour before the heat drove them back to the Mehari.

"What's going to happen to Ben's firm?" he asked, as they drove back.

"I don't know."

"If you ever need any money, Pym, you have only to ask."

"How much have you got, kid?"

"About sixty thousand."

"It's always nice to have rich friends, but I don't want to think about the advertising agency now. I'm on holiday." She patted his knee. "I wonder how Nick and Wendy have got on this afternoon?"

Nick sat naked on the edge of the pool, his feet in the water and his mind a thousand miles away in an equally hot television studio where critical voices snarled at him about his book. A woman who looked as if she could strangle an elephant was bent on dismantling his thesis. She hit him with a foaming torrent of abuse and a volley of questions, each of which landed on a painful spot. He was unfair, he was misinformed, he was prejudiced, he had – worst crime of all – misinterpreted his own evidence. The leader of this feminist fusillade made a Russian hammer-thrower look dainty. He withdrew from the reverie with a gloomy sense of foreboding.

In his kitchen Rupert Puckle had discovered the Russian world service on his Philips short-wave radio, and was now engrossed in a melancholy panegyric about a gaunt and obscure Russian city that was, he learned, full of history. Starved of electronic entertainment, he repeatedly swung through the wavebands in search of a friendly or even just comprehensible voice. The Russian world service, lecturing him in English, was a find.

Wendy sat on the bed in her room and wondered whether to take her clothes off. She had watched the others adjust happily to nudity: if she was ever going to try it, this was her opportunity. She stripped naked and looked at herself in the mirror. She had a nice figure. Her breasts weren't as large as Pym's but they were round and firm. The only thing that spoiled her appearance, she realised now, was the white part that the sun hadn't seen. Perhaps this afternoon could put that right. She ran a comb through her hair, and then combed her pubic hair as well. Nervously she went downstairs.

Nick had dislodged thoughts of television nightmares by slipping into the pool. He swam a slow length and congratulated himself on the healthy life he was leading after months in a smoke-filled room. He dived to the bottom of the pool in search of a glinting coin, failed to find it and pushed himself to the surface.

Wendy was approaching, with a bottle of Spanish champagne.

"I thought I would join the nudist club," she said, only slightly embarrassed.

"I thought you were wearing a flesh-coloured leotard," said Nick, standing in the pool. "What a lovely body you've been hiding, he said ejaculating into his cocoa."

She opened the champagne and filled two glasses which she put on the poolside table. Nick found himself staring up at the neatest bottom he had ever seen.

"Would you like the loan of my body?" he asked.

"How much?"

"Fifty pounds an hour."

"Fifty pounds an hour?"

"I'm willing," he said, "to pay more."

She laughed and handed him his glass, and then lay down on her back in the sun. He drained his glass, climbed out of the pool and sat down on the grass beside her. Glancing down he was relieved to see that his body was showing great control.

"I wonder how Simon and Pym are getting along?" he said. "Do you think they are at it?"

"At it?"

"Sex."

"Certainly not. No thanks to him, though. He would if he could."

"Would you care?" he asked, reaching for the champagne bottle.

"Of course I'd care. I married him, didn't I? I'd sooner he went to sleep with a man. I wouldn't feel so insulted. It would be biological."

"You're happy then? I had a strong feeling that couples who live together wind up not liking each other very much."

She lay, eyes closed, on her back and thought for a while. "I must admit that he sometimes gives the impression that this isn't where he wants to be and I'm not who he wants to be with but I'm the best he can have for the moment. Perhaps all marriages are like that? Sometimes I wonder why people bother to do it."

"It's a tradition," said Nick. "It's called Holy Acrimony."

She opened her eyes and looked up at him.

"There's something else I wonder," she said. "Can I ask you a personal question?"

"Absolutely."

"How big is it?"

"How big is what?"

"That."

"I don't know, Wendy," he said blankly.

"It's pretty big, though, isn't it?"

"Compared to what? A telegraph pole? A cricket stump?"

"Simon's," said Wendy. She sat up suddenly to look at it. It responded, gratified, to her attention.

"Can I measure it?" she asked with a smile, and produced from nowhere the pink tape-measure that she always took on shopping trips. "Stand up."

Nick stood up. She took his penis in her hand and laid the tape-measure along the side. Under her gentle touch it swelled alarmingly.

"Twelve centimetres – no, fourteen. Hang on – sixteen centimetres. Is it going to stop? This is a very small island."

Nick didn't say anything.

"Ah, that seems to be it," said Wendy. "Just over twenty centimetres."

"What are centimetres?" asked Nick. "My erections haven't gone metric yet."

She put the tape against him again.

"Eight inches. Have you got a licence for it?"

She held it for a moment and then let go.

He gazed in dismay at his erection that was now throbbing quietly in the sun.

"You're not going to leave it like that?" he asked.

"Why not? Isn't this the way to treat an up-and-coming author?"

"Up, but not coming," Nick croaked.

"What do you want me to do with it? Wrap it up and send it to the *Guinness Book of Records*?" She threw the tape-measure to the ground and walked over to the edge of the pool. "What I can't understand," she said, "is why you don't pitch forward on to your face. You seem to be flouting some fundamental law of balance."

He growled at her in an American accent. "Get your svelte carcass over here, Mrs Venables. I wanna show you something."

"I can see it from here, blue eyes. They can see it from Algiers. It's probably a blip on the screen in Tashkent. Squadrons of fighters are being sent up to investigate."

He came up behind her and put his hands round her waist. "You're a girl I'd waive my stud fees for," he said. He slid his hands up her body and cupped her cool breasts. This mood seemed to change her attitude and she relaxed into his embrace. He lifted her up and turned her round, and he was in her almost immediately. Her feet met willingly behind his back, and her hands behind his head.

"Oh Nick, oh Christ, oh Nick," she said.

Gripping her by the hips, he moved her up and down while she gasped, head back, in the sun. It seemed to last for ever, perhaps because of the discomfort of the position, and Nick moved her faster as her gasps grew louder in the hope that they would finish before somebody stumbled across this bizarre poolside spectacle. But it was Nick who stumbled at the climactic moment, and they fell into the water in each other's arms pumping away and creating a tidal wave which rushed out of the pool and vanished into the parched grass of Rupert's lawn. They floated apart eventually, Wendy on her back, smiling at a cloudless sky, and Nick paddling in mid-pool as he wondered what post-sex juices might remain in this water as evidence to the others of their act. He felt like a man who had run a marathon with a sack on his back, and he pushed himself gently to the edge of the pool and climbed out to lie on the grass.

Wendy stayed in the water. "Thanks, Nick," she said.

Nick raised his head and looked at her. Nobody had ever said thank you before.

"My pleasure," he joked and flopped back on the grass. "An emission of mercy."

"What happened to the twenty centimetres?" she called, but he was wrestling now with a nasty bout of post-coital guilt. Wendy, on the other hand, was distinctly perky. She jumped out of the pool and came over to kick him.

"One more time then?" she said. "It's just a question of locating the missing centimetres."

He smiled up at her. "Do you feel guilty?" he asked.

"I feel terrific. I'm on holiday, aren't I? Anyway, life's too short to waste. Get up, you lummox. And I mean up."

He had seen this before in a woman, the transformation wrought by good sex, and he wondered what her sex life was like back in Wimbledon.

The man who knew most about that appeared just then in the Mehari with Pym. They jumped from the vehicle and came across the lawn.

"Good lord, my wife has no clothes on," said Venables.

"If you can't beat them, join them," said Wendy, pouring herself champagne.

"Simon had a fight on the beach with a German," said Pym. "You should have seen it!"

"Who won?" asked Wendy.

"Simon did. He threw the Kraut into the air."

"My hero!" Wendy said, offering him a drink.

"I hope you've been behaving yourself," Venables said, "and not disturbing the author?"

"She was very good," Nick said.

But he was too ashamed to look him in the eye.

They woke each morning to a silence broken only by the shrill sound of the cicadas, and Rupert's water-sprinkler fighting its daily battle to keep the coarse, springy elephant grass a sort of green. They became used to the ants in the kitchen, the mosquitoes in the bedrooms, and the occasional lizard. But by the time they had accustomed themselves to the gifts of endless sun, cheap champagne, ever-open bars and a peaceful, timeless existence which soon embraced the Hispanic tradition of post-noon inertia, the holiday was over.

A final shopping expedition on their last day was conducted in a flurry of credit cards. Perfume, pearls, liquor and leather vanished into an increasing number of plastic bags bearing the names of many grateful shops. Venables bought Spanish jeans; Nick stocked up on Antaeus Pour Homme aftershave, declaring that helpless women would soon be dangling their bodies hopefully before him. The women spent wildly, as if they would never see a shop again. Bumping into the tourists who crowded the town now, they were glad that they had chosen a holiday home in the country where visitors were hard to find. The foreigners packed the shops, conforming amusingly with their stereotypes: fat and morose Germans, loud and condescending Americans, Scandinavians blinking in the sun, and pushy and ill-mannered Britons who imagined that the reason why they were not being understood in their native tongue was that they were not talking loudly enough.

Afterwards they ate green ice-cream in a plant-bedecked tea-room while a man who looked like a heavyweight boxer played the piano rather gracefully. He yielded eventually to live television coverage of a bullfight in Seville, in which a gored *banderillero*, carried in a rush to the safe side of the ring, was met not by a doctor but by an importunate television man who thrust a live microphone into his crumpled face. But the man's anguish was nothing compared to the bull's, and Wendy groaned in disgust.

"She's found a new cause," said Venables. "She'll be printing Boycott The Bullfight posters and tee-shirts by the end of next week."

"Something should be done," said Wendy.

"Not by you, though," said her husband. "You haven't put the rest of the world right yet."

That evening they took Rupert Puckle for a steak in the Dumbo Bar at Cala Fons. They gave him cheques which totalled £600, the amount he had asked for the use of his villa. It had been a cheap holiday for them, and a cheap three weeks for him – they had paid for all the food and drink in the house.

Wearing tonight a green velvet smoking jacket with extravagant curled lapels, he said: "I'm going to be lonely when you've gone." He had kept out of their way for a lot of the holiday, but now he was going to miss them. Nick began to see him, not as an object of envy with his life in the sun, but as a sad figure, with his eccentric clothing, his lonely life and the Russian world service on his battery radio.

"What are you all going back to?" he asked.

They were eating the best grilled steak they had found on the island, and sitting in a cave at the edge of the harbour.

"I'm the only one who is going back to work," Wendy said. "Isn't it amazing? All this lot get out of bed when they feel like it."

"I'm going back to become rich and famous," said Nick. "It's a pity you don't receive British television in this paradise."

"I'll read about you in the papers," Rupert said. "Even if they are a day old."

Venables had no idea what he was going back to, but he was looking forward to it. The future was hazy but bright.

"I'm going back to count my money," he said. "Once I get out of bed." He felt a different man without his moustache, a cheerier figure who was no longer the victim of circumstance, but a man in control of his own destiny, even if he was not yet sure what that destiny was.

He smiled across at Pym. She had been a lot friendlier to him since the fight on the beach, but tonight she wasn't smiling at anybody.

"I dread to think what I'm going back to," she said.

part four

RESOLUTIONS

In seventy years the one surviving frag-
ment of my knowledge, the only indis-
putable poor particle of certainty in my
entire life is that in a public-house lavatory
incoming traffic has the right of way.

Hugh Leonard

TWELVE

BEN BROCK sat tense and upright at his office desk in Chelsea and listened to his world falling apart. His two-week tan already looked more like a terminal pallor.

"I've always concentrated on getting the business," he said, "because I thought if I did that, everything else would look after itself. Anyway, finance bores me."

His desk was covered with ledgers and documents and account sheets, upside down to him but the right way up to Cliff who sat opposite, consulting first one set of figures and then another.

"I'd better give you the whole picture, Ben. But I warn you, it isn't pretty."

Ben stared out of his office window at the clouds that were spoiling an English summer, and thought of the others sipping champagne by Rupert's pool.

"Shoot," he said.

"Turnover last year – six million pounds," said Cliff.

"An excellent result," said Ben. "I awarded myself a hundred thousand pound bonus, I seem to remember."

"I'll be coming to that," said Cliff. "Of that six million, thirty per cent, about one and three-quarter million pounds, came from Shackleford Ciderhouse. Government action against the drug industry has cut our turnover target for this year nearly in half. Those are the two facts to keep in your mind." He flipped through some sheets. "Let's have a look at expenditure. The lease on these offices, five thousand square feet, fifteen-year lease, rent, rates – a hundred and forty thousand a year. Salaries: enormous. We have an eighty thousand pound tax bill on the bonus you gave yourself last year, and a corporation tax bill of nearly a hundred and fifty thousand for 1981, due next month. The corporate tax-flow is no good. Cash has been syphoned out of the company for backhanders to people like Glen Nardini, an apartment in Paris, holidays in the Seychelles and some, I may say, for your own enjoyment."

"What does it all add up to?"

"I make it that as from now, with our overheads and the loss of Shackleford Ciderhouse, we're losing about fifty thousand a month."

"That much?"

"It's a high-salary business, Ben. There are a lot of people doing very well in this agency."

Ben stared at the upside-down financial evidence and thought for a long time before asking: "Can we survive?"

Cliff thought for a long time, too.

"Not in my opinion," he said. "And there are other things you should be thinking about."

"Like what?"

"Your house. It's part of the guarantee at the bank."

"I'd almost forgotten that."

"The Revenue will go for the company assets, the bank will go for the house."

"Dear God."

Ben had been gradually attuned to the possibility that his agency might go under, but had always imagined that he would salvage some money, perhaps a lot of money. The prospect of losing his house filled him with panic.

Cliff continued to search through his papers.

"Glen's apartment in Paris," he said. "Is it in his name or ours?"

"His."

"Terrific."

"You'd better lend me some money, Cliff."

"I haven't got a hundred pounds in the world. My wife spends it all."

"A penniless accountant doesn't exactly fill you with confidence. It's like dealing with a spotty dermatologist, or a dentist with false teeth."

"Come on, Ben. Be serious. What are you going to do?"

"I'm open to suggestions. I read somewhere that a financier was somebody who could borrow money on the strength of what he owes."

"My advice is don't borrow. Look at the prospects. What are they?"

"If your analysis is right there are no prospects."

"So what is the point of borrowing? It only increases the debt."

Ben stared at, or through, his desk. "The point of borrowing," he said, "is to buy time. To stay in business until business improves."

"What makes you believe it's going to improve?"

"I've got to believe it's going to improve."

"It would have to improve bloody quickly to save this agency," said Cliff. "Losses of fifty thousand a month can't be sustained for long, and even if you were right, and there is going to be a turn-round, where can we borrow money from? The banks know too much about our affairs to lend any more, and the interest rates aren't very amusing at the moment, either."

"I have a couple of friends who have recently struck it rich," said Ben. "Perhaps I can prise them apart from their loot. A hundred thousand would buy us two months. It could make all the difference."

Cliff's conviction that this new idea was a bad one was conveyed without words: an embarrassed silence, a mild frown. He knew now that he would soon be looking for a new job and it didn't matter very much to him. In his line, there were always jobs and the strain was someone else's. Fortunes were made or lost, but his cheque arrived every month. He would never be rich but he would never be broke, so long as he could control his second wife's penchant for the snootier department stores. He looked across at Ben who was sitting now with his elbows on the desk and his head in his hands.

"I've got to fight, Cliff," he said. "I didn't get this far without fighting."

Cliff didn't say anything.

"I'm not a man you can rely on to do the decent thing if shown an empty room and a revolver, Cliff."

"Why don't you go to see your friend, Johnny Fix-It? If he can fix this, he really is a miracle-worker."

The suggestion brought Ben to life.

"That is not a bad idea, Clifford. If I wasn't so distracted I'd have thought of it myself. Johnny Fix-It! The very human being!"

Half an hour later, after a telephone call had elicited the desired invitation, he turned his Bentley towards Cheyne Walk and followed the Thames east with the faintest flicker of hope. He stayed with the river all the way to Blackfriars, glancing at its murky depths and reflecting that it was at this stage in their careers that many ambitious young men had jumped in fully dressed without so much as a good-bye.

Johnny Fix-It was in his best scatological form. "I'm farting like a trombone today," was his opening remark. "I had better warn you. How are you, Ben? You look terrible. What is it – angst, dyspepsia, ptomaine poisoning?"

"Probably," said Ben, sitting down. "How are things with you?"

"I'm having a *belle époque*, mate."

His face was almost as red as his hair. He wore the same huge glasses but the lenses were now tinted in blue.

"Have you been in the sun?"

"I've been down in Banus, planning my future. Do you know that property values are going up there by twenty-five per cent a year? You could buy, sit there for four years, sell up and come home and you'd never have to work again."

"That sounds too good to be true."

"Most of my schemes sound like that. What can I do for you, Ben?" He walked over to a filing cabinet against the wall.

"What does one come to a miracle-worker for?"

"A miracle?" suggested Johnny Fix-It. He bent down to pull a file from the cabinet's bottom drawer. A fart which shamed thunder rocketed from his trousers. "Do you know I once singed a man's beard at a party by setting light to one of my own farts? He was quite surprised."

"Difficult sort of thing to anticipate," said Ben. "Is that my file?"

"Yes. I'm getting quite organised. I've got the goods on all my clients here."

"Am I one of your clients? I hadn't realised."

"You've picked my brains enough to qualify. How's Pym?"

"She's away on holiday. I had to come back. I'm in trouble, Johnny."

Johnny Fix-It opened his file on Ben. "I heard," he said. "The drugs business is on the floor. What are we talking about? The melting bank balance syndrome?"

"Melting? Mine vanished weeks ago."

Johnny Fix-It grimaced at this. He loved to deal with money.

The absence of money depressed him, and presented a different and unwelcome set of problems. "How much are you losing a month?"

"Cliff guesses fifty thousand."

"Jesus!" said Johnny Fix-It.

"Jesus isn't available, so I've come to you."

"What do you want, Ben?"

"I need a loan to keep me going until things look up."

"How much?"

"A hundred."

"A hundred thousand without security? For once I can't help. That's megabucks, Ben."

"What about all this Arab money that is supposed to be swilling round London?"

"If it isn't being lost in the casinos, it's being used to buy racehorses. I can't get my hands on it. Don't think I haven't tried."

Ben sat dismayed, staring at his own lap. There was something terribly final about the way that Johnny Fix-It dismissed his problem. "I might as well hang myself," he said.

Johnny Fix-It shut Ben's folder and pushed it to one side. "You're too young for a pine box, Ben," he said. "My advice is go into liquidation, and start up a new firm with a new name."

"I'm not selling bloody jeans," said Ben. "I've got clients, I've got long-standing accounts, I've got goodwill."

Johnny Fix-It, for once, was too polite to answer this. It was clear enough to both of them that this was just what he didn't have.

Ben looked up and saw that Johnny Fix-It's mind had already moved on to the day's next problem.

"I've got a couple of friends who have just made a bit of money," he told him.

"Rich friends would be the answer," said Johnny Fix-It, shifting slightly on his seat. A fart like a roll of drums reverberated round the ceiling. "I was thinking the other day – if farts were blue, people would be more careful."

Nick Bannerman fell impatiently on the parcel that had been waiting for his return and sliced it open quickly with the help of his bread-knife. When he had dragged the contents from its rumpled clothing he gave it a long kiss. Teams of men working in long shifts in a North Country printing works had, in four weeks, transformed his untidy manuscript into a book – or, at least, the proofs of a book. Photocopies of the 300 pages had been spiral bound into a floppy paperback for revisions and corrections.

He opened it slowly, studying the title and his name below it, the address of the publisher and the printer, the copyright line, and, finally, the first page of *Battered Husbands* and what had become, during the last rewriting, its opening sentence:

Even in sexual intercourse it is the man who does the work.

He smiled happily at his provocative introduction which looked so much better in ten-point type than it had done on a typescript that had been hammered through a very old ribbon. What he had written now seemed truer, less refutable. Its message came at you much harder. He put the proof copy on his desk, contemplating with pleasure the hours he would soon spend reading it, and turned to another bulky item that had been keeping it company on his mat.

This was a large, board-backed envelope from Arthur Scott which contained the royal blue dust-jacket that his book was going to wear. The big red word BATTERED had been battered just as he had promised, and the blood that dripped from it, past the word HUSBANDS, just missed staining his own name in white capital letters below. On the back was a photograph of Nick looking, he decided, deceptively macho, in a black roll-neck sweater, and wearing a much-rehearsed expression of arrogant male certainty.

On the inside of the dust-jacket, Arthur Scott had produced, after several hours of writing and re-writing, a simple but compelling blurb that would introduce the bookshop browser to Nick's pugnacious message:

> Every once in a while a book appears that changes our perception of the way we live. This original and passionate work marks such an occasion.
>
> In the wake of the Women's Movement which has monopolised

media attention since the publication of *The Female Eunuch* in 1970, Nick Bannerman asks: What about the men?

His startling and unexpected thesis is that in the 1980s it is the married man whose life is barely supportable.

Away from the home for an average of twelve hours a day to provide money for his family, and then hopelessly restricted in his social life by the demands of that family, he silently endures an existence that is filled with stress. The man who cracks and flees is cruelly cheated by our divorce settlements and faced with bills that hound him to the grave.

Nick Bannerman, a belligerently heterosexual bachelor of thirty, examines the laws, the traditions and the conventions which fence in and eventually mould today's husbands.

His image of the married man – "a butterfly nailed alive to the board, a pin in his chest, but his wings still fluttering" – leaves a disturbing picture in the reader's mind of what today's burdensome existence has done to the once-proud male.

Nick found, with a considerable feeling of relief, that reading this message improved his own opinion of his book. It seemed to lift it from the ranks of other topical books – the diet volumes, the pop psychology, the quick, superficial guides to lasting sexual satisfaction – and elevate it to the significant, even important. Delving again into the brown envelope, he found a letter from Arthur Scott.

"First, the good news. I have sold the US hardcover rights of *Battered Husbands* for a twenty-five-thousand-dollar advance, and it will come out there in November. This is tremendously good news for you because it opens up the possibility of an American paperback deal which could involve real money.

"Next, I have decided against offering paperback rights here until the book comes out. I am now so optimistic about the stir that it will create that I am certain you will be offered more money if we wait so that the paperback people can see the book's strength.

"I hope you approve of the dust-jacket. We are very pleased with it up here. The proofs should have arrived separately and we need any corrections you want to make ASAP. Everything now is urgent.

"I hope you had a good hol. Now let's get on with the work of making your book a big success."

The thought of another £15,000 or so emigrating across the North Atlantic to establish a new home in his growing bank account gave him a strange sensation. This new reality bore no relation to the reality he had always known, and he could feel a strong surge of incredulity waiting to break surface. He began to see himself as a man at a fruit-machine, the mechanism of which has fractured at exactly the right moment so that dazzling gold coins gush forth in an endless cascade, falling around his feet and finally submerging them. What he was waiting for now was the tap on the shoulder that would wake him up.

Too excited to stay still, he paced round his flat barely noticing how the dust and the fluff had accumulated during his holiday. For the first time he began to wonder whether *Battered Husbands* could be a meal ticket for life – whether he had already reached that magic milestone when it would not be necessary for him to work again. He came back to earth when he remembered Arthur Scott's command: everything was urgent now. He sat at his desk, picked up the proofs and found a pen, and began to read.

He was engrossed in his work, picking up the odd mistake, changing the occasional word, when there was a knock on the door. It was unusual. He hardly ever received a visitor.

Ben Brock, with wet hair, white shorts and a dirty yellow tee-shirt, stood on the step. His eyes looked as if he had missed a couple of nights' sleep.

"Hallo, Nick. Can I come in?"

This was the last moment that Nick wanted a visitor. He had never enjoyed work so much before.

"Of course," he said. "How are you, Ben?"

Ben walked in slowly, pushing the door shut behind him. "Are these the proofs of your book?"

"I'm just correcting them."

"How does it look?" Ben asked, leaning over the desk.

"Well," said Nick, "I like it."

"How did the holiday finish? Pym seems to have enjoyed it."

"It was wonderful. To think that I've been ignoring holidays all my life."

"I've never seen you look fitter. Mind if I sit down?"

"Please do. Want a drink?"

"Coffee."

"From the mountains of Colombia," said Nick, switching on his electric cooker. "It was a pity you had to quit early, Ben. Did everything go all right?"

"No. Everything went all wrong."

Nick stopped what he was doing for a moment and glanced at his visitor. He realised that he was in some distress.

"Why aren't you working?" he asked.

Ben ran a hand through his wet hair.

"I've been swimming," he said. "Swimming up and down the pool and thinking."

"About what?"

"My money problem."

"Is it bad?"

"It couldn't be worse."

Nick handed him a cup of coffee. He sipped it immediately and then put it on the desk.

"Reason I'm here," he said. "Some time ago you came to me and asked to borrow some money."

"Did you lend me any?" Nick asked. "I've got a terrible memory."

"No, I didn't. I hadn't got any."

"I always thought you were a millionaire."

"There was a time when I could have sold the agency for a million pounds if I stayed on as working chairman for five years. That didn't mean I had money in my pocket."

"I see."

"Unfortunately, that time has passed. I missed it. It's nearly the only mistake I've ever made. But I didn't want to work for somebody else and anyway we were on an expansion kick then and for all I knew the agency was going to be worth another million if I stuck at it. Anyway, the boot is now on the other foot, and I've come here to see whether you can lend me any money.

Quite a lot of money, actually." He picked up his coffee again, embarrassed.

"You're talking to the wrong man, Ben," Nick said.

Ben looked up at him. "I rather got the impression that you were making a fortune out of that manuscript?"

"Book money is a bit like advertising money."

"How's that?"

"It's elusive, it's intangible, it's mysterious. It's always on the way but never seems to arrive. It's blocked at a station up the line. It's all part of the magic of publishing."

"I see," said Ben, looking grim.

"I'm hoping to make money when the paperback rights are sold. At the moment I have received precisely two and a half thousand pounds. I'm owed that much again, but not yet, and I've just heard that the hardback rights have been sold in America for an advance of twenty-five thousand dollars. But it could be months before I see it."

"You can't help me then."

"I'm sorry, Ben," said Nick, worried now that Ben was about to cry. "In a year's time I may well have money coming out of my ears. You're twelve months too early."

"I'm in the shit, Nick. I could lose my home."

"It's as bad as that?"

"It's as bad as that."

"Talk to your bank manager."

"He's the man who's going to grab my home."

Nick finished the coffee he had made for himself and took the cup to the sink. It was full of unwashed plates – he had been preoccupied with the morning's post. Now he was distracted by the problems of Ben. What he wanted was to get back to his proofs.

"Why don't you go to see Simon?" he said. "He really has got a fortune doing nothing in his current account."

The bank statement that awaited Simon Venables on his return from holiday told him that he had £57,765 in the bank. Allowing for the foibles of the bank's computer, he imagined that, give or take a thousand, this was about right. For two days he struggled against his natural impulse to hoard. Money that was difficult to earn had never been easy to spend. But his need now was to impress Pym with a real display of wealth, and soon he found himself in a car showroom, sitting at the wheel of a new beige Mercedes 500 SEL.

"How much is it?" he asked the young salesman.

"They're expensive cars," said the salesman, looking at him doubtfully. "But we can arrange hire-purchase."

Venables, in old sandals and his Spanish jeans, scowled at the man. "I don't need HP, thanks," he said.

Half an hour later, he was driving it alongside Richmond Park, the surprised salesman beside him and drawing his attention to the vehicle's more irresistible points. Venables had always been bored by cars and contemptuous of anybody who discussed them outside a working garage, but now, as the smoke-stained trees fled past the electrically controlled windows of the Mercedes, he found himself listening to phrases that he could scarcely believe had meaning, and delivered by the young salesman with the compulsive fervour of an evangelist on the make. Contactless, transistorised ignition was followed by four-speed torque-converter automatic transmission. The lighting system had asymmetric halogen low beams, and the passenger compartment, he learned in a rare moment of comprehension, was a safety cell. The battery of instruments in front of him, he decided, would make lifting Concorde a doddle.

"It has air conditioning and cruise control," said the young man.

"Cruise control?"

"It takes the car along without you having to put your foot on the pedal. You set it to the speed you want."

Venables, who had eschewed luxury since boyhood, found that he liked driving this vehicle.

"What did you say it cost?" he asked.

"With extras, about twenty-eight thousand."

"Extras? It seems to have everything."

"You can have alloy wheels, leather upholstery, electric sunroof . . ."

Venables contemplated this extravagance and discovered that it didn't hurt. What was the point of having money if you hid it? Tomorrow we die. It was just the sort of purchase that would change the picture Pym had of him. His final, decisive thought was that he wasn't saying good-bye to the money – he could always sell the car and get most of it back.

He wrote a cheque for £28,142 in the showroom. His hand-writing barely wavered.

"By the time the cheque has cleared, we'll have fixed up insurance, numberplates and all that caper," said the salesman. "Can you pick it up Friday?"

He was a smartly suited young man who looked a bit of a drinker. By Friday his attitude had lurched towards the obsequious, and it was obvious to Venables that he had not really expected the cheque to be cleared.

"Everything is in order, sir," he said with a new respect in his voice.

Venables drove home, overwhelmed by a wonderful feeling of irresponsibility. He knew that this money should have been put into bricks and mortar, but the future was too uncertain for that kind of investment at the moment. Wendy, of course, would be furious at his profligacy, but her attitude to the money disqualified her from consultation.

He parked the car in the road outside his flat and stood on the pavement for some time admiring it. He had worked all his life and not been able to afford a car like that.

As he climbed the stairs to his flat, he met Ben Brock coming down.

"Ah, there you are," said Ben. "I've been ringing your bell."

"Come up. Come in," said Venables. "You haven't seen my humble abode, have you? I'm afraid it can't be compared with a mansion in the Surrey hills."

"Huh," said Ben.

Venables was shocked at the change in him. The last time they had been together, on holiday, Ben was brown and relaxed. Now his face was white, his beard was flecked with grey, his eyes were sunken. His hair needed a comb. He was still wearing the expensive suit of the advertising executive, but it looked in need of pressing.

"Do you fancy a gin?" Venables asked. It didn't look as if tea would be adequate.

"Lots of tonic," said Ben, sitting down. "How's things, Simon?"

"Getting better all the time. How's Pym?"

"Pym's all right. Greg's all right. At least, I think they are. I've been a bit wrapped up elsewhere lately." He stroked his beard and sighed. "I'm in trouble."

Venables found some ice for the gin and handed Ben the glass. "Well, I gathered that," he said. "The last time I saw you, you were dashing home to deal with some crisis in the advertising jungle."

"Quite. Some crisis. If I don't raise cash pretty damn quickly I'm sunk."

"How much cash?"

This was the moment that Venables had been waiting for – the moment when he gained instant access to Pym's pantheon of heroes. The man who saved Ben Brock Advertising. Perhaps a seat on the board would follow, maybe even a takeover bid.

Simon Venables Advertising.

"That's the point," said Ben. "I wondered whether you could help with this money you won on a horse. You are really standing between me and the precipice."

Venables sat down with his gin and then noticed that Ben's was already empty. He got up and produced a refill.

"Isn't it funny?" he said. "It's only a few months since I was trying to borrow some money off you."

"Is it?" said Ben. "I don't remember that. It's all 'on paper' money with us so I don't suppose I lent you any."

"No, you didn't."

"Well, don't hold that against me."

"I don't." He was day-dreaming about the situation after he had bought his way into Ben's firm. The benefits might not all relate to Pym. When the tide in the industry turned, perhaps he, too, would have a luxurious home in the country.

The thought made him bold enough to ask: "How much money do you need, Ben?"

Ben's expression, once the epitome of arrogant self-confidence, somehow managed to combine misery, discomfiture and despair. "What I am trying to do," he said, "is buy a month's time while I dig out some new accounts. The firm is losing fifty thousand a month, so I suppose that's what I need."

Venables sucked a lot of air through his teeth.

"Out of my league," he said.

"I thought you won about fifty thousand?" Ben asked suspiciously. "Not that I have any right to ask," he corrected himself.

Venables pulled that week's bank statement from his pocket and handed it across. Then he stood up and walked over to the window.

"If you look at that piece of paper you will see that I had fifty-seven thousand at the beginning of the week. And if you look out of this window you will see a brand-new Mercedes 500 SEL that I bought this morning. It cost twenty-eight thousand. I think that means I have about twenty-nine thousand in the bank."

Ben stood up and stared resentfully at the new car.

"A bit flash for you, Simon, isn't it?" he asked.

"I'm getting myself a new image."

"So am I – pauper," said Ben, and sat down again. He finished the gin and put the glass on the floor. "That's it then. I've had it."

Venables was uneasy now. Ben Brock seemed to be shrinking physically in front of him, and there was nothing he could do. His new-found wealth had proved to be embarrassingly inadequate. Ben tugged his beard, shook his head, stood up and headed for the door.

"Listen, Ben. Even if your firm goes bust you'll be all right, won't you? You'll come out of it with something?"

Ben stared at him distantly. "I don't know why you think that," he said. "I'm not privileged. Quite the reverse. When a plane crashes the first-class passengers not only die as well, they often die first."

The following week, to take his mind off a recurring picture of Wendy in the nude, Nick placed a new loose-leaf pad on his desk and began to agonise over the novel that he had promised Arthur Scott. He really had little idea what *Memoirs of a Streaker* was going to be about, despite some hopeful outlines he had passed along to his publisher over lunch. The novel had begun with a title, which he imagined was the reverse of other writers' methods of working. The hero would be a retired streaker, now perhaps a coach to a new generation of streakers, and the book would relate the stories of his naked dashes in many surprising places and the trouble that it brought upon himself. He could picture the completed work ("Takes a hammerlock on your emotions" – *Birmingham Bugle*) but he wasn't sure how to write it. He knew plenty of stories about streaking and would work them all into his book. There was a friend in Brighton who had stripped naked in the lavatory and then streaked for a bet through the refined atmosphere of a rather select restaurant to the horror of the diners; but their horror was matched by his when he completed the circuit to find the lavatory locked and in use. He had fled the restaurant, crossed the road and cowered waist-deep in the icy waters of the English Channel until friends, who were numb with laughter, could liberate his jeans. This would be one of the memoirs of his streaker, isolating a problem of the trade: reclaiming the clothes. He knew many stories like this but doubted whether, laid end to end, they would fill a book. He could make a few up, of course, embellish the others, and bestow upon the whole a riveting storyline that would carry the reader with a minimum of pain from the first page to the last. But would it make a book or merely an anecdotal hotchpotch? Perhaps a few profound thoughts, if any ever arrived, would lift the entire venture from farce to philosophy, with the intrepid hero mulling over, between streaks, some of the serious issues that arose through merely being alive. He stared at the empty page and was engulfed by a huge depression.

Where were the words going to come from?

Last night he had endured a vivid dream about somebody opening a shop that provided death on demand for the terminally ill, the incompetent suicides and the people who couldn't get hold of the Exit pamphlet which described a swift and painless route to the next world, if there was a next world. You paid the shop £10 and you made an appointment for when you wanted to go. They were very kind to you, organised your will and other associated legal problems, and gave you a cup of tea that sent you to sleep. It was all over quite quickly.

Now, puzzled by his novel, he wondered whether to scrap or postpone it, and turn the dream into a book. He could call it *The Dead-End Shop*. There had been a lot of death in the newspapers lately, and perhaps that is what had provoked the dream: Ingrid Bergman had died, Sir Douglas Bader had died, Princess Grace had died after a road accident. The Lebanese leader, Bashir Gemayel, had been killed by a bomb. Less celebrated people were dying by the score: 48 in a helicopter crash in Germany; 59 in a coach crash in Switzerland; and this month's record, 800 Palestinians had been massacred by Lebanese Phalangist forces in the refugee camps of Sabra and Chatilla outside Beirut.

The subject seemed immediately to be too depressing to handle, and he wondered instead whether he should write a thriller. As usual, he had a title ready for that, too: *Corpses Don't Cough*.

Stalled by indecision, and somewhat in anticipation of events, he began to draw up a list of the records he would require when the invitation arrived from the BBC to appear on Desert Island Discs: *Cavatina* by John Williams, *Black Sheep Boy* by Tim Hardin, Elgar's *Chanson de Matin*. There would have to be a Beatles song to remind himself of what it had been like when the world was young. He chose *Norwegian Wood*.

His attention wandered to the view from his window. Once again, Mrs Vaughan was preserving her figure with a few unhurried lengths of her pool. He tore his gaze from the spectacle with reluctance – the self-employed had to concentrate. For a moment he could almost envy that vast majority who could enjoy any distraction, or even do nothing at all, confident that they would be paid as usual at the end of the month.

The trick now was to get words on paper – any words. It could develop a momentum. He found himself writing the letters of the alphabet down the side of the paper, and against the line that carried A he wrote: Assaulting an antelope. Greatly encouraged, he wrote "Buggering a barn owl" on the next line. Could he, while he was waiting as it were, complete an alphabet of bestiality? Copulating with a camel came easily, and so did deflowering a dormouse, and then the words flowed: enticing an elephant, feeling a ferret, galvanising a gorilla, humping a hippo, interfering with an iguana. He paused to read this sudden outburst of words, and then hurried on. Jerking off a jackal, kissing a kestrel, licking a llama.

Turning to the window for inspiration, he saw Mrs Vaughan easing her bottom on to the pool's rim and, looking up, she saw him watching. She beckoned him to come down.

He didn't hesitate. Trying to write a book seemed to be a horrifying prospect now that he really was a writer. If you weren't a writer, of course, there was nothing to it. He grabbed his bathing costume and left the flat.

"Come on in, the water's freezing," Mrs Vaughan said, when he reached the pool.

Nick changed in a small shed at the edge of the lawn that

contained sunchairs, a lilo, numerous tennis rackets and a bag of golf clubs. When he came out, Mrs Vaughan was back in the water, swimming doggedly from one end to the other as if she had a daily target that must be met. Nick dived straight in and gasped: this wasn't Spain.

"I hope I haven't tempted you away from your work," Mrs Vaughan said when she reached his end of the pool. "How is the writing going?"

"It seems to have stopped." His brain was still wrestling with his uncompleted alphabet. Massaging a marmoset, he thought. Nookie with a nanny goat.

"How can somebody who leads such a monastic existence be qualified to write a book about women?" she asked. She pulled herself out of the water again and sat on the edge to look down on him.

"What makes you think I lead a monastic existence?" he asked.

"If you've had any women in our flat you've been damned furtive about it. The only visitor I've ever seen is Mr Brock."

He nodded sadly. "They haven't exactly been queueing up at the gate, have they?"

"I don't know why. I think you're terribly attractive."

Nick looked up at her damp face. She was smiling down at him. Her blonde hair had been pinned up so that she had swum her quota without getting it wet. As he watched, she unpinned it and let it fall, an implicitly sexual gesture that momentarily hypnotised him. The phrase "poking a parrot" arrived at the centre of his mind.

"I have met some women," he told her, "in answer to your question."

"Well, you ought to do more than meet them, Nick. How old are you?"

"Thirty." Sodomising a sturgeon, he thought. Titillating a tortoise.

"Dearie me," said Mrs Vaughan. "You'll soon be past it."

Nick had lost his place in the alphabet. Yielding to a yak. Ravishing a rhinoceros. Wasn't there an animal called a vakari?

"How is Mr Vaughan?" he asked.

"He *is* past it. When my daughter had a baby girl it seemed to kill his desire stone dead."

Nick didn't know that Mrs Vaughan had a daughter, let alone that her daughter had a daughter.

Grope a granny, he thought.

THIRTEEN

BEN BROCK had always imagined that the worst thing that could happen to a human being was to be nailed down in a coffin, but the things which happened to him now made that fate seem like a mild setback.

The first indication that his fight to save the agency was lost came when the bank called in his financial director, Cliff, and demanded weekly accounts and a cash-flow forecast. The answers that Cliff produced seemed to frighten the bank. The manager phoned Ben.

"The game's up, I'm afraid, Mr Brock," he said.

"I've been trying to buy time," Ben replied, with an attempt at his old confidence.

"It's run out," said the bank manager. "We can sustain you no longer."

Ben was now plunged into a nightmare sequence of events over which he had no control. The bank obtained a creditors' winding-up order on Ben Brock Advertising, and hired an accountant to act as Receiver and collect all debts owed to the agency. A bailiff arrived in the Chelsea offices to stop any further flow of funds. The chequebooks went, documents were removed from the safe – even the petty-cash tin vanished.

When the cleaning lady came in for her money, Ben paid her from his own wallet.

"I'm sure everything will be all right in the end," she said.

"Why is it that the less education you have, the more optimistic you are?" Ben asked Cliff when she had gone. But Cliff was too worried about his own future to frame a reply. He was bitterly regretting the surge of ambition that had persuaded him to abandon the safety of the City for a glittering salary in the uncertain world of advertising.

"We should have diversified," he said, staring blankly out into the street.

"I tried to get a couple of cosmetic accounts, but it wasn't any good," Ben told him. "They just said we had no track record where cosmetics were concerned. Anyway, I was never a belt-and-braces man."

"What are you going to do?"

"I think I'll start a new venture in darkest Soho. Topless Handjobs – something like that. Orgasms faked while you wait."

"Christ!" Cliff said, shaking his head. "You can still joke now? You're losing everything, Ben, you realise that? The bank has the deeds of your house. The cars will have to go. They'll even be selling this furniture."

Ben didn't say anything. He had been living on the edge of the precipice for so long that it was almost a relief to topple over. At the same time, what was happening to him was too terrible to seem real. He hardly listened as Cliff talked on about the immediate future: "If the Receiver becomes the Official Receiver, he will act as banker for our creditors. He'll pay the Inland Revenue first, and the corporation tax. Staff salaries aren't top of the list. They'll auction everything in these offices to raise money and they'll pay what they can to everybody except you. Ben, you're bankrupt."

The ugly word hung in the air between them as neither spoke. Ben's vision now was of ending up with his wife and son in a council hostel. His plan had always been to send money off at favourable moments to a secret account in the Isle of Man, or, maybe, Switzerland, but the spare cash had always been needed to sweeten somebody, and there had never been any hurry to put this plan for his financial future into action. There were a few thousand pounds in a building society that had been intended for Greg. Presumably he would now have to reclaim that. It would keep them going for a couple of months.

A dreadful silence had fallen over the other offices. No typewriters typed. No phones rang. The sound of human voices tossing ideas round a room had been quelled. For a while none of the staff came in to see Ben. They sat at their desks considering their own private disasters. In an era of high unemployment it was no great surprise to find that you had lost your job, but new jobs with these salaries were not easy to find, and cruelly difficult to get. After a time one or two senior members of the staff came in to shake Ben's hand and express their sympathy, but he could sense more than a tinge of resentment behind their polite words:

passengers don't normally thank the driver who crashes their coach.

It was well into the afternoon before he fully realised that he was no longer running his own firm. The Receiver, a tall and appropriately corpse-like man in his late fifties, told him he needed to use Ben's desk.

"I might as well go home," Ben said.

"Leave the car and keys," said the Receiver.

The loss of the Bentley was a fresh blow and the Aston Martin, highly polished and little used in his garage, would have to go too.

He walked out of the building suddenly, and crossed the road to a wine bar, but found that he felt too sick to drink. He wandered round aimlessly for some time, unable to focus his thoughts. He tried to cheer himself with the idea that what he had done once, he could do twice, but then decided that this wasn't true. What a man had done twice he could probably do three times, but if he had only done it once there was no guarantee that he could repeat it.

He caught a train to the country like any other commuter, and read the evening newspaper on the way. As usual, all the news was depressing, but the darkest moment still awaited him. For when he had walked the mile home from the station, a new experience for him, he discovered that a For Sale sign had sprouted from the laurel and rhododendron hedge at the front of his lovely house.

Wendy Venables' anger at the discovery that her husband had spent £28,000 on one motor car was defused somewhat by the suspicion that she might be pregnant.

By the middle of September she was three weeks late. Her stomach was bloated and her breasts were sore. She stopped wearing jeans and belts and found instead some dresses, skirts and loose tops. She had abandoned the Pill on marriage, in the hope of starting a family, but the sexual activity which had followed that long-forgotten ceremony in the spring would have made it superfluous anyway. The prospect of a baby now horrified her, particularly the difficulty of persuading Simon that he was the father. Back here in Wimbledon – cutting sandwiches at Morsels, or pursuing her latest cause at home (ironically helping to raise money for the National Society for the Prevention of Cruelty to Children) – she could still blush with shame at the nude frolics of the previous month. She blamed the sun, she blamed cheap champagne, she blamed her husband's lack of interest; she could not blame herself. She pictured Nick occasionally, always aroused and with no clothes on, and during one quiet spell in the sandwich bar had nearly phoned him for fun; but this was Wimbledon, not Spain, and at the last moment her instinct that it would be a girlish blunder persuaded her to replace the receiver. She would see him soon, anyway. He had promised a party when his book came out in October. Perhaps she would have a surprise for him.

She was sitting at the table in her flat drafting an appeal. "In the last hundred years nine million children have been helped by the NSPCC. Even today 40,000 need our help every year. We need your help every day. Telephone calls cost . . ."

Simon came in, whistling cheerfully. The ownership of a Mercedes had conferred a certain cockiness on to what had once been a self-effacing personality. Either that or he was seeing Pym.

"Do you fancy a ride in my limo, Mrs Venables?" he asked. "We could eat out." After her criticism of the car's arrival she was surprised to be asked, but today she was grateful: difficult days lay ahead.

They cruised north over Putney Bridge to Fulham. The styling of the seats and the smell of the new upholstery were a taste of luxury after her miles in the van.

"What do you think of it?" he asked.

"It's very nice, but is it you?"

"Why shouldn't it be me?" he asked irritably. "If I can afford it? What is this boring, pedestrian image people are trying to saddle me with? I'm thinking of wearing leather jackets and dyeing my hair."

"I don't think Pym would like that."

"Pym? What's Pym got to do with it?"

"I don't know." She was irritable herself, and easily upset. It went with her condition – whatever her condition was. But she was determined now to keep a grip on her mood, and she cursed herself for bringing up Pym. It could sour the evening, and her plan for the evening had suddenly become clear. It was not too late to inveigle her husband into a sexual act which would confuse the subject of paternity if a baby was on the way. The only problem was inveigling her husband into a sexual act.

They found themselves soon afterwards in a dimly lit bistro north of the river that offered Scotch salmon steaks, with bacon and herbs, hollandaise sauce and salad elona. They started with asparagus. The clientele, young, loud, confident and loaded, made Wendy think about money, and when the food arrived she decided to raise the subject of her husband's bank account.

"What are we going to do with it?" she asked.

"We?" said Venables. "I thought you wouldn't dirty your hands with gambling money?"

"What's thine's mine," said Wendy. "You can't leave thirty thousand in your current account. You could be making more than fifty pounds a week in interest."

"It can stay there while I decide," he said. "There's plenty of time."

"What about Morsels Two?"

The possibility of extending the sandwich-bar empire never occurred to Venables now. If the money wasn't enough to save Ben Brock Advertising, it was still sufficient to use as bait to prise Pym from a bankrupt husband. "It's more than we need for that," he said. "I may have a bigger idea."

"Well, don't leave it too long. I could double it in three years."

Venables picked up the wine that had arrived belatedly and filled their glasses. "I'm sure you could, Wendy. You're a clever girl."

She drank the wine and looked at him over the rim of the glass. It was time to push the conversation in a certain direction. "I have a body, too, you know," she said.

Venables started. "What's that supposed to mean?"

"It means what's happened to our sex life?"

Venables picked up his own wine. "Is it that bad?"

"Bad? It's non-existent. You know that."

He knew that. It had been a silly question, but her own had caught him off-balance. "I haven't felt like it lately," he said weakly. He could see Pym's brown body in the sun and then, with an effort, his wife's worried face between the bottle of wine and the *grissini* that stood, like a flower arrangement, between them. "The job loss emasculated me," he suggested.

Wendy recoiled at the dishonesty of this. "The honeymoon was

226

an orgy, of course," she said. She wanted to bring up Pym again – that was where this conversation naturally led – but it wasn't a rift that she was trying to create.

The subject was dropped as Venables picked up the menu.

"Do you fancy some spotted dick?" he asked.

"Does it have to be spotted?" she asked sadly.

Ben found his wife holding back tears. She sat on one of the patio's bright, white seats looking at the lawn which she had recently adorned with croquet hoops, while Greg circled her awkwardly on a new three-wheeler.

"They're going to sell the house, Ben," she said. "Can they do that?"

Ben looked at his wife, and his son and heir, and then slumped in one of the comfortably cushioned chairs that he used for early-evening drinking in the summer.

"We're broke, Pym. It's all over," he said. Disbelief, depression and anger, which had followed one another over the last few hours, were now replaced by a mind-numbing impotence. "They can do whatever they like. The agency has closed."

"We're bankrupt?" She asked the question, but she couldn't look at him. Greg stopped his circuits of his mother, fascinated by a word he had not heard before. "Bankrupt!" he shouted.

"Yes," said Ben.

One tear broke through now and rolled down Pym's cheek. "Does that mean we have no money?"

"We have a little. We'll have to rent a flat."

"I love this place," she said, and began to cry properly. "They can't do it to us."

"They can," said Ben. "They can do anything."

At this, Pym plucked her son from his tricycle and held him protectively in her lap. "Poor Greg," she said. "Poor Greg."

"He's got more money than either of us," said Ben, "in the building society. In fact, he's going to lend it to us."

"How long have we got left here?"

"Until they sell the house. They could have thrown us out now and changed the locks but they're being gentlemanly about it."

She put Greg back on his bike. "Do you want any supper?"

"I couldn't eat. But I could drink. Let's hit the champagne."

"Yes, let's." She went inside and fetched a bottle. As she was pouring it, Nick came round the side of the house clutching a brown parcel.

"I thought I'd find you here, champagne flowing," he said. "How are we all? Hallo, Greg."

"I'll get another glass. Sit down, Nick."

"You've brought us a present," said Ben. "How kind."

"I have," said Nick. "It's in this parcel."

"I guessed that's where it was," said Ben.

Pym gave Nick a glass of champagne and while he took a sip she unwrapped the parcel and then held up a copy of *Battered Husbands*, its bright-blue dust-jacket shining in the evening sun.

"They can't wrap the chips in that," said Nick. "It's a signed first edition. I should put it in the safe."

"It looks wonderful," said Pym. "I like the dripping blood effect."

"Who is the handsome chap on the back?" asked Ben, taking the book.

"It's a pictorial representation of me," replied Nick. "A photographer took it with one of those camera things."

"I like the first sentence," said Ben. "Does the rest hold up?"

"It's a beautiful book, Nick. Thank you very much," said Pym. "Mind you, I don't know that I am going to care for its message. When is it published?"

"October eleventh. Copies are now being rushed to the critics."

Ben flipped through the book. "When's the launching party?"

"That's what I came to see you about. You can imagine, my flat's on the small side for a literary knees-up."

"I catch your drift," said Ben, "but I can't help."

"Oh," said Nick.

"Did you miss the For Sale sign?" Pym asked.

"What For Sale sign?" asked Nick.

"The one by our gate," Ben told him. "We're broke, Nick. The agency has folded. The bank is selling the house. By the time you hold your party, we could be living in a tent."

"Jesus," said Nick. "I'm sorry."

"I'm fairly disconcerted myself," said Ben. "You have to put a brave face on life's little reverses."

"We've lost everything, Nick," Pym said. "Do you want some more champagne?"

They all laughed at the incongruity of it, but it was the champagne that helped the laughter.

"Do they get everything in the house as well?" Nick asked. "You have a cellar of champagne, haven't you?"

"They've got no what's-it on that," said Ben. "What's the word? You're the writer."

"Lien."

"That's it. They've got no lien on the things in the house unless they can prove they were bought with company money for invest-ment and resale. And they can't."

"Greg can keep his teddy bear," said Pym.

Greg, sitting on the patio now and driving an imaginary car with a steering wheel so large that he could barely reach its rim, smiled at the news. "Take your face away," he said to Nick.

Nick poured himself some more champagne and picked up the book which lay on the table. It had only arrived that afternoon – a parcel of six free copies – and the sight of it thrilled him. It was fatter than he had expected and looked solid and important. The cover had worked beautifully and would surely leap out from rival volumes in the bookshops.

He was in a mood to celebrate, but he had gate-crashed a wake.

"What are you going to do?" he asked.

"Look for a flat," Ben said grimly. "What does it cost to store furniture?"

"Perhaps they won't be able to sell the house?" Nick sug-gested.

"Oh, they'll sell it. It'll be the biggest bargain on the market. They'll sell it below value just to get some money back."

"That would be very silly," said Pym, frowning. "These houses are going up by a thousand a month. They should hang on to it as an investment, and let us carry on living here."

"I'm afraid banks don't think like that. They can lend billions to South America without hope of return, but me they can squeeze."

He emptied the champagne bottle into his glass, but it didn't seem to improve his mood.

"Cheer up," said Nick. "It's easy to make money. You proved it."

"I also proved it's a damned sight easier to lose it."

*

The bank's metropolitan view of the world led it to put the house into the hands of a Kensington estate agent whose customers sought splendid homes in the capital, and not thirty miles away among the trees. The For Sale sign at the gate, in a private drive used only by those who already lived there, was another mistake. The house remained unsold.

Ben rang Nick. "We're not out yet. You can have the party here. If you pay me for the champagne, we can use mine."

"If I pay Pym will she do some food?"

"In our situation, she'll do anything for money. How many are coming?"

"About thirty. I sent Rupert Puckle a book, and he is so curious about it, and about your future, that he is flying over specially. Can you put him up?"

"Will he pay? What sort of evening is it going to be?"

"It's a literary soirée, Ben. Indistinguishable from any other piss-up you've attended."

The Saturday before publication was one of the last fine evenings of the summer. The guests arrived like moths at a light and spilled over Ben's vast patio on to a lawn that was no longer the immaculate green turf it had once been. Firing his gardener was Ben's first economy, particularly as the house was no longer his.

Johnny Fix-It arrived in red corduroy trousers and an iridescent shirt to murmur a few sympathetic expletives at the collapse of Ben's firm. In a new mood of sombre realism, he revealed that the depredations of the Thatcher government had reached him, too, putting back his departure to the fleshpots of Banus. "It's only when you've got a Labour government that you can make any money," he moaned.

Arthur Scott appeared in the company of a wild-eyed poet from Trincomalee, in the north of Sri Lanka, who now lived in Hampstead producing small volumes of esoteric verse, praised by the critics for its "prestidigitation", and published by Arthur Scott to balance his list against its bawdier fictions. The publisher himself, in a light-grey suit and pink shirt, was in buoyant mood.

"It's looking good, Nick," he said, grabbing his arm. "It's looking good. I don't want to build up your hopes, but it's looking good."

"What are you talking about, Arthur?" Nick asked. "In what

way is it looking good?"

"Newspapers ring up and ask for your photograph. It looks like they're planning big write-ups. The *Sunday Times* may want to take their own picture of you. They're deciding on Monday whether to buy an excerpt. I've had the BBC on the phone about six times. I tell you, this book is going to explode on the public!"

Nick shivered. "Are you sure?"

"I'll say this much," said Arthur Scott. "It's looking good. What did you think of the finished book, by the way?"

"It looked good," Nick said evenly.

"One of our better efforts. You stay by your phone next week, Nick. Promoting a book is a full-time job."

Rupert Puckle, with a tan that made the poet look pale, arrived from Heathrow by taxi in a thick Fair Isle sweater against the British climate, and drifted among the guests in search of a lady he could take back to his island exile. "I'm getting lonely, old boy," he told Nick. "I want a woman to keep me warm this winter."

"You haven't read my book, Rupert," Nick said.

"I have. I loved it. I want to be battered. You associate with the opposite sex yourself, I noticed."

"Noticed?"

"I watched you and Wendy by my pool. Tremendous performance, I thought."

"Blimey," said Nick, feeling uncomfortable.

"My lips are sealed."

"Thank God for that."

"Why? Has He promised to keep His trap shut, too?" A wink followed this enquiry, and Nick felt a certain relief. "The one I fancy is Pym. What a woman!"

Nick hurried off to greet the other guests. He had gone to parties for years before he realised that he hated them – he had gone to them with an optimism that owed nothing to experience. But tonight's was different. It was his party, although, he now saw, there were guests he had never met. Friends of Ben's had drifted in, too.

He saw a Mercedes turn into the drive and cruise into the car park. Wendy got out. He went over to meet her.

"It's my husband's new toy," she said. "Hallo, Mr Bannerman."

"Hallo, Nick," said Venables. "Loved your book."

The previous week he had sent them a signed copy along with an invitation to the party.

"He read every word," said Wendy. "It's changed his life."

"And you?" asked Nick. "Have you read it?"

"No!" she said, with theatrical emphasis. "I don't want it to spoil our friendship."

He laughed to conceal his disappointment; he had wanted her to like this book. She was wearing a loose rubiginous frock that matched the autumn leaves. She looked pale.

"I'll read it one day, Nick," she said. "At the moment I don't want to find out how hostile you are to my sex."

They walked round to the patio where bottles of champagne stood in rows of ice-buckets.

"In India women are regarded as unproductive and uneconomic," he told her. "I don't go that far."

She looked round the garden at the guests. "I'm glad, Nick," she said. "Would you mind if I only drank orange juice?"

Rupert Puckle came over with Ben. "Hallo, Wendy, darling," he said. Ben kissed her cheek.

They were joined by Venables and Pym. "I've been showing your wife my new motor, Ben," he said. "She was most impressed."

"Don't confuse her with wealth," said Ben. "I'm about to buy her a bicycle."

"It's funny seeing you lot with your clothes on," said Rupert Puckle. "The nudists dressed. It doesn't seem right, somehow."

"I wish you wouldn't mention it," Wendy said. "I find the whole memory very embarrassing."

"You shouldn't," said Rupert. "You've got a lovely bum. I know about bums. How many times have I followed the perfect bottom, only to discover on overtaking its owner that she had buck teeth and the beginnings of a moustache!"

Nick pulled himself away from this conversation, embarrassed himself now that he knew Rupert had been watching. He had the duties of a host to perform.

A couple of men he had invited from the Valiant Sailor were arguing about how you weigh your own head. "If you lie on the ground with your shoulders on the floor and use the scales as a pillow . . ." said one. A girl, who seemed to be all eyes and legs, came up and asked him: "Are you a filter or a drain?" Ben's speakers in the trees relayed an album from Fleetwood Mac.

Nick found himself alongside the poet, deserted by Arthur Scott, who revealed a nasty tendency after a few drinks to talk about things like the "existential dilemma". One of his arms was much fatter than the other. Had he been ill or was he a tennis champion?

"Tell me about your poems," Nick said politely.

"They are romantic," the poet replied earnestly. "I'm not apologetic. It is only in the future that any age receives its name, and our poetry is still unnamed. But if human rights and romanticism come hand in hand then these poems of mine can be a flag. Why are we surrounded by neurotic, sex-repressed people who carry their lives like a millstone?"

He looked up at Nick with eyes that seemed to burn straight through him.

"I don't know," said Nick. He was beginning to see why Arthur Scott had escaped.

"Exactly," said the poet. "I am Blake. I am Whitman. I am Williams. I'm a sensual man. I have spent nights on the mountainside with satyrs and nymphs. Women are the muse. All poems come through them." In an astonishing juxtaposition, he rounded off this proclamation by picking his nose.

"When you get to the bridge give me a wave," Nick told him.

Pym had produced a sumptuous buffet on the patio and guests were now collecting cutlery and filling plates. With Venables trailing Pym, Nick looked round for Wendy. She was sitting on the grass eating smoked salmon.

"I don't think I can take any more of this love and affection," she said. "Look at him."

"Look at who?"

"Simon. He's besotted. I don't know what you wrote in your book but he's become very stroppy."

"How?"

"He won't do the washing-up any more."

"Are you sure he read the book?" Nick asked. "He didn't just skim through it?"

"I told you. Every word. You're his hero now. Do you think it's going to get big coverage in the papers?"

"It's beginning to look like it. How are you Wendy, anyway? And why aren't you drinking champagne?"

233

"I may be pregnant. I'm waiting now for the result of tests."

Nick looked at her quickly, but her cool profile was bent in concentration towards the slicing of her salmon, and the news was left to stand on its own. A wave of apprehension swept over Nick.

"Does Simon know?" he asked.

"No."

"Is he the father?"

"No."

"But you will convince him that he is?" Nick suggested.

Wendy put down her knife and fork and looked at Nick. "If the baby has blue eyes and a penis that keeps hitting the nurse in the face I doubt that even Simon will be deceived about paternity," she said.

Nick looked round nervously. "Don't talk so loudly," he said. There were guests everywhere. One of the men from the Valiant Sailor had grabbed a passing girl a few feet away.

"You're a female," he said. "I know. I've met lots of human beings." He kissed her on the mouth as she struggled to escape.

Wendy said: "He'll have to know eventually. A pregnant wife isn't something he could miss."

"Ring me when you know," Nick said. "We must talk."

They were interrupted by the girl who had escaped from the clutches of her admirer. "He tried to put his tongue in my mouth," she told Nick.

"You're lucky."

"Lucky?"

"That it was only his tongue he tried to put in your mouth."

"That it was only your mouth he was trying to put something in," said Wendy. The girl wiped her lips with the back of her hand and found her glass of champagne, standing precariously on a square handbag on the grass. "Right," she said.

Nick turned back to Wendy, but another distraction loomed.

"Congratulations," said Johnny Fix-It. "It looks as if you will get on television again under your own steam."

"I hope so," said Nick.

"If you need an accountant give me a bell. A voice from a burning bush tells me you could soon be into a heavy tax situation."

"Which voice was that?"

"I've been talking to your publisher. He's very optimistic on your behalf."

"You can fix tax problems, can you?"

"Fix them? I can get you a tax rebate when you haven't paid any tax."

A splash told that somebody had chosen to use the pool. It wasn't a warm enough evening for swimming, but alcohol had made the idea attractive for one guest – a girl, evidently, from her excited shrieks that were amplified by the water.

At the other end of the garden, where the darkening October evening had turned Ben's brightly lit patio into a stage, Venables was having a bad time. He had finally got money, he had taken off his moustache, he was driving a car that few could afford, he was a new man. But the world failed to recognise him as such. Pym's attitude to him had not been altered by his new wealth despite her own financial disaster. His car failed to impress her: she was used to Bentleys and Aston Martins. In his frustration he drank steadily.

"Do you want money?" he had asked Pym, during a stroll round the garden. "Anything? I'd like to help."

"If you want to lend Ben money you should talk to him," Pym replied sweetly.

This answer, he thought, was as welcome as a chastity belt to a nymphomaniac. "I don't want to lend him money. I want to lend you money."

"But I don't have money. Ben has the money."

"Not at the moment, he doesn't. You're broke, Pym. Money would be handy." He gulped champagne as if it were beer.

"I don't touch money, Simon. I leave all that to Ben."

"That's not the way Nick tells it in his book."

"Well, we're an old-fashioned couple. You know what they say – love is a woman's prison."

Venables hurled more champagne down his throat. He didn't like the way this conversation was going. "What's that supposed to mean?"

"I am my husband's woman."

"The way he treats you, you shouldn't be," Venables said angrily.

Pym started to collect the used plates that were lying around the lawn. "Listen, Simon. Ben has just gone bankrupt. It would be a right cow who deserted him now. What sort of woman do you think I am?"

A man appeared behind her. It was Rupert Puckle who wrapped his arms round her waist.

"I think you're a very sensual woman," he said.

Venables stumbled off furiously, in search of the Brocks' luxurious downstairs loo where, booby-trapped unknowingly by a recalcitrant pubic hair, he urinated blissfully down his right trouser-leg. Waiting in mounting frustration for the cloth to dry, he saw a packet of cigarettes left with matches on the windowsill. He took one out and lit it immediately. It tasted wonderful.

Nick, mingling dutifully with the guests, was approached now by a middle-aged lady, a neighbour of Ben's, who had heard that he had written a book. "My husband doesn't like me to read books," she said. "He thinks it will give me ideas. I turned round and said to him, 'Ideas are what we need at the moment.'"

Nick was always surprised at how talkative people were, considering how few of them had anything to say that was worth hearing.

"'We don't have to get our ideas from a bunch of Commie writers,' he said. 'What do they know?' I turned round and said to him, 'What do *you* know?' That shut him up."

This wasn't small talk: it was microscopic. Even a racehorse was disqualified for boring.

"Tell me," said Nick, "why are you always facing the wrong way for your conversations?"

"You tell me something," said the lady who never listened, "why has Ben got a For Sale sign outside? That's what everybody in the road wants to know."

"I didn't notice it," Nick told her.

An unseen signal suddenly produced a hush among those people nearest the patio, and the bearded figure of Ben Brock appeared in the middle of the crowd clutching a copy of *Battered Husbands*. Guests who had been sitting or standing on the lawn wandered towards him.

"I want you all to fill your glasses," said Ben. "We're going to drink a toast."

More buckets containing bottles of champagne were produced and glasses were filled.

"You haven't heard of this book yet, but next week you will," Ben shouted. "It is written by your host tonight, Nick Bannerman, and I want you all to drink to its success."

"Hear, hear," said Arthur Scott, and even people who had no idea that a new book had been the *raison d'être* of tonight's revelry, raised their glasses to the bright-blue volume in Ben's hand.

FOURTEEN

THE RECEPTION that awaited *Battered Husbands* was even more extraordinary than Arthur Scott had predicted or Nick Bannerman had hoped.

The *Sunday Times* paid £3000 to extract the meat and filled the front of their Review section with selected pearls that were set around a picture of Nick, taken in bathing trunks on a sunbed beside Mrs Vaughan's pool, and headed "The Swimmer and the Sex War". The following week they received just over 2000 letters which broke six to four in Nick's favour, and ten proposals of marriage which the newspaper forwarded, they said, "with some apprehension".

Then the critics moved in.

The Times sent the book to an Oxford don and part-time book reviewer who, under a characteristically mysterious headline, "Mutiny in the Potting Shed", examined the sociological implications of a soaring divorce rate, the growth in single-parent families, and the newly won legal rights of the live-in lover, all of which led him to ponder whether, in the twenty-first century, marriage would have ceased to exist as a practical possibility for an ambitious man. The *Daily Telegraph* reviewed the book on its leader page, using the publication to argue that the balance in society was, indeed, now weighted against the married, working man. It called for an "urgent look at the ancient laws which load so much on the fragile shoulders of a mere male".

The *Observer* gave the book to a leading feminist who chewed it up and spat it out in 800 angry words that seared the page: "After a struggle that has lasted half a millennium and advanced the cause of women by no more than a centimetre or two, men have hit back with a lanky and lugubrious writer called Nick Bannerman who, on the evidence of this untidy mess, wouldn't know a woman from a gerbil, or a gerbil from a gerund."

The *Daily Mirror*, under a white-on-black headline that said "Bannerman carries the banner for men", analysed the financial settlements from six recent divorces, and concluded that Nick's book should be required reading for every member of the Cabinet. The *Daily Mail* ran an editorial headed "Daily Male?" which wondered nervously whether Britain's overworked husbands were too tired to do other than compromise in domestic squabbles, and thus become skivvies in the home.

The *Sun* launched a search for Britain's "most hen-pecked hubby" and, to Arthur Scott's delight, offered copies of the book for the hundred best readers' letters.

The *Spectator* gave it a column of qualified praise under the one-word headline "Rumblings", and concluded drily: "Mr Bannerman, apparently, is a bachelor and on this showing likely to remain so." *Mayfair* gave it a paean of praise under the headline "Ball-kickers kicked", and *She* made a point of announcing that the book did not deserve the favour of review, much less to be bought. *Private Eye* ran a spoof feature, "Women Are Awful, by Nick Wankerman", but the printing was so poor that Nick couldn't read it.

One of the new, trendy women's magazines sent to interview him a butch young girl with, it seemed to him, the sad eyes of a trainee lesbian. Her scathing indictment of his subversive ideas appeared under the headline "The Pig in the Attic", a reference to his alleged male chauvinism and the flat over the garage in which he lived. "Bannerman, predictably, lives alone in a small, grubby flat where his evident sexual frustrations are channelled into a quiet fury at a female sex he neither knows nor understands," she wrote.

While Nick snipped the cuttings out and pasted them, chuckling, into a new scrapbook, the publicity people at Arthur Scott's sifted through the acres of opinion and discovered enough fulsome bouquets to make *Battered Husbands* sound like the publishing event of the decade. After two weeks, the book was in its third printing, having ousted the twenty-ninth edition of the *Guinness Book of Records* from the number one spot in the non-fiction bestseller list. Corgi and Penguin engaged in a bitter struggle for the paperback rights, a battle which Penguin won with a £50,000 advance. The £50,000 became £25,000 now and the other half on publication in one year's time, and the £25,000 became £15,000 when Arthur Scott had deducted his forty per cent of paperback money.

"If I had a job, I'd give it up," said Nick.

One morning he rose early to reach Broadcasting House before the rush of commuters filled the trains. He was author of the week on *Midweek* where Libby Purves asked him if he had ever met any women. He called her "women's Libby" and an acrimonious wrangle ensued which wasn't helped by another guest on the radio chat show, a mauve-topped gender-bender who suggested, ironically, that he was obviously in thrall to some despicable sexual perversion.

Arthur Scott, listening uneasily in his Hampstead hideaway, rang directly the programme had finished to tell him that it was all "tremendous publicity" and he would order a fourth printing that day.

"When are you going to get me on television?" Nick asked.

"They all want you. It's just a question of picking the right programme."

"Hurry up," said Nick. "I want to be famous."

"You're famous already, Nick. We've sold the book now to fifteen countries. I did very well for you at the Frankfurt Book Fair. You'll be getting reviews you can't read from *Corriere Della Sera*, *Die Welt*, *France-Soir*, *Le Monde*, *Algemeen Dagblad*, *De Telegraaf* and *Journal de Genève*."

"They'll blast it," said Nick. "Europeans think all Englishmen are queer anyway."

"They're paying good money," Arthur Scott told him. "There's another twenty thousand pounds in foreign advances coming your way. You'd better get yourself a good accountant. In the meantime, go and have a look at Foyles' window."

Nick left Broadcasting House with a growing feeling that he had moved in the last week into a dream world where anything could happen, but nothing was real. He wandered along Oxford Street towards Centre Point, and turned into the Charing Cross Road. He half expected the crowds to applaud as he went by. What he did not expect was the sight which met him when he reached the country's biggest bookshop. The whole of one of Foyles' windows was devoted to a huge picture of his face, surrounded by dozens of copies of his book. THE NEW SENSATION said a banner stuck to the inside of the window. At the bottom, a matching banner said THE MEN HIT BACK! – an exultant message only slightly marred by some external graffiti which declared firmly: BOLLOCKS TO THE WOOFTA.

His mind was a ferment of conflicting ideas, demanding ac-clamation and privacy at the same time. Privacy won and he fled from the scene before other window-gazers noticed the re-semblance between the bellicose author in the window and the shy man standing alone on the pavement.

He caught a train to the country and hid behind his newspaper.

Two days later the phone rang.

"Is that the belligerently heterosexual Nick Bannerman?" a man asked.

"It's me, love." He recognised Venables' voice.

"Simon here. Can I come and see you?"

"Of course."

"This afternoon?"

"I'll be just here."

He had taken to staying in, feeling the need to make a few mental adjustments, although to what he wasn't quite sure. He cleaned the flat as it had never been cleaned before, and tidied up the area where he wrote. He read several books that had been waiting unread for months, and he constructed a wall chart from graph paper to track the progress of his bank account – an exercise which was rendered useless almost immediately as the soaring curve of his wealth, fuelled by schillings and francs and guilders and kroner, flew off the top of the sheet.

Unworried by bills, he had delighted his newsagent by ordering five papers a day. His book had become a topic of the moment and, following the reviews, a bitter correspondence was going on in both *The Times* and the *Daily Telegraph* about the male's role and responsibility. Nick felt confirmed in his central thesis by the happy discovery that the women letter-writers who dwelt most forcefully on the financial and domestic duties of a husband managed to reveal parenthetically that they were now widows. As the instigator of this correspondence he yearned to participate, but with his views on sale in every bookshop in the country he didn't want to deflect buyers with a free synopsis.

He heard the Mercedes coughing in the drive and got up to open the door to Venables, who came in looking distinctly glum. He was wearing a white shirt with old jeans and a pair of Kickers. A new cigarette hung from his lips.

"You don't smoke," said Nick, pushing a chair towards him.

"I do now," replied Venables. He ignored the chair and studied the view of the Vaughans' swimming pool from Nick's window. "I heard you on my car radio the other morning. Very good, I thought."

"Thank you," said Nick. "What can I do for you, Simon?"

Venables moved uneasily round the room, finally coming to rest on the chair that Nick had provided. "It's about Wendy," he said. "She's expecting a baby."

Nick had become so preoccupied with his success that it had never occurred to him to link Venables' visit with Wendy's putative pregnancy.

"That's nice," he said blankly.

"I'm not sure it is," Venables said, looking straight at Nick for the first time since he had come in the room. "The thing is – have you had intercourse with her?"

Stunned by the directness of the question, Nick decided to stall. His replies could implicate Wendy.

"It depends what you mean by intercourse," he tried.

Venables' reply came back over the net so quickly that he was thrown even more off balance. "Insertion concomitant with ejaculation will do for now."

"Regardless of orifice?" Nick suggested.

Venables threw himself back in his seat impatiently. "Why do you have to make everything so complicated?"

"I'm a writer," said Nick. "Leave simplicity to the simple. You refer to a commingling of our reproductive equipment?"

Venables stared at him. "Have you fucked her?, is my question."

"Yes," said Nick. "Once." The answer jumped out before he could think of another evasion. Venables' reaction was the one he least expected.

"Right," he said, jumping up. "I'm going to have Pym." He headed for the door and turned briefly when he reached it. "You haven't heard the last of this, Nick."

Nick watched him go without replying and then got up to shut the door that had been left open. A few minutes later he dialled Morsels.

Sally, Wendy's assistant, answered. A full two minutes elapsed before Wendy came on. She sounded strange.

"I don't like your book, Nick," she said at once. "It's hateful. I spent the last three days reading it and I was shocked."

"Shocked?" said Nick, confused. He was still worrying about Venables.

"It has an animosity towards women that I found quite frightening," Wendy was saying.

"Do you mean there was nothing you could agree with?" he asked.

"Nothing."

"I'm sorry about that," he said, but he was angry and hurt. Wendy was not one of those wives who rode their husbands like a brutal jockey, changing whip hands when necessary if he seemed to be losing direction. Surely there was enough in the book for a fair-minded woman to discover something which met with her grudging acquiescence?

"That's not what I rang about," he said. "I've had Simon here. He said that you're pregnant, and he seemed to think I might be the father."

"What did you tell him?"

"Eventually the truth."

Nick listened to a long silence. How could she describe his book as "hateful"?

"I can handle him," Wendy said. "Where has he gone?"

"To see Pym, I believe."

"Much good that will do him. Thanks for ringing, anyway."

Nick replaced the receiver and leaned against the wall. It hadn't been the conversation that he had expected. He stood there for a while, a perplexed frown on his face. He had been prepared to offer her whatever comfort or support she needed, but she seemed to have written him out of the script. Had the book changed her view of him – or had the book changed her? He sat down at his desk to consider the awful possibility that what he had written would achieve exactly the opposite of what he had intended, and come to be regarded as an instruction manual for the world's women, producing an infinitely more lethal regiment of termagant feminists, amazons, vixens, all much better informed on how the battle should be conducted, thanks to his work. He thought of the animals whose numbers are supposed to be reduced by new chemicals and poisons, but who grow stronger because of them. He thought of rats in giant refrigerators who grew fur coats ...

The phone rang. After today's interruptions he looked at it suspiciously. It was a local radio station in the north of England.

"We've got a studio discussion going on up here about women's rights, Mr Bannerman," said the producer, "and somebody had the bright idea of bringing you live into the programme on the phone. It's a chance to plug your book – we've spoken to Arthur Scott, of course."

"Fine," said Nick.

"Just make yourself comfortable and I'll plug you in. Don't speak until they've introduced you. Okay?"

"Let me at them," said Nick.

There was a click and a buzz on the line, and then Nick found himself listening to a radio programme.

". . . two kids under the age of five and no husband, you can't go to work even if you want to," said a woman. "Hire a nanny and your wage becomes her wage."

"That is a specific economic situation," said a man who sounded as if he were the chairman. "But the broader picture that you paint is of women getting the rough end of the deal as the law stands today. Interestingly enough, a new book out this month suggests exactly the opposite. It is called *Battered Husbands* and with any luck I've got the author, Nick Bannerman, on the line now. Hallo, Mr Bannerman?"

"Hallo," said Nick.

"Your book suggests, I gather, that men are getting a raw deal today?"

"On every front, yes," Nick replied. "It's all work and no play, it's one bill after another with too little time for leisure, it's worry and responsibility and early death, and if you want a divorce it's financial crucifixion. Marriage is a health risk."

"Powerful stuff," said the chairman. "But surely women, who mostly lack the earning power of men, are entitled to some protection under our laws?"

"Of course they are, and they've got it. They've got too much. Have you read my book?"

"I read an excerpt in a Sunday newspaper."

"Well, I don't see how you can interview me if you haven't read it. The fact is that a man is hog-tied financially from the moment he says 'I will' or 'I do' or whatever the fateful words are that misguided bridegrooms utter. Did you know that one woman got her husband thrown out of the house that he had owned long before he met her? It's in the book. You should read it."

"I think I'd better, Mr Bannerman. It doesn't sound to me as if you have a lot to say in favour of the fairer sex?"

"The unfairer sex. No, I haven't," said Nick. "I think they're a dangerously unpredictable species."

When the interview was over he sat at his desk surprised at how angry Wendy had made him.

Venables eased his Mercedes into the Brocks' drive with a contented smile on his face. The pangs of guilt which had accompanied his longing for Pym had gone for good, released by an unfaithful wife. He parked the car at the front of the house and heard Pym's voice at the back. He walked round. She was kneeling on the patio in a yellow bikini playing with Greg who, completing a total tan in the last of the summer sun, was naked.

"Hiya," said Venables, lighting a cigarette. "Hallo, Greg."

"Hallo," said Pym, surprised. "What brings you here?"

"I had to see Nick. I thought I'd drop in to see you. It's a social call. How's Greg? Nudism runs in the genes, I see." He sat at one of the patio's tables and pulled an ashtray towards him. "Where's the patriarch of this clan?"

"Are you drunk?" Pym asked, looking at him.

"Drunk? No. Mildly elated, yes. Why?"

"Your language seems a trifle flowery, like someone who has had a pint or two. The patriarch of this clan is playing golf with Rupert."

"Rupert? Is he still here?"

"He seems reluctant to go. I think he's being kind, cheering us up in our hour of need." She let go of Greg who, displeased by the interruption, took a plastic football off to the lawn. "Do you want a drink?"

"I'd like that," Venables said. "Gin?"

She brought a bottle of gin, two glasses and some bottles of tonic on a small black tray, and sat at his table. He picked up a women's magazine that she had been reading, and studied a large colour picture of a veteran beauty. "Still a fashion plate in her sixties," he read, "she said that the secret of her beauty was that she neither drank nor smoked, slept long hours and consumed forty glasses of water a day."

"That's my aunt," explained Pym. "I got the idea of modelling from her."

"Forty glasses of water a day?" said Venables. "I suppose they took the pictures between visits to the loo?"

"It worked wonders for her complexion. How much tonic do you want?"

"All of it," said Venables. "I have to think of my complexion. Have you thought of going back to modelling? In your hour of need?"

"I'm too old."

"You're not too old. You look magnificent."

"Thank you, Simon."

"How is Ben taking it all?"

"He's surprisingly resilient, considering. The thick skin that got him to the top. I was wondering whether this little setback will change him politically."

"I've never heard him discuss politics."

"Oh, when I met him he thought people should pass an intelligence test before they got food. But now – perhaps he'll join the Labour Party."

"I doubt that. I've met Ben's type. What he'll do is make another fortune."

"And you, Simon," said Pym, picking up her glass for the first time, "why are you elated?"

"I've just heard that Nick has been making love to my wife."

"When?"

"It must have been that afternoon that we were on the beach. When I had the fight. He seemed a bit strange when we got back."

"And this makes you elated?"

"It kind of gives me *carte blanche*, doesn't it?"

"To make love to somebody else, do you mean?"

"Exactly."

"Blimey, what a spooky reaction."

"Spooky?"

"That wouldn't be the normal reaction of a husband, would it?"

"I've no idea," said Venables, slightly put out. "It was certainly mine."

"Have you chosen anybody yet?"

"Yes, you."

Pym laughed. "Would you mind awfully if I didn't?"

"I think I would. Yes." He felt that he had put this quite reasonably. The sagging top of her bikini was already causing a mild tumescence. If Wendy could quietly have intercourse with Nick, why couldn't he do the same with Pym? Her husband, after all, had a woman somewhere. Everybody was at it except him. The isolation filled him with resentment.

"Any more news on those pictures upstairs?" he asked. It seemed a good moment to nibble at her loyalty to her husband.

"I wish I'd never told you about them," said Pym.

The eerie cry of one of the new telephones reached them from the house, and Pym jumped up. Propelled by lust, he followed her.

The phone calls around here were often enough from desperate desk-bound salesmen who plucked a name from the directory and urged strangers, in tones of warmest familiarity, to consider the benefits of double glazing, cavity-wall insulation, or even life insurance. This one asked Mrs Brock whether she had had her photograph taken lately. A new studio had opened locally, and for the first month special colour portraits, frame of your choice, were on offer at a reduced price.

Venables, standing close to listen to the salesman's forlorn spiel, found himself untying the top of Pym's bikini and dropping it to the floor. Standing behind her, he cupped both breasts in his hands, the realisation of a dream that had haunted him since he first stepped into the Rueda Bar in San Luis.

Pym, fending off both Venables and the salesman, was unable to give her full attention to either and soon Venables was kneeling in front of her and kissing her breasts instead. She pushed him away angrily with the hand not holding the phone, and told the man from the studio: "I'm a professional model. I've got all the pictures of me I can stand, thanks." The man, undeterred, had another question. "My husband hates having his picture taken," Pym told him.

"If he's got clothes on," Venables said from between her breasts.

Pym slammed the phone down and pulled herself away with such force that Venables fell over on his back. He lay on the floor with a smile on his face.

"Behave yourself, Simon, for God's sake," Pym said, picking up her bikini.

"I enjoyed that."

"Well, I didn't. Pack it up."

"I could take up molesting housewives in earnest."

"Not this housewife. Get up and behave properly."

He rolled over on the floor and kissed her naked foot.

"Get up, you randy lump," she said, kicking him.

"Why don't we just hop into the bedroom for half an hour? I have something to show you."

"I've seen it. How is the gender-reversal problem, by the way?"

"You can't hurt my feelings, Pym," Venables said, still lying on the floor. "I'm in love with you. Why don't we go to bed?"

"I went to bed last night. Daytimes I get up."

"Ah, there you miss out. Love in the afternoon, while both parties are fresh, is what we want."

"It's not what I want. Will you get up, Simon, and stop abusing my hospitality?"

"Is that what I'm doing?" He climbed to his feet, contrite now. "Okay, sorry. You knock me sideways, you see."

"I ought to. Let's forget it. Come and finish your drink."

They went back out to the patio.

"Christ!" said Pym. "Where's Greg?"

Her eyes scanned the garden in one wild sweep, and then she was running and shouting.

"Greg!"

She ran along the edges of the lawn, still shouting, peering into the bushes where a boy may hide. Venables, torn abruptly from a sexual episode that he was still savouring, followed her at a quick walk, looking in the directions that she missed.

So she came to the dip before him and ran down to the pool where she let out a shrill, short scream. Venables ran now, and as Pym hurled herself into the pool he could see the tiny body, face down on the bottom, before she hit the water.

She came up very quickly clutching him and laid him on the grass beside the pool. She crouched over him, shouting at him, and then she laid him face down and tried the artificial respiration she had learned at school. The she turned him over and pressed his chest. Then she tried the kiss of life. But in the end, holding her dead son, she only screamed.

*

His conversations with the Venables, one in the flesh and one on the phone, drove Nick at opening time to the gloomy Edwardian seclusion of the Valiant Sailor where he climbed on to a bar stool as if he never intended to leave it and ordered a pint of the best bitter while he decided what to drink. He found that even at this early hour he was sharing the bar space with a lot of customers. Next to him was a blonde with a black parting and an older man who was exploring a tin of Hedges snuff.

The landlord was a man who had reached this tenancy after a lifetime in the officers' mess. He wore a blazer with a prized badge on its pocket, and a tie that signified some cherished but obscure regimental connection. His attitude to his customers had always made them feel privileged to be served.

"How is the book going?" he asked Nick, as he handed him change. "I saw your picture in the paper."

"Selling well," Nick told him, counting coins. "I shall soon be able to afford your prices."

"You the writer?" asked the man with snuff. "I nearly wrote a book myself once, but never had the time. It was going to be about a trip I made, hunting for koodoo on the Kapiti Plains. I was going to call it *Green Hills of Africa*. A good title, I thought."

"Didn't somebody do something like that?" Nick asked.

"I expect so," said the snuff man. "I've been pipped at the post all my life."

"Why don't we talk about the book he has written, rather than the book you didn't write?" asked the blonde.

"People should confine their conversations to the things they know about," said the man. "That's why I always talk about myself."

Nick drank his beer and tried, by the direction he faced on his stool, to extricate himself from this. Things had been happening too quickly lately, and he wanted peace to think. But Mrs Vaughan came in just then and headed straight for him with a broad smile. Why did people always imagine that you were pleased to see them? he wondered. They approached you without a flicker of self-doubt.

"I bought your book," she said. "You naughty boy."

"Naughty?" He put some money on the bar.

"All those unkind things you said about women, Nick. Women will do anything for you if you treat them properly."

"Well, they've never done anything for me, but thanks for buying the book. What will you drink?"

"Gin," said Mrs Vaughan. "Are you going to be on television?"

"I believe I am."

"Let me know when, this time. I want to record it."

The bar was filled now with a considerable early-evening clientele who evidently did their drinking between work and dinner. Nick bought himself another pint before the service slowed. He drank deeply and studied his neighbours. There were local businessmen who had reached this select area by the arduous route of the eighteen-hour day, and pin-striped men who had arrived from the City in chauffeur-driven limousines. Mingling among them, social astronauts trolling for compliments, were ladies for whom money was the only true aphrodisiac.

Like a snowball thrown slowly towards him, the white face of Simon Venables came at Nick through the crowd. It was a face distorted by misery.

"Whisky," he said, gripping the edge of the counter. "Large."

"Have my stool," Nick said, standing up. "You look dreadful."

"Thanks," Venables replied, and sat down. "Something terrible has happened. Greg was drowned in the pool."

Nick listened, horrified, to Venables' story.

"Where's Pym? Shouldn't I go to see her?"

"She went off in an ambulance with the body."

Nick felt sick. He handed Venables a large whisky, and stood in silent awe as he considered this new tragedy to hit the Brocks. First their money, then their home, then their child. It was almost biblical in its intensity, he thought. Their next meeting was not something he was looking forward to. He felt even sicker now – at the selfishness of his own reaction.

Venables was holding an empty glass.

"She blames me," he said, in utter desolation.

"You?"

"I was fooling around with her in the house. Flirting with her. I distracted her. The kid wandered off."

"Is that fair?" Nick asked, handing the empty glass to the landlord. His chief concern now was that Venables would burst into noisy tears.

"Quite fair," Venables said mournfully. "If I hadn't gone round to see her the boy would still be alive. She's right. It was my fault."

Nick gave him the new Scotch and for some moments they were both silent. The genial hubbub of bar-room conversation went on: nobody knew that a boy had drowned and, if they did, would the conversation stop? Life goes on, and death was a part of it. The television news bulletins were largely a procession of coffins – terrorists' victims, political leaders, yesterday's show-business stars, murdered children – and people barely noticed. But Nick continued to feel sick. For a while he ignored his drink.

"Where was Ben?" he asked.

"I don't know," Venables replied. He knew that Ben was playing golf with Rupert Puckle, but he couldn't be bothered to say it. Ben would come home to the news in his own time.

"She blames me," he repeated.

"How were you to know?" said Nick. "You're not used to looking after children."

"I took her mind off him." He glared into his whisky, yearning to be punished, but Nick could already see what his punishment would be: the enmity of Pym. He decided to introduce a different mood into this melancholy tableau before Venables started to cry.

"I have spoken to your co-habitee," he said.

"My what?"

"Wendy. I rang her."

"She hated your book. It made her quite angry." Venables seemed relieved at the change of subject, and particularly welcomed this one.

"She told me."

"'This is not a book to be tossed aside lightly,' she said. 'It should be thrown with great force.'"

"I didn't know she read Dorothy Parker."

"God, I thought for a moment she was being original. Why did you phone her?"

"To tell her you had been to see me. To ask her how she was."

"And?"

"There is nothing between us now. Not that there ever was."

Venables was twiddling an empty glass. "I don't know what attitude one is supposed to take these days to someone who has been to bed with your wife. Three out of four marriages end in divorce. One in five kids are illegitimate. It's a brave new world. Perhaps I'm supposed to write you a cheque." He held his glass up until the landlord noticed.

Nick picked his way through what Venables had said, and fought off a desire to tell him proudly that bed was not where they had been, and that what had actually occurred was a glorious, monumental, vertical, alfresco fuck. But he wanted to appease him now, and the important thing was not to make the sexual episode too real to him. He said: "I think the attitude that you are supposed to take is that it is in the past and finished. It *was* only once. You should also try not to be too bloody hypocritical about it. You have been trying to have Pym all summer."

"Do you think I'd feel differently if I'd succeeded?"

"You would have to, wouldn't you? I'll have a gin, by the way."

Venables bought a single gin and a double whisky. "Wendy and I were very happy until the spring," he said. "Then we got married and stopped enjoying ourselves."

Nick drank the gin. "My book came out too late for you."

"What about you, anyway?" asked Venables, turning slightly in his seat to look at Nick. His speech was already a little slurred. "Haven't you ever been in love?"

The face Nick saw now was Helen's, with her dark hair and wide-open eyes. "There was a girl once," he said.

"What happened?"

"I'm told she married someone else."

"Typical! Typical of bloody women! I liked your book, Nick, even if Wendy didn't." This whisky was disappearing even faster than the others. He bought himself another, leaving Nick with his gin.

"I'm a useless bastard," he announced when he had drunk it. "Old Ben can make a million. You can write a book. What can I do? Nothing. What am I going to do? No idea. Got a bit of money now but no idea what to do with it."

"Open another Morsels," said Nick. "Build an empire. It's obviously what you should do."

"Do you think so?" asked Venables, looking at him carefully. "Is that what you'd do, Nick?"

"Certainly."

"You know, you're a good bloke, Nick."

They stumbled from the Valiant Sailor at closing time, the friction dissolved by alcohol, and found that Venables couldn't stand up.

"Come on," said Nick. "You can sleep on my sofa."

251

"Good idea," agreed Venables. "Better not drive."

They walked along the private drive, with Nick's arm offering Venables necessary support. The huge white underwing of a barn owl soared over their heads.

"Friend of mine drank and drove once," said Venables. "He had a white Rover. The police stopped him and gave him a breath test. Then he got into the police car and drove off. The police didn't notice. They got into his car and drove off." He looked at Nick. "The police had white Rovers, you see."

"I understand," said Nick.

"Bloody funny, it was."

In his flat Nick found some blankets and made up a bed on the sofa. Venables had left home that afternoon to tear his throat out, and now he was sleeping on the sofa.

"I've treated Wendy badly," he confessed when he lay down. "Mind you, I'll be called over the holes tomorrow."

"Or hauled over the coals," said Nick.

"It was my fault," Venables said, but he was asleep before Nick could find out whether he was talking about Wendy or the tragedy of Greg.

When Wendy Venables had made the necessary preparations in Morsels for what she called "feeding the five thousand", she served herself a coffee and took a fifteen-minute break, usually with the morning newspaper. But this morning she had difficulty in concentrating on the paper's news. Simon had disappeared, and last night she had slept alone for the first time in years. She knew that he had gone to see Pym and guessed that he had drunk too much to drive home. He was very fussy about drinking and driving which was why she had spent so much time driving him in her van. She had rung the police but there was no record of an accident. She had rung the Brocks but there was no reply. Half worried, half angry, she realised that she had not been giving her marriage the attention it deserved. Her guess was that Simon would come strolling in soon with a hangover. She decided to be sympathetic.

She picked up the newspaper and her eyes bounced off the

maze of type and drifted down the page. She didn't have the concentration this morning for other people's problems. The stories got shorter and shorter and her gaze eventually settled on a one-sentence filler at the bottom of the page that she thought she could handle: "Gregory Brock, aged three, son of Mr Benjamin Brock, head of the London advertising agency which collapsed last month, was found drowned yesterday in the family swimming pool." She dropped the paper and murmured, "Oh, no." She knew that she must go to see Pym, but Sally was out shopping and she would have to wait until she got back. She picked up the paper and read the story again. This time she noticed a cross-reference at the bottom to a feature inside. Greg, it reported, was the seventh child to die in a family swimming pool this summer. Classes which attempt to get a young child accustomed to water were actually dangerous, said the article. "Not only does the child lose its fear of water, but the parents think of him as safe, and grow complacent. An inquisitive child knows very little fear and one with no fear needs protection." The article concluded by saying that children, anyway, can drown in very little water: two this year had drowned in nappy-washing water, one in a washing machine and at least one in a bucket.

Driving as carefully as her new condition demanded, Wendy headed for the country in her Austin van with the deepest sense of foreboding. She could not even guess at what possible link there might be between Simon visiting the Brocks and the death of their baby, but he must have been there because Nick had told her he was going.

An hour later, having been overtaken by almost every car using that road, she turned into the Brocks' drive, pale with nerves. The For Sale sign, still in the hedge, seemed to mark this space out as a scene set for tragedy.

She rang the front door-bell and waited a long time. The usual display of cars was gone and she began to wonder whether the house, too, had been deserted when the door was opened by Rupert Puckle.

"Hallo, darling," he said miserably. Today he was wearing a dark-blue dressing-gown but beneath it were not pyjamas but a pair of beige slacks. "Come in."

Wendy followed him into an empty house.

"Where's Pym?" she asked. "I've just read the news in the paper."

"It's terrible," Rupert said, and sat down. "This family seems to have a curse on it."

"How on earth did it happen?"

"Simon was here chatting to Pym. Greg wandered off. They found his body in the pool. Sit down."

"I can't. It's too awful. Where's Simon now? I haven't seen him since yesterday."

Rupert looked up at her. "Simon? Haven't seen him. But Pym is in hospital. Ben beat her up. She has broken ribs and God knows what."

"Beat her up?" Wendy asked numbly.

"He was crazy with grief. He loved that boy. He just slammed into her and then cried for two hours. If I hadn't been here I think he would have killed her, I really do."

"I must go to see her."

"Yes, that'd be kind. I'll draw you a map."

While he was doing it the phone rang. Wendy answered.

"Simon here."

"Where the hell are you?"

"I'm in Morsels. I'm helping. It's very busy."

"Sally told you I was here?"

"Correct. Sorry I didn't get home. Nick and I drowned our sorrows. I couldn't phone, let alone drive."

"You could have phoned this morning."

"I was whizzing towards you in my Merc, dearest. How's Pym?"

"In hospital. Ben beat her up."

"Oh God!"

"I'm going to see her now. I'll catch up with you at Morsels this afternoon. Don't stray."

He was silent so she replaced the phone.

The hospital was a new complex of single-storey buildings that sprawled over several acres. Wendy, with a bunch of freesias bought from a flower shop that had been thoughtfully marked on Rupert's map, walked through open-plan wards where the privacy of a single room was created instantly by a swish of orange curtains. She had to ask and ask again before she discovered Pym in bed in the corner of a large ward. She was lying on her back staring blindly at the white ceiling. A card on the wall above her head said DOCTOR MANATT.

The arrival of Wendy did not produce any noticeable change in her expression, but her eyes followed her briefly as she deposited the flowers in a jar at the side of the bed and then found a chair against a distant wall that she brought over. She sat down and put one hand on Pym's hands which were joined, death-like, on her chest. "I'm so sorry, Pym," she said. "Are you in much pain?"

Pym's pale face and dark, sleepless eyes remained motionless for a minute and Wendy thought that she couldn't speak. But suddenly, with some discomfort, she framed a reply. It arrived in a slow whisper.

"The pain," she said, "is irrelevant."

"It's Greg?"

"Of course," she muttered between clenched teeth, as if the movement of any part of her body, even her jaw, was going to hurt. Wendy decided that she should talk, and not ask questions, to entertain or at least distract Pym whose eyes looked frighteningly like those of a person who was preparing to relinquish her grip on life.

"I feel half to blame myself," she said, and was pleased to see Pym's eyebrows raised questioningly, as if this was a possibility that she had not considered. "Simon should never have been there, he should never have been pestering you. I'm afraid I've been rather cold towards him since he lost his job and took up gambling. In a way, I've driven him towards you because of the way I've behaved. It's all going to change. He didn't even come home last night. He stayed at Nick's. I actually missed him. I want someone there when I wake up. If I had treated him properly he wouldn't have been chasing you and this wouldn't have happened."

She paused and looked round the ward. Not many patients had visitors. From the opposite bed a woman who had been kept down to six stone by an overactive thyroid gland stared across at her wretchedly. Wendy began to wonder whether there were things she could do in the hospital world: there were enough people in need of help here. When she got home she would write to the hospital's League of Friends.

"My news is that I am pregnant," she told Pym. "A little keepsake from our holiday."

Pym moved to say something, and Wendy had to lean forward to hear.

"Deaths," she said, "and births." It occurred to Wendy then that Pym had been given some pain-killing drugs which made her sleepy. Perhaps it would be kinder to leave her and call again when she felt better.

A young black nurse appeared, pushing the tea-urn trolley.

"Mrs Brock is very tired," she said. "She hasn't slept yet and we have given her something."

"What has she got exactly?"

"Four broken ribs and a fractured jaw." The nurse filled a teacup from the urn. "And a broken heart," she added. "You should leave her now. Come back in a couple of days."

"I will," said Wendy. She turned to Pym whose eyes had at last closed. "Pym, is there anything I can get you? Is there something I can bring in?"

"Yess." The word arrived promptly this time, sounding like a hiss.

Wendy leaned forward. "What?"

"Bring Ben in," Pym muttered without opening her eyes.

"I will. Don't worry. Where is he?"

There was a long wait this time before the listless reply emerged.

"I've no idea."

Ben was in a brothel in Shepherd Market. He had arrived there by a circuitous route having begun his drinking in the Ritz, and then strolled up to the Mayfair Hotel before crossing Berkeley Square and heading for Claridges. He had then crossed Grosvenor Square and made his way down South Audley Street to the Dorchester where a binge that had begun with champagne ended with Chivas Regal.

The pain that he now felt was outside his previous experience. That one man should have had to endure his series of disasters filled him with horror and disbelief. He had hoped that a few drinks in some of London's most expensive watering-holes would make his financial collapse seem less real. The drink, he hoped, would ease his misery.

After three hours neither of these hopes had been fulfilled and he made the short walk to Shepherd Market. He lay now on a four-poster bed in a spotless and well-furnished room above a betting shop. He was fully dressed in one of his best dark suits with a blue shirt and a red tie, partly concealed now by his beard.

Lola came from Huish Episcopi. On his first visit here, Ben had laughed at her false name and imagined that Huish Episcopi was in Turkey, but he was wrong on both counts. Lola had been christened Lola, and Huish Episcopi was a village in Somerset. She was a pleasant well-built woman in her mid-thirties. Somewhere there were two sons. Somewhere else there was their father.

She said: "I read about your boy, darling."

Almost any woman looked good to Ben when there wasn't another one around. It was only when another woman appeared that you could make a comparison. But now he lay on the bed feeling quite drunk.

"I don't want to talk about it," he said. "If I talk about it I'll cry."

"I'm so sorry," said Lola. "How did it happen?"

"I wasn't there."

Lola skipped into the kitchen and made him a coffee. She was wearing a very short white dress with nothing beneath it. She had long black hair that reached her waist.

Ben closed his eyes and wondered why he was here: sex was the last thing on his mind. He was managing now not to think about Greg all the time, and was worrying about Pym. He had hit her before, but never like that.

Lola brought him the coffee and he sat up on the bed to drink it.

"What do you want to do, darling?" Lola asked. "Or is this a social visit?"

Ben drank his coffee and considered the question. He imagined that he was one of Lola's more unpredictable customers. A sexual appetite whose voracity was once a legend, had been stringently modified by the arrival of herpes. Ben lived too close to the pharmaceutical industry, itself defeated by the virus, to be careless about his health. So coition was expunged from his shopping list at Lola's, and replaced by a variety of sexual diversions involving hands, mouths, bottoms, jam, cream, polaroid cameras, video cameras, tape recorders and mirrors. It won't be long now, he thought, before I'm on the bondage trail.

"Do you want to take pictures?" Lola suggested.

Ben finished his coffee and wondered to what new depths his life could fall. If he didn't get a grip on it soon, he would end up dossing on the Embankment, wrapped up in old newspapers, and fighting off the Salvation Army.

257

He put the coffee cup down on the side table and got off the bed.

"No, I don't," he said. He handed her a £20 note. "I must go to see my wife."

FIFTEEN

ARTHUR SCOTT found himself, for the first time in his career as a publisher, with the television network at the disposal of his new author – although as the invitations flowed in they each bore a murmured hint that their interest in talking to Mr Bannerman would wane somewhat if he were to appear elsewhere first.

Arthur Scott was solely interested in selling as many books as possible and with this in mind he declined invitations to see *Battered Husbands* shunted into an afternoon programme or buried among the chat-show transvestites. He rejected, as well, the moving viewers of breakfast television, and eventually decided against an early-evening magazine programme where a superficial interview would be hastily conducted and, on all known form, brutally cut short to make way for the latest cure for baldness or a skate-boarding duck.

He chose the important current-affairs programme, *Vista*, which filled forty-five minutes on Monday evenings. *Vista* was versatile and thorough. One week they would discover, in that cruel stretch of land that links the Americas, an eighteen-year-old widowed mother of three who would be interviewed through an interpreter to an aural backdrop of gunfire. The following week they would be back in the London studios for a prurient seminar on the boom in incest. The viewing figures were colossal.

Vista promised to devote the whole programme to women's inhumanity to man. There would be charts, graphics, filmed interviews with enraged and newly impoverished men, an MP or two, a garrulous bishop, and, at the heart of the fun, a studio discussion between the author of this important book and a well-known feminist obtained, the jovial producer promised, by calling "Rent a Lez".

Her name was Lorna and her friend came, too. Lorna was a lean, pale, thin-lipped lady with a complexion like the newsprint which carried her angry column in a Sunday newspaper. Lorna had been known to advocate castration for even quite trivial offences. She shook Nick's hand with perceptible distaste. Her friend, Eunice Gilberthorpe, was also not unknown to this sort of programme. She ran a Rape Crisis Centre in Wapping from where she would toss nervous journalists excoriating but deeply quotable remarks about the male sex. She was short, plump and crop-haired but potentially, Nick decided, quite beautiful.

"Two against one," he remarked as Hospitality provided them with gins before the programme.

"Your book stinks," said Eunice Gilberthorpe.

"Save your anger," said the producer. "We want a lively programme."

They were drinking in a small room that had all the charm of a railway-station waiting-room. Through a window in one wall they could look down on the studio floor. It was a huge area but they would only be using a small part of it. Black screens and a few chairs had created their own small room.

People filed in now as transmission time approached. The garrulous bishop, who seemed to be about seven feet tall, was followed by two scruffy men; one, with a squint and a red beard, looked to Nick like a refugee from the booby hatch. It became clear that he and his partner were Members of Parliament. Finally, a good-looking young man called Felix, *Vista*'s presenter, was introduced to them all. His face was vaguely familiar to Nick who seldom saw television. He had reached his present eminence, uniquely, via both Fleet Street and the Old Vic.

"I loved your book," he told Nick over a gin. "My marriage broke up last year and my wife has got everything, the house, the children. It's very unfair. I'm paying them nine hundred pounds a month, and surviving on just over a hundred pounds a week."

"A pity you're supposed to be impartial," Nick told him.

Lorna and Eunice glared at them malevolently.

The producer outlined the programme's shape, and then led them down to the studio floor.

Felix was installed at a big marble desk that looked like a sar-cophagus. Behind him was the picture that viewers would see as he talked to the camera. It showed a balding, harassed man standing alone, and the words, a foot deep to one side: UNFAIR TO MEN?

"I don't like that for a start," said Eunice Gilberthorpe.

"You'll get your chance to speak, Eunice," said Felix.

"Sixty seconds," came a voice from the darkness.

Nick looked round at the strange setting in which he found himself. It was so intimate that he didn't feel at all nervous. He was glad now that he had insinuated himself on to *Tell The Truth*, to get an early taste of the television business. On a monitor above the cameras a muscle-bound tot was vaulting over some gymnastic obstacle in Budapest, the trailer, perhaps, for a later sports show.

Nick sat to Felix's right, and Lorna and Eunice sat grimly on Nick's right. The bishop and the MPs waited on the other side of the presenter, anxious to share the fruits of their second-hand wisdom with the world.

"Exciting, isn't it?" Nick said to Lorna.

"Like watching paint dry," she said, ignoring his smile.

"Twelve million people are about to hear about my book!"

"It's disgusting," said Eunice Gilberthorpe. "Jesus didn't even have a microphone."

"Ten seconds," came a voice from the darkness and an eerie silence settled over them all. It was broken by Felix, cued by an unseen hand, who was suddenly addressing a distant camera in the brisk tones of an accomplished presenter: "Good evening. Britain has the highest divorce rate in Europe. More than a million children live in single-parent families. Something has gone seriously wrong with the marriage business. A book published this month suggests that men should never have got involved with it in the first place, that they get a raw deal when they are married and an even worse one when they are divorced. In fact it seems to be saying that it is only a simple-minded man who would get married at all. Later we will be talking to the author and to representatives of women's movements, to two Members of Parliament and to a bishop who agrees that marriage is under threat. But first, a report from Gavin Anderson."

Silence fell in the studio.

"We're on cine," said Felix. "You can pick your nose now if you wish."

His face on the monitor had been replaced by Gavin Anderson's filmed report.

Nick leaned towards the presenter. "Can I quote your case?" he asked. "It sums the whole thing up perfectly."

"Oh, please don't," Felix said, holding up both hands. "My image is that of a happily married father of two."

Gavin had found the man who had been thrown out of his own house, a story that Nick had recounted both in his book and in his radio interview.

He was so familiar with it that his gaze wandered from the monitor to a group of people who were watching the programme from behind the cameras. And then he saw Helen. He remembered now something that he had forgotten in his mother's letter, that she was in television. His heart jumped and his concentration was scattered. She looked a little older, she was wearing glasses, but she was still the pretty girl that he had never taken to the theatre in King's Lynn. He wondered whether she would recognise him, whether she was here to watch him. But he was Nick Bannerman now, and the boy who had fled his home in embarrassment and humiliation was called Tony. She moved behind a camera and he lost sight of her as a voice called: "We're coming back to you in one minute."

A production assistant walked over to Felix with a copy of *Battered Husbands*. He held it so that the cameras would catch the cover.

"Ten seconds," said a voice.

Suddenly Felix was talking to a camera.

"A new book, *Battered Husbands*, has been written by Nick Bannerman, who is described by his publisher as a belligerently heterosexual bachelor. Mr Bannerman – you've got something against women?"

He saw himself on the monitor, swallowed, and launched himself on the air waves.

"Not women. Marriage. Most marriages that I know are unsatisfactory for the woman and a burden for the man. There's total incompatibility of interest. From a man's point of view, I have never understood its attraction. A woman wants children and needs the economic support, but what's in it for a man? He gives away most of his wages in return for not being allowed to go out for a drink at night."

A cameraman's laughter drifted across the studio.

"Your book goes rather further than that. It's an attack on the Women's Liberationist Movement?"

"I don't think it is." He glanced at the dolorous duo on his right, leaning forward in their seats ready to pounce, and thought: Get your retaliation in first! "If the women's libbers want female gynaecologists, rape crisis centres and better pay, good luck to them. I have always been in favour of equal pay. I'm not trying to put women down. I'm just asking, politely, if they'll get their heels off our throats. Let me give you an example. Only this evening, in this studio, I was talking to a man whose marriage broke up last year. He said to me: 'It's unfair. My wife has everything – the house, the children.' He has to pay nine hundred pounds a month . . ."

Felix, startled at this, turned quickly to the women. "Heels off men's throats?" he asked Lorna, who was introduced to viewers by a caption across the screen.

Lorna was off. Male arrogance, insensitivity, sexual incompetence, trivial pursuits, financial dishonesty. The off switch was missing. There was something feral about her, Nick decided. She had the ears of a fennec fox.

He elbowed his way back in as she drew breath, and talked about the male hormone, testosterone, which made men sexy, ambitious and prematurely dead. That was the way men were, nature's handiwork.

An outburst from Eunice followed this, a startling history of repression that had reduced women to second-class citizens all over the world.

Nick made some propitiatory noises. He agreed about the past. He was talking about the present. But his concession seemed to infuriate the virago on his right whose need was for confrontation. She made to speak but he jumped her.

"Men are a minority group in this country now, even without a war to trim their numbers," he said. "They don't want to control women. Why do women seek to control them? The women live for ever. All men want is a longer, happier life."

"What a man wants," shouted Lorna fiercely, "is a three-foot-high woman with a flat head which he can rest his beer on while she sucks him off."

"And a protruding chin to rest his balls on," shrieked Eunice, bubbling now with a fury that Nick found inexplicable. He had seen too little television, and was shocked by the language of this exchange. He knew that barriers had fallen in matters of obscenity, but he hadn't realised that it had come to this. Embarrassed, he fingered his ear nervously and found a ball of wax had transferred itself from one to the other. Appalled by his crassness, he massaged it discreetly into his right sock.

"There's something entirely bogus about the way these sisters stick together," he said, recovering. "Women won't even vote for each other."

"We're coming together," snarled Eunice. "Don't you doubt it. And then the men had better watch out!"

"You've won the war already. What do you want – a massacre?"

Lorna smiled for the first time. "A massacre would be nice," she said.

Felix, sensing a loss of direction, moved in.

"Mr Bannerman, the figures suggest that quite a lot of women, knowing what they know, wish they had been born men. But I have never heard of a man who wished that he had been born a woman."

"Yes, and they want to be bachelors, not husbands."

"Fine," said Felix, swivelling round in his chair. "Also with us tonight are two MPs, who have been much concerned with legislation about the family, and a bishop who has, you might say, a vested interest in the continuing popularity of marriage."

Nick sat back, happy at the way the programme had gone. He was becoming addicted to television and wondered what programme he would appear on next. He gazed over to where Helen had been standing. She was staring at him.

He dragged his attention reluctantly back to the refugee from the booby hatch who, mindful of the female half of his electorate, was engaged on a demolition job on Nick's book. It was cynical, superficial, chauvinistic, inaccurate and ultimately harmful. Nick could take any amount of this: he knew that nobody believed MPs. But the man's vanity intrigued him. He was the latest in a long line of humourless polytechnic lecturers who had burst out of the classroom into politics, craving an ever-larger audience for their mendacious spiel.

"I'm happily married myself," he said. "Perhaps Mr Bannerman's view of matrimony is warped by the fact that nobody has married him."

Nick wondered what sort of woman would be prepared to curl up at night with this hairy little twerp, but now it was the bishop's turn, and he was "desperately anxious" to tell people what God said. Nick could hear television sets switching to other channels all over the country. Soon it was over and he saw his name rising with the credits on the monitor above the cameras.

"Thank you everyone," shouted the voice that had previously been restricted to counting down the seconds. Nick stood up.

"That was fine," Felix said, shaking his hand. "You'll sell some books tomorrow."

"That's the plan," said Nick, watching the departing figures of Lorna and Eunice. "Back to your bean-bag classes, girls!" he called, and received, as a valedictory message, an energetic V-sign.

He headed now for that area behind the cameras where Helen had been standing. She was still there, talking to the production assistant, but as Nick approached across the studio floor her eyes followed him all the way.

"I've been looking and looking and looking at you," she said.

"Hallo, Helen."

"I thought 'Can it be?'"

He kissed her cheek, and he fancied she trembled in his hands. When she smiled up at him he knew that five years ago he had made a terrible mistake.

"It's certainly me," he said.

"With a new name, or is that just a pen name?"

She was wearing a tight red dress, sexy and business-like at the same time.

He told her: "It's my name. I changed it on the night I last saw you. You look lovely."

"You're wearing well yourself. You do a good interview, by the way."

"Is that a professional assessment? I hear television is your game."

The production assistant, an intruder at this reunion, drifted off, leaving them alone among the cameras.

"You *hear*? Don't you see me?"

"I don't have television. I live alone in a tiny flat that I share with my typewriter."

"And I always imagined you seeing me on the box."

She was telling him more than she knew. She took both his hands in hers and looked up at him with the big eyes that had hooked him all those years ago.

"Why did you go, Tony?"

"Nick. Embarrassment. Humiliation. You know what my mother was like. A normal life was impossible. I had to start afresh."

"A new start. A new name."

"It worked. But I have often thought of you. Aren't you doing well?"

"Welcome to post-print journalism. Have you ever been back?"

"Never. And I never shall."

She shook her head at his implacable will.

"You're a hard man."

"I had a hard mother."

She looked up at him for a long time and then suddenly released his hands. She scooped up a handbag that was hanging from a chair. "How extraordinary our meeting like this."

"I must get a television set and see you more often. What programme are you on?"

"Oddly enough, this one. But it was a man's subject tonight."

She led him away from the cameras and on to the studio floor. They stepped between chalk marks, a discarded clip-board, a ball of paper. The bishop and the two MPs, unconcerned at the dead cameras, were still tugging at the state of matrimony, its secular benefits, its spiritual thrust.

Nick decided that at the first opportunity he would take Helen to dinner.

"I've read your book," she said. "It's a fine polemic. You're going to be rich."

"Do you mean you didn't recognise my picture on the dust-jacket?" he asked.

"My husband always removes the dust-jacket when he reads a book."

With too many other things to think about tonight, he had forgotten that she was married. He remembered that his mother's letter referred to a politician.

"Who did you marry?" he asked quietly.

She pointed at the man with the red beard, and he suddenly realised that she was here to collect him.

"He's going to be Prime Minister one day," she said.

Not that little fart, he thought. "It wouldn't surprise me at all," he said.

"At least, that's what he tells me."

"Well," said Nick, "he must be right sometime."

He watched her walk over to him and take his arm. He didn't acknowledge her arrival, but continued with a speech that still had some way to go.

Standing alone on the studio floor, Nick felt that what had been an exciting and successful evening had been suddenly transformed into something that was pointless and sad.

To his horror, he discovered there were tears in his eyes.

Not many miles south, in their gloomy flat on Thornton Hill, the Venables watched Nick's performance in silent fascination. Venables was enthralled by seeing someone he knew so well appearing on television, but for Wendy the programme was more traumatic. Nick's attitude to women, provocative in the book, had come across as even more aggressive when challenged in the studio. Her heart sank, and as her heart sank her stomach began to hurt.

"He was good, wasn't he?" said Venables. "He kept his end up."

"Kept his what up?" Wendy asked, holding her stomach.

On the screen now was a commercial for Top Toys' new battery-driven car for children, aiming, from two months out, at the Christmas market. A bright-eyed blond boy of about five was driving it round the zoo at Regent's Park, watched by an admiring audience of elephants and giraffes. Venables studied this advertisement with almost as much interest as the programme that preceded it: Mel Schwarzbaum's batteries seemed to be doing their job.

"Top Toys is surviving in my absence," he said, but Wendy had left the room.

Sitting ringside at the Brocks' disasters had been disturbing enough and Nick's evident anti-feminism had hurt her too. But now she could think only of her own pain. She sat on the lavatory and discovered that she was passing blood.

Venables sat alone, staring at the television. An inarticulate silhouette was mumbling about his addiction to illegal hallucinogenic substances. Venables turned the sound down. He had problems of his own but he didn't go bleating about them on television. Any chance he ever had of winning Pym had gone. The death of Greg had finished all that. His wife was pregnant and it still wasn't certain who the father was. He had no job, nor the prospect of one. His only consolation was that he now had money, and he was disappointed to find, after the years of fretful yearning, what a small consolation it was. An added complication was that with Pym removed, even as an extremely speculative figure in his future, he now felt a renewal of interest in his wife, in her dark good looks, her quiet certainty, her new sad moods that reached out for affection from somebody. But his marriage was an area of some turbidity, and when he tried to think about it he became confused. Instead, he poured himself a gin and tonic and lit a cigarette. If he hadn't gone back to smoking before, he would certainly have been puffing by now. He turned the sound back up on the television. A tiny man with an accent that was difficult to understand was slapping black-and-white clouds all over a map of Britain; troughs of low pressure were lurking to the west, apparently, threatening rain. He was replaced by a beautiful sight: a golden four-mile beach at the back of which were not hotels or shops but only high green hills populated by sleepy, satisfied sheep. He recognised Woolacombe in Devon, and then Croyde and Braunton. Topping up his gin and saving on the tonic, he had his first idea for months. Looking at the screen, filled now with a long-distance shot of the island of Lundy from the Devon coast, he realised suddenly the insanity of living in a third-floor rabbit hutch in Wimbledon when, a few hours down the road, there were places like Devon offering space, air and visual pleasure. He was no longer tied to the capital's dingy suburbs by work, nor to anywhere else. He sat watching the changing picture – it was a wildlife programme about birds, he gathered – and plans formed in his mind. A gull swooped over a cliff and landed precariously on a ledge. It glared haughtily at the camera. Below it, the provisions boat chugged towards Lundy, and then viewers were back on the cliffs looking at the towering north Devon coastline. Venables thought of all the people who headed that way during their brief summer escape. Presumably they ate sandwiches?

Wendy returned from the bathroom looking deathly white. She walked to the sofa and, instead of sitting, lay down on it, eyes closed. Venables, engrossed now in his dream, did not look up. Every picture of Devon added a shimmer of reality to his plans. He said: "I've just had an idea!"

His wife's one-word reply, "What?", sounded so strange that he looked across at her.

"Devon," he said. "We sell up and move. We sell Morsels, we sell the Mercedes, we sell the flat, and we head for the land of sunshine and cream teas. What do you think?"

"Wonderful, Simon."

"We start a new business down there. Not just sandwiches. We could buy a restaurant. We could buy a guest-house. We could even afford to buy a small hotel. Everything's cheaper down there. Go west, young man!"

"Can we afford a small hotel?" Wendy asked. She sounded as if she might cry and he looked across at her again and saw how pale she was.

"Of course we could. We'll make at least twenty thousand on this bloody rabbit hutch, the Morsels lease is worth quite a bit, and what with my ill-gotten gains . . . you okay?"

He stood up and went over to her.

She shook her head, not trusting herself to speak.

"What's the matter?" he said, suddenly alarmed. "What's the matter, Wendy?"

She began to cry then, which frightened him even more. She was a girl who never cried.

"I'm not pregnant any more," she told him.

In the country beside a grey pond that stretched into the pine trees for half a mile and was the coveted home of a weekend sailing club, there was a luxurious hotel whose restaurant gazed out on to the water. In the summer there were bathers as well as boats, and in the winter intrepid motor-cyclists rode daringly across the pond's ice roof.

Ben took Pym to the hotel for dinner soon after she had left hospital. Rupert Puckle, who had flown here for fun and found himself immersed in tragedy, was with them. His return had been postponed a dozen times as fresh duties were heaped on him in the Brocks' home. Yesterday there had been a damp day of grief which he had organised: a quiet funeral, a coffin no bigger than a suitcase, a rainswept burial beneath the trees. They had invited no one.

The Brocks' path towards reconciliation, forgiveness and healing had been made easy by the fact that each of them was overwhelmed by such guilt they found it impossible to blame the other. Ben was horrified by his own behaviour, dismayed and ashamed. Pym would never forgive herself for allowing her son to stray.

United by guilt, they clung together like survivors on a raft.

"We must look a cheerful bunch," Pym said, when the coffee arrived.

Rupert Puckle, one of whose jobs was to lift the spirits of those around him, said: "I don't think we stand out. Nobody over thirty ever looks happy unless they've got a slate loose."

Ben wondered whether it were true. A cheerful face in the street was not an everyday sight. It was certainly a long time since he had looked cheerful.

He ordered brandies.

"I suppose you'll be going home soon?" he asked.

"I'll start looking for a cheap ticket tomorrow. I can feel an English winter coming on. The things I want to do, like sitting in the sun and drinking beer, are a bit difficult in England where the sun never shines and the bars are always shut."

The brandy arrived and Ben drank some. "It was our climate that made us great, Rupert. We couldn't lie around stupefied in the sun like those foreign people. We had to work to keep warm. The Germans are the same."

"You're blaming two world wars on the climate? They have a coup in Bolivia every day. No, I'll settle for the sun, old boy. I save a fortune on woolly clothes and heating bills."

Pym had found and was eating a Bendicks chocolate *crème de menthe* that had arrived gratis with the coffee. All vestige of her summer tan had gone.

"I envy you," she said. "Our future looks rather different."

"I was wondering about that," said Rupert. "So much else has been going on we haven't had time to discuss it. What is your future exactly?"

"Uncertain, I'd call it," said Ben. "No home, no job, no money. The opposite of rosy, I'd say." He looked at the white skin on his left wrist which had once been concealed by his Patek Philippe watch.

"And your plans?"

"I'd like to open another agency. On a smaller scale, perhaps. Certainly with cheaper premises. Looking back on it, opening up in Chelsea was a bit of an extravagance. I could have operated just as well out of town."

"I have money multiplying in Sweden faster than I can spend it," Rupert said. "I live a frugal existence. The sun, the pool, the vegetable garden, the bridge club on Mondays. Money? Who needs it?"

"I do."

"Precisely, old boy," said Rupert. He put down his brandy. "Why don't you and I start a new agency? I've always rather fancied the oversimplifications of the advertising world. Guinness is good for you. Things go better with Coke. Beanz meanz Heinz. You're never alone with a Strand. What happened to Strand, by the way?"

"The advertising campaign killed them."

"Oh dear, I thought advertising was intended to promote sales?"

"Yes, well, we all make mistakes. Listen, are you serious?"

"Perfectly. Joint owners. My money, your talent."

"That's wonderful, Rupert," said Pym. "Isn't it, Ben?"

"It certainly is. You won't make any money for two years, Rupert. After that you'll be rolling in it."

"That's fine. I can wait." He beckoned the waiter for more brandy. "You'll have to work, Ben," he said.

"I'll work. I'll work seven days a week."

Rupert looked shocked. "I don't think that will be necessary. If you work seven days a week it's either incompetence or greed."

"You can get pretty greedy when you're bankrupt," Ben said grimly. "What shall we do? Draw up an agreement?"

"Yes, let's go and give the lawyers some money."

"What are you going to call this agency?" Pym asked.

"How about Punch, Low and Run?" Rupert suggested.

"I might give you a job as a copywriter," said Ben. "Hey, I haven't felt so cheerful in weeks!"

Pym, watching, saw a deadness that had lingered in his eyes start to lift. He produced a pen and an envelope from his pocket, and started to write a list of places where an office could be opened within easy reach of London.

The mail that now began to flow into Nick Bannerman's flat filled the first hour of his day with a consistent mixture of surprise and laughter.

"Dear Blue Eyes," wrote a Ms from Maesteg, "I should like to take you to me bedroom, remove your trousers, and cut off your balls." From the other end of the island, from Balmungie, where the chill winds off the Moray Firth had failed to cool her anger, a woman whose domestic status was unrevealed sent him an eight-page account of menstruation, its physical realities and psychological traumas, along with an invitation to Nick to respond with an equally candid description of any comparable ordeal regularly confronted by men.

A vicar's wife in the New Forest wrote to tell him that marriage was a sacrament and, as with so many other things in this world, if the spiritual approach was lacking, confusion and dismay would be the certain consequence. A homosexual drag artiste in Hamburg, who hadn't seen the book but had read about it in the newspapers, sent him unwelcome sympathy; and a proposal of marriage arrived from Hay-on-Wye with a photograph of a young schoolteacher who said that Nick's declaration that marriage should be a fifty-fifty contract was a darn sight better arrangement than that endured by any of her married girl-friends.

The angriest letters came from London where literacy and frustration evidently coagulated in the same bed-sitters. A cliché-strewn missive from Battersea demanded: "What are you – some kind of nut? You think the chicks have got it made in this God-forsaken male environment? It's the women who are battered, deserted, cheated and kept on the breadline, even today, and you must be a naive simpleton if you can't see it. Look in a betting shop, or a pub or go to the dogs, and see where the housekeeping money goes. And I could introduce you to some wives who would tell you what happens to them when they complain. What's it like out there in Cloud Cuckooland, you brainless fink?"

Some messages were not written. His own press cuttings reached him daubed with blood from an undisclosed orifice. A plastic male nude arrived with its sex organs chopped off. But after two weeks the front runner in the abuse mail was a giant turd, wrapped in tin foil, and tied with a red bow.

At first, Nick responded enthusiastically to this public interest in his work. Where he felt that he had been misunderstood he took the trouble to explain himself; where he felt that his reader was misinformed he typed out an immediate corrective. But soon answering the mail became a full-time job, and he eliminated those who wrote to him because they had read about his book in the newspapers and confined himself to correspondents who had actually bought it. Even this eventually became too much, and finally he replied only to those letters that he felt, for one reason or another, deserved it. He studied the others, though, with fascination. He discovered that a popular myth was true: green ink *was* the preferred choice of mentally unstable letter-writers.

The letter that he had been expecting arrived, like the others, with the help of Arthur Scott's secretary. It came from that flat, chilly stretch of land between the Thames and the Wash, and bore a familiar handwriting.

"Dear Tony," his mother wrote, "I am writing to let you know that your father died on August 12. It was a painful death for him and not very much better for me. I wrote to you in the summer after we had seen you on some television panel game to tell you that he was far from well, but either my letter didn't reach you (I wrote to the television programme) or you were not sufficiently interested to get in touch."

Nick put the letter down at this point. He was only mildly interested in his mother's reaction to the discovery that her son had written a book, but the death of his father hit him with an unexpected force. He had been a quiet, ineffectual man with whom he had finally lost patience, but now that he had gone there was room for remorse. His life had been one long pointless sacrifice, a sad truth about millions of men, but Nick had at one time been the beneficiary. His father had given him the security in which to grow, and in the early days had taken an interest in his development. If, after a decade or so, his interest had waned, Nick didn't find it reasonable to condemn him. He had been reluctant to punish, and he never used physical violence. It was the abdication of all responsibility to his mother that Nick found hardest to forgive. The life had been depressing, and so was the death. In one tiny corner of the earth's surface he had slaved away for sixty years, not enjoying himself very much, and then he was gone. To what end? It was typical of the world's cruel timetable that he had died just a few weeks too soon to read the book that he had, to a large extent, inspired.

For a long time Nick sat staring at nothing, remembering childhood events involving his father: a ride on the back of a motor-cycle, his first kite in the park, the laborious erection of a tent on the back lawn. All that had been before he was ten. By the time he was eleven his novelty value had diminished, and his presence in the family had been reduced to an item on the expenditure list.

Nick picked up his mother's letter again, with an effort.

We buried him near his father's grave at Sheringham. The Boyds came from Cromer. Perhaps you can imagine how difficult it was to explain your absence. I tried to pretend that you were abroad, but a few weeks later we all saw you on the *Vista* programme and they rang up to ask whether it was you, and whether Nick Bannerman was your pen-name.

I bought your book on my monthly trip to Norwich and read it with great sadness. From the moment you joined the newspaper I always thought that you would write a book one day, but I never imagined that it would be anything so bitter. It seems to be a very one-sided view of the complex relationship between men and women, but I hope it makes you rich. Perhaps you will be able to repay the money you took when you left here so callously. I am not hard up, don't think that. Your father's insurance, that I persuaded him to take out when we met, has paid just over forty thousand pounds. It is the principle that I am talking about.

It was strange that you were on *Vista*, because that is the programme that Helen is on. She is a lovely, bright girl and it is a pity that you never married her. I asked in my last letter whether you married, but I see from your book jacket that you have not. Reading your book, I doubt that you ever will.

I also asked whether you will ever return to East Anglia, but I shall probably never get an answer to that. I can't pretend to understand you any more, but I wrote because I thought that you should know about your father. He left you a little money in his will.

Your mother

Reading his mother's laborious handwriting, Nick gasped at her crocodile tears over the death of a romance that she herself had evilly sabotaged. He stood up, unable to stay sitting, and paced up and down the flat, talking aloud to himself.

The whole letter was typical of her – the whining sense of injustice, the small concern for her husband's death, the demand for money, the hypocrisy over Helen, the carefully arranged windfall for herself, the embarrassment at what others thought and, dangling insultingly at the end, the bait about his father's will. Well, he would write in confidence to his father's bank manager about that. She hadn't even liked his book.

SIXTEEN

AT TWO O'CLOCK on Wednesday, 10 November, Nick Bannerman sat at his desk with his telephone resting between two bottles of champagne. In Russia Leonid Brezhnev was about to die, but Nick's attention was focused in the opposite direction. In New York it was 9 am.

The midday post had brought him a letter from Arthur Scott and a copy of *Time* magazine. *Battered Husbands*, published in America the previous week, had received the accolade of a review in *Time* and Nick had flipped through it to catch its flavour. After the novelty of the first flurry of Press cuttings, he had developed an antipathy towards reading about himself which he found difficult to explain.

But the *Time* review sang. It was headed "Turn of the Worm".

> YOU thought romance was coming back? Postpone the celebrations. Nick Bannerman, a laconic Briton, has been to the sex war and his report from the front is not encouraging for the moony June brigade. He presents a grim picture of the modern husband trapped in the pincer of domestic duty while waiting for an ulcer or worse.
>
> The male as victim, thwarted by women, is, of course, not new, but never has the case been so comprehensively put. The tone is angry and then some. With gloriously abusive prose, and a highly selective eye for facts that hurt, Bannerman hurls thunderbolts that do for men

what *Watership Down* did for rabbits.

Folded into his polemic are some poignant vignettes of lives that have been destroyed when love is replaced by litigation.

Though written in a popular style, Bannerman's book does not sidestep the moral dilemma at the heart of his cold war. We could be friends, he says, but first get your dainty shoe off my face.

The review went on to fill a page which included the same picture of Nick as had appeared on the dust-jacket of the British edition.

He put the magazine down and picked up Arthur Scott's letter. It had the nicest first sentence he had ever read: "By Wednesday evening you will be very rich." Nick touched the bottle of champagne, but didn't open it. It was still only Wednesday afternoon.

The source of this impending wealth was the auction of the book's American paperback rights. "Wait by your phone," urged Arthur Scott's letter – but Nick couldn't wait. He phoned.

"Paperback firms will ring the hardback publishers with their offers and they're going to ring me after each one," Arthur Scott said. "The auction will close at noon – that's teatime here."

"And the signs are good?" Nick asked.

"The reviews are good, which is more important," said Arthur Scott. "You know what a feminist place America is. The women go from beautiful young things to hard-faced harridans without any intervening period of gentle lover. Your book is a real novelty over there. Already there has been an offer of half a million dollars for the paperback rights, so that becomes the floor."

"The floor?" Nick said.

"Yes. It's on the table."

"The floor is on the table?"

"You got it. As I hear of each bid I'll give you a ring. Have you got the champagne on ice?"

"On my desk, actually."

"Good luck, Nick."

Nick replaced the receiver. The champagne was on the desk, and the floor was on the table. Everything seemed to be in order.

At quarter past two the phone rang.

"Bantam have gone straight in at three-quarters of a million," said Arthur Scott. "You won't forget your poor friends, will you?"

"How much of this do I get?" Nick asked.

"About eighty per cent."

"Is the floor still on the table?"

"We've left the floor behind. We're going upwards."

Nick hung up and reached for his cigarettes. He lit one quickly, and began to contemplate sudden, unimaginable wealth. What was he going to do with it all? Ben bought a Bentley and Simon a Mercedes, but Nick had never owned a four-wheeled car in his life. He had no wife to adorn with jewellery, no children to spoil. He didn't even have a house. Should he buy property? Should he invest? Should he travel? The dazzling array of choices that now lay before him were so attractive that he decided to do all of them. He would become friends with his unknown bank manager, and get himself a stockbroker. He would buy a house that kept the world at arm's length. He would arrive in faraway places with strange-sounding names, clutching only a passport and a platinum credit card. At the back of these dreams one disappointment nagged: he had no one to travel *with*.

Just after three o'clock Arthur Scott rang to say that the bidding had topped a million. The hardback publishers in Manhattan, who were presiding gleefully over this spiralling contest, predicted now that this book was going to affect every marriage in America. It was the book that everybody had been waiting for, but nobody had thought to write. Was Nick Bannerman producing anything else?

Nick Bannerman was drinking champagne. It seemed silly to drink it on his own, but he couldn't leave the telephone, so he drank it by himself from a half-pint mug that had found its way back to his flat from some long-forgotten public house. When the money arrived he would buy himself a proper champagne glass, maybe two. It was hard to imagine a life without financial restrictions, but he tried. A white Lamborghini, an apartment in Nice, a wardrobe from Savile Row? The first bottle of champagne disappeared at the speed of lager. In his excitement he had forgotten lunch. He toasted two slices of bread and covered them with smoked-salmon pâté, collected absent-mindedly on his last supermarket tour. The second bottle of champagne produced ideas. He could see himself now on a South Sea island, dispensing gifts to the natives and enjoying, in return, the voluptuous charms of ladies in grass skirts. He lived with several of them in a hut on a long white beach, drinking rum and eating coconuts. Ironically, it was cheaper than living at home. The royalties remained unspent, earning prodigious interest and doubling in seven years, while he languished in his sunny hut, contracting sexual diseases unknown in the research hospitals of the world's largest cities. The dream soured somewhat at this stage and he shifted his baggage to Antibes. Coffee with Graham Greene every morning was only the half of it. The palm-fringed seafront was awash with crumpet, a vista of topless girls in search of rich and frustrated bachelors, the most famous of which he was.

The phone rang.

"One and a quarter and still going," said Arthur Scott. "There's an hour left and there are some very determined bidders."

"Do you mean one million two hundred and fifty thousand dollars?" Nick asked. He was still in the south of France.

"That's it. You're going to be a dollar millionaire. Have you got an accountant?"

"I know one."

"What are you doing, Nick?"

"I'm drinking champagne on my own and dreaming of a life of luxury."

"It's no dream, Mr Bannerman."

There wasn't much champagne left but Nick filled his mug and continued sipping. His predominant emotion now was one of fear. To what extent were these dollars going to change his life? To what extent did he want them to change his life? "This isn't going to change my life," said the football-pools winner, and everyone guffawed. Within months these unchangeable lives were in chaos, with alcohol problems, broken marriages, crashed cars and often, incredibly, debts. The tragedy of success!

Nick drank some more champagne and resolved to tread very carefully. The arrival of wealth on this scale deserved a better reception than fear or a neurotic anxiety about how money should be used.

Money equalled freedom: it was that simple.

The champagne ran out before the final call. It came through at ten past five, ten minutes past noon in New York. Nick picked the receiver up nervously. He had visions now of an aborted auction, of legal squabbles and petulant withdrawals, with an unsold book at the end of it. Things had gone too well.

"One point five closed it," Arthur Scott said. "You're practically a sterling millionaire till the tax man catches you. Congratulations!"

"One and a half million dollars?" Nick said. He wanted to hear it spelt out, not abbreviated. "Can it really be true?"

"There's nothing unreal about it," Arthur Scott replied. "They'll sell two million copies at five dollars each and owe you more within two years. I'd like to be there to celebrate with you but I've a dinner date tonight."

"Don't think me mercenary, Arthur, but when do I get a sniff of this loot?"

Arthur Scott sighed. He knew more than most about writers' obsession with money. They spent so much time worrying about numbers it was a wonder they found any time for letters. "I should be able to get you the first dollop in a month. The rest will fall in another tax year. Perhaps you should live in the Isle of Man?"

"I don't want to live in the Isle of Man, Arthur."

"I don't blame you, Nick. All those beatings and motor bikes. How's the new book coming along?"

"Slowly, Arthur."

"Another small matter, while you're on the phone. The television programme you were on –"

"*Vista.*"

"Yes, *Vista*. They want to know whether you would go back and face a studio audience of angry female viewers who have been demanding your head ever since they saw you."

"I'd love to."

"Could you handle it?"

"I'd do anything to get on television, Arthur."

"Give them a ring, will you?"

When he put the phone down he felt dry-mouthed from the champagne. He stood up for the first time in two hours. He was a rich man. It didn't feel any different.

He went over to the window and opened it wide. Cold November air rushed in to dissipate the afternoon's cigarette smoke. The darkening sky was its normal mixture of grey and black. He could afford an air ticket that would lift him through all that.

That was his first idea on how to start spending the money, but looking out of his window he suddenly had a second one. When he leaned out he could see the telephone number of the estate agent on the For Sale sign in the Brocks' hedge.

Like a man who has been at the heart of a nasty road accident and is then hit by a passing car as he climbs from the wreckage, Ben Brock was slowly rebuilding his life. It was well within his capabilities if he gave it all his attention. He was giving it all his attention.

This afternoon he had driven Rupert Puckle to Heathrow Airport in his wife's Golf after signing an agreement with him which made them joint owners of a new advertising agency which would be launched in the new year on Ben's know-how and Rupert's money. Its name would disguise Ben's earlier failure with a sonorous spoonerism: Buckle and Prock.

He was pouring his wife a glass of La Ina sherry when the doorbell rang: Pym was being pampered for the first time in years. The dinner that her sherry preceded had been cooked by Ben. It was something that he had once enjoyed doing until the demands of work began to damage his domestic life. He poured himself a sherry and sat on the sofa with Pym. It seemed as if the terrible things that had happened to them had brought them closer than they had ever been.

"Rupert will be back in the sun by now," he said, looking out at the lowering clouds.

"That's what you need," said Pym, "a business partner who keeps out of the way."

"All we have to do now is find somewhere to live. Are you okay?"

"I'm fine."

If Ben had learned one thing this year it was that life wasn't quite as easy as he had supposed, a discovery that had made him noticeably gentler.

The doorbell rang again, a prolonged cry this time.

"I thought it rang just now," said Pym.

"I didn't hear it," Ben said, getting up.

Nick Bannerman burst into the room, waving his hands in

circles like a man doing a soft-shoe-shuffle routine.

"I'm a millionaire. I'm slightly pissed. I want champagne," he said.

"What?" said Pym. "What, Nick?"

"The paperback rights went in New York this afternoon for a million and a half dollars."

"That's nine hundred and twenty-three thousand pounds," said Ben instantly. "The pound was one point six two this morning."

"I'll leave the figures to you, Ben. I want flagons of drink, then I'll give you some more news."

"Good news?" asked Pym.

"You'll like it, Pym. You'll invite me to stay for dinner."

"You're welcome to dinner anyway, Nick. We can get pretty bloody obsequious when millionaires drop in."

"Nick – wonderful!" said Ben, appearing with champagne. "When all else has been taken from us we shall still have a little champagne left for our friends." He opened it with a pop. Nick took a glass and retired to an armchair.

"What news?" Ben asked.

"I've just bought this house."

"Bought it?"

"Well, I've spoken to the estate agent. I'm seeing the bank manager at nine-thirty when I shall provide him with evidence from Arthur Scott of this upcoming wealth, and I'm visiting the estate agent at ten. No mortgages, no surveys, no farting about. By lunchtime it will be my house. Do you want to hear my plan?"

"I'm fairly interested," said Ben quietly.

"You can have it rent-free for a year. At the end of that time you can either buy it or start paying an economic rent. Okay?"

"That's too generous."

"No, it's not. The way property values are soaring round here the rent is neither here nor there. I'll be making over a thousand a month just by owning it. And I got it cheap. The bank were desperate to sell. They were with the wrong estate agent."

Pym was up and kissing Nick now, spilling his champagne. "What a wonderful man you are!"

"I always thought so."

Ben stood up, and shook his hand. "You've removed the last of my worries. I signed an agreement with Rupert today to launch a new ad agency in the New Year. I'll buy this house back in twelve months' time."

"I hope you do," Nick said. "It's too big for me. What I need is a slim, dark-haired temptress. Know any?"

"They'll be like bees round a honey pot," Pym told him. "Watch out that it isn't your money."

"From what I saw on holiday, I don't think it would be his money," said Ben. "Now if you'll excuse me, the chef must withdraw to the kitchen."

"A man's work is never done," said Nick. "Have you read my book?"

"He's different," said Pym when he had gone. "He's quite different."

"I'm glad, Pym. Is everything okay?"

"It is now with *your* news. I was hating the thought of leaving this house." She looked round the room and then her gaze came back to Nick. "I hear Wendy lost her baby."

"I didn't know that."

"She rings me often to see how I am."

"She doesn't ring me. She hated the book."

"I know. I loved you on television, by the way. I watched it in hospital. Nobody would believe that I knew you."

"I'm on again soon, facing a horde of angry women." He looked round at the house he had bought and saw on the piano a new, gold-framed picture of Greg. "*Take your face away!*" he seemed to be saying.

Whose baby had Wendy lost?

He emptied his glass and stood up to fetch the bottle. The news today was arriving a little too fast.

Ben brought the dinner in on a trolley. "The wine list is limited," he admitted. "I think we have Mateus Rosé."

"A fine wine," said Nick. "Kindly fetch it."

Ben had produced steaks in a mushroom sauce, *sauté* potatoes and cauliflower. Nick, who had eaten carelessly today, was now ravenous.

"Do you take credit cards?" he asked.

"Our landlord always eats free," said Ben, opening the wine. "Try this, sir."

Nick tried it. It tasted good.

"In the old days, Ben," he said, "when you were a millionaire –"

"Before I became a pauper?"

"Yes, in your pre-pauper days when money was coming out of your ears, did you find that it changed you? I mean, am I going to feel different in a minute?"

"It did change me a bit," Ben admitted, sniffing wine. "I became less tolerant. I was less tolerant of people who had no money. I thought they were stupid and lazy not to have it, because I'd worked bloody hard for mine. I thought *you* were lazy. You never had two pennies to rub together yet you didn't even get a job. You just had a few mysterious freelance assignments and some bloody book you were writing."

"Ben thinks he made his money because he worked harder than other people," said Pym. "He *did* work harder than other people, but he also had luck. He could have worked twice as hard in another job and made no money at all."

"But did he *feel* different?" Nick persisted. "I want to feel different. I never have to do a day's work again and yet I feel the same useless prat that I felt yesterday."

"The change will come," said Ben. "You'll be stomping on the faces of the poor in no time at all."

"No, I won't," said Nick, but before he could elaborate on this denial the doorbell rang again.

"We're getting some callers today," said Pym, getting up.

"It's probably a charity collector," said Ben. "Tell them we've got a dollar millionaire hiding in here."

But it was the Venables who came into the room, hand in hand. They were both wearing jeans and sweaters.

"Hallo, hallo," they said. "We've come to say good-bye."

"Good-bye," said Ben.

"Hallo," said Nick.

"Sit down while we finish our dinner," invited Pym. "Pour yourselves some champagne."

"What are we celebrating?" Wendy asked.

"Nick has just made a million dollars from his book and Ben and Rupert are setting up a new advertising agency," Pym told her. "What about you? Was that a tiny Metro I saw in the drive? What happened to the Mercedes?"

"We've sold it," said Wendy happily.

"We've also sold the van, the flat and Morsels," added Venables. "We're going west tomorrow."

"Always go west or south," said Ben. "But if you have a choice, go south."

"We're going south-west," said Wendy. "We've bought a small hotel in Devon."

"What a marvellous idea!" said Pym.

"No kidding?" said Ben.

"You can all come and stay," Wendy told them. "We have twelve bedrooms."

"Will we have to cross your palm with cupro-nickel?" Nick asked.

"Plastic cards will do," said Venables.

Nick looked at him in surprise. The last time they had met Venables had been in drunken despair but now, as optimistic as a man who buys next year's diary in July, he could see a wondrous future. He had regrown his moustache, Nick noticed. Perhaps that had something to do with it.

"Congratulations, Nick," he said.

"I knew that book would make you rich," said Wendy.

"Thank you," he said. He was trying to think of the word that described her appeal and then it came to him. She looked so *clean*! Today, for once, she also looked happy, but she recoiled from his gaze.

"How are you, Pym?" Venables asked.

"I'm fine, Simon, thank you." She replied without looking at him.

Ben stood up. "I think I had better fetch some more champagne to cover all these various celebrations," he said. He reappeared with two bottles. Full glasses were passed round. Congratulations were passed backwards and forwards like parcels in a game.

Nick Bannerman had drunk so much champagne in the last few hours that he seemed to have bubbles in his head. But he could still think clearly enough to face what had become during this eventful year a familiar but unwelcome truth: that in this noisily celebrating quintet he was the odd man out.

The *Vista* studio was crowded with women who were looking for blood. They were not, it seemed to Nick, a fair cross-section of their gentle sex, but a maliciously chosen minority, virulent and demented, to whom, in all probability, terrible things had happened at the selfish hands of the Fascist male. One gap-toothed gorgon was six feet tall in high heels with wild, gingery hair. Another, with two-tone head and dark glasses, wore a man's waistcoat and smoked a thin cigar. Nearly half had that sad fatness which is the fate of women who eat their way from unhappiness to obesity. Most were white-faced and tight-lipped with eyes that burned with injustice. Nick looked at them as a fox, if it had the opportunity, would examine a pack of hounds.

From behind this pack, jostling for their correct places in the studio seating arrangements, came another woman, slim, small, stunning. She wore a brown two-piece over an orange blouse that had an elaborate floppy collar. Her delicately applied television make-up accentuated her saucer eyes.

"Hallo, handsome," she said. "We certainly pushed your book into the bestseller charts for you, didn't we?"

"Hallo, Helen. You look remarkably happy."

"Well, I start a month's holiday tonight. And then it's always a pleasure to see you. Are you looking forward to this programme?"

"Less and less as time passes."

"It'll be okay. Don't worry."

"Are you the presenter?"

"I sure am. This is women's night on *Vista*. We're going to kick you round the kitchen."

"Thanks a lot."

"Stay for a drink afterwards?"

"I'll need it."

The meticulous preamble to a live television programme was now in progress as studio hands, lighting technicians and programme assistants hurried about making last-minute checks on their end of the action. Helen sat at the same marble desk that had been occupied by Felix on the earlier programme, but the words behind her tonight, which would appear on the screen with her face, asked UNFAIR TO WOMEN? She sat there calmly, shuffling notes, and her face came up on a monitor to Nick's right, zooming in and out of focus as cameramen prepared for the countdown.

The next half hour was a nightmare for Nick, an orgy of invective and abuse, of remonstration and denunciation, as wave after wave of insults and epithets threatened to engulf him. His book's message was twisted beyond recognition, and the new, false picture demolished in tones of near hysteria.

Outnumbered, beleaguered and defeated by decibels, his only relief came when the attack shifted momentarily from the personal to the general. A girl from Casper, Wyoming, who had come here, oddly enough, to get the Americans out, said that men were only needed for reproduction, anyway, and a few studs, preferably restrained in a cage, would solve that problem. Her companion, who had the hands of a steeplejack and was wearing the new fashionable baggy trousers that made a woman's bottom look like a sack of potatoes, said that to most women a man was just a wallet.

Helen presided over the fracas with an impartiality that she eventually jettisoned before the programme's main guest was submerged. But when she insisted that Nick was being misrepresented and should be heard, she was assailed herself with cries of "Traitor!" "Stool pigeon!" and even the masculine "Judas!"

The programme came to a lively conclusion followed by a jammed switchboard from viewers' telephone calls that were mostly sympathetic to Nick.

Helen led him gently away from the scene of battle, not to a bar but to her own office on the sixth floor. It was a small, sparse office, like hundreds of others in this building, with a desk, two chairs, a filing cabinet and a cork-covered wall that was crammed with memos.

"This doesn't look like a bar to me," said Nick. "It has the appearance of an office."

"But lo!" said Helen, after shutting the door and pulling open the filing cabinet's bottom drawer. "What have we here?" She lifted out two glasses and several bottles. "Gin, Scotch, Bacardi?"

"Scotch and water, please." He slumped on one of the chairs and rubbed his face. "Where did you find that rabble?"

"Those are real viewers. They wrote in. In their thousands. You touched a raw nerve, Tony."

"Nick."

"Sorry." She handed him a whisky, poured herself a gin and sat on the edge of the desk. He was reminded of what nice legs she had. "They were pretty brutal, weren't they?"

"They weren't even civilised. They had the knife out for you in the end."

"I've seen worse. I've seen a fight on the studio floor in midtransmission. People are getting angrier. You notice it in the street. I wonder why?"

"I think they're learning to express themselves."

Drained by the programme, and depressed now by this close

look at the ravishing woman he should never have left, he had emptied his glass already. He looked up at her lovely face and smiled, but the thought of the husband who waited somewhere made him feel empty. She smiled back and took his glass. For a building whose frantic productivity filled twenty million screens every evening, the office was strangely quiet.

Helen came back round the desk with a much larger whisky.

"I have a confession to make to you, Nick," she said.

"Confess," he said. "I've forgiven you already."

"It's about the rather rough passage you had this evening."

"Don't worry about that," he said. "I love television, it's all publicity to me. I'm a born show-off, anyway. It comes from all that solitary endeavour at the typewriter."

"It was rough, though. Wonderful television, but rough on you. And I instigated it."

"How do you mean?"

"I was responsible for it. It was my idea. I saw the letters flowing in and I said, 'Let's get Nick Bannerman back on the programme and throw him to the wolves.'"

"Really? Why?"

She seemed faintly embarrassed.

"It was the only way I could get to see you again."

The silence of the whole building seemed to settle now in this room. Helen picked up her glass and drank from it for the first time.

"You don't say anything," she said.

"What can I say?" he replied. "I was so embarrassed by my mother that I thought I couldn't face you again, but I don't think a day has passed when I haven't thought of you. We all make mistakes, and I made a beauty."

"That's nice to hear," Helen said, putting down her glass. "All I made was a terrible marriage and it was all your fault. I intended to marry you, you see."

Nick sat motionless. He felt as if he was floating.

"Once I had seen you again I knew that was it," she said. "Nick, would you do something for me?"

"Anything," he said, not looking up.

"Kiss me."

He stood up then and took her in his arms. He kissed her gently and then hungrily, and then her head was nestled against his chest. Her words came up to him, muffled.

"Will you do something else for me?" she asked.

"I would like to."

"I know that I'm married, and that you hate women," she said, "but will you marry me?"

A shiver ran down the back of his body from his skull to his heels.

"Yes, please," he whispered.

Puerto Banus had erupted so recently on the European coastline that it wasn't even on the maps.

It was a magical waterfront village of tall, thin white buildings that looked as if they had been constructed with a child's toy bricks – some covered by carmine bougainvillaea, others hiding behind palm trees – and all of them facing a tiny harbour that was packed with more than 400 boats. The boats ranged from slick racers to graceful multi-million-pound yachts, and they had, according to their nameplates, reached this unlikely rendezvous from distant origins in Panama and Monrovia, Helsinki, Houston and Hong Kong.

Along the waterfront were restaurants, bars and boutiques, differently canopied and shaped, and between the bars and the boats were the cars, parked ostentatiously at the water's edge: Corniches and Lamborghinis, Ferraris and Camaros, many with Arabic numberplates.

Nobody in Banus looked as if they had ever worked. Even the visitors, transported briefly to this unreal playground, did not seem to have earned their way here by anything so tedious as a job. They looked as if they had been delivered, smiling and gaudily dressed, without having endured the gruesome quotidian of life at an office desk.

It was three days before Nick and Helen were to find Puerto Banus, but it was only six hours after the *Vista* programme that the first sun-bound plane with vacant seats lifted them through Heathrow's clouds. Armed now with a deck of credit cards, Nick was buoyantly prepared for huge and unexpected expenditure.

They reached the south of Spain an hour ahead of the dawn. Malaga Airport gave them a bleak welcome, but a sleepy taxi-driver greeted them with a smile. Nick asked for a de luxe hotel.

"Mucho pesetas?" the man asked.

"Si," Nick told him. This was what money was for, this was how it should be spent, not on extravagant possessions to impress the less fortunate, but on the quality of life itself.

The driver put their hastily assembled luggage in the boot of his Renault and headed west in the darkness. After thirty miles Helen finally fell asleep on Nick's shoulder, but he stayed awake, excited, as dawn revealed grey mountains to his right and the sea below on his left. The road followed the coast for mile after mile, and the mountains were replaced by fields of sunflowers and olive groves and then there were mountains again.

The taxi pulled into the grounds of the hotel as the sun rose in a blue sky.

"Where are we?" Helen asked.

"Andalucia."

"I mean the hotel."

"It seems to be called Los Monteros."

"I've heard of that. It's the best hotel on this whole coast."

"The best is good enough," said Nick. He paid off the taxi with pesetas bought at Heathrow.

As they unpacked in a suite of luxurious splendour, he looked for a hint of regret in Helen, or of anxiety, but there was no suggestion that she was having second thoughts. Not even the sleepless night could quell her bubbling feeling that she had escaped from something awful.

"Come on," she said. "I noticed when we came in that they do proper breakfasts here. None of your continental bread roll and coffee. Would you like to kiss me first?"

"Yes, I'd better," Nick said.

Afterwards, in the rare pleasure of warm November sunshine, they had a look at the hotel. It had four swimming pools, ten tennis courts, a sauna and gymnasium, and an exotic Japanese garden with a waterfall near which lived a family of flamingos. The grounds dropped down through pine trees to their own Mediterranean beach where a beach club had two more swimming pools, a restaurant and bar.

"I could live here," said Nick. "I'm an expert on Spain, you know. This is my second visit this summer."

"How many times have you been altogether?"

"Actually, I've been abroad only twice in my life."

"All that has got to change," said Helen. "Travel broadens the view. I was reading about Spain on the plane. Some people think it's a bit backward, just because it had its civil war only the other day. But this article made the point that Spain was a centre of civilisation when mediaeval Europe was the pits. It said that when London was being besieged by Viking bandits, Cordoba's half million inhabitants were strolling well-paved streets quoting poetry from a library of four hundred thousand volumes."

"What – all of them? Were they all reciting poetry?"

"Well, I suppose that some of them were listening. Shall we lie on the beach?"

They went back to their rooms and found bathing costumes. They were so excited by what they had done that sleep was impossible. The only regret that Helen had was about the speed of their leaving England: there were dresses that she would have brought, clothes that she would need. In a panic to get to the airport, she had tossed into her case whatever was to hand – a toilet case, a travelling iron, a hair-drier, a yellow sundress, two bikinis. And then she had written a note to her husband. He was in Glasgow, speaking at the Queen's Park by-election.

She had thrown on, for the journey, white jeans, a black sweater, and a brown suede jacket.

"You look terrific," Nick had said.

It was a long time since she had heard that.

They walked down to the beach and found sunbeds. The temperature was in the seventies.

"What did you say in the note?" Nick asked.

"It was a masterpiece of brevity. I just said 'I am going to Spain with Nick Bannerman.'"

"What will he do?"

"Probably call a press conference. Publicity is his drug. If he was on every front page accused of murder he'd be thrilled to bits."

She wondered: Why don't I feel guilty? But she knew the answer immediately – there was no room for guilt in her heart because it was so full of joy. She looked at Nick, lying eyes-closed at her side, and thought: What a miracle! I've got him back!

A buffet lunch of gourmet proportions was laid out on a long table in the beach club. It ranged from lobster to fillet steak. They filled plates, bought beers and sat under a Cinzano umbrella of red, white and blue. A swarthy man with a guitar was singing a Spanish song.

"How long does a divorce take?" Nick asked.

"Why? Does it matter?" she asked.

"I'm impatient."

"Look," she said. She held up her left hand and took hold of the gold and platinum wedding ring on her third finger. Slowly she slipped it off and dropped it into her bag.

"That's better," he said.

Their lack of sleep caught up with them after lunch. Back in their room they undressed and fell into bed. For the first time in nearly six years they made love.

"Christ!" said Helen. "I'd forgotten what you were like. Are you going to do that often?"

"How often would you like?"

"Do it again."

He rolled on to his back, taking her on top of him and staying inside her. "I could cry at the wasted years," he whispered.

When they woke up it was the following morning. They had slept for fifteen hours.

Helen suggested a trip down the coast, a sight-seeing, clothes-buying jaunt that would take them not only to Marbella, but all the way to that locked-up piece of Britain in the Med, Gibraltar. She wanted to hire a car but Nick had a better idea: in a taxi he could hold her.

What had recently been a barren coastal road was now the prey of every developer in Europe. Old white villas that had stared across at Africa for a hundred years suddenly found that they had a thousand neighbours. Men laboured, cranes swung, new homes sprouted on the hills like mushrooms. The Saudi king had built a palace on a hill, but first he had built the hill. The palace was like the White House, but three times the size. "Three hundred days of sunshine a year", was the slogan of the real-estate men who urged you to stay and get yourself a ten-year mortgage, a beachfront apartment, a luxury penthouse, a secluded villa with a pool in your own lush, sub-tropical garden. In these sun-shine latitudes, the building of a simple home became "a creation of elegance and grandeur". Some arrivals had required little persuasion to stay: the coast was a favourite haunt of British villains-on-the-run. The Arabs, too, were in flight from their own prohibitions, drinking, gambling, women. Judging by the posters, Arabic was the second language in this sun-baked corner of Europe.

Watching the scenery unfurl from the back of their taxi, Nick and Helen, in jeans and tee-shirts now, thought of damp London streets and dark skies, the different lives that people led. The road bent south at Estepona, still following the coast, and the rock of Gibraltar loomed in the distance, and then they could see another country, another continent, as Africa and the mountains of Morocco were suddenly visible on the horizon. The world seemed to Nick to be shrinking, becoming more accessible through the modern wonder of plastic credit cards. When the taxi-driver faltered, uncertain of where they wanted to go, he waved him on, keen to see more. The road left the coast now and ploughed inland to San Roque, and then curved round the bay of Algeciras so that they were looking at Gibraltar from the west. A sign directed them up a side road to a restaurant by a beach.

It was a fish restaurant that dispensed such rare delicacies as seaweed omelette. It was set in a white courtyard with a eucalyptus tree in the middle. Both the walls and the ceiling were spotless white canvas attached to white brick pillars. They ate *dorada*, a delicious white fish that arrived entombed in salt and was exhumed by the waiter at the table.

They broke the journey back to buy clothes. While Nick shuffled his credit cards, Helen, in two hours, bought two short evening dresses, one in printed silk and one in soft jersey cotton; a peach designer jumper with beads; a straight skirt; some black evening trousers; a cream double-breasted jacket; some silk underwear and a pair of strappy sandals.

On the third day they found Puerto Banus.

Nick had seen the sign on their journey down the coast and remembered that this was the place that Johnny Fix-It talked longingly about, the glamorous spot where he hoped one day to own a boat. Walking hand in hand along the waterfront that evening they agreed that it was, indeed, extraordinary. Nick bought several postcards, aerial views of the port, to surprise the Brocks and the Venables.

He was telling Helen who Johnny Fix-It was when he saw the Menchu Bar that Johnny had also extolled.

"We'll have to go in for a drink, just so that I can tell him," he said.

Yet somehow it came as no surprise to see Johnny Fix-It sitting at the bar in white shorts and a suitably vulgar Puerto Banus tee-shirt on which the "B" of Banus had deliberately slipped a few inches. He was drinking gin and looking at *The Times*.

"Good God!" he said, amazed. "I was just reading about you!"

He pushed *The Times* at them before Nick could introduce Helen. A short story at the bottom of the front page carried their raciest headline for years: MISOGYNIST ELOPES WITH MP'S WIFE.

"I said he'd call a press conference," said Helen.

"What does it matter?" Nick said. "Johnny, this is Helen."

"I know it is," he said, pushing his glasses into place to study her. "I get a hard-on watching *Vista*, without you coming in here."

"What are you doing here, Johnny?" Helen asked politely.

"I'm just down for the weekend," he said, cagily. "Wonderful place, isn't it? It's full of hot money, you know."

"You're planning to move here, I'm told."

Johnny nodded with more energy than was really necessary. "Just as soon as I've structured it financially."

"Lucky you."

"As the man said, the harder I work, the luckier I get. Can I buy you two lovebirds a drink?" He produced a new Spanish wallet bulging with 5000-peseta notes.

"Gins," Nick said, and looked round the bar. It was unlike any bar he had ever seen. Two rooms had been knocked into one and furnished like an Arab's tent. There were fans in the mosaic ceiling and pillars of split cane and hessian, with plants and lamps in all the corners. The seating was wickerwork armchairs and loungers, but the bar stools had golden legs.

Through the door the view was a forest of masts.

"You've made a bad mistake, Nick," Johnny Fix-It said, handing them drinks. "It makes me cry to think about it."

"What mistake has he made?" asked Helen quickly.

"He's made a million bucks and he's going to pay tax on it. You should have told me you were writing a mega-book. I could have helped you." He stared sadly into his drink, appalled at all the money that was going to be handed to the government to waste.

"How could you have fixed that?" Nick asked.

"I'd have dreamed up a scheme," Johnny Fix-It said. He looked surprised, as if his reputation had been impugned. "It's what I'm good at," he explained to Helen.

"I heard," she said. "But what on earth could you have done?"

Johnny Fix-It rubbed his nose and thought.

"Well, here's one idea off the top of my head. When you finished the book you should have sold the copyright to my company in the Channel Islands for, say, ten thousand pounds. You would pay tax on the ten thousand and that would satisfy the Revenue. The rest of the money, a million dollars, whatever, would then flow tax-free into Guernsey, and I would give it to you after taking back the ten thousand plus, of course, a small fee for myself."

"But you would never get the money from the Channel Islands into England without paying tax on it," Helen said.

"Well," said Johnny Fix-It, "I've done it before."

"Is it too late?" Nick asked.

"I'm afraid it is. The book states quite clearly that the copyright is yours."

Nick drank his gin. "Perhaps I'll come back to you on that when I write another book."

"You writing another book? What about?"

"Helen has been giving me some ideas."

"He's going to write a book called *Unfair To Women*. I've been telling him about the other side of the picture."

"Might as well milk both teats," said Johnny Fix-It admiringly. "Why don't you write it under Helen's name. *Unfair To Women*, by Helen Bannerman. It would get a lot of publicity that way."

"I'm not Helen Bannerman," said Helen. "But it sounds nice."

"You're going to be, though," Nick told her. "This marriage business has been greatly maligned."

The tantalising future hung before him now and he experienced a surge of happiness that was almost child-like. He laid his picture postcards on the bar and pulled a pen from the top pocket of his shirt. He felt an unaccustomed contentment and security which filled him with a preternatural love of the whole world. He took the top off his pen. This new chapter in his life might even begin with a pretty postcard to his mother.

To Have and To Hold   Deborah Moggach

Viv was giving her sister, Ann, the best present she could think of – a baby. How Viv, Ann and their husbands cope with this extraordinary situation is the subject of this tender, triumphant and utterly absorbing story. Now a powerful TV drama.

Castaway   Lucy Irvine

'A savagely self-searching tale . . . she is a born writer as well as a ruthlessly talented survivor' – *Observer*. 'Fascinating' – *Daily Mail*. 'Remarkable . . . such dreams as stuff is made of' – *Financial Times*

Runaway   Lucy Irvine

Not a sequel, but the story of Lucy Irvine's life *before* she became a castaway. Witty, courageous and sensational, it is a story you won't forget.

A Dark and Distant Shore   Reay Tannahill

'An absorbing saga spanning a century of love affairs, hatred and high-points of Victorian history' – *Daily Express*. 'Enthralling . . . a marvellous blend of *Gone with the Wind* and *The Thorn Birds*. You will enjoy every page' – *Daily Mirror*

A Daughter of the Nobility   Natasha Borovsky

A magnificent and spellbinding blend of fiction and history, set in the Russia of Nicholas and Alexandra. 'An enchanting tale that richly recaptures the glorious days of Imperial Russia' – *Booklist*

Love, Honour and Betray   Elizabeth Kary

Destined to love, doomed to part, Seth and Charl become part of a seething drama of treachery, tragedy, pain and desire. History and romance entwine spectacularly in this climactic story, as highly charged and memorable as any story told before now.

FOR THE BEST IN PAPERBACKS, LOOK FOR THE Ⓟ

PENGUIN BESTSELLERS

Dreams of Other Days Elaine Crowley

'A magnificent and unforgettable story of love, rebellion and death. 'You will never forget Katy and the people of her place . . . a haunting story' – Maeve Binchy, author of *Light a Penny Candle*

Trade Wind M. M. Kaye

The year is 1859 and Hero Hollis, beautiful and headstrong niece of the American consul, arrives in Zanzibar. It is an earthly paradise fragrant with spices and frangipani; it is also the last and greatest outpost of the Slave Trade . . .

The Far Pavilions M. M. Kaye

The famous story of love and war in nineteenth-century India – now a sumptuous screen production. 'A *Gone With the Wind* of the North-West Frontier' – *The Times*. 'A grand, romantic adventure story' – Paul Scott

The Mission Robert Bolt

History, adventure and romance combine in the most exciting way imaginable in this compulsive new novel – now a major motion picture.

Riches and Honour Tom Hyman

The explosive saga of a dynasty founded on a terrible secret. A thriller of the first order, *Riches and Honour* captures the imagination with its brutally chilling and tantalizing plot.

The World, the Flesh and the Devil Reay Tannahill

'A bewitching blend of history and passion. A MUST' – *Daily Mail*. A superb novel in a great tradition. 'Excellent' – *The Times*

Lace Shirley Conran

'Riches, bitches, sex and jetsetters' locations – they're all there' – *Sunday Express*. 'One of the most richly entertaining reads of the year' – *Options* magazine

Lace 2 Shirley Conran

The gilt-edged obsessions and unforgettable characters of *Lace* are back in this incredible novel of passion and betrayal set in the glittering, sensation-hungry world of the super-rich.

Out of Africa Karen Blixen (Isak Dinesen)

Passion and compassion, intelligence and an acute understanding of an alien culture. Now the subject of a major motion picture.

The King's Garden Fanny Deschamps

In a story which ranges from the opulent corruption of Louis XV's court to the storms and dangers of life on the high seas, Jeanne pursues her happiness and the goal of true love with all the determination and high spirits of one who is born to succeed . . .

Paradise Postponed John Mortimer

'Hats off to John Mortimer. He's done it again' – *Spectator*. A rumbustious, hilarious new novel from the creator of Rumpole, *Paradise Postponed* is now a major Thames Television series.

The Garish Day Rachel Billington

A sweeping, panoramic novel of spiritual and sexual crisis. 'Rachel Billington's marvellously readable novel . . is a real treat. Telling insight and poker faced humour' – *Daily Mail*